Critical acclai

A *Globe and*
A Writers' Trust Best B
A 49th Shelf Books ~~of the Year Selection~~

"Timely…a gripping page-turner." —*Elle Canada*

"Bush's deeply resonant ecological retelling of *The Tempest* showcases a 'brave new world' as ironic as Shakespeare's: brave because it is startling, dangerous and inescapable for those left alive; new because it really isn't, merely the whirlwind humanity has sowed for its children to reap." —*Maclean's*

"A page-turner that confers a moral imperative of our time." —Writers' Trust of Canada

"Reminiscent of E. Annie Proulx's *The Shipping News* with a slight magic realism take on Newfoundland, and a tinge of John Wyndham's *The Chrysalids*, set in a post-Tribulation Labrador." —*The Telegram*

"A fascinating and prescient story. With climate change as the backdrop, Catherine Bush's lyrical portrait of the northern island landscape and a young woman's passion for the land offers a frightening warning of how big business will surely adapt to the changes to benefit itself. Bush's story is compelling—we watch the hurricane unfold, as only a brilliant writer can show us—and offers a moving and soulful primer for climate survival." —Shani Mootoo, author of *Polar Vortex*

"Atmospheric and dramatic, *Blaze Island*…introduces food for thought about apt responses to our predicament and what sacrifices might need to be made to stabilize the natural world." — *Toronto Star*

"A prediction of what is to come should we fail to heed the mounting evidence of the current climate crisis." —*Quill & Quire*

"An elegantly crafted story that also proves to be a sizzling ecological thriller." —*Vancouver Sun*

"*Blaze Island* is a fierce box of wind. Open its cover and you feel at once the fury of the weather to come, the future of the planet in novel form." —Brad Kessler, author of *Goat Song*

"It's a book that has stayed with me, that I think about almost daily and has the power, I believe, to awaken people from their apathy. For people who are not apathetic, it has the power to encourage us to do more: to not give up." — *Carousel Magazine*

"Compelling and beautiful.... In the famous end of *The Tempest*, Prospero asks that the audience free him and the other characters from the dream of the play. *Blaze Island* amounts to a similar request. To deny or ignore our changing world is to stay willfully dreaming." — *Bookshelf.ca*

"Characters are vibrantly 3D and come together in a hot mess of passion and conflict. There are deep and daunting questions raised and readers will never look at a cloudy sky the same." — *Alphabet Soup*

"Alan (Milan) Wells, a Prospero for the Anthropocene, is a climate change fugitive, a prisoner of conscience on a self-imposed exile to Blaze Island with his daughter Miranda. There's a gorgeous tension between them. His decisions impact her like weather, imposed and out of her control." — *Hamilton Review of Books*

"*Blaze Island* asks the reader to consider the hows and whys of decisions made in crisis. Through the actions of the characters, Bush communicates the triumphs and shortcomings of society's approach to the most pressing issues." — *Nuvo Magazine*

"As you'd expect, the novel poses morally complex questions. It does so with the tautness of a thriller and the luxuriant precision of poetry." — *Atlantic Books Today*

CATHERINE BUSH

BLAZE
ISLAND

a novel

Edited by Bethany Gibson.
Cover and page design by Julie Scriver.
Cover image adapted from Christine Koch's *Voice of Fire IV*, 2018, reduction linocut ed.
23/25 V.E., 22.86 x 45.72 cm (photograph courtesy of Gallery 78), christinekoch.com.
Tracy K. Smith, excerpt "An Old Story" from *Wade in the Water*. Copyright © 2018 by
Tracy K. Smith. Reprinted with the permission of The Permissions Company, LLC
on behalf of Graywolf Press, Minneapolis, Minnesota, graywolfpress.org.
Printed in Canada by Friesens.
10 9 8 7 6 5 4 3 2

Library and Archives Canada Cataloguing in Publication

Title: Blaze Island / Catherine Bush.
Names: Bush, Catherine, 1961- author.
Identifiers: Canadiana (print) 20200211943 | Canadiana (ebook) 2020021196X | ISBN
9781773101057
(softcover) | ISBN 9781773101064 (EPUB) | ISBN 9781773101071 (Kindle)
Subjects: LCGFT: Novels.
Classification: LCC PS8553.U6963 B53 2020 | DDC C813/.54—dc23

Goose Lane Editions acknowledges the generous support of the Government of Canada,
the Canada Council for the Arts, and the Government of New Brunswick.

Goose Lane Editions
500 Beaverbrook Court, Suite 330
Fredericton, New Brunswick
CANADA E3B 5X4
gooselane.com

What seas what shores what grey rocks and what islands
What water lapping the bow
And scent of pine and the woodthrush singing through the fog
What images return
O my daughter.

   —T.S. Eliot, *Marina*

I have done nothing but in care of thee.

   —William Shakespeare, *The Tempest*

Pressing changes are underway. Everything is becoming
something else, unpredictably. A completely new outlook is
required. The challenge for now and the foreseeable future is
to extract ourselves from what men have engineered: a planet
long on the edge of catastrophe.

   —Elena Ferrante

...And then our singing
Brought on a different manner of weather.

   —Tracy K. Smith, *An Old Story*

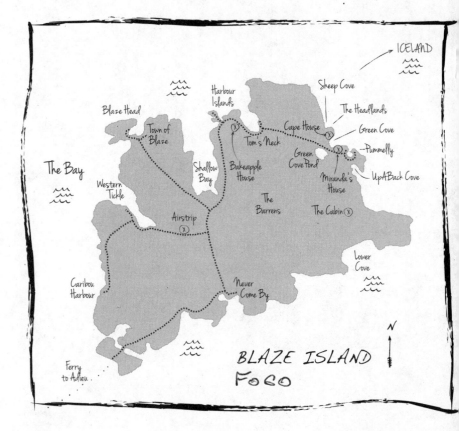

PROLOGUE

She will give her daughter all this.

Fresh bread that broken open is as soft as milk. The year's first strawberries. New radishes, crisp as apples.

It is mid-May and almost a decade into the new millennium. Already the lilacs are over. The silver maple and the copper beech are thickening with leaf. The tiny flowers of the lindens send out a subtle sweetness. In the heat, all these things arrive earlier than usual but they arrive nonetheless.

For a day she will abandon her painting. She and her daughter will take the train into the city. Breathless, as soon as the train begins to move, their fingers crowd into a punnet of strawberries, they cannot help themselves. With each bite their tongues pucker with pleasure, their lips grow soft and pink. When her daughter, beloved Miranda, offers the woman beside them a strawberry, the woman, dignified in her flowered dress, tells them her name is Aurelia. One strawberry, then another, so that the three of them are joined in this bliss, the fever and harmony of the moment, their devotion to it.

In Penn Station, she will take her daughter's hand as they descend into the subway's depths, hot already, air with the taste of metal. Released, they climb out of the darkness, into a cacophony of towers. On the sidewalk they pass a woman playing drums with such ferocity her dreadlocks sweep the air like comets, as a dove-white pigeon arrows a path overhead.

In the park, they will tug off their shoes and run barefoot, heat enfolding them like a dress. There is so much she cannot give her daughter, but for now there is still this—bread, strawberries, enough beauty to swell their hearts and break them open.

. . .

Blustery when Miranda went to bed, the wind wrenched her from sleep just before midnight. Gusts moaned in the chimney as Ella, the dog, pressed close to her side. The wind moved into her. The walls shook. Light slivered through the floorboards from the kitchen below. Slipping from bed, she pulled on her jeans, wool sweater, slippers. Ella, a slim shadow, leaped to the floor. At the rear of the house, wind smashed against the windows, swooped into Miranda's stomach, hurled rain like nails at the glass, pressing out of the southeast, where their autumn storms usually came from.

At her entry, her father started from the kitchen table, shutting the lid of his laptop. Still in his work coveralls, he was not a tall man but feral and muscular, his beard close-cropped. Something rushed across his face, which he tried to hide, and his discomfort made Miranda's skin prickle, attuned as she was to his every fluctuation.

"What were you looking at?"

"The wind map," her father said and opened his laptop again. When the page reloaded, the wind swirled like sleet against the blue earth, its green strength darkening to red. For days they'd tracked Hurricane Fernand, Category 5 then 4 then 5 again, winds topping 250 kilometres per hour as the hurricane churned up the east coast of North America, ripped away trees and homes in Florida, flooded land and roads and cities in Georgia and North Carolina, flattened towns. In dismay Miranda had stared over her father's shoulder as he paced through news sites at photos of crushed and roofless houses, floating cars, uprooted trees, the pictures sinking into her before her father clicked them out of sight.

Don't look, he kept saying. But she had — at a brown sea swelling through a Manhattan subway station she remembered travelling through so many years ago —

On Blaze Island, two decades into the millennium, they were still too far north for most hurricanes, but as the oceans warmed, hurricanes drew closer all the time.

"You said the hurricane was moving out to sea."

"Wind's come round." Her father, who went by the name of Alan Wells, ran a hand through his greying hair until it stood up in gusts. "She's swerved, though we'll still only get the brush of her outermost wings."

They had their own power, stored in a shed full of batteries, a small windmill supported by guy wires, solar panels fastened with metal bolts to rock and roof, and their small house, alone in its sloped fields with a view out to sea, almost never lost electricity in storms, even when a hard wind knocked out the town's. Her father had planted trees as a windbreak, cedars to the north of the house, alders on the slope to the east. He'd insulated the walls when they'd moved to the cove eight years before, the summer Miranda turned eleven, so the rooms were snug, the wood stove pluming heat.

"How about a game of gin rummy?" He extracted a pack of cards from the utility drawer. "And tea, if you're not going to sleep."

It seemed her father wasn't about to sleep either.

As Miranda pulled mugs from the cupboard, her father came close and squeezed her shoulder. "We'll be fine. We live in a world of wind out here. We're storm-seasoned."

It was true. Hurricanes might swerve their way, but ordinary winds on Blaze Island were like nothing Miranda had experienced before coming to this place: winds like a huge body pummelling her body, winds strong enough to knock her over or lift her off her feet, winds that sometimes made it impossible to move at all. Wind had ripped a car door out of her hands, unlatched the storm door, pushed so hard against their house that they were trapped inside. Winter blizzards rearranged the landscape so that from one day to the next Miranda barely recognized where she was, shoved snow so high against their back door that their closest neighbour, Pat Green, had to plow his way down their lane to dig them out.

Long ago, in a rented house on the tip of Cape Cod, in the midst of Gabrielle, the first hurricane Miranda had lived through, her beautiful mother had been the one to suggest card games. While the wind slammed against the roof and threw seaweed at the windows, Jenny Erens lit an oil lamp and seven-year-old Miranda found cards in a drawer, both of them trying to tempt her moody father, who stared fixedly into the storm, to join them.

In the darkened utility room, when Miranda went to fetch milk, the leftover wind from Hurricane Fernand grew louder, a hoarse cry, high, low, a force loud as a train hammering the walls. The wind, wild even for the island, made her stall. Through the dark window she searched for the slope leading up to the vegetable garden, through the saplings that her father had planted over the years, here in a place where there'd been no trees for centuries.

"Do you remember that storm chaser, the one who went from place to place recording the sounds of typhoons and hurricanes," her father called from the kitchen. "We heard him on the radio, speaking from a shack in the Philippines in the midst of a typhoon, Talas, I believe it was, saying that every storm has its own voice, depending on whether it's blowing through trees or power lines or over city or ocean. Some sound female and some male. This one sounds female, don't you think?"

Did it? From the middle of the kitchen, her sleek black body trembling, Ella let out a bark.

"What is it?" Miranda called to her as the kettle switched off.

"It's just the wind," said her father, ruffling Ella's fur. Yet Ella, who had been born in Nain, on the northern coast of Labrador, who had known hard winds her whole life, stayed tense.

In the mud room, Miranda switched on the outside light. Yellow poured onto the doorstep. At the edge of the bridge, on the steps, lay a slumped form. A hand gripped one of the wooden railings of the bridge the way a drowning man might clasp a piece of driftwood or the edge of a raft to stop himself from being swept out to sea. Shock funnelled through her as the body lifted his head, black hair plastered to his scalp. No one Miranda had ever seen.

She scrambled into her boots and jacket without thinking, wrenching the sticky handle of their everyday door. Beyond it, the wind bucked against the wooden storm door, held in place by hooks, wrestling with Miranda as her fingers stumbled to release the bottom hook. When she undid the top one, the door would swing open and bash into the stranger. What choice did she have? The hook leaped free, and the door slammed out of her hands, pulling her with it.

She was in the blast. Wind and rain tore at her. Wind ripped through her jacket, her hair, her skin, her mouth. A monstrous fury. Was this the worst, the edge of the hugest hurricane ever to pound up the coast? She was nothing to it. Wind would carry her away, but there was someone else, a boy, a young man, trying to pull himself up the steps to her house. She had to help.

She reached out. There was a tug on her hood, her shoulder, an immense strength wrenching her back as she struggled forward, pulling her into the house while the rain bit her face. Her father. There was ferocity in him, her stern protector. "Get inside." He'd thrown on his rain jacket, a rope wrapped around his waist.

"I'll hold onto the rope," Miranda said, giddy and reeling. They were both in the doorway. Wind and rain swept into the room behind them.

"No you won't," her father said. "Tie the rope to the bottom banister."

The house would be his counterweight. In the first hurricane ever to brush the island, Hurricane Jose, he'd struggled outside in the middle of the night to close the door of their store shed, which had swung open, and been caught, swept off his feet, forced to crawl back to the house, inch his way back. Eleven then, Miranda had slept through all of it. He told her the story the morning after, leaving Miranda with nothing but bolts of panic and remorse. Without knowing it she'd almost lost him, the only parent she had left. After that, Alan had strung up ropes between their outbuildings whenever high winds and storms were brewing.

Now, soaked to the skin, she stumbled back through the kitchen, ordinary and warm, cards and mugs still on the table. There was a howling behind the sitting room door, Ella, whom her father must have locked inside. Miranda's heart surged into the storm again. To the stranger. Breathless, she tugged the rope around the banister as tight as she could with a knot her father had taught her.

When the rope went taut, it caught the leg of a kitchen chair and toppled it, pitched the table up against the wall. In the mud room, her father was a silhouette beyond the door, wind pouring into the house, rain like savage stars all around him. Braced against the railing, he lowered himself to reach the stranger. Everything in the room rippled and shook. The empty egg basket took flight. Miranda almost tripped over the rope. Her father hauled the stranger up the steps as the wind screamed. On his hands and knees, the young man was close enough that she could extend a hand to him once more, she and her father working together. The stranger's hand, cold and wet, grasped Miranda's. While her father grabbed his jacket, she pulled him in, battling the wind for him, dragging him over the lintel.

He whispered something as he collapsed to the floor.

Time grew large enough to contain her father, still outside, letting the wind flood over him, as if he wanted to meet the storm, truly see it, feel it, know it. He was shouting into it. Miranda drew in one long, ragged breath. Then her father too was inside, tugging the storm door closed. Once more they were barricaded from the weather, the dark mud room askew, hats pulled from hooks, water pooling across the floor where the stranger lay, a lime-green anorak slick against him. Cold water streamed across Miranda's skin, her hair heavy as a pelt on her back. Stunned excitement flew through her. Her father shook himself the way a dog will after a fight, the room still too full of wind for speech, his skin shining. The stranger closed his eyes. Was he hurt, was he badly injured, dying? The clasp of his hand left its trace on hers. Miranda knelt beside him.

"Don't touch him."

Then it was her father's turn to crouch over the prone body. "Are you in pain?"

Groaning, the stranger curled into a little ball. Like a child. But he shook his head and the tremor of a smile passed across his face. "I'm winded."

Slowly he struggled out of his soaked jacket, Miranda taking hold of each sleeve as he loosened his arms from them. That he was alive and unharmed seemed miraculous. On her father's rain-slick face, there was an expression of kindly, immense, partly suppressed curiosity and relief. They weren't supposed to invite strangers into their house. They weren't supposed to welcome any visitors, at least not people from away, but how could they turn away someone flung onto their doorstep like this?

"What's your name?" Miranda asked.

"Frank," the stranger whispered.

Her father asked, "Frank what?"

After an uncertain pause, in the same hoarse voice, the stranger replied, "Frank Hansen."

Her father nodded with a peculiar expression that made no sense to Miranda. "You can tell us more in a moment, but first let's get you up and out of these clothes. You must be half-frozen and bruised after battling through all that." Alan guided Frank by the elbow as he staggered to his feet. There was shock in him, as if he hadn't yet landed where he was.

He had pale brown skin and high cheekbones, narrow eyes, black hair. A little cotton scarf was knotted around his neck and his cable-knit sweater had holes in it, threads dangling from the cuffs. His tight, muddied jeans were ripped at the knees. From his pocket, he pulled a slim metal phone, soaked like the rest of him, and seemed not to know what to do with it.

In eight years, Miranda could count on her hand the number of times someone from away had stepped inside their house. People from the nearby village of Pummelly stopped by. Caleb Borders used to come all the time. For some years, his mother, Sylvia, too. But from off-island, other than the three young scientists, Anna, Agnes, and Arun, who had visited her father, no one, ever.

. . .

Caleb paced the parlour of his great-aunt Christine's B&B with a restlessness that wouldn't leave him. Nearly midnight. Wind and rain battled against the wide window. Outside lay the world he knew, the small village of Pummelly curved around its flat and treeless harbour, the ocean smashing beyond the outer ring of rocks.

As the evening had worn on and the storm unexpectedly worsened, his great-aunt, who lived just down the road, had called his mother and asked for company, her last guests having left a week ago and her husband having set off some years previous for the grand hotel in the sky. Though he'd have preferred to hold out on his own, his mother, Sylvia, would have none of it, so Caleb was forced to accompany her through the driving rain along Little Harbour Road to his great-aunt's house.

In her parlour, the weather channel blared its endless reel of disastrous news about the hurricane, all the way from Florida up into New England: exploding power plants, flood waters stretching as far as the eye could see. Now the damage included houses with siding stripped away and gushing rivers where there'd once been streets in St. John's, down on the

Avalon Peninsula, where Caleb's aunt Mona and his great-aunt Magdalene lived. From her armchair, his great-aunt Christine was speaking into her phone, telling someone how she'd been trying to reach her sister Magdalene all day. Caleb was halfway across the room when the lights went out, the television plunging into silence. From the kitchen, where his mother had been filling jugs of water at the sink, she gave an exclamation as Caleb held the blue light of his phone to the window, his own face shining back at him, rain streaming over the glass.

His mind surged down the road that led out of the village and into Green Cove, where the girl lived with her father in their little white house. Let her be safe. In the old days, when a gale blew, he would have called her on the land line to see how she was faring, since the land line was all the girl had. Sometimes the pain of being cut off from her still felt like being stabbed. His thoughts swept farther, across the cove, anxious, down the lane on the far side and along the track that led to Cape House, up on its promontory, surrounded by black spruce and field and scrub, waves splintering below.

Everyone had known some wind and rain were coming, the far reaches of the hurricane as it moved out to sea, but no one had predicted such a blow as this. The wind, blasting at Cape House on its landward side, would be broken by spruce trees — as long as the trees themselves didn't break.

Already Cape House had survived so much. Used as his uncle Charlie's sheep shed for years, it was half boarded up when Caleb convinced his uncle to pass the wrecked house on to him. No one else wanted it, and his uncle no longer cared to keep a flock of sheep. In those days, teenagers would break in to drink out of the wind, leaving cans and bottles strewn across the wooden floors. The sheep lived in what had once been the dining room and parlour, shut in by planks nailed across the doorways. Boards covered the tall bow windows. Hay bales filled the breezeway and were stacked along the far kitchen wall. As a boy, Caleb sometimes stopped by, riding on quads with his uncles and cousins. Later he started biking out to the house by himself, his cousins, that pack of boys, leaving him to his own devices. He brought a broom to sweep the kitchen floor free of straw and cans and bottle caps and swirling dog hair. A hammer to nail down loose floorboards. A wooden fisherman's daybed, with an ancient quilt flung over it, clung to a corner. Sheep hooves clunked from the parlour. Caleb had stood on the bridge outside the back door, scenting the land like a fox, as a dragonfly hovered. He had let himself imagine the views out to sea through the boarded-up windows, right to the edge of the blue horizon. The house itself whispered to him. He felt at home out there, at ease in a way he never did other places. Out there, the colour of his skin, so unlike that of everyone around him, didn't matter.

Sand brown. Dark hair, thick with waves. That's what his reflection showed him. He looked nothing like his cousins or his tall, pale, red-haired mother, that much was for certain. Not her lips or eyes but someone else's. His mother had told him how she'd discovered she was pregnant a year to the day after her own mother had died and this had seemed a beautiful omen. A fine story, yes, but a fatherless one.

There was a man out there somewhere, or there had once been, a man his mother refused to speak of even now. Caleb had searched their house on Little Harbour Road for clues, for photographs. The old kind you printed out. The photos on his mother's computer began with their arrival on the island, when he was two, and from their earliest days in Pummelly there was only a scattered one of himself as a wary-eyed, chubby toddler.

As a boy, he'd walked awestruck under the high and still-grand ceilings of Cape House, past the rippling wallpaper, the wide staircase up to the second floor. There was a hand pump outside the back door and clear spring water poured from it. When the girl arrived in his life, he brought her out there, herself an outsider, too, with her solar-panelled house and wind turbine spinning in its field. They sat on the broken bridge and watched fox cubs tumble in the long grass. Waving away stouts and nippers, they followed the path that led beyond the house, hugging the rocky shore all the way out to the headlands. Caribou grazed in the marshy fields beyond the scrubby borderland of spruce trees, their mottled bodies moving slowly in the distance, ankles clicking, heads raised as the wind carried to them a human scent or the sound of footsteps above the crash of waves.

Now the house would be protected by the new shingles Caleb had tarred and nailed to the roof, the new clapboard he'd laid over the blue sheets of Cladmate tacked and taped between the strapping. This he told himself as he paced. On the inside, he'd stripped the parlour walls, added pink insulation and a plastic vapour barrier. He was fixing things slowly, carefully, room by room, sanding the parlour floors, installing snug windows, safeguarding the old house as best he could from the new weather, the new storms carrying winds up from the Caribbean like the trade ships of old, bringing them all this way north.

The wind had shifted, from a southeasterly, into the east. There must be cracks in his great-aunt's house, slivers around the airtight windows through which the wind whistled and sang. Safe where he was, Caleb longed to be elsewhere, out at Cape House, feeling the wind in his bones as it hit those walls. Helplessness rose in him, and a different urgency, the desire to repair another thing, to discover the act of salvage that would bring the girl back to him. There must be a way. He had a house. He'd told her his dream and seen a bright light in her eyes as he'd done so. When they'd kissed, she had been slow to pull away.

From the dining room, his mother called, "Caleb, stop pacing. Come join us." His great-aunt had the Scrabble set out, pieces clattering on the table, the squeak of a cork as his mother poured herself a shot of whiskey. Candlelight shivered up the walls, wind gusts coming at them now from every direction. The very rocks beneath them shook.

Caleb was in the dining-room doorway when the air itself turned suction, a vacuum pulling at him, popping his ears. His great-aunt glanced behind her at the weather glass on the wall as a shudder ran all through the house. A boom sounded. The back door burst open, as if ghosts were plunging in along with the storm.

He was first at the door, rain already soaking their jackets and boots. The coat tree toppled. He had to struggle through a thicket of downed cloth in order to reach his boots and thrust his feet into them. One thought spurred him on: he had to get to Cape House to find out what had happened there.

A loose piece of siding clattered down the rain-veiled road as his mother's voice burst from behind him. "Caleb, what do you think you're doing?"

He couldn't say, Driving out to Cape House.

That *was* cracked.

He couldn't say, Looking out for my future.

Grabbing him by the arm, his tall and still-strong mother wrenched the door closed as his great-aunt's tourist booklets took flight in the dark all around them.

. . .

They settled Frank in a chair by the wood stove. It would take him hours to undo the laces of his boots, Miranda thought, having stepped out of her rubber boots in seconds, her father also, these boots like a second skin, almost all they ever wore. Nevertheless Frank tackled the tight, soaked laces with fumbling fingers. Released from the sitting room, Ella bounded to sniff him, impolite, ecstatic. The heat from the stove heightened the salt smell of his clothes. There was sand in his hair, mud on his knees where his skinny jeans had ripped and more sand all over him. It was impossible to stop staring. He, too, kept halting as if to take in where he was.

"I'll get you some dry things," Miranda said, attempting to break from her trance.

Frank was tall, taller than her father, long-legged. Upstairs, in her father's wind-loud bedroom, she pulled jeans from his chest of drawers, a sweater, decided to forget about underwear. She was back in the kitchen before thinking about a towel, he'd want a towel as well.

"So you drove all the way from Boston," her father was saying. He'd already embarked on some kind of interrogation, Ella curled in a ball at Frank's feet.

"Yeah." Frank seemed reluctant to say more. "I took off right after the hurricane began moving north again, ahead of any mandatory evacuation call. You could still buy gas most places. I confess, I drove fast."

He seemed relieved by Miranda's reappearance. She explained things—bathroom upstairs on the left, spare room on your right, towels in the chest of drawers in the bathroom. By now he'd managed to remove his sodden boots and socks. He had long, slender feet. Miranda couldn't help staring at them. Reaching out a hand to him in the storm had felt like a dream. This didn't. No, it felt like a different kind of dream. What kind? Excuse the mess in the spare room. Watch your head on the ceiling beams.

"Thanks, Miranda."

He was an American. In his voice she heard traces of the voices of her childhood, from her life before.

"No whiplash?" her father asked. "No concussion?"

Frank touched places on his body where he said he was stiff. He shook out his right arm. The kettle was boiling again. The wind had turned from the southeast into the east, billowing against the mud-room walls. On his way out of the room, Frank stopped to lean against the table, Ella now at his heels. Miranda called her back.

He was upstairs, in the bathroom, no doubt taking off his clothes. Pipes shuddered. In the kitchen, Miranda tried not to think about the stranger's naked body. Downstairs, it was just the two of them, she and her father, as it had been since they'd come to the cove and made a new life for themselves in this wild and far-off place. There was a deliciousness to be felt in walking for hours over rocks and scrub with the wind in her ears, by herself or in the company of her dog, feeling the long strides of her own body, becoming unhuman as her father said, Ella making her own loops outward. But now, Miranda's body seemed to be undergoing another rearrangement, the entire surface of her skin quickening.

Earlier that evening, her father had received a phone call. He didn't receive many calls. Neither of them did. As soon as he saw the number on the screen, he had headed out of the house, away from Miranda, so that she'd caught only stray words as the door closed behind him: *How was the flight?* And: *Haven't heard from Agnes. Arun's trapped in Boston.* When he re-entered the house, he said nothing about the call and didn't mention who had been phoning him. Flight, Miranda thought. This had pricked her attention. Also: Arun. And Agnes.

Now, as her father dropped two tea bags into the teapot, poured hot water in, and set the tea cozy over it, she could ask him about the call. Or now, as she carried the pot to the table, soothed by its ordinary warmth, as her father placed Frank's wet boots by the stove. The way her father moved was so familiar it was like something inside Miranda, and some part of her was reluctant to disturb this ease.

Footsteps clunked down the stairs. Frank burst into sight at the foot of them, black hair towelled and tufted. The clothes altered him. The sweater was one that eighty-five-year-old Mary Green had knit, from wool that Miranda had dyed with Sylvia Borders's help. Sylvia had spun the wool from the sheep of Pat Green, their neighbour and Mary's oldest son. The jeans barely reached Frank's ankles. He had to hunch beneath the ceiling beams in order not to knock his head. The socks were thick wool, a pair of Miranda's making.

"Magnificent," said her father. Given his usual feelings about strangers, would he, as soon as the weather settled and

Frank got his bearings, ask him to leave? The thought plucked at Miranda as she hung Frank's wet clothes on the drying lines strung around the wood stove, ripped jeans, a thermal shirt of some slippery high-tech material, bedraggled sweater. The wind jittered through the cloth. Her own jeans were patched where she'd carefully mended them.

"I don't suppose you have a dryer," Frank asked, handing over his black boxers.

"Wind and wood stove's our dryer," said Alan as Miranda pegged the damp boxers to the line. Moments before Frank's body had touched them and something moved into her fingers like an electric spark.

"Aha," said Frank. "Well then, it'll be a bit festive in here."

Miranda asked if he wanted a cup of tea. Her cheeks flushed. Boston, he'd come all the way from Boston. Frank gave her a radiant smile.

There was brightness in him, but then a wave of wooziness seemed to wash over his body. Alan told Frank to sit down. Did he want to lie down? Frank shook his head. But he began to shiver. Miranda bolted upstairs to yank the quilt from the spare room bed and when she handed it over, Frank wrapped himself tightly in it, sinking into a chair. He was so slim. Ella watched him, dark-eyed.

"You came on the ferry?" Alan's tone was kind, almost fatherly.

"The one that left at six o'clock. The wind was blowing but not like now."

Miranda's mouth was full of questions, even though her father was the one asking them.

"Wouldn't it have been wiser to find somewhere to pull in for the night?"

"Everything was shut up. I couldn't find a motel so I pulled over for a while, but then I decided to keep driving."

"All the way across the island."

"I didn't know how far—. At last I came to the top of this big hill. By now the wind was trying to push me off the road. At the bottom I saw water, but I could make out the other side in my headlights so I thought I'd gun it, which is stupid—next thing I knew I was in the current. The car struck something and tipped, water started pouring in through the floor. I was trying not to panic. I managed to get the window open before the electrical cut out—"

A needle of concern creased Alan's forehead.

"I squeezed through and dove—"

"I'm guessing you were in the cove, and this is the brook you're describing."

"It was totally dark. The current was so strong, I was sure I was going to be swept away. My mouth was full of salt water, there were rocks—and then I saw your light way in the distance. My feet touched sand, I grabbed hold of some grass, I thought, All I have to do to live is reach the light. I crawled across a big field. It took a long time but I kept clawing my way forward."

"You're lucky to be alive." The ghost of another possibility twitched across her father's body. The feeling passed through Miranda as her father reached out and touched Frank's arm. Who knew how many hours he'd been out there.

Some people were saved from accidents. There could be this huge, stupendous grace. Exhilaration rose in her. Frank stumbled to his feet, wrapped in the quilt. "Thank you for hearing me howl at your door and rescuing a stranger on a night like this."

"Miranda heard you," said Alan.

"Ella did."

Frank wrapped his quilted arms around Alan, then Miranda. It was like being hugged by a tent. She had never been hugged by a strange young man before. The steady warmth of his body stunned her. The surprising strength of the hug. Frank patted Ella's eager head.

At the counter, Miranda cut slices of bread and slathered them with butter and jam to calm herself, bread her father had baked that morning, partridgeberry jam she'd made the previous fall. She handed a slice to Frank. The moist bread in her mouth felt delicious, the slide of butter, tart burst of jam, she ate avidly, something to set against her unsettled body, against the wind still flooding all around them, Frank's presence, his hug. Tremors moved up through her feet. They could measure the wind's velocity and atmospheric pressure in the weather notebooks that she and her father kept, but sometimes measurements were nothing compared to how the wind felt. The house had firm bones, even as it shook, and it had stood through centuries, through so many, many storms. In Nova Scotia, even down on the Avalon, people were dying, homes destroyed, birds and animals drowned as well. Their house would surely stand through this gale. Except the winds, and storms, were getting worse.

Storms move in a circle: her father had taught her this, and Miranda had learned to feel it. Would the three of them play cards, would they stay up all night? Should she tell Frank to go to bed? Possibly the wind was lessening as it turned. No. The next instant, gusts piled at the house from every direction.

"Pressure's still dropping," Alan said, after checking the electronic barometer mounted on the wall in the utility room. "Really dropping, it's plunging." Then it was as if all the air was sucked out of the house. A great clobbering began from above. Never in Miranda's memory of other storms had anything quite like this happened. Her heart boomed. The clobbering stopped. They were still here. She was. Her father. Frank. Ella. Let everything, everyone, every creature around them be okay.

"How about a joke?" said Frank in a disembodied voice. "What did one hurricane say to the other?" He answered before Miranda could. "I've got my eye on you." He winked.

"We're still standing." Her father peered through the kitchen window, let out a ghost of a laugh. "It's a full moon and high tide so waves will be high in the cove and likely spill into the fields, but they won't reach us here on our slope. We'll be all right."

They hadn't lost power. Miranda poured more tea as her father asked Frank if there was a particular reason he'd decided to drive all the way from Boston, just ahead of the most massive hurricane to hit the North American east coast since weather records began?

"Birds," blurted Frank.

"Birds," said Alan, with a stir of incredulity.

"Accidentals, ones that get tossed far off course, you know like Caribbean or European birds blown astounding distances, so you get singular sightings, ones for your life list, especially now, sadly, since bird numbers are plummeting. Once off the coast of Maine I saw a red-billed tropicbird."

"You're a serious birder then," said Alan.

"Trying to be," said Frank. "There's an island near here, the Grand Funk Island, where there's a bird sanctuary. I'm trying to get to that."

"You mean Funk Island," said Miranda.

"Oh, yeah, right," said Frank as if caught out.

"Once we saw a flamingo, out in the cove, after a storm," Miranda told him.

"A flamingo?" said Frank in astonishment.

"Out there—you can't see now, where you, where the brook goes out to the sea. It stayed for a day. At first we didn't believe it." She turned to her father for confirmation and found him giving her an assessing look. Pointing to the pair of binoculars perched on the windowsill, heat in her cheeks, she told Frank how they'd stared in wonder at the improbable bird, so pink it couldn't be anything else, though too far off to photograph. Another time, they'd spotted a purple gallinule out on the rocks. When Frank looked puzzled, she told him this was a shorebird from the Carolinas and Florida—with yellow feet?

At that Frank nodded vigorously and said he was sure he'd seen them in the past.

"There've been more accidentals in recent years, given the new storms pushing up from the south, so you may well have come to the right place," said Alan. "Though the middle of the night, you have to admit, is hardly the best time to look for birds."

Frank had an engaging smile, and some bravado seemed to rise in him in the face of her father's persistence.

"I figured I'd eventually find someone to take me in."

He was smiling yet not in the room. Black hair matted to his forehead, quilt pulled tight as he peered out above it, he looked as if the wind had forced its way inside him. Miranda wanted her father's questions to stop.

Lying in bed in the dark, her bedroom warmed by the wood stove below, she felt lonely, even with Ella's body pressed against her, hard as a barnacle. The wind had swung around to the north. *I will look after you.* This had always been her father's promise. On the other side of the wall lay Frank, in the bed that her father had brought into the house when the first of the three young scientists came to visit. Their beds faced away from each other through the wall, Frank's head so close to hers she almost didn't want to think about it. The mystery of her father's phone call nudged her again, the words, *How was your flight?*

Who else was here? Where were they?

Frank creaked the mattress, startling her. Through the wall, came his muffled voice. "Good night, Miranda."

The wind had calmed when Miranda slid from bed, into the dove grey of early morning. Ella a shadow at her heels, she stepped outside as silently as she could. Small cumulus clouds scudded across the sky. Yellow burst over the grassy eastern hills that led to the village of Pummelly, beyond their own shimmery slope of alders. The wet roofs of their ring of outbuildings glistened. The green wind flag that her father had mounted when they first moved to the cove leaped softly atop its pole. The wind turbine stood in the field beside Pat Green's sheep pasture, on the way up the lane, supported by cables and posts drilled deep into the ground, switched off by her father before the storm. The solar panels hadn't fallen from the roof. The hens burbled in their house. In a moment Miranda would feed them, Rosie, the loudest, the bossy one, always the first at the grain. That nothing seemed fundamentally altered calmed Miranda to the bottom of her soul.

Until she moved away from the house. In the distance, down in the cove, where usually pale sand formed a wide crescent, banked by flats of marram grass, spread water, nothing but water. That was the first shock. On the inland side, a torrent rushed out of the low spruce forest, a river so fierce it had cracked the road open, slabs of asphalt broken like teeth and tossed aside. In the froth lay Frank's half-submerged car, shattered glass and bluish metal. Miranda's breath caught. Somehow he'd pulled himself from that. A line of alders, thin black poles, stood between road and water, all that was left of the beach and the land behind it, the morning tide still rising. She squinted. The footbridge that ordinarily crossed the brook, on the shore side of the road, was missing. Most of the alders and dogwoods lining the road were underwater. Never in all her years in the cove, in all the storms she'd lived through, had the road been ripped open and the beach in Green Cove completely vanished.

Swift and silent in his approach, her father, beside her, viewed the scene through binoculars with similar intensity. On the high hill beyond the cove, the highest on the island and the one that everyone called Telephone Hill, the cellphone tower leaned at a rakish angle, some of its support wires dangling, receptor panels askew.

"Look at that," Alan said.

"Is he still sleeping?" Somehow Miranda couldn't bring herself to mention Frank by name.

"I believe he is." Her father pulled out his phone. "It's always cheering when a high pressure system follows a storm and the sun shines down on us, even though we're without a road, not to mention no cellular or internet connection, it looks like."

Through binoculars they took turns examining the wreck of Frank's car. And the gaping road and vanished beach and the broken cellphone tower on its hill above the flood, all laid bare by sunlight sharp as a knife. Lacking a cellphone, the disabled tower meant little to Miranda. No strange birds, only a pair of common murres flew past. Alan scanned the hills around them. Ella dove into the long grass.

They had their own satellite connection, separate from the island's large dish located in the town of Blaze, the biggest community on the island, and usually they didn't lose the internet in storms. Pulling the extension ladder from the storage area beneath the house, Alan said he'd climb to the roof to check on the state of their smaller dish. Quietly. No sign of any problem with their connection, he told her as he descended, Miranda holding the ladder hard to keep it steady.

The storm must still be messing up signals high in the atmosphere. Or there were problems elsewhere. Wherever their internet server was. Maybe in one of those places she'd glimpsed online. Washington, DC, where hundreds might be dead, she'd read over her father's shoulder. Closer places. Drowned cars and flooded neighbourhoods in Halifax. The tidal marshes breached, cutting Nova Scotia off temporarily from the rest of Canada, making it another island.

Likely the stranger, Frank, had followed the same roads they'd sped along in their own flight north nine years before—the journey her father insisted they keep to themselves. They'd crossed the border from the United States into Canada, travelling on the all-night ferry from Sydney, Nova Scotia, then the second small ferry that, pointing out to sea, had brought them to Blaze Island.

There had been brilliant skies the morning after Hurricane Gabrielle, which had ripped shingles from the roof of their vacation house in Provincetown. On the beach the next morning, sand crystals shining in the light, seven-year-old Miranda had walked wonderingly with her mother past house after house torn open by the storm's ferocious tide. Every house beyond the breakwater had its seaward wall swept away, rooms exposed like underwear. Their house, the first within the breakwater, was spared. Her mother took Miranda's hand and squeezed it. Then she gave an exhalation and darted off.

When Miranda caught up to her, not far away, her mother was kneeling on the damp sand left by the retreating tide, digging with her long fingers, tugging at something small and white. She pulled out a slim tube with a little bowl at one end. A pipe, she said, a very old clay pipe. Eighteenth century, probably. There was more: shards of glazed pottery, pieces of beach glass in rare colours, red and blue. How had she known these things were there? A long time ago, Miranda's mother said, people had tossed such things into the sea and the sand had swallowed them, but a strong storm tide will unearth them and return them to the surface. Storms stir up the past. She opened Miranda's palm, dropping the objects into it, closing Miranda's fingers into a fist to cup the treasures, her now-lost fingers making a heat around Miranda's, as if she were removing the image of the violated houses and replacing them with this. Her mother had painted a version of that scene, them, the beach, the houses, flickering figures beneath shining, semi-translucent layers of colour; it was one of the paintings Miranda and her father had been forced to leave behind in their flight.

Outside their house in the cove, her father was saying, "I'm going to head in to the cabin now to check on things there. Given the night we had, I'm worried about water damage. Any leaks would be devastating to the computer equipment. I won't be long. Thing is, I also need to get hold of Caleb. He's supposed to be running a rather urgent errand for me to Tom's Neck this morning."

Miranda had the distinct sensation that her father was both confiding in her and not telling her everything. It was not an unfamiliar feeling. The cabin, forty-five minutes away on foot, less by quad, was where her father had taken to doing much of his work in recent years. His weather studying and weather monitoring.

The afternoon before, he'd been out there, far off along the shore, when a small plane had buzzed as it circled in its descent, noticeable because such a rare occurrence. Working in the garden, Miranda had dropped her pitchfork at the sound. There were no regular flights to the island. Something medical, she wondered, cumulus clouds already gathering. Perhaps someone seeking safety before the coming storm?

"You could stop off in Pummelly," she said, though her father wouldn't want to go by Caleb's house, given the chance of encountering Sylvia.

Storms stir up the past.

There was mist in the air as, for the last time, Miranda's father locked the door of their house in Princeton, New Jersey, red brick with ivy climbing up the walls.

Only one person had come to see them off that early July morning, weeks after Miranda's tenth birthday. Her father's colleague, white-haired Adolphus Rowe, marine biologist, once of Newfoundland's Trinity Bay, leaned his bicycle against a red-brick wall. Just after seven o'clock, maybe it was simply too early for the neighbours to stop round to say goodbye. Their bags and boxes were already in the car, packed in the back seat, the trunk, the roof rack. All else that had belonged to Miranda was gone. Sold. Given away. How swiftly she'd learned that your life can be ripped without warning from your hands.

In the driveway of the Princeton house, Adolphus gave Miranda a bear hug. He hugged her father hard as well, whispering something urgent in his ear. Knapsack in one hand, thermos in the other, Miranda climbed carefully into the front seat, trying not to disturb the weather all around her. Her haggard father said that it was her choice, to sit in the front seat beside him, since she was tall enough, or in the back where she always sat. Wherever she was, her mother's absence in the front seat was the shadow in the car that neither of them could escape.

The rain began as soon as they turned the corner from Prospect Avenue onto Harrison and grew heavier by the time they reached the interstate. The rain was all the tears Miranda couldn't shed. She'd cried so much she no longer felt like crying. Rain punished the windscreen. Her father didn't remove his sunglasses. He was wearing a ball cap, something he never used to do. And growing a beard. With wiry dark hair covering his cheeks he was barely recognizable as the father Miranda had known, which brought her equal measures of unease and relief.

They had arrived in the US from England the year Miranda turned six, travelling across the Atlantic by steamer, which no one did anymore. Her father had insisted on it. When she was two, they'd flown to England from Canada but when it came time to return to North America, her father said there'd be no more flying. They had to keep their carbon budget down, all three of them together.

Miranda remembered the week at sea, the swells, standing on deck with her mother, gaining her sea legs while staring at the horizon all the way from Southampton to New York. Manhattan-born Jenny was happy to be coming home, back into the orbit of her art school friends, the Chelsea gallery that represented her, her family. To Miranda, everything was new: their house in Princeton, people's voices, the trips into the city, as her mother called it, her grandparents' Upper West Side apartment. Even her father, appointed first director of the new Climate and Cryosphere Center at the university, seemed new and shiny, and there was something new in the way people looked at him, with wide warmth and thrilling respect, and the people themselves were new, these Americans. They invited the three of them to dinner. They didn't hesitate to embrace Miranda.

Yes, her father worried about the weather as he always had, but he was excited by his work, the centre, their life. A lot of weather made up the climate, he told Miranda. Climate was weather over long periods of time and this was what he studied. He'd always had a galvanizing energy. In Princeton this energy seemed intensified. Her parents biked Miranda to school each day, sometimes together, sometimes one or the other. Her mother, home from her studio in a building near the university, burst through the door in a rush. Absorbed in his work, her father looked up from his laptop at the sight of Miranda and held open his arms. *Sweetheart*, he said softly, as if he found something about her eternally surprising. And disturbing. She didn't know what or why but she allowed the surprise to feel good and pleasure to ripple through her. Happiness flew between all three of them.

Milan Wells met Jenny Erens by chance at an art opening. Once, Miranda's parents had loved telling her these stories. Briefly at loose ends, Milan was just back from months on a field campaign drilling ice cores that told the story of ancient climate in the Arctic. Still with longish hair and darkened face, a snow-goggle tan that left him with white owl-like eyes, he walked into a Manhattan art gallery with the geochemist whom he was visiting. Five years out of art school, six months out of a relationship with another painter named Helen Krane, Jenny spotted him as soon as he walked in the door and sought him out as he stood, arms crossed, in front of a painting of an iceberg. Milan asked Jenny if she'd ever seen a real one. He showed her photographs of icebergs on his phone. So unlike the artists all around them, he told her stories about the world of snow and ice that he studied, the cryosphere, where he'd been weeks before. Abandoning the gallery, they walked to the river, imagining the warm world around them covered in ice as it had once been.

At her loft in Brooklyn, Jenny showed Milan her museum-sized paintings of forests, cities, people, paintings whose transparent layers of radiant colour seemed almost as alive as the two of them standing close together, hands entwined, bodies rustling. He told her how his Czech-Canadian mother, Magda, after giving birth to him in a hospital in east-end Toronto, had named him for a writer whose work she loved. He had one name from each of his parents, Milan from his mother, Wells from his English father, both of them immigrants to the new land of Canada. Born in winter, in the midst of a snowstorm, Milan Wells had loved snow from the moment of his birth.

He didn't leave Jenny's loft until he'd convinced her to run away with him, north to Waterloo, Ontario, where he was teaching at the university, and where, he told her, Amish drove around in blue clothes and hats in their horse-drawn buggies and lived in houses where they used no electricity at all.

—

As Miranda and her father sped north up the interstate, I-95, she stared west towards the river and the misty towers of Manhattan where her mother had grown up. Shabbat dinner in her grandparents' apartment, the five of them gathered around the table as her grandfather Adam lit the candles, gone. Her friends in Princeton, Uma Srinivasan, Ellen Markowitz, vanished behind Miranda like fluttering scraps.

She had seen her grandparents only once since her mother's death. Bones showed through the skin of her grandmother Sarah's face and her silent grandfather's long-fingered hands had stiffened. They barely hugged her father, as if, though they couldn't say it, they blamed him for what had happened to their daughter.

Uma Srinivasan, whose mother dropped her off and picked her up in a large white van, had loved to brush Miranda's hair. They told each other's fortunes, folding paper into triangles to make a fortune teller, Miranda sliding her hands into the paper folds. When Uma pointed at the four, Miranda walked her fingers back and forth. Unfolding the final tab, Uma read out the words, You'll be famous. Then it was Miranda's turn. Six. Blue. You'll fall in love. How soft Uma's hair had been between Miranda's fingers. Before Miranda's departure, they'd taken each other's pictures on their phones, but then Miranda's father had taken away her phone, which she'd only had for six months, downloading her photos and music onto his laptop. Rage and helplessness poured through her. She tried to squelch the feelings. He said they both had to give up their phones and numbers for security reasons. He looked like he wanted to say more but couldn't. There was anger in him but it wasn't directed at her.

—

Storms can arrive without warning.

One day back in February, her father had walked into the kitchen of the Princeton house, where at the wide butcher-block island Miranda's mother was helping Miranda with a page of Spanish homework. He spoke in a voice Miranda had never heard before: "Jenny, someone's hacked into my email account—either it was an inside job or whoever did it leaked what they stole. Because stuff from my emails, it's all over this climate-change denier's blog, from my correspondence with Ian Petersen about our research—sections, phrases taken totally out of context. Someone forwarded the link to Paul Fletcher and he sent it to me. The guy's twisting things, making it sound like I've altered data to show warming. It's all lies. He's misusing words like *proxy*. You know these guys, they pull their own graphs and numbers out of nowhere, or it might as well be nowhere, but they have a way of sounding convincing. I'm worried."

"It's one man's blog," Miranda's mother said. "Is it that big a deal?"

"Yes," Miranda's father said in his newly unrecognizable voice, sounding as if someone had squeezed their hands around his neck and, when they let go, left his vocal cords raw and bruised. "The *New York Times* just called." He stood in the kitchen doorway. Miranda touched her own throat softly. "He's a big deal among the deniers, and they've got big money behind them, the fossil-fuel companies hiding behind fake scientific institutes. They're all desperate to undermine us because getting off carbon means rewriting the geopolitical landscape, not to mention our whole economy—"

"Ian Petersen, Paul Fletcher, the others, the scientific

community will support you, won't they?" said Miranda's mother. On her feet, she pressed Miranda's father's cheek with one hand, kissed him, messed with his hair.

"Yes, but the ones I'm closest to, my colleagues, they're implicated, Jenny. Don't you see? These guys, blog guy, they want to sow doubt any way they can, they'll play dirty, they don't care, and people don't want to believe the truth. I stuck my neck out by saying climate science is a moral issue, we can't ignore the numbers going up and up—. Now they've targeted me and this thing's going to break—"

"Don't let the bastards grind you down," said Miranda's mother.

In response her father's face made the strangest contortion, a ripple of volatility and panic.

What Miranda knew was this: her father was director of the centre but he was also principal investigator of several research campaigns and the lead author of several important papers. When she was younger and they lived in England, he'd gone away a couple of times for months, from spring into summer, up onto the Greenland ice sheet to drill down into the ice and pull up long white cores that were a record of deep time, tens of thousands, even a hundred thousand years. He studied the bubbles of gas in ancient air trapped in the ice, how these changed through time, including recent time.

The summer after they arrived in Princeton, he went north once again. And the summer after that. Her mother, seized by a new restlessness, said it was necessary. He was doing important work. He took ships to reach Greenland, not planes, and a reporter wrote an article about his unwavering commitment to the implications of his research. In the accompanying photograph, her father looked charismatic and dashing. But he was very far away. Meanwhile Miranda accompanied her mother to her studio, where she sat in a corner and drew while her mother painted: a skyline overlaid with miniature human figures and smooth blue water, layer upon layer of shining paint; tiny, ghostly wolves running along an avenue of towers, among the blurry yellow taxis; paintings that made you look close to see what they were hiding. The two of them went into Manhattan by train, tried on vintage dresses in small boutiques that smelled of old perfume, hung out in boisterous cafés with Jenny's artist friends, sometimes staying overnight at Miranda's grandparents' apartment, sleeping together in her mother's childhood bed.

Her parents limited Miranda's online access but sometimes, wistfully, she looked her father up. He had his own website. So did her mother. Miranda looked her up, too.

Her father's interests were: understanding natural and anthropogenic climate and environmental change through the lens of atmospheric composition and chemistry; the atmospheric CO_2 budget; interactions with atmospheric, cryospheric, and ocean systems. She understood, from her mother, that he was lead author on a particularly import-ant paper showing evidence that certain gases, once stable, had begun to rise sharply in the atmosphere. People need to do something about the rising gases, Miranda's mother said. That's why her father had sounded the alarm, as other climate scientists had tried to do before him. *We're in deep shit,* he'd said in an interview after the important paper was published. Miranda found this online, learned that his blunt words were repeated everywhere. This was why journalists had called and sent him hundreds of emails. It was brave of him, Jenny said to Miranda, but there are risks. Ordinarily scientists are supposed to keep quiet and stand behind their data. When Miranda asked what the risk was, her mother said with a grimace, Of saying things people don't want to hear.

What entranced Miranda most on her father's website were the photographs: her lean father bundled deep in a red parka against a bright white landscape, little orange tents dotting the flat white land, a snakelike river of blue winding through thick grey ice, her father pulling a core of ancient time up on a pulley. In the first photograph he stared narrow-eyed out of the frame, peering urgently at the world as if from far away, the father she knew and not the father she knew.

In the wake of the email hacking, people were saying other things about him. Even her classmates seemed to know something had happened. It was in all the papers and everywhere online and on TV. From the seat in front of her, Nathan Reid, who'd never liked her, turned and announced, Your Dad's a liar. No, he's not, Miranda said. Maybe he got something wrong, said Cassandra Leon, who sometimes gave Miranda candies, and sometimes laughed at her accent.

One day Miranda came out of her bedroom as her father stepped from his second-floor study, saying goodbye to someone on his phone. Startled, his eyes darkened, as if he were holding a secret only it wasn't a secret he wanted to be hiding.

"Hello, Miranda," he said. Talking to her seemed painful, as if someone still had their hands gripped around his neck. "I've been summoned before the board of my research centre. They're concerned about the hacking, but they aren't so kindly disposed to my having told the world we're in trouble. Apparently my message is too negative. It attracts the wrong kind of attention. Somehow that's my fault."

His laugh rose into a high octave, into that nearly strangled place. Miranda reached out a hand, and to her surprise her father took it. The tips of his fingers were as cold as ice.

"The university administration wants to meet with me. Next it'll be Congress. The accusations are a joke, yet everyone's taking them very seriously." He squeezed her hand, then dropped it as if it were a hot coal. "I shouldn't be telling you these things. Go out and play."

Their house held a new, tense quiet: Miranda entered rooms in which subdued conversations between her parents lingered. *They're saying proxy means fake when it just means we have to rely on evidence to infer temperature. You can read about it in fucking Wikipedia.* Sometimes they raised their voices at each other, which made Miranda's stomach hurt. *Don't be reckless!* she heard her mother shout. Her father's words, *We're in deep shit,* echoed inside her. Were they? Some days she couldn't eat anything at all. Her mother's plan to bring home a parrot faltered. Her father was suddenly around the house all the time.

He told Miranda in a brusque yet mournful voice that the university had asked him to step down temporarily from his directorship while they investigated the allegations against him. He said it was an official process; it didn't mean they believed the lies. Yes, other scientists had spoken out in support of him but there was bound to be social push-back when you assailed the status quo and what you said meant people needed to alter their lives radically. The deniers were in bed with the biggest companies and politicians who couldn't stomach the scale of intervention required, who wanted to go on making huge sums of money from oil and gas instead of keeping the fossil fuels in the ground. Banks, the whole financial system, were sunk deep into fossil fuels. Meanwhile her father wandered about, upstairs and down, wearing a tuque and down vest indoors as if some penetrating cold had entered him. At Miranda's bedtime her mother curled up beside her in her little bed and sang her lullabies.

One night Miranda and her mother came home to find her father sitting on the bottom stair in his tuque, cradling a glass of whiskey. "I've agreed to go on the *Julio O'Brien Show* along with the guy who first accused me, blog guy," Miranda's father announced with a frown.

His words made her mother go still. "But there's no debate, Milan," she said. "It'll be ugly. Don't do it."

"Do I have a choice?" Miranda's father replied, as an ugliness passed across his face as well.

Miranda's mother didn't want Miranda to watch her father on the *Julio O'Brien Show* with the man her father sometimes called the worst of the deniers. It was on a school night, far too late, but when Miranda wouldn't stop crying, her weary mother relented.

And there her father was, shining with handsomeness, debonair in his sleek suit, the fake studio skyline behind him, seated next to Julio himself, the man with the biggest gestures and knowing smile. The other man, in the rumpled jacket and tie, with a bulldog stare behind dark-rimmed glasses, was Canadian, as they were, her father had told Miranda. How an economics degree gave him climate science expertise, her father had no idea, though this man kept interrupting him—

"You make these outrageous statements, Millie, based on dubious data. You have no proof—"

"The data's only dubious because you say it is," said Miranda's father, and despite his obvious frustration there was still swagger in him, which made Miranda's stomach spark.

"Science provides consensus, Tony, based on the organized accumulation of data and the continual scrutiny of evidence. We have consensus."

"Like I said, you have no proof—"

"No one can prove anything about the future," Miranda's father said with a shaft of anger. His face went still, as if he wished, more fervently than anything in the world, to retract what he'd just uttered.

Because the man in glasses and rumpled suit, waving his arms like a conductor, repeated the words as if his own certainty were a form of salvation, until the studio audience took them up like a chant. *No proof. No proof. No proof.*

Their voices seared into Miranda, as Jenny leaped from the sofa, remote control in hand.

The next day and the day after, Miranda didn't try reaching out to her father. There was something newly frightening about him, which made her fear that any comfort she had to offer would fail, and then what would happen? She overheard him on the phone muttering about someone threatening him with a lawsuit: *The bastards aren't just lying about me, they're trying to muzzle me!* Another time she entered the kitchen as he said something about an envelope of white powder delivered to his office. *The university's talking about giving me a security detail—*

As soon as he saw her, he broke off.

. . .

First thing in the morning, Caleb went to see how the animals had weathered the storm, up in the small, ochre-coloured barn tucked into the hillside beyond the house he shared with his mother at the end of Little Harbour Road. He forked the goats some hay from the loft and asked them how their night had been. Gabby and Jewel seemed restless in the wake of all that wind. Noelle was eager to press her head against him and have him rub her nose, while Fleur's yellow, square-pupilled eyes met his as she mashed at a mouthful of hay. Caleb released the girls into their paddock and scattered a bowl of food scraps from his great-aunt's kitchen for the chattering hens.

The power was still out but the house and stores were untouched, only a few loose roof shingles scattered on the ground. Impossible to know how far the outage extended, whether around Pummelly, across the island, or beyond. Or where the damage was. There was no television or Instagram to tell him. Not even his phone seemed to be working now. It wasn't the battery, he couldn't get a signal. He switched it off, desperate to get out to Cape House as soon as he could.

When he'd left the old man's place at the end of the previous afternoon, after picking up the visitors from the airstrip and delivering them to their guesthouse in Tom's Neck, the old man had asked him to return first thing in the morning. Now it was the morning after a storm worse than either the old man or any online weather report had predicted. Surely everything would move more slowly because of it.

The old man. For the past year, Caleb could no longer bring himself to say the name of the man who'd once been almost a father to him. Weather watcher, hunter, builder of homes and wind turbines, a man whom Caleb had known most of his life and would once have said he loved. My boy, the old man had been accustomed to calling him: Do you want to come out and set some rabbit snares, my boy? I'm going in to the woods to cut firewood, my boy, do you want to come with me? And Caleb, who had lived all his life with a father-sized hole in him, who as long as he could remember would stand in front of mirrors touching his own face and wondering about the missing man who'd fathered him, who whenever he went to St. John's searched the streets, his eyes casting restlessly over every brown-skinned stranger, had swooned towards these words.

Now—the girl's name, too, was a sharp pain on his tongue. So—Caleb shut the door to the goat barn, its painted white star visible in darkness or fog—better to avoid their names altogether.

In his great-aunt Christine's kitchen, Caleb's uncle Leo, his mother's older brother who lived farther along Little Harbour Road, was leaning against the counter, boots off, ball cap glued to his head. Brassy hair in tufts, still in her quilted nightgown, Christine had pulled out the propane camping stove once used at the cabin built by her husband, the cabin Leo and his family frequented now. A blue jug of water stood on the counter. The mood in the room was cheerful. They were islanders, used to weathering storms. No power outage thwarted them. From the table, Sylvia, dressed in sweater and jeans, handed Leo a can of Carnation milk and mug of tea.

"If the power stays out," Leo, the tallest of the three Borders brothers, was saying, "I'll get the generators going here and at our place. Have some of last year's wild meat in the freezer I'd rather not feed to the gulls."

"Leo says road's washed out in Green Cove," Sylvia called to Caleb. She was still beautiful, threads of grey in her long red hair, strong enough to haul Caleb in from the storm the night before, but he glimpsed gauntness in her at certain angles and there was a self-protective hunch to her shoulders that never used to be there.

"That's right," said Leo, who worked for the island's road crew, who was sometimes cool to Caleb one-on-one but on the whole accepted him. "Pat Green says culvert's washed out in the brook, road's gone, beach gone, cell tower took a hit, brook's higher than he's ever seen it. Can't get a call in to the town or RCMP, but those on the other side will figure it out soon enough."

"The road's gone," Caleb echoed.

"Yes, boy," said Leo. "Some young American drove right into the flood last night. Buddy's some stunned. Car's a wreck, still in the brook, but he got out, Pat says. Made it to the Wells's place. I'm off to take a look, fetch some water from the pond if I can. Windward side of Pat's mother's roof tore off in the night. Must have been that great gust. Pat was on his way there when I met him."

"That one, oh my goodness, yes," said Christine. "The door burst open, the wind sucked the water right out of the toilet bowl, and the weather glass, never seen it drop so low, right to the bottom of the dial."

Warm air forced up over colder, that's when a barometric pressure drop formed. So the old man had taught Caleb. The girl said she felt those pressure drops right inside her spine.

"There's no getting out of town," Caleb said to his uncle.

"That's right," said Leo. "According to Pat. Wind's too high yet to go anywhere by water. You'll have some trouble getting around the brook. More than a trickle, I'd say. So until we muster a crew to tackle the road, we're on our own out here, right at the edge of the things, just like in the rare old times."

"Not quite like the old times," Sylvia said acidly, under her breath. Then, turning to Caleb, "Where do you have to be to in such a hurry?"

She had, as ever, a penetrating stare. She didn't like the fact that he still worked for the old man. No, he'd have to say, her feelings were stronger than that. She didn't trust the old man at all. She was full of questions about what he was up to. Was it really just weather monitoring as he said? If so, why was he so secretive about it? Back when they still talked to each other, he never would answer her questions, that much was for sure.

The night before, she'd asked Caleb if he had any idea who'd flown in that afternoon. Not in a plane with propellers. Everyone wondered, since flights were so few, and word travelled swiftly around the island, faster than a car could drive across it. Why are you asking me, Caleb had replied, shifting under her gaze, her curiosity that bordered on suspicion, as if his mother had sniffed out that he knew something he wasn't going to be able to tell her.

As for Cape House, he wasn't sure how she felt about that either. She'd come out there with him a scattered time.

She'd brought out herbs to burn and cleanse the air of the place — of sheep stink and ghosts. It was to the girl that he'd told the story of the old house's origins, how it came to be built in such a remote spot, even more isolated than where her little white house stood on the near side of Green Cove. More than a hundred years ago, a ship's captain named Aeneas Green claimed to have had a vision of a house standing up on the rocks of that shore. With the money he'd made whaling, he spared no expense when building the house, solid beams for the joists, nine panes of glass in the upstairs windows. In those days you paid for glass by the pane. The more panes, the richer you had to be.

Some said the old captain had built his house in such a remarkable location in the hopes of wooing a wife. Yet no wife materialized. For years, old Ane Green lived alone by the sea with no company but his faithful dog. At night, from town or across the cove, people saw his oil lamp shining. In the end, he closed off every room but the kitchen. Cracked. Possibly. He was buried in the town cemetery, Caleb told the girl, alongside all the Greens and Borders and other families who'd come across the sea and lived in Pummelly for centuries.

He had to get out there. Not by car. Could he ford the brook? Or take the quad, go the long way, around Green Cove Pond? Paths through the barrens would be marshy after so much rain, but with luck they'd be passable. How were people elsewhere on the island faring, Caleb wondered: in Tom's Neck and Harbour Islands and Shallow Bay, across the high barrens in the town of Blaze, in Caribou Harbour and Western Tickle and Never Come By, the villages over on bayside?

Usually, if travelling by road, he'd have to pass the turnoff to the old man's place on the way to Cape House. From his uncle's words, it sounded like that house had avoided damage, which relieved Caleb, for the girl's sake. Was the stranger who'd crashed his car one of the men who'd arrived by air yesterday? They had no car. If not, then another American. Odd. Why would any visitor be driving across the island in the middle of the night in such a howl? Unless he was cracked. Or some kind of storm chaser.

"I'm off to Cape House," Caleb told his mother, "to see how she held up."

"Are you planning to fly?" Her voice was light but pointed.

"My wings are a bit out of practice so I thought I'd take the quad."

"Stock up on gas now, boy, because without a road, we won't be getting any more for a spell," said his uncle Leo. "Can't go far, true, though we'll need it for the generators."

Caleb's great-aunt had the frying pan out, intent on feeding all of them scrambled eggs and toutons.

"Christine, my dear, I need to be on my way," said Leo, dropping his mug into the sink and tugging his cap across his brow. "I'm off to Mary's with some two-by-fours for Pat and Brian. Then on my way to the cove." There was vigour in his uncle: he wanted to be out there, doing things. The storm's aftermath only intensified that urge.

"Why not wait till later," his mother called to Caleb. "Land's soaked, brook's up. Go with Leo, fetch some gas for Aunt Christine." And to Leo, "Tell Pat and Brian and Mary herself if you see her that I'll walk around the harbour with a tincture for her."

To Caleb these were heartening words, since his mother hadn't been taking much interest in her tinctures lately.

"I'll follow Uncle Leo on the quad. And fly home first and get the gas cans." He hoped, for now, these words would satisfy her.

Plenty of people were out and about on the harbour road early this bright morning, men in their trucks, others on foot. It was almost a procession, everyone caught up in the release from the usual that a fierce storm can bring. Beneath his helmet, wind pressed across Caleb's scalp. He and the old man were the only two men in the village who didn't own a truck. He'd taken the old man's advice: You don't need a truck, get a car solid enough for winter, all-wheel drive if you can afford it, take the quad when you need to go off-road, hitch up a wagon to haul things about. His uncle Tom had offered him a rusted half-ton when he got his full licence, one that neither of his own sons wanted, and Caleb had said no, proud of himself.

I'm thinking of the future and you should, too, the old man had told him. Need to get our fossil-fuel use down as much as we can. In those days, Caleb took pride in doing exactly what the old man said.

Ahead of him, Ed McGrath was leaning in the window of his uncle Leo's truck. Stearins speared themselves across the sky, preparing for their autumn flight to the other end of the Earth. Seaweed lay plastered against the harbour rocks, puddles at roadside. Caleb checked his phone again. No signal. He wondered again how bad the lashing down on the Avalon had been. Funny to have no way of finding out how his aunt Mona and great-aunt Magdalene were, the phone a slim bit of uselessness. Likely there were text messages out there, wandering through the air. Up in the Alberta oil fields, where his cousins worked, they'd be fine, though they'd been plagued by forest fires all summer and must be anxious about everyone at home. Perhaps they knew more about what was going on than he did. Then there were the things no text could tell him: how the caribou had made out in the storm, hunkered together in the lun of the hills, how foxes had fared and rabbits and birds and whales and fish.

At the gas pump outside Vera McGrath's general store, Vera's husband Dan had a generator going already to power the pump. Cash only. Voices flew in all directions, no need for phones after all. Did you hear Ned Pratt lost a whole wall of siding? Gerard Pratt was up on his roof in the worst of it, banging nails into his shingles so they didn't rip off. Must not have used enough tar to stick them down in the first place. My goodness, the cats were galing around the house. And Mary Green? Cyril Foley found her in the kitchen in her nightgown, ready to haul a pair of buckets upstairs where there's no roof left. When he told her to stay where she was, she insisted he go up and rescue two things: the portrait of her son Joe who was lost at sea and her extra set of teeth.

"More lives than a cat, that one," said Dan McGrath.

When his turn came, Caleb pulled the quad up alongside the pump, fixed the nozzle inside the mouth of the first can before pushing up the metal lever to start the flow of gas manually, black numbers on their little white tabs ticking over to count the price. Dan was already rationing gas. Caleb could fill up one can but not the other. He'd leave the filled can for his great-aunt in Leo's truck and ask his uncle to deliver it.

Along the road, Pat Green, angular and grey-haired, waved at Caleb from the roof of his mother's house. A blue tarp flapped in the breeze from the far side of the roof. Leo was passing two-by-fours up to Pat's younger brother Brian, stocky, hair buzzed short. High above, a black-back circled. A mattress leaned against one wall, rugs on the clothes line. Caleb pulled off his helmet.

"Caleb, you're the giant one, help us nail the tarp to the roof beam before this breeze yanks it off," Pat shouted.

Being, in fact, the smallest one, therefore useful, Caleb was best able to balance high on a roof ridge. At least up there he'd be able to ask Pat himself about the washout.

The tarp was temporarily held in place by nails through the corner grommets, a southwesterly rippling the tarp. As soon as Caleb reached the top of the ladder, Pat handed him a hammer and a pouch of roofing nails. "Down in Green Cove, is the road really gone?" Caleb asked.

"Yes, boy," said Pat, pulling a nail from between his teeth. "Brook sawed a hole right through it."

"Water's high?"

"Yes, you'll not be driving through that."

"Did you by chance get a peek at Cape House?"

"Now, Caleb, couldn't see much from where we were, other than that the house is standing and your roof looks to be on."

A year and a half ago it was, in the spring of the year he turned eighteen and a few months before he finished school, Caleb had gone to visit his uncle Charlie, home in the harbour on one of his spells between oil-sands shifts. Five years since Charlie, the youngest of his mother's three brothers, trim and small and wiry, had left the fish plant and gone to work out west, driving a great rig across the tar sands because, for the moment, that's where the money was. Standing in the kitchen of Charlie's big new house built with the oil money, Caleb, already nervous, wasted no time: "I'd like to buy your old sheep shed from you."

With a wink Charlie said, "Now what do you want with that old palace? And what'll you pay me for it? Bottled rabbit or fish? And are you hoping for sheep to go along with it?"

Caleb said, "I fancy living out there."

"Is that right?" Charlie laughed. His handlebar moustache jiggled when he spoke. Was there derision in his laugh? He handed Caleb a mug of instant coffee. "What does your mother think about that?"

"She thinks it's a fine idea." This was far from the truth, which Charlie probably intuited. His mother knew nothing of his plans. But Caleb wasn't intending to live with his mother forever.

"There's no power," Charlie said, rubbing his moustache. "She's in a lonely spot. Sylvia will think you're cracked, boy."

"I'll do like Alan Wells does, with the wind and the solar."

"You will, will you," said Charlie. He paused. "She's a lot of house."

"I'll turn her into a B&B, I'm thinking. Aunt Christine says someone should take over when she retires."

"In the village, boy, not out on a cliff. Why not let me find you a job out west when you graduate?"

Caleb said, "I want to stay on the island."

Charlie's son Phil was out west and Tom's son Jim had left the island the year before. His other cousins Danny and Gerald, who were in his class, planned to bolt for the mainland as soon as they could. But no one ever really thought of him, solitary, a mongrel, as being like the rest of them.

"What do you say I give it to you," Charlie said. "My boy doesn't want it. You'll want money to fix her up. Don't come after me if she falls down."

"She won't," Caleb insisted.

Caleb wasn't sure Charlie believed he'd do anything with the near ruin. Yet they'd trekked out there, his three uncles, the old man who wasn't really that old, and himself. They determined that while a wreck, the house was a salvageable wreck, despite the sheep shit and the risk of worsening storms.

His uncle Leo said, "You'll want an earthmover out here to deal with the septic."

His uncle Tom, the loud one, simply shook his head. Luckily Caleb had his job working for the old man. It didn't pay a lot but it was something. Steady. On the island. He told the men he'd do as much of the labour himself as he could. It would take time, yes. But what it would be to live out there in that remote spot beside the sea. Despite the storms. You could make a fine and self-sufficient life. Not necessarily alone either. He and Charlie had shaken hands on the deal.

"Says he has a dream," Charlie said with a shrug.

From his rooftop perch, Caleb peered across the harbour. Out at sea, the tiny islands called the Little Fish were barely more than ridges above the horizon, white smudges of foam bursting against them. High pressure shrank them, low pressure made them loom. Lots of power still out in the water.

A glaucous gull flew overhead, wingspan wide as a flag, and all at once Caleb was higher in the air looking down, only his vision was not his vision. Sometimes this happened to him. Seeing another creature, without warning, he'd lose his own body and enter its skin. How much wider the circumference of his sight, it was like being able to see behind him, the glint of water from the cove back there, the little boxes below, moving figures, an electromagnetic wind stirred up and sailing in grey-blue swoops, the retreating storm a chaos of energy, a tug in the pattern of the air from far off even as it dissipated.

Down below, the girl approached on her bicycle. Caleb dropped back into his own body, wobbling on the roof beam. She had to have seen him. Was that a wave? As she wheeled her bicycle right up to Mary Green's house, she disappeared from sight.

White-haired Cyril Foley was down there somewhere, voice rising. "How was it down in the cove last night, Miranda? No lun where you are. Did the wind sound like it was throwing rocks at you, too?"

Caleb couldn't hear her reply. He hammered the last nail in, almost hitting his thumb. He was on the ladder. Careful now. Her father was nowhere around. This was a chance, wasn't it? Once, when he'd gone to the house to apologize and speak to her about the future, knowing her father to be in at the cabin, she'd run inside. Another time, she'd shut herself in the chicken coop. It wasn't his intention to distress her further. Another time, out on the shore path between Green Cove and Pummelly, he'd seen her approaching at a distance, and though she'd turned away, there was indecision in her turn. She'd looked back at him over her shoulder, mouth open, as if wishing to speak.

As Caleb reached the ground, Cyril Foley came around the corner of the house. "Text for you," Cyril said, holding out an envelope.

"Where's—?" Caleb couldn't bring himself to say her name.

It was like casting a spell: if you moved too quickly the creature you were trying to entice would vanish.

Everyone in the village would know that himself and the girl, born mere months apart, who had for so long spent so much time together, no longer did. They had not spoken in over a year. Since the day he took her out in speedboat to see the icebergs.

Down on the beach, after the old man had heard the girl's version of what happened, he'd shouted at Caleb, told him he was to have nothing more to do with his daughter. No more going inside the house on the cove. Now it was as if there were thorns around it. When necessary, the old man asked him to step into his study, housed in a shed across the yard. Or they met at the old man's cabin. Despite all this, the old man hadn't fired him. The separation was a test through which Caleb had to redeem himself. He'd turned the boat in the wrong direction, yes. But he could atone for that. He'd upset the girl. Yes. But he had apologized. One day they would go back to the way things were before. Only better. He had the best possible future to offer her. How could the old man and the girl herself not see this? Once more he would be able to speak to her softly and share his deepest thoughts. Only in the future, they'd do more than speak.

"Miranda's gone to see Mary," Cyril said, as Caleb took the envelope.

Caleb knew how much the girl loved Mary Green, and Mary herself had always taken an interest in the girl, who helped her in house and garden now that Mary's hands had grown arthritic. Planted potatoes for her in old plastic fish tubs, lettuces in Mary's small, glass-walled greenhouse. A painting the girl had made hung in Mary's parlour. Not from watercolours, as Caleb had first thought, but inks concocted from wild substances: lichen and moss and berries and plants and seaweed and tree bark.

When he reached the road, the girl was wheeling her bicycle farther around the harbour. Splintered pieces of wood and shingle, likely from Mary's roof, lay strewn at roadside. The girl was not as tall as his mother, but her body rippled with firm and fluid movement, that kind of grace, her hair falling long and dark across her back. She'd knit the blue wool cap that clasped her head. One day he'd peel it off so gently and run his fingers through her hair. Caleb knew her to be shy but she wasn't always studying herself like the other girls they'd gone to school with. Everyone at school had treated them like some kind of couple.

There was nothing on the outside of the envelope. Caleb ripped it open. When a couple of bills fell out, he stooped to catch them. The folded note inside was from her father.

What had he expected?

He would call out. Before he could, the girl turned. Saw him, frozen as he was, gave a true and unmistakable wave.

. . .

Mid-morning: Miranda had delivered her father's message. She'd stopped for a cup of tea with Mary Green, who, from the rocking chair in her daughter Susannah's kitchen, seemed stubbornly unrattled by her night's adventure. Ahead, as Miranda cycled over the hill leading out of town, lay her small white house, alone at the end of its lane. Her heart surged towards it. The blades of their wind turbine, which her father had switched on earlier that morning, spun in the field near the road.

Down in the watery cove, where the swollen brook cut the road in two and churned into the tidal water that had stolen the beach, a black truck was pulled up, three figures gathered at the jagged edge of the washout, two in coveralls and a third in a lime-green jacket. The big black truck belonged to Leo Borders. At the turn into her lane, Miranda hesitated. The men gestured to the remains of Frank's car, still submerged in the torrent. A wheelbarrow with a handful of logs tossed into it stood abandoned by their roadside woodpile. Above all this, the sky swung big and wild, thin clouds like the white ribs of a great creature spanning it. The thought of Frank's crash juddered through Miranda once more. She listened for any sound of her father's quad returning from the cabin along the track that led into the barrens, heard nothing.

The wind, soft out of the west, carried another sound across the cove to her. Was that the buzz of a drill? From Cape House? The sound rose and faded.

The black truck left the cove, making its way in her direction. Caleb's uncle Leo, who had an uneven, gap-toothed smile and still sometimes went duck hunting with her father, waved. Her father and all three of the Borders brothers had gone hunting together ever since she was a child. In those days, Caleb and his cousins sometimes went with them. She'd never gone, nor had Sylvia, Caleb's mother, though Miranda was content to eat the duck. By now Caleb's cousins had all left the island. A year and two months since she and Caleb had last spoken. How did it feel? It felt like a part of her had gone missing. There'd been relief, after the initial shock wore off and the bruises on her chest faded. Then came the loss. The contours of the loss kept changing — shifting between guilt and anger, regret and unease. All these feelings slipped through her in pulses. When she saw Caleb, which was as little as she could manage, or heard him, which was more often, when he came to get instructions from her father, something stirred in Miranda. Restlessness. Longing? It was perplexing. Why couldn't the wind carry the feelings away?

Leo Borders swung his truck into the lane, trucker's cap pulled over his brow. At his side, his brother Tom, oldest of the Borders brothers, gave a nod. From behind Leo, Frank extracted himself from the jump seat, long legs in flight as he leaped from the cab.

"We'll come by later when tide and brook's lower and pull her out then," Leo said, peering down at Miranda through the cab window. "Now tell your father, Miranda, the road's going to take some repair. I'll get a call into the town as soon as the phones are working, but we'll likely be enjoying our own company for a few more days."

Their own company plus a stranger's: Frank had come to stand, tall and unusual, beside Miranda. A new day and he was still here, emphatic by daylight and filling her with an awe that made her both want to observe him and run in the other direction. As the men pulled away, Frank told her the car was totalled, obviously.

"You can borrow anything you need from us."

The storm had left him with even less than she'd had upon arriving on Blaze Island. Under his lime-green jacket, he wore the sweater she'd loaned him the night before. The rubber boots, a pair of her father's, must fit him well enough. He'd retrieved his skinny, ripped jeans and by daylight looked a little more at home in his borrowed clothes. Miranda wondered what it would feel like to draw him. The cheekbones, the black hair, the lips. Her skin prickled. He didn't seem distressed as much as floating on a cloud of shocked equanimity.

"Your father asked me to bring down some more wood so I was doing that when Leo and Tom showed up." It felt strange to hear the men's names in Frank's mouth. Together he and Miranda tossed a few more logs into the barrow, then set off, Frank manoeuvring the wheelbarrow joltingly over the lane's puddled ruts. When a pair of sanderlings flew past, he glanced at them.

"A bit freaky seeing everything by daylight." Frank raised his sunglassed face to the wide, bright arc of blue. "What I drove into. What might have happened, the horror of the hypothetical. Then there's everything else, which is spectacular and awesome. This sky, for instance."

"Are you okay?"

"I have some beautiful bruises coming in but otherwise I'm fine." He seemed distracted, now, by the wind turbine. No accidentals yet, he told her.

When Miranda asked Frank if her father had returned, Frank said no. She was about to ask if anyone else had passed by on a quad, thinking of Caleb, only Frank was already inquiring about the village. Miranda told him: missing shingles, a missing boat, and one woman's roof had blown off.

"Do you often get hurricanes out here?"

"It was really only the edge of one," Miranda said.

"But, like, is that becoming more common? Hurricanes coming farther north?"

"I guess so." She wasn't sure why she didn't want to admit this.

In the yard, within their run, Rosie, the most assertive of the hens, hurried in their direction, Mimi murmuring behind her, the hens' stippled, brown-gold plumage winking in the sunlight. Sylvia had given Miranda the eggs, and she'd hatched all eight of them under a grow light in the bathroom. There were three eggs in the laying box, one warm, all of them blue. Frank peered at the eggs in Miranda's hands and said he'd never seen a blue egg in his life. "I've heard of green eggs — and ham. But not — what would you call this colour? Pale sky?"

"They're Ameraucanas, and they only lay blue eggs."

"Do blue eggs taste different than brown or white ones?"

"Our eggs taste — a bit like the sea, a bit like the grass, intense. You have to try one."

Frank turned to her with what felt like sharp scrutiny. "Apologies if this is kind of forward, but you and your father — your accents don't sound like you're from around here."

"We've lived out here a long time." Miranda had a violent wish for her father to reappear. Frank was a visitor. Naturally he was curious. About them. Was it wrong to tell him things? Her body stiffened. She asked if he'd grown up in Boston.

"No, no, all over. Like, Florida, Virginia, New England. My parents are very, hmm, peripatetic?"—Frank gestured to the solar panel fixed to the rocks beyond her father's office shed—"And everything's off-grid?"

Miranda nodded, tucking the eggs into her wool cap.

"Is your father some kind of survivalist? I did happen to notice the rifle hanging on the rack over the kitchen door."

Again, her muscles contracted. Was there a name for what they were? "He hunts. Everyone around here hunts. We live close to the land. And try not to use too much power."

She had no experience describing her life to a stranger. On the island, her life had its peculiarities, but this was different. She'd expected her father back by now. He'd implied that he was only making a quick trip in to the cabin, but perhaps he'd stopped by the village on his return.

On the other side of the door, Ella gave eager yips. She leaped into the air when the door opened—"Ella, watch the eggs!"

There was a thud behind Miranda. Frank swore. Crumpled against the bridge, he lay clutching his forehead, Ella all over him. "You need signs on your house telling tall people to duck."

Miranda had to put the eggs down and call off Ella, haul her away from Frank by the collar. He'd survived a car crash, crawled through dark fields in a hurricane, been dragged through their door, only to smash into her door frame the next morning, a red welt forming on his forehead. Now he struggled to his feet and hunched through the doorway as if afraid the door itself might hit him. A moment before he'd had almost a detective's curiosity.

After soaking a tea towel in cold water, Miranda told him to lie on the fisherman's daybed, which Frank did, cloth over his forehead, long legs dangling off the end but no, he said, no concussion. At least he stopped asking her questions, although there was something about him that kept tugging her troublesome past out of the deep.

. . .

During the weeks after her mother's death, Miranda woke in the dark of the Princeton house to the sound of her father sobbing. Her own tears were long silent streams, while her trembling body hovered somewhere up above the Earth.

One afternoon, she came upon her father at the kitchen table, head buried in his arms. He started up, pale cheekbones like fists, and told her that something else had happened. The major funding that supported his research hadn't been renewed, because of the allegations against him. They weren't true, but he hadn't yet officially been cleared. Without funding, he had to let his research team go, all his post-docs, his graduate students. The university couldn't fire him because he had tenure, but the administration had decided to dissolve the centre, which effectively meant he had no job.

"They're saying they're concerned about an unsafe environ-ment for students," he said. "Unsafe environment! Because of the threats and the protests and the sniper but oh, oh, the irony!" He gave a raw and reckless laugh, almost a scream, which he then tried to stifle.

"Listen, Miranda," he said quietly, "the thing is, our house belongs to the university, and the university wants it back, so we're going to have to move."

"Where will we go?" Miranda asked in a whisper, nearly mute.

"Dearest one, I'm not sure yet, but I'll figure out something. I love you more than anyone and I'll find a good, safe place for us, I promise from the depths of my soul." Gathering her into his arms, her father held her and rocked her and for just a moment it was possible to feel safe.

"Where are we going?" Miranda asked him on that July morning as, with all their remaining belongings stuffed in the car, they sped up the interstate. Raindrops quivered at the edges of the wipers and smeared across the windshield. They were in Massachusetts now.

"North," her father said from behind his sunglasses.

Would they drive as far north as the Arctic, was it even possible to drive to the Arctic?

"You said we were in trouble," Miranda said, pushing the words out of her mouth. "Does that mean we're going to die?"

"No," her father said sharply. "Everyone dies but we're not going to die now. We're going to be fine."

Somewhere in New Hampshire, he said, "We're not at war but sometimes things feel like a war, there's so much money and power arrayed against people like us, and those people are swaying other people not to believe that humans have anything to do with the warming weather. It's no use my speaking out any more because I've been compromised. So we're going to retreat. We'll leave others to take up the cause. Things will change, sweetheart. It'll just take some effort and time."

As he spoke Miranda felt like she'd been in unknown places with him. He was speaking to her, not as if she were a child but someone else.

That night, in a lonely motel room in Maine, they watched reports about the unusually heavy downpours. Stretches of the I-95 behind them had flooded so high they had to be closed, said a male news anchor. A story came on about a woman who lived outside Bar Harbor, trapped in high water on a country road near her house. She reversed her van only to have the current catch it, forcing her to struggle out the van door, clutching her three-year-old son. She tried to hold onto her child, but the water grabbed him, swept the boy away. The next time Miranda looked at the TV, a moose was being borne downstream by racing flood waters. Miranda's father, lying on the other twin bed, switched off the television, removed his sunglasses, and turned away from her, curled in on himself. He gave a sob, which he seemed to be trying to strangle. She wanted to touch him but didn't know how, and so, on her own twin bed, in the wan light of the single bedside lamp, Miranda lay absolutely still. If she lay still enough, for long enough, maybe the police and the searchers would find the boy alive and the moose wouldn't drown and the rain would stop falling. When her father turned at last in her direction, he stared at Miranda as if he were shocked at the sight of her and had no idea who she was. Heart speeding, she closed her eyes.

The next day they crossed the border into Canada. At Saint Andrews, New Brunswick, the clean-shaven border guard took their Canadian passports, asked Miranda's father to remove his sunglasses and state the reason for his return.

Her father handed his sunglasses to Miranda. Clearing his throat, he said, "I miss the pristine landscapes of my home and native land."

"Do you have permission from the child's other legal guardian to be travelling with the child?"

"My wife just died." His tone made the border officer clear his own throat while Miranda's father asked her to pass him the bag at her feet. After rustling in it for a moment, he handed the guard some paperwork.

Evergreens blurred past outside the car windows. The air still streamed with rain. Then they were on a ferry that would carry them through the night to another province that was an island out at sea. In the night, Miranda woke to find her father, on the bottom bunk, still in his sunglasses, staring at maps on his laptop, edges of land and water, water as far as her eye could make out.

When she woke again, she was still in the ferry cabin but her mother was in the room, poised on the single chair, on top of their discarded clothes, watching Miranda. Her wild dark hair tumbled in waves down her back. She had on the flowered raincoat and red boots she'd been wearing the last time she'd left the house. Everything in Miranda's body surged towards her. A smile swept over her mother's perfect lips. She raised a finger to them.

Under Miranda's pillow was the black sweater belonging to her mother that she'd stuffed in her suitcase in the rush of leaving. Every night before sleep she buried her face in it and, breathing in her mother's scent, felt her ribs close around her grieving heart. Every night she was overcome with the longing to steal her father's phone, call her mother's number, tell her where they were. In her knapsack she kept one of her mother's business cards. Jenny Erens, artist. Before leaving the Princeton house, she'd looked one last time at her mother's website, all the paintings now sold or placed in storage. In a box Miranda had packed one of her mother's smallest canvases, thin figures in a forest overlaid with a shining layer of ghostly buildings; her paintings were like time, a map of time. Miranda wanted her mother to know she'd brought the painting, and that her father had a bigger one, wrapped in brown paper. Every speck of Miranda's body closed around the possibility of *if*: if she had not called out to her mother on the last afternoon wanting her to take one last look, if she had not been wearing her pink running shoes, her mother would have lived.

Every day that spring, her mother had raced off to her studio in an old building halfway between their house and the university to work on new, large paintings for her second solo show, but that particular afternoon, mid-May, after school, she was rushing off somewhere else. Miranda's father was also elsewhere. At his office, Miranda's mother said. The babysitter hadn't yet arrived. Some people had gathered outside his building, Jenny said. She was going to join Miranda's father and offer her support. All this sounded vague, as if there were other things Miranda's mother wasn't saying, but her impetuous energy was the same as ever, bold and vivacious and urgent. As soon as she left a room you leaned into her absence.

In the front hall, smoothing red lipstick over her lips, Jenny said to Miranda, "Danielle just texted me. She'll be here any moment."

Even then, Miranda had tried to slow her mother, holding up her phone because she wanted her mother to look at the film she was making with Uma, about pandas, using two stuffed toys, a real piece of bamboo, and a painted scroll with stars on it that read, Let Us Live. And, hurrying as she was, Jenny had stopped long enough to look at the pandas, the stars, the words, as if sensing Miranda's need and pleasure, to marvel at the little film and praise her. If only the film had been longer or there'd been no film at all. If only her mother had stayed. Instead she'd stood there wavering, glanced at her phone. She kissed Miranda on the forehead, rustled her hair, told her she loved her, the movie was beautiful.

"I'll be back soon," she said. With one last hug and the snap of her bike helmet's chin strap, she was gone.

Five o'clock then six o'clock passed. Danielle, the babysitter, who'd arrived as Jenny departed, left for a swim class. When the land line rang, Miranda decided not to answer it. She was in the kitchen texting Uma when her father burst in the front door. His face. It was like someone had struck him with an axe. He said there'd been an accident.

If only she had clung to her mother's coat and screamed and refused to let her go, if only she'd fallen sick, if only her mother had taken Prospect not Ivy on the way to the protest organized by climate-change deniers outside the building that housed her father's centre then she would not have been hit by a car as she biked the last stretch, a car driven by a known climate-change denier, a man with an assault rifle in the back seat, though whether he'd had the heart attack before or after he swerved into Miranda's mother and crashed into a tree, instantly killing himself, no coroner could determine.

Now her mother was in the news, not because of her painting, though she was described as a painter and wife of—. Because while the accident couldn't be directly attributed to the protest it was nevertheless tangled up in it. In the hospital room, Miranda reached out a trembling finger to touch her unconscious mother's swollen and nearly unrecognizable face, her head shaved, tubes running all over her, as her father, in his heart-wrecked voice said to the doctor, "Yes, you can withdraw life support."

In their cabin on the ferry as it travelled across the Gulf of St. Lawrence through the night, her beautiful mother held up cards, no, tiny paintings that moved, only it was impossible to see what the figures in them were doing. The boat beneath them swayed. As Miranda reached out, tears forming, her mother's faraway face reassured her softly, Your father will find you a new home.

When Miranda woke next, her father, dressed, was packing their bags. He looked at her as if he actually saw her and gathered her to him.

The next day the rain let up a little. That night, in a motel in Badger, Newfoundland, her bearded father announced, "We're almost there."

"Where?" Miranda asked. Anticipation had left her. It felt as if they'd been travelling forever and were never going to stop.

"You'll see," her father said. Now, despite the blankness of his sunglasses, a tendril of new warmth lived in his voice. "Soon. I promise, sweetheart. We're not going to drive forever."

—

They came at last to a place that was barely a place at all called Adieu, pronounced A-dew, as they discovered in the store where Miranda's father stopped to buy gas. It was dusk. Every night Miranda had lain as still as possible in her bed. The rain had finally halted and her father's sobs had quieted, too. Although it seemed impossible to go any farther, they followed a long and lonely road that led them at last to a wooden booth on a perch of land facing the wide and empty ocean.

"Yes, boy, you've found us," said the man in the white booth, drawing out his *yes* like a net you'd catch things in. Ahead lay only a boarded-up trailer with a For Sale sign nailed over another sign that said Chip Truck, and closer to the water, one low wooden building, a dock, and some white lines painted on the pavement. "Are you sure we're in the right place?" Miranda asked nervously. Everything seemed so desolate. Her father said they were and they were waiting for another ferry.

Soon other cars and trucks began to form a line behind them, which made the place feel somewhat less forlorn. A woman walked about with a small white dog. Yet where could the ferry possibly be taking them, how far out to sea? Miranda's father stepped out of the car. He took off his sunglasses and eyed the world around him with more interest than Miranda had seen him take in anything in months. Gulls shrieked from the rooftop of the low wooden building. There was no more rain but the clouds hung low and grey.

They had to leave the car in the ferry hold for the crossing. Upstairs, people gathered inside the cabin, laughing, chatting, men and women her father's age or older, in sweaters and jackets, who must live in whatever faraway place they were travelling to. There was a machine that served coffee. One of the women, in a red jacket, waved. Miranda's father headed outside, onto the passenger deck in the bow. Surging from its mooring, the boat swung round so they were facing the sea, bracing themselves against a sharp north wind, a wind ready to lift Miranda off her feet if she gave it a chance. Still pale and gaunt but without his sunglasses, her father seemed to be drinking in the wind, his mouth wide open. A thin green line appeared in the distance, hovered, then vanished in a grey roll of fog. Miranda gripped the railing. On their right, a few small islets, dotted with evergreens and seemingly without houses, swept past.

Alone, she stumbled through the wind to the stern where the ferry's wake streamed out behind them, widening across the bay. The wake pulled her old life with it, turning everything Miranda had ever known into a milky froth. When she pushed her way to the bow, her father held out a hand to her, a hard, sure grip.

"Say goodbye to the rest of the world," he shouted in her ear. "We're going where no one will ever find us."

Hand in his, Miranda struggled to find her balance and not be swept away.

Back in the car, waiting for the signal to drive off the ferry, he showed her where they were on a paper map. "Here's Blaze Island," her father said, "and here," he pointed to a dot at the far end of the island, "is where we're going to spend the night."

They clanked off the ferry into fog so thick it was as if the world had disappeared or they themselves had vanished off the face of the Earth. Somewhere in Miranda's depths stirred a kernel of curiosity, beneath the still tight clutch of bewilderment and fear.

"I can't see anything," she said.

"We've survived so many storms, blizzards with visibility far worse than this." Her father spoke as if she, too, had been along on his adventures. "Miranda, my love, we'll weather the weather together."

He said if they were careful they had enough money to live for years. In this new place, they would start a new kind of life. They would leave his enemies far behind. Once more he reached out his hand and she grasped his fingers tight in hers. "Say it with me now."

"We'll weather the weather together."

"One more thing. Actually two. First of all, don't mention the word *climate*. Not to anyone. Nothing about my being a climate scientist. And, second, from now on I'll have a different name. A new name for a new life. You'll still be Miranda but I'll be Alan, not Milan. Alan Wells and Miranda Wells. Let's practise."

. . .

The afternoon before the storm, Caleb had arrived by car at
the island's airstrip, a half-hour's drive from Pummelly. In
the middle of the island, it was small as these things went, a
long ribbon of pale pavement enclosed within fencing topped
with barbed wire, surrounded by bare rocks and ponds and
scraggly tuckamore, the small trees leaning northeasterly,
pushed by the prevailing winds. If you ever got lost on the
island you oriented yourself by the lean of the windswept trees.

The old man had told him that the visitors were due to
arrive by two, but the wind must have been with them because
when Caleb pulled his car into the parking lot, the gleam of a
plane was already on the tarmac, parked close to the terminal.
Terminal was hardly the word for it. Or maybe it was, since
the large shed, with an uneven patch of pavement out front,
resembled a place at the end of the Earth. On the other side
of the fence, four men stood near a small, sleek jet. Not a
turboprop. Three strangers clustered around Alfred Harder,
who worked for the airport authority and drove out to the strip
whenever a flight came in, who was staring in wonder at the
luminous aircraft. A light wind pushed out of the south, the
sky already thick with cloud.

There were no commercial flights to the island, other than when the ferry broke down for over forty-eight hours. Then the government put on a small plane to carry people across the bay. You lined up in the turquoise-walled terminal, in a room that held an ancient wooden desk. Behind it, Alf Harder or Mitch Buckle wrote your name down by hand in a lined notebook. Then you waited to hear whether or not your name was called and if you'd made your flight.

Two of the men standing close to Alf Harder were extremely tall, well over six feet. A mane of white-gold hair cascaded to the shoulders of one man, who had a presence that commanded attention as soon as you set eyes on him. Caleb assumed he was going for a hipster look, although he was older. A silk scarf protruded from the chest pocket of his jacket, which was made of some soft, ridged fabric. Corduroy. And sneakers. Aiming for boyish as well, was he? The other man was slim but stiff, younger, hair neatly cut. He didn't seem at home in his sporty outerwear, as if he'd let someone else dress him or he'd had an idea of the journey and dressed to fit it, only the idea was nothing like where he actually was. The short man wore a leather jacket so shiny it looked fake.

Words floated to Caleb as he approached the gate. Hurricane Fernand. Started the day at Midway in Chicago, well out of the way of it, yeah, but have a lot of business on the East Coast. Grim. Unfolding disaster. Will be in the thick of it soon. Stopped off in Toronto. Fly into Logan or LaGuardia, whichever opens up first.

The man with the mane was like the stag with the biggest antlers, a great rack, like the creature who'd stepped into the road in front of Caleb one misty morning as he drove along the highway between Pummelly and Tom's Neck. He'd swerved. The animal had almost killed him.

Where was the pilot, Caleb found himself wondering. Who was the pilot? None of them seemed to fit that part, though the antlered man was talking to Alf Harder about ramp presence, advanced cockpit environments, unbelievable short runway performance.

A woman stood beside Caleb. He jumped. Where the Jesus had she come from? Anna Turi. The old man had told him she'd be with the others. Eyes on them, he'd somehow failed to notice her. She must already have come through the gate and been in the terminal building. Also: her appearance was so unlike any other time he'd set eyes on her.

Her long hair hung loose, the colour of autumn grass. Always before Caleb had seen it braided or knotted on top of her head or stuffed inside a hat. On her two previous visits to the island, she'd been bundled into jeans and rain jacket. Well, no, the first time he'd set eyes on Anna she'd been wearing pyjamas, when he'd walked into the old man's kitchen and immediately bolted out again, in shock to find a third person, an unknown person at that, standing at the counter chopping onions and tomatoes first thing in the morning. The shock still reverberated through Caleb whenever he remembered that moment. Five summers ago, that was.

Now, bright red lipstick coated Anna's lips. High-heeled black boots ran up her legs and her hands were stuffed in the pockets of a white trench coat, cinched at the waist. City clothes. Caleb supposed there was no one particular way that Anna ought to look, yet her transformation unsettled him, as Anna had a habit of doing. She did not seem at ease. The real question was, why was she here, and with these men?

"Hello, Caleb," Anna said in her lilting, lightly accented voice. She was watching the men closely.

"Have a good flight?"

"Gratifyingly uneventful."

On the other side of the gate, Alf Harder, in boots and well-worn coveralls, was telling the antlered man that the plane ought to be safe where it was. "When the wind blows, she'll blow out of the southeast. May be a spot of rain and a bit of a breeze."

"Well, we plan to be on our way by the end of the afternoon," said the antlered man. "The hurricane's heading out to sea last radar I saw."

"Here for a visit, are you?"

"Reconnaissance," said the antlered man with a brilliant smile. "Heard about this place. Anna told me about it, actually. I've an interest in remote locations. They appeal to my soul. Somewhere out of the direct line of hurricanes, that's of interest these days, for all kinds of reasons. Heard it's beautiful. Happened to be heading this way. So I wanted to see it for myself."

All this seemed performed for Alf Harder's benefit, yet it was hard to tell if Alf was taken in. Caleb wondered if Alf Harder, who lived in Tom's Neck, knew about Anna's connection to the old man. Caleb kept waiting for Alf to ask the antlered man if he was here to visit Alan Wells, bracing himself, because the old man's involvement was supposed to be secret, but Alf didn't ask.

The two other men, the tall and the short, came through the gate after Alf and the antlered man, who disappeared into the terminal to take care of paperwork. Wind tugging at her dark blonde hair, Anna made introductions. Len Hansen was the tall man in the crinkly windbreaker with many pockets. He had a distracted handshake and was juggling a leather attaché case and his phone. Tony McIntosh possessed a hungry, greasy air, smudged glasses. His handshake was firm but moist.

"This is Caleb Borders, who works for us," said Anna, glancing over her shoulder as if to make sure Alf was out of earshot.

Inside Caleb a shout rose: he might work for the old man but he certainly didn't work for Anna. However, the old man had given him reason to understand that it might be best, in front of these men, to keep his mouth shut.

"We've booked a guesthouse for you," said Anna. "Even if it's for a few hours, you'll have somewhere to make yourselves comfortable, refresh, wash up."

Oddness hung all over this meeting, Caleb thought. But then, in the last while, there had been a buildup of odd events.

Two months ago, the old man had asked Caleb to book all three rooms in Teresa Blake's guesthouse in Tom's Neck, called Bakeapple House because of the salmon-orange colour of its exterior walls, for a week. Caleb told Teresa, as the old man had told him, that the guests would appear sometime in this window, he wasn't sure when. The old man would pay for all five nights regardless, with one stipulation, the breaking of which would have the direst of consequences: his name was not to appear anywhere on the reservation. He'd give her a fine gratuity to ensure that. Then, as instructed, Caleb went next door to Margaret Hynes's restaurant, Never The Like, the best on the island, found Margaret in the kitchen and told her that Alan Wells wanted her to cook for some people staying at Teresa's guesthouse in the middle of September—at Teresa's place so they could dine in private. Meals of hand-caught fish and foraged greens and local berries. Also, when speaking to them, she was never to mention the old man's name, for which compliance she would also be paid. Handsomely. The request made Margaret grumble, What are they, royalty? But when she heard how much the old man was willing to offer her, she agreed.

A week ago, the old man had stepped out of his office shed, holding out to Caleb, who waited in the yard, a small stack of white cards. Business cards, it turned out. With Caleb's name printed on the front, no less. Everything beneath might as well have been in another language. Caleb Borders, Site Manager. The ARIEL project. Underneath all that was his actual phone number.

"I'm expecting visitors in the next few days," the old man said. "If all goes well, three men are flying in with Anna. If they ask you any questions about who you work for and what you do, show them one of these. Otherwise, keep these cards to yourself. They're only for emergencies."

All this seemed cracked, though the old man's manner was undeniably serious.

"Are you going to tell me what a site manager does?" Caleb asked.

"Looks after a property, takes care of things, pretty much what you do now," said the old man.

What Caleb did now was chop wood and stack it, at the house and in at the old man's cabin, pick up groceries, run errands, sometimes going all the way across the bay to Gander to pick up supplies and packages from the post office box the old man kept there. That was mostly it.

"The important thing is," said the old man, with the same intensity, "you're not, under any circumstances, even if they ask, to mention my name. If anyone from here asks you about the visitors, say they're Americans, they're here for a quick look around the island."

"Right," Caleb said, slipping the cards into the breast pocket of his coveralls. "A quick look. Got it."

Then the old man had upped his wage, which aroused a crowd of complicated feelings in Caleb, gratitude, and also pain alongside the conviction that the old man must still value and trust him, despite all that had happened with the girl. Hope, yes, a strong bolt of hope.

And so, frightened of troubling a temporarily calm surface, Caleb had not asked more about the what-was-it-called project.

The antlered man, when he reappeared outside the terminal, moved towards the car as if he expected the air itself to part around him. His body had assertiveness and rhythm. Up close, you could see that much of his hair was silver. He was perhaps around the old man's age. The old man had authority, too, but it was that of an intensely physical man, coiled. It made a different impression. The antlered man was saying to Alf, "Heard from my wife who's outside DC, some flooding but she's safe. My daughter's out west, so well out of the trouble. Son's far enough inland he ought to be fine, though as usual it's been radio silence on that front."

Alf Harder climbed into his red truck and waved goodbye.

Without consulting the others, the antlered man settled himself in the front passenger seat, a white canvas knapsack wedged between his knees. A pack of crows was making a murderous racket in a nearby spruce. Who were these people? The wind rose fitfully, clouds swooping past in grey swells. The car wasn't big. It was more usually used for carrying lumber and tools and other building supplies, but Caleb had done his best to tidy it.

"All right, Anna," said the antlered man, "we're here. I could have cancelled given the havoc on the coast, but I didn't, because our meeting, our being here, feels even more necessary. Time to start throttling back on all this climate variability, so let's get this show on the road."

"Yes," Anna said. She slid into the middle of the back seat. With a glance over the car at each other, the other two men climbed in on either side, pressing their thighs up against her thighs, glimpsed by Caleb in the rear-view mirror as he tried to make sense of the antlered man's perplexing words.

"Roy Hansen," the antlered man said. He extended his hand, taking notice, it seemed, of Caleb for the first time.

"Is that your plane?" Caleb asked. Then, "Who's the pilot?"

"Who else?" Roy Hansen said with a forceful laugh. He shook out his mane of hair. "I pilot many, many things."

"Hey, Roy," said Len Hansen from behind them. "I'm not getting any service, are you?" The two men shared the same last name, a similar chin and mouth, though other things about them seemed decidedly different.

"I'm not either," Tony McIntosh announced.

Caleb started the ignition. Roy turned his sleek silver phone off, then on again.

Anna said, "Some providers don't work out here. Isn't that right, Caleb?"

Leaving him to affirm this.

"That's impossible," Roy Hansen said. "My service works everywhere on Earth."

Anna's phone pinged: it did seem to be working. She retrieved it from her pocket. Caleb checked his, just to be sure. He made the turn onto the gravel access road. Goldenrod and yarrow swayed at roadside. The horizon was a jagged line of pine.

Caleb turned to Roy Hansen. "You can make a call on my phone if you want."

Again, Roy Hansen laughed, a laugh that was superficially friendly yet utterly patronizing, as if he, Caleb, were a child, as if one call were as useless to Roy as a hundred. "Thanks," he said.

The laugh made Caleb stiffen.

A pilot, Roy had called himself. Yet he didn't seem like a pilot to Caleb. Granted, his knowledge of pilots was limited. Were these visitors like the old man's other visitors—here to study the weather? Roy had spoken about climate variability. Somehow these ones did not feel like the others. Roy Hansen's manner seemed a little king-like. Tempus, the name unfurling up the plane's tail, was an American airline company, Caleb knew that much, founded by a man who'd started out in a rock band, gone from rock star to airline mogul. Caleb took another look at Roy, the hard jaw, silk scarf in his pocket, the way he shook out his cascade of hair. Time flies, we fly faster, that was the Tempus motto. Ads, jingles, you saw and heard the phrase everywhere. Caleb had never flown Tempus but his cousins had, on trips to Disney World.

He turned onto the highway, ponds to either side of them like open mouths, harrier hawk on an updraft. Caleb's mind swooped up into the hawk; he pulled it back.

Anna said, "Unfortunately, it looks like we'll have to move the meeting to tomorrow."

"What the hell do you mean?" Roy Hansen demanded, swivelling.

"Our director says the storm's tracking farther north. Where our base is, it's in a remote part of the island. There might be problems getting you back."

"It's a small island. It can't be that difficult."

"Nevertheless, that's what he says. He's out there now."

"Text him back. Why can't he come to us?"

Caleb tried to make sense of all this. It sounded like the old man was in at his cabin, and this was where he wanted Anna to bring the men. On the island the blow wasn't predicted to be so bad, however destructive the hurricane had been elsewhere. What had the old man heard? And why couldn't he come to Tom's Neck? The wind was rising, but there was no storm yet. Unless the secrecy of whatever they meant to discuss demanded that the meeting take place somewhere remote. Not at the guesthouse or the old man's house. Maybe the old man had his own reasons for insisting on a delay; he'd booked the men rooms in Bakeapple House after all. Caleb wondered how much Anna knew about the old man's plans. More than he did, he didn't doubt.

"He says it has to be tomorrow," Anna said after her phone had pinged again. Caleb would have said she was holding a lot in. He didn't sense much warmth in her towards the visitors.

A restiveness had grown among all three of the men, as if they were on the verge of revolt.

"What do you want to do, Roy?" asked Len.

"Okay, look," said Roy. "We might not be able to fly out again today, anyway. I don't particularly want to go speeding directly into old Fernand. Truth is, I value myself enough to take self-preservation into account. So, let's say we reschedule for first thing in the morning. It's an inconvenience but we can work with that. Then we're out of here. Got to get the whole eastern seaboard moving again as fast as possible. If this meeting weren't so crucial, your interests, our interests mutually convening to address the climate problem in a timely fashion, I'd be out of here now. But we need to talk."

. . .

While Frank stretched out on the daybed, Miranda cleared the breakfast mugs and oatmeal bowls abandoned hours before. She needed to check on the garden. There'd been no time before leaving on her father's errand, his urgency pressing her onward. As she'd set off, she'd caught sight of a brief, worrying flap of loose plastic from the greenhouse on its slope behind the house.

From beneath the tea towel, Frank asked if the internet was working. There was someone he needed to get in touch with. He paused. His mother. But when Miranda went across the hall into the sitting room, the small hub of the modem still blinked red. On the counter, Frank's drowned phone lay buried in a bowl of rice. At least for now, they remained each other's only company.

Dropping dishes into the sink, Miranda told Frank she wanted to raise goats. The day before, their neighbour Pat Green had passed on word about a man selling a pair of doelings across the bay. She'd called the man's number and left a message. Now, given the storm, who knew how long it would be before she heard back. If she did. Once, she might have asked Sylvia for doelings, just as, for many summers, Sylvia had kept them stocked with fresh milk and cheese.

"We can ask in the village for someone to take you out to the Funks, only you'll have to wait for the water to settle, and you'll want to offer to pay for gas. Maybe Tom Borders, he has a speedboat."

She'd leave Frank in the house while she ran up to the garden.

"Miranda—" Frank began, as if he were about to ask her something else. Then he broke off.

"Why did you come here to look for your accidentals if Fernand wasn't even supposed to come this far north?"

"Well," Frank said, "its winds were so huge, I thought better stay out of its reach but be close enough that some interesting birds might be blown my way. Admittedly a gamble."

Did that make sense? "I have to take a look at something."

Frank pulled the tea towel from his forehead. "Can I come?" It seemed cruel to refuse him. He asked if he could borrow their binoculars, plucking them from the table where Miranda had left them that morning.

The path to the greenhouse and vegetable plots led behind the chicken coop and up the low slope where alder saplings rustled in the breeze. In her father's boots, Frank walked as if the ground might jump up and hurt him. Near the top of the slope, Miranda felt him stop. He'd raised the binoculars, pointing them to where cove met sea, where big waves burst in white splashes against the rocks. A storm petrel winged over the water, one that the wind might have blown in from far offshore. For a moment Frank followed it, wondering aloud if it was a Leach's or a Wilson's, but the next moment he was peering at something else.

"Miranda, what are those—those funny things in the field

on the far side of your house, beyond the trees and the solar panel?"

There were two of them, plus the wind sock. Weather monitors, one stick-like and metallic, the other like a tiny white house on a pole, both set far enough from the house that its shadow never touched them. Every afternoon at four o'clock, no matter what she was doing, if she was at or near the house, which was most days, Miranda went to meet her father. He, too, shaped his life around the indelible ritual of their daily weather measurements. In every kind of weather they walked out along the footpath and into the field. For years, this repetition had been set against all other aspects of her life. At the end of the previous afternoon they'd been out there as the wind began to rise.

The monitors stood beyond the windbreak of conifers that her father had planted to cut the strength of the north winds, the persistent nor'easterlies, the newly powerful nor'westerlies. One day they would live amid field and forest, he said.

The tall, insect-like monitor, its sensors exposed atop a metal pole, communicated data directly to the computer in her father's study. At the top, the small spinning cups of the anemometer measured wind speed. Alan had nicknamed the monitor Marty, after a character in a movie he'd loved as a child. The other one, its sensors enclosed behind louvred panels, painted white to deflect sunlight, they called Iceland, since Iceland was the next thing you'd see if you craned over the horizon. They had to collect its data by hand. While her father sang out numbers, Miranda inscribed them carefully in a notebook, the wind billowing the pages as she wrote. On rainy days, she scribbled in a rough, water-soaked pad, and transcribed the numbers afterward, seated at a small side table in her father's office, beside the row of notebooks, nine years' worth now, lined on a shelf. Up above her hung a photograph of her laughing mother on the beach in Provincetown, still a pang at the sight. Her father believed in keeping both manual records and electronic ones. Because you never knew, he said. The handwritten might outlast everything else.

After they'd written down these measurements, her father hiked back to his study, powered by the open book of the solar panel fixed to nearby rocks. Some minutes later, he returned with a small white weather balloon jumping at the end of a tether, the helium he'd pumped inside the balloon lighter than air. When he handed the reel of nylon cord to Miranda, she unspooled it, letting the balloon and the radiosonde, the panel of instruments dangling from it, rise. At each point where there was a red mark on the cord, she stopped to let the probe send data back to her father's computer until the balloon was no more than a tiny thumbprint high in the air. Wind throbbed through the cord into her arms, currents pulling the distant balloon sideways, buffeting her as she reeled the balloon back to earth.

At high tide, her father walked to the shore and measured the sea's shifting height against the rocks. He recorded the weather details of every storm. In winter, they marked the height and date of each snowfall. With a broom they brushed snow from both solar panel and weather monitors.

Some of this Miranda told Frank. Describing her life to a person from away made her feel like she was standing on a tall hill looking down at herself through binoculars. Or staring at something in a notebook.

"Are you part of a government weather network?" Frank asked, still peering across the fields.

"No." Miranda spoke quickly. They weren't, as far as she knew. She was pretty sure her father kept his activities to himself. "It's just for us, or anyone around here who's interested in the weather."

"What do you monitor exactly?"

"Wind speed, wind direction, air pressure, temperature, humidity. Precipitation at ground level. Solar radiation."

At this, Frank gave her a stare. "Solar radiation?"

"Amounts of sunlight."

"So are you noticing a lot of changes over time?"

"Some," Miranda said. She really didn't want to face more questions about her father and what he was up to. There was the past, his past, which he'd ordered her to keep hidden, when his speaking out about the dangers of the world's warming weather had overturned their lives. But there were mysteries in the present as well.

"Is your father some kind of meteorologist? Professional? Amateur?"

The wind shifted. When Miranda closed her eyes, the wind swept over her, out of the southwest, batting her face, ruffling in her ears, a soft wind but one that nevertheless had force. She tried to concentrate, let it flow through her, around her, allowing Frank's troublesome questions to fall away. She did not wish to talk about her father, she really didn't. The wind was always there. She lived in a world made of wind. Wind was her father, mother, sister, brother. Wind was changeable, yet a wind like this, in its constancy, steadied her. She held out her arms.

Frank's voice broke through again. "Miranda, are you okay?"

"The wind's checking off. It's moved back into the south-west, that's our prevailing wind. The air is full of currents like the sea. When you close your eyes it's easier to feel them."

Frank grew quiet. When Miranda couldn't stand it any longer, she opened her eyes to find him, at her side, eyes closed.

"I'm not very good at this," he said. "I'm afraid to admit I have absolutely no idea what direction the wind is coming from."

"It teases you, it swirls, but mostly it's pushing at your left cheek. Can you feel that?"

She was close enough that she might have reached out to touch his smooth skin with her finger, sunlight making flecks on the barest hint of stubble. "What I feel is a lot of air moving about," Frank said. "I suppose I need practice, don't I? Miranda, will you teach me more about the wind?"

An Arctic tern flew past, swift, bent-winged, a tiny air moustache, preparing for its long autumn flight south to the very bottom of the world. But Frank had his eyes closed and anyway the tern wasn't an accidental, only a migrant.

"A south wind arrives here over water, cold in the spring, then warmer. A west wind comes over land. A north wind's a cold wind. Winds that have 'east' in them bring rain. Never go fishing in a wind with 'east' in it. Fish in a north wind because it blows towards the land," Miranda said.

"Never go fishing in a wind with 'east' in it, okay, got that." Frank grinned. When a pair of goldfinches swooped past, chirruping, he startled, but Miranda told him goldfinches weren't so unusual anymore. Though they never used to come to the island, there'd been more in recent years, their range shifting north as the weather warmed.

Silently they stood there, eyes closed, as the smell of sun-warmed moss and lichen and the salt brine of the sea rose around them. The wind was agile and tender and calming. A gull called, while the shadow of a cloud passing overhead was a small, dark break of coolness.

"Do you do this often?" Frank asked.

"There's so much wind out here, it feels good to stop and listen to it." She'd point out the wind flag her father had erected in the yard, back when he was helping her learn her wind directions. There were other places she could take Frank to stand in the wind and listen to the sea.

"So was that storm last night bad for out here?" Frank asked. "It may not strictly speaking have been a hurricane by the time it got here, but it was pretty hair-raising to be out in, I can attest to that."

"It was unusual," Miranda said quietly. "It wasn't supposed to reach us."

Frank opened his eyes, which was a sensation brushing against her. "So *is* your father some kind of scientist?"

Miranda had to admire his persistence. "He's retired. It's a hobby. He's just very interested in the weather." She hoped Frank wouldn't ask how her father came to have retired so young.

By now the greenhouse was just ahead, strands of plastic rippling where they shouldn't be. The storm had shredded some of the plastic walls to pieces. Miranda let out a cry.

The fishing net, one of Tom Borders's castoffs, which surrounded the greenhouse, protection from coyotes and foxes, had been flung to the ground but hadn't blown away, still fixed to its metal stakes and their rock protectors. It was so random what a storm wrecked and what it saved.

She and Caleb had built the greenhouse together, nailing the sheets of plastic to a wooden frame. When Miranda took hold of a post and tried to shake it, the frame stood firm. She'd wanted to grow tomatoes in this cold and rigorous place and she'd succeeded. She longed to tell Caleb both that the storm had ripped through the plastic and that the frame hadn't budged.

But here was Frank, coming up behind her. She lifted the latch of the greenhouse door and stepped inside where the smell of the tomato plants was still intense, the fur of it, though the plants themselves were limp and salt-blackened. Maybe they should have built the greenhouse out of glass. They'd spoken of it, yet glass was more expensive. The storm might have broken the glass. The plastic, though made from fossil fuels as her father pointed out, could be replaced. She had plans to build a second, bigger greenhouse as well.

"The storm did all this?" Frank asked, fingering ripped plastic from the doorway.

Miranda nodded. The good thing was she'd already picked the tomatoes. They were in crates in the utility room, had Frank noticed? He hadn't.

"You'll need more plastic, which may not be immediately easy to come by, I realize, given the lack of a road, but it looks fixable. If I can be of any assistance, let me know. I've built tents out of plastic, which may be a transferable skill."

Tents out of plastic? "Where did you do that?"

"Oh, at protests and encampments all over the world."

She was trying to square this information with her image of him as a birder. "For birds?" She meant protests for —

"No, people." Frank offered a generous smile. "Protesting monetary policy and obscene cutbacks and neo-liberal tax cuts for the rich. Capitalism, in other words. It's what I do when I'm not birding."

Miranda wasn't sure what to say. News of the rest of the world reached her, in fragments, from far off. She went online mostly to look at plant catalogues and biodynamic farming sites. Other demands tugged at her. All the living things around her. It felt better to push the rest of the troubled world away.

The three vegetable beds were enclosed within a fence of slim spruce poles, cut and lined up in a row, on end. *Longers*, Miranda told Frank as she opened the garden gate. In the first bed, some of the long-fingered greens of the onions and garlic were bent; the dark thatch of the rows of potatoes and turnips, frilly carrot greens, red-veined beet greens, all thrust upward, tiny worlds of water pooling on the leaves. Miranda bent to touch them, speaking soft words. The hills along the oceanside had protected them, and the fence, too. Beyond it stood the row of alder saplings that she herself had planted as a windbreak. It had been back-breaking labour to dig up the saplings and transport them by quad from the cove. They would need more protection in the future. She would move more. Trees, they needed to plant more trees, her father always said, and every summer he planted more young ones up beyond the house. A ripple of alder leaves would surround them. Miranda stood up.

In the second bed, the lettuces were wilted, arugula

flattened. She knelt to pinch off blackened leaves between finger and thumb. "But look," she said as Frank drew close. Beneath the blackened leaves were smaller ones, which, in the sun, had already begun to revive. "And even a storm like that can't touch the kale." There were three different kinds: dark-green and purple, tough stalks, resolute, leaves wrinkled as brains.

There was sun and wind colour in Frank's cheeks as he stared curiously down at her. "I have to admit I'm usually paying more attention to humans than plants. I used to travel a lot, until I—started to rethink the whole idea of flying. One of my roommates, she grows a few vegetables. The point is, I don't really know what all these things are."

Pointing to each row, Miranda named what was in it: red potatoes and white, two kinds of carrot, cabbage beside the kale. Frank offered up another dazzling smile. "So you and your father, you're probably all about food self-sufficiency, too, am I right?"

"Only we haven't figured out how to grow tea or canned Carnation milk or chocolate." Her father sometimes groused about the impossibility of finding good olive oil on the island, as if this were one thing he did miss about the outer world. Then Miranda said, "Actually I do most of the gardening." For some reason she wanted Frank to know this.

"You do?" She was awarded with an appraising look. "I'm truly impressed, Miranda."

In the spring, she and her father had dug out the third bed. Miranda had planted more rhubarb, a row of raspberry canes, red and black currants. Rhubarb was hardy and grew all over the place. Raspberries already flourished wild on the island. The currants, she'd see how they took. She was even thinking about apple trees. Her plan was to sell produce to other islanders who no longer grew things—and visitors, too, when there were visitors; there were always some adventuresome travellers. Salad greens beginning in the spring if she built a bigger greenhouse. It was a short growing season but they were so far north there was lots of midsummer light. Of course the wind could be a challenge. And the ever more unpredictable weather. Margaret Hynes, who ran the restaurant in the next village down the road, had begun to buy produce from her. Lettuce grown by the sea tasted like no other.

She told Frank about harvesting berries that grew wild on the bare hills and in the protected places among the rocks, how everyone had their own secret spots for picking: bakeapples in July; blackberries, blueberries and partridgeberries coming into ripeness now; cranberries, marshberries after the first frost. She made jam. Canned vegetables. There were needles and buds of the spruce tree to gather. Her cheeks were burning. Why could she not stop talking? Where was her father? All the previous winter, during the long evenings while the wind blew around their little white house, she'd been thinking about what to do with her life. She would feed the people around her. She'd drawn up crop plans for the beds and pored over online seed catalogues. Lettuce see, her father had joked, peering over her shoulder. Who knows what might turnip, he'd said. Beets me, Miranda had replied.

Once she would have talked things over with Caleb and felt the stir of his encouragement. There were vegetable plots on the other side of the cove where Caleb's uncles had grown potatoes. Caleb had put in a crop in the spring. Once she and Caleb had spoken of growing things together, farming on the land, farming at sea; seaweed would be their carbon sink. Sometimes when she knew that Caleb wasn't around, she'd walk down the Cape House lane and from there out along the trail that led around the headlands.

Now, kneeling in front of a raised bed of potatoes, fingers in the soil, heat rose in her limbs, as, under Frank's watch, she loosened the earth around a handful of nubs, then tugged on the greens until the whole plant came free. The moist soil felt good on her fingers, luscious. All this, the air, the soil, could be set against the storm and its damages. How to describe that lusciousness, or draw it; she loved to draw things, like her mother. Yes, the nubs were firm enough and ready to harvest. Miranda rubbed dirt off a potato and handed the nub to Frank, who seemed about to hand it back until she rubbed one clean for herself and bit into it.

His face.

"You can eat them raw when they're fresh," she said. "They're crisp. Like an apple?"

Crouched at her side, Frank finished his. "Do you ever get lonely out here?" he asked. The dome of the sky was huge. Robin's egg blue. At least she'd convinced him to stop asking her about her father.

"No," Miranda said. Sometimes, out on the headlands, hiking by herself on the far side of the cove, she'd be overcome by fierce joy. The silence of the land was its own singing, beneath the shatter of waves, her blood beating a sensuous pulse.

Certainly, when Caleb had been in the picture, she hadn't been lonely. Almost every day he'd stopped by or she'd gone to his house or they'd set off on the trails together. And if they hadn't seen each other, they'd spoken. She'd never spent much time with the few girls her age on the island, the ones she'd gone to school with who spent all their time texting each other. Most of them had left by now. It had taken time getting used to life without Caleb. A part of herself remained shuttered away, where the hardest feelings couldn't catch her. She'd had to learn anew to keep herself company. There was Ella, found homeless in the streets of Nain as a puppy, sent south to them four years ago by Luke, brother of Agnes Watson, one of the young scientists come to visit her father; Ella, whom Miranda had trained and who went everywhere with her, who came trotting up now, grass seed in her fur, tongue at a pant. There was her father, often busy but always a presence.

"Do you ever think of leaving, like to go to college?" Frank asked. He said *college* the American way, meaning university, something Miranda remembered from her old life.

"No," she said. "My life is here. I'm going to farm."

Was that, distantly, the soulful roar of her father's quad?

"Hey, Miranda." Maybe Frank registered the sound, too, because a new urgency seemed to take hold of him. "I'm wondering, do you happen to know if there are other scientists on the island? Like climate scientists?"

That word. It aroused a small panic in her. It heated up her skin. "Not that I know of."

"Okay, I'm going to take an insanely wild gamble and ask something else. Have you by any chance heard of something called the ARIEL project?"

"The what?"

A very strange question, alarming even. That sound. It was her father returning, surely it was.

・ ・ ・

The night of their arrival on Blaze Island, Miranda's father, who had been Milan and had become Alan Wells, hefted their bags upstairs to their room in the Pummelly B&B, run by a brassy-haired woman who introduced herself as Mrs. Christine Brett.

"Now, Alan, mind the ceiling," Mrs. Brett said, her father's new name banging in ten-year-old Miranda's ears. The ceiling was close above their heads. Beneath his trucker's cap, her bearded father barely spoke. Once the door to their room closed behind them, he threw himself onto one of the beds and pulled a pillow over his head. Miranda climbed into the second bed, listening as a new world creaked and pressed around her.

By daylight, when she tugged at the curtains in their room, the village revealed itself, a belt of wooden houses cinched around a harbour, the land flat except for a low rise of rocks beyond the houses. Across the room, her father lay unmoving. When she called to him, he stirred enough to tell her that he was too tired to get up. She should go exploring by herself. Miranda ate breakfast alone in a dining room looking over the harbour, her only company cheerful Mrs. Brett, who served her scones and a boiled egg and asked her questions she didn't know how to answer. As soon as she could, Miranda slipped away and set off along the main road, where she discovered that there were no restaurants, no cafés, no shops other than one small, weather-beaten store with a single gas pump outside it. On the far side of the harbour the road came to an end. Sea pounded against rocks. She was on the far side of an island, facing another small hummock of rock called Sheep Island, only she didn't know that yet. There were a few dots of other tiny islands out there, above the yellow horizon, then nothing. Shivering, she imagined the sea reaching out to tug her into its depths, no mother or father to wrestle her back to land.

By now it was August. Occasionally there were other visitors in the dining room at breakfast: Gillian and Warren from Toronto, Michael and Gregory from Witless Bay. What's your name, they asked Miranda. Where are you from? She told them the things her father had instructed her to say. We're on vacation. We're from Waterloo, Ontario. Waterloo, where the Amish are, said Gillian. Miranda gave a nod. She ate her eggs quickly and toasted some bread for her father, who never came downstairs for breakfast and in fact rarely got out of bed at all. Sometimes, when she brought the toast upstairs, he was asleep. Or he was buried under the sheets and blankets and not asleep. When he spoke, his voice was raw and gravelly. One morning Miranda awoke wondering, What if he dies? She lay there, paralyzed. Her father turned his pale face to her.

Dear one, he called her. "Please walk about our new home and tell me what you find." So she went out. She wanted to do the thing that would make him get well and come back to her. When she kissed him, his beard prickled her skin.

On the far side of the harbour, a footpath traced its way behind the houses, along the ocean shore. Out there great slabs of red and black rock tumbled against each other, and flat grey rocks were littered with broken sea urchin shells. The wind blew at Miranda, off the ocean. Overhead, a gull dropped a sea urchin from a great height, then swept onto the rock to stab its beak at the broken shell and eat the exposed flesh. Miranda's hands curled inside the mittens Mrs. Brett had loaned her. Mittens, in August. How was she to make a new life in this raw, ferocious place? Was this what her life was going to be like from now on?

Her father must have had some conversations with Mrs. Brett, because Mrs. Brett was feeding Miranda not only breakfast but other meals: fried fish for supper some days, fried bologna others, moose stew and moose meat loaf the rest. Mrs. Brett taught Miranda words like *duckish*, the light at the hour that darkness falls, and explained that lunch was a meal or a snack eaten late at night. In the evening, they played cards together. Or bingo, the calls broadcast on the local channel from the Lion's Club on the other side of Blaze Island.

Mrs. Brett told Miranda that her dear husband had passed some years ago. "And your mother, is she at home in Ontario?"

Miranda shook her head.

"Do you live with her sometimes, my love?"

Miranda shook her head again. Her father had said, if someone asked, she could tell them her mother had died. Passed, Mrs. Brett had said. "She's passed," Miranda whispered.

"Oh, my darling." Mrs. Brett pulled Miranda onto her lap, holding her close, the way her mother used to, only Mrs. Brett's body was larger and had a solid warmth that was different than her mother's fervent embrace.

In the Princeton house, on nights when Miranda had trouble sleeping or when her mother wanted to be close, Jenny would climb into Miranda's bed and stroke her face while gazing at her as if all she wanted was to drink Miranda in and reassure herself of something. In the dark of the room in Pummelly, heart aching, Miranda whispered to her.

Weeks went by. One day, in the general store, which everyone called Vera's after the name of the woman who ran it, as Miranda deliberated over a chocolate bar and a carton of chocolate milk, wondering which would tempt her father the most, she turned to find a boy staring at her. Dark-haired, close to her own age. He was in line at the cash alongside a tall, red-haired woman. Miranda stared back. The woman wore a hand-knit sweater, jeans, rubber boots, and her hair travelled in a long red braid down her back. There was something formidable about her beauty. By the time Miranda paid for her chocolate bar and left, the pair were some distance ahead, an odd couple walking side by side along the main road. They took the Little Harbour Road turnoff, the one that led past the Catholic church to the B&B, but by the time Miranda reached the turn, they'd vanished.

And then she forgot about the woman and boy, because when she entered Mrs. Brett's kitchen, she found her father, thin as an egret within a thick pullover, still bearded, but out of bed, drinking a cup of tea with Mrs. Brett. His dark hair was wet and combed, he must have had a shower. Though there was fragility in his every movement, as he turned his head and the wind cried at the windows, he was up, he was on his feet.

With a crinkled smile, he said to Miranda, "Mrs. Brett has found us somewhere to live."

—

Magdalene Trewitt's house stood across the road from the B&B. It belonged to Christine Brett's sister who lived in town and had already shut it up for the season. The water had been turned off, but it could be turned back on. The house was small, two storeys stuffed with large pieces of furniture. From the window of her bedroom in Mrs. Magdalene's house, Miranda spotted the dark-haired boy trudging along the road through a driving rain, first thing in the morning, a knapsack weighing down his shoulders. Yet she'd seen no school in Pummelly.

The school, Mrs. Brett told her, was in the centre of the island, now that there were so few children there was only need for one school. On this point, her father, who seemed uncertain about other things—how long they were going to stay, what he wanted to eat—was adamant. Over dinner, their first night in Mrs. Magdelene's house, he announced, "You're not going to school. I'll be your teacher. And I'll teach you things more useful and important than anything you'll learn in school."

Like the names of all the things that grew around them.

They began to take walks together, slowly at first, for her father had shockingly little strength. Miranda was the one leading him up the path beyond the white house at the end of Little Harbour Road, the one with the paddock full of goats, both of them bundled in sweaters, clad in gloves and wool hats. She held his hand sometimes and waited for him, when, hunched, her father stopped to catch his breath.

Out on the path, he pointed at things. Ground juniper, with the prickly needles, had blue berries, he said, which were edible but they weren't blueberries, which grew on a smaller, shrubby plant with shiny leaves. Labrador tea had leaves that almost looked like needles and, when pinched, gave off a sharp scent. He handed a sprig to Miranda. A vivid spike of purple flowers was fireweed. Small stems of cotton grass were topped with cloud-like puffs. They stopped to picnic on a rise where the air had a green spice to it. The plants that grew here, close to the ground on this wind-hugged shore, were not all that different from those he used to see on his field trips in the Arctic, her father told Miranda, sounding wistful as she passed him a thermos lid full of steaming tea. It feels like a homecoming, he said and reached out thoughtfully to touch a frond of cotton grass. He plucked a small red berry, partridgeberry, known as lingonberry in Europe, he said, from greenery clinging to a rock. In Miranda's mouth, the berry was a bright burst of tartness. Marshberry, her father said, holding out a different kind of berry, adding, Northern berries are full of nutrients. Miranda repeated these words to herself: *Labrador tea, partridgeberry, marshberry.*

Wherever they were in this land, they were immigrants, and in some sense they would always be, her father said as he gazed out over the water. He had been the first in his family born in a new country, and Miranda had been born in the same country, but then, because of his work, they had moved, from country to country. Both of them were cut off from the places their people came from, the old countries full of stories of hardship and war: people forced to flee, lands overrun. He, too, had almost never seen his grandparents while growing up or where his parents had been born. Now here they were, getting to know a new place. What better way to live than to open themselves to the land on which they found themselves and invite it to shape them?

"Yes," Miranda said, glad that being immigrants was something that bound them.

For thousands of years, her father told her, a people called Beothuk had paddled their canoes among these islands and built their summer fishing camps onshore, before the Europeans came. Now that the Beothuk were gone, killed by the Europeans, they could nevertheless remember them and sense the traces of their presence. Miranda closed her eyes.

Day by day, the wind and sea air brought colour back to her father's cheeks. His stride grew stronger. He remained quiet, he was not Miranda's old father. What was he going to be, she wondered, now that he was no longer a scientist? Nevertheless, in his company, amid the wild wind that constantly boxed her ears and weather that was sunny one moment, raining the next, something in her began to relax.

One day her father stood her on top of a rock covered in lichen, a rock that didn't look like the other rocks so close to the shore. He said the rock was a dropstone, and an ancient iceberg had abandoned it there, on land once underwater as the great glaciers that covered North America retreated. He asked if she could identify the direction the wind came from, wind that was like a big cloth all over her, bashing her face, her arms, her legs.

"Where is it strongest?"

"There," Miranda said, and pointed to her left cheek.

"What direction is that?" asked her father, the wind entering and buckling his jacket. "Where's the sun? Where does it rise and where does it set?"

"Southwest?" said Miranda.

"Yes," said her father.

Forty million years ago, where they were standing had been

the peaks of high mountains, he said, the top end of the Appalachian chain that ran like a spine all the way down the east coast of America and marked where even more ancient supercontinents once collided. As they lay on the ground side by side, the thunder of great waves eroding the rocks that had once been mountains entered their bodies. The past, Miranda's past, which had already seemed far off, dissolved even more in the face of this ancient geography. Could you be an immigrant of time, she wondered, squeezing her toes in her boots. Her father turned to her, smiling, his revived face full of wonder. Her teacher. He touched her cheek. Love, she felt it brush her skin. Here was a kind of magic: that she, once more, could be a cord, pulling him onward, out of the worst of loss and grief. She squeezed his hand. A flock of eider ducks flew over them, wings clacking, and the moss beneath her body was a soft bed.

Back at the house, Alan instructed Miranda to scrunch up old supermarket flyers, place a layer of bunched-up balls inside the wood stove, sticks of kindling over these. He balanced a log on top. When she held a match to the paper, a little flame lit. Everything seemed hopeful, until a cloud of smoke sent them running out of the house. Soon, though, when she held a match to wood and paper, the flames lit neatly and the wood burned. She learned to clean out the wood stove too, carrying buckets of ash into the yard.

Some mornings, her father baked bread. He taught Miranda to knead the dough until it was supple. In a quiet cove they picked blueberries until their fingers turned blue and came home to make a pie, pastry and all. They were barely apart. They went out even when it rained and the wind was high. They went out in all weather. Almost all. It was as if her father couldn't tear himself away from the land and the weather.

Sometimes they arrived home at the end of the afternoon to find tinfoil-wrapped dishes on the doorstep, or in the back porch on top of the washing machine, or even waiting for them on the kitchen table. Pork chops and potatoes, moose stew with doughboys, macaroni and cheese, meat loaf topped with ketchup. The women of Pummelly were cooking for them. Kimberley Green, Wanda Travis, Vera McGrath, Della McGrath, Irene Foley, Susannah Pratt, Rita Borders. Slowly they met people, out on the road, or in Vera McGrath's general store. By now everyone seemed to know that her father, a former weather forecaster, had lost his job and Miranda's mother had died.

"Forecast too much weather, did you, boy," joked Dan McGrath, which made Miranda's father nod and wince simultaneously.

One late afternoon, as the light turned duckish, there was a knock at the back door. No one locked their doors in Pummelly, no one ever used the front door, and most everyone entered a house without knocking.

They were sitting in the parlour, studying a book about clouds that Alan had found in a store in the town of Blaze, a store that sold wool and sweaters and T-shirts, along with books about wildflowers and trees and local geology. He'd bought a copy of each book. These were to be Miranda's school books.

"Go see who it is, Miranda, will you?" said her father, sliding the book under a sofa pillow.

At the back door stood the red-haired woman, taller and younger than most of the women who'd come bearing casserole dishes. Up close her fierce beauty felt like cliffs and the sea. Sea air was a perfume around her, in her large, loose sweater, dark jeans, and rubber boots. She was holding out a jar of jam, the deepest ruby. There was abruptness in her manner, hard edges not entirely rubbed smooth. She said she was Sylvia Borders, Christine Brett and Magdalene Trewitt's niece, daughter of their sister Eva, now passed, who used to live in town. Tom and Leo and Charlie Borders, who lived along the road with their wives, those were her brothers. The Borders boys. She lived in the white house with the green roof right at the end of the road, the one with the goats in the small field on the hill behind it. "I've seen you go by on your way up Lighthouse Hill."

By this time, Miranda's father had appeared, shaggy-haired, bringing his own air of abruptness. Sylvia Borders stepped inside. She repeated her introduction and handed Miranda the jam.

Her father said, "That's very kind." There was an awkward silence.

"Would the two of you like to come for supper?" Sylvia had a quick-moving smile. To Miranda she said, "Have you met my son, Caleb? He's often wandering about."

Caleb must be the dark-haired boy.

To Miranda's father, she said, "I'm sure you could go out hunting with my brothers if you wish." She added, "My brother Tom brought me a brace of eider. I'll roast one. Eider or turr, though turr's more fishy, so I believe I'll offer you eider."

—

The wood stove poured heat into Sylvia Borders's kitchen. In the centre of the wooden table, a beeswax candle burned. Sylvia's kitchen was nothing like Magdalene Trewitt's or Christine Brett's. For a start, all sorts of dried plants hung from the exposed rafters. Shelves full of jars lined the walls, jars filled with mysterious dried leaves. In the back kitchen were more shelves of preserves: jams of vibrant colours, bottled meat and fish. It was like no kitchen Miranda had ever been in before. The dried plants gave the room a rich, earthy aroma that mingled with the woodsmoke. Red, floor-length velvet curtains hung over the door to the back kitchen and the door to the parlour. To keep the drafts out, Sylvia said as she tugged them closed. She opened a bottle of dandelion wine, which she said she'd made herself. Out of the flowers, Miranda's father asked and Sylvia said yes and added that dandelion was a good liver cleanser.

"You can make honey out of dandelion flowers as well, Alan, though you'll want at least forty pounds to do that."

"That's a lot of harvesting," said Miranda's father as Miranda repeated his new name to herself. How strange it was to hear others say it. He'd put on a clean sweater, combed his beard, and while he seemed interested in his surroundings there was some part of him still wandering elsewhere, as if he hadn't yet fully arrived.

Sylvia brought the roast duck to the table. There were no rings on any of her fingers. No wedding ring. She carved the duck, asked Caleb to pass around the potatoes and pickled cabbage, something Miranda had never eaten. She'd never eaten roast eider either, which tasted rich and had a hint of salt in it.

Yes, she'd grown up on the island, in Pummelly, Sylvia said, her long red hair flowing over her shoulders. Then she'd left to go to university. She had a degree in sociology. She'd come back to the island when Caleb was small. In those early days she'd done some work in elder care up at the hospital. Had they been that way yet, up along the road to the town of Blaze?

"Yes," Miranda's father said. He asked if she did that still, and with a quick shake of her head Sylvia said no.

Later, she'd trained as a massage therapist, though most people on the island considered such a thing a luxury and weren't inclined to pay for it. She sold herbal products made from the plants that she foraged and dried. Some people still liked the old medicines. She pointed at the plants hanging above their heads. She sold jams. And knitwear. She included Miranda in her gaze though her comments seemed to be directed mostly to Miranda's father, who, like Sylvia, spoke with a halting tentativeness.

While it might make sense to leave the island for work, Sylvia said, she had no wish to give up her life here. "It's not a life I could have anywhere else. It's possible to live at least partway outside a monetary economy in a place like this."

Alan's attention twisted into focus at these words.

"Christine says you're planning to stay the winter," Sylvia continued. Candlelight made patterns on her fair skin.

"That's the plan," Alan said.

"Winter's hard out here."

"I've lived through some harsh weather." Alan flexed his hands until the knuckles cracked. "We'll adapt. I want to live a quiet life close to the sea, in a northern place, whatever the weather. That's the sum of my aspirations."

"Low-pressure system coming in tomorrow," Sylvia said. "Sky's clear enough tonight to see the dark side of the new moon. Likely rain if you're thinking of heading out."

Caleb took Miranda to visit the animals. The goats, Jewel, Noelle, Gabby and Fleur, had prickly hair on their long noses and banged their heads against Miranda's hand. Their bright, curious eyes made her never want to leave them. Caleb's small body moved with solid purpose as he forked the goats some hay. There was authority in the way he closed up their barn for the night. The goats were a kind called Nubians. When he spoke he ducked his dark head bashfully. His skin was much darker than his mother's, darker than anyone else Miranda had yet met on the island.

His mother took the does off-island to visit a buck and this was how they bred them, Caleb said. They drank the milk and in the summer made yogurt and cheese. They'd tended the ten hens by hand when they arrived as three-day-old chicks. He told Miranda how he'd given each chick her name, as he locked up the hens in their house, too. A fox lived in the hills beyond town, Caleb said. He'd seen her there and in the cove, down where Pat Green's old, abandoned house stood.

The night air was salty and moist. Miranda listened to the goats chewing hay in their barn, a soft, bewitching munching.

Caleb said, "*Pummelly, Pummelly*, it's the sound the pebbles make when waves rock them at shore."

"You mean the waves pummel them," said Miranda.

Caleb picked up a stone and hurled it with a force that came close to Miranda then violently retreated.

—

One autumn afternoon, as Miranda walked by herself around the harbour, white-haired Mary Green, tiny and sharp-eyed, beckoned from her back door.

Over partridgeberry muffins and tea with Carnation milk, Mary told Miranda the story of how, in the spring five years before, she and her friend Wanda Travis had outrun a polar bear.

One fine day, the two of them decided to walk to Lower Cove, an abandoned settlement down the shore where Mary had lived as a child, a distance of a few hours on foot. At first glimpse, Mary reckoned the large white creature glimpsed through spruce on a headland was a horse. Yet who kept a white horse on the island? Then she and Wanda were running as fast as they could, tripping over branches and the cords holding up their rubber rain pants. Luckily, Mary said, the wind blew the bear's rancid, fishy scent to them, not theirs to him, and their rain gear helped conceal their smell.

They reached the cove but Mary had forgotten to bring the key to the cabin. Neither of them had a portable phone. Rather than risk the long walk back, they determined to spend the night on the cabin roof, Mary boosting Wanda from the railing of the bridge, Wanda hauling Mary onto the roof after her. My, what a sight we must have been, Mary said, though by then there wasn't even a bear to see it.

At last the sound of a purring motor reached them. When a speedboat turned into Lower Cove, they were after waving frantically to Ferg Foley, come to visit his own cabin farther along the shore. Mary said he didn't believe her when she told him they'd been spotted by a polar bear. He showed no interest in searching for the tracks of the vanished animal, but he did take them back to Pummelly in his boat.

Two days later, word came that a man had shot and killed a polar bear on one of the Little Blazes, the small, uninhabited islands that lay close to Blaze Island in the bay. Ferg stopped by Mary's house to apologize and say that he should have taken her at her word, but the story of two old women outrunning a polar bear seemed too fantastical to be believed.

Back around the harbour, Miranda went to find Caleb Borders who was up in the goat barn, doing chores. As she patted the goats' shifting flanks, Miranda asked him if he'd ever seen a polar bear.

Two years ago, Caleb said, he was buying flour at Vera's when a polar bear walked into the village, down the path from UpABack Cove. Before anyone could call wildlife, it shook its greasy yellow fur, turned and walked back out again.

"What would you do if a polar bear showed up outside your door?"

"I'd only pull out a gun if I had to." Pitchfork in hand, dark hair falling into his eyes, Caleb seemed friendlier than at their first meeting.

"But where do they go when they've come all this way south?"

"I don't know, Miranda," Caleb said solemnly, "but I don't suppose they find their way home again."

When Miranda told her father these stories, over a supper of stewed cod and kale and bread, he laughed at Mary's story, said Ferg Foley's response was more evidence that humans were very good at believing only what they wished to believe.

A moment later, Pat Green hollered through the back

door that he'd dropped a load of wood for them at roadside. Calling out, Alan grabbed a bottle from the top of the fridge and poured a dollop of whiskey into two cups of black tea.

Tall, lean Pat was a teacher who'd spent years up in the Arctic, at schools in Rankin Inlet on the shores of Hudson Bay and Pangnirtung on Baffin Island, places Miranda's father had also been. He'd admitted as much to Pat. The shared landscape seemed to have bonded them, though Alan never mentioned ice cores drilled from glaciers, only that he'd spent time out on the land.

"Miranda's been telling me polar bear stories," Alan said as Pat folded his long legs into a chair. "Your mother's, for instance. Here's another. I was out hunting with some Inuit friends, up on Devon Island, north of Baffin, got caught in a spring blizzard, which blew for three days, the tent humming and vibrating like a bad radio signal the whole time. One day I woke up to what I thought was a different kind of wind, shaking then not, shaking then not. The next moment, a pair of claws rips right through the nylon."

"Just what you needed, a little breeze," said Pat as he downed a mouthful of tea.

"I fired out the front and managed to scare the creature off." There was something theatrical about her father's manner, yet the story was a true one that Miranda had heard before. He was after something. She wasn't sure what.

"Sea ice up north is thinner so more find themselves stranded out on the ice, unable to return to land," Pat said. "They'll be caught on ice floes when ice breaks up in the spring and end up floating south on the Labrador Current. I've seen paw prints out near Green Cove Pond big as dinner plates."

"Is that so?" Alan said meditatively.

"Harry Pratt keeps a record of all the weather around here. Clouds that don't behave the way they used to. Fog coming out of the northwest. It never before did that. Cedar waxwings, that's a bird we never used to see. And the ice, it's not the same ice, there's not so much of it for a start, pans don't raft against each other on shore the way they once did."

Her father's body grew still. "Do you think Harry Pratt would talk to me?"

Outside in the falling light, Alan and Miranda said good-bye to Pat, who set off in his big grey truck, a plume of exhaust settling over them.

A moment later, Sylvia Borders, tall and lanky in her rubber boots, came walking in their direction, with a profound, curious air that seemed to reach right to Miranda's depths. "Good evening to ye," she said.

Alan, not unfriendly, said, "We're inspecting the wood that Pat has so generously dropped off for us."

Crossing her arms over her thick sweater, Sylvia agreed that it was very kind.

"Pat mentioned that Harry Pratt keeps a record of the weather in Pummelly." Her father's body, next to Miranda's, was ticking, almost twitching.

"Yes," said Sylvia. "Useful, given all the weather weirding, as I've heard some call it."

"Does anyone around here deny the weather's changing?" Perhaps her father was recalling his enemies, Miranda thought. Once, with something like anger, he'd let loose that they were still a force out in the world, growing stronger as the weather grew more unpredictable. There'd been a spate of wildfires in California—she'd glimpsed this on his laptop —whole towns going up in smoke.

"Hard to do when you live as close to the wind as we do, when you step out the door and feel what's happening for yourself," said Sylvia. "The weather's always been changeable but it's never changed like this."

Alan ran a hand through his unruly hair. Sylvia asked if they'd like a half-dozen eggs. When Alan said yes, and she strode back to her house to fetch them, his eyes followed her, his preoccupied attention furrowing into Miranda.

That night, as her father tucked her into bed, words burst out of him as if he couldn't help himself. "Maybe we should visit Harry Pratt and ask to look at his weather records."

"Why?" Concern roiled in Miranda. Wasn't the whole point of their coming to the island that her father had abandoned his old life as a scientist?

"Or we'll invite him round here for a cup of tea." Her father kissed her forehead.

That winter, they weathered blizzards fierce enough to make the walls of Mrs. Magdalene's house sway. There were days when the wind blew so hard they couldn't go outside at all. When at last Miranda stepped out on the bridge, the wind beat at her so strongly she couldn't move. Inside, she sat by the wood stove with her father, turning the pages of the books on plants and clouds and geology as the house groaned. In the afternoons, seated at the kitchen table, he taught her to touch type, so that she could transcribe weather stories, he said. When, on a fair and windless day, they went to Harry Pratt's drafty house on the far side of the harbour, out on

Careless Point, her father brought along a notebook and small tape recorder. He took notes as Harry offered them green tea, unfurled printouts from an antique computer and spoke about the strong, hot summer winds that had begun blowing out of the south, high water in the harbour, winter winds that came without snow.

A sudden thaw in February brought winter rain like no one had ever seen. Then snow so deep it buried the village for two days. Alan dug pathways between their house and Christine Brett's place and Caleb and Sylvia's. He helped Caleb and Sylvia clear paths to the goat barn. Every day he seemed to move with more strength and vigour, excited by the prospect of their upcoming move to the little white house on the near side of the cove — Pat Green's old hay store. Alan had asked Pat if he could buy the abandoned house and some of the land around it and, after some coaxing, Pat had agreed.

Inside Mrs. Magdalene's house, wood stove piled high, her father stamping snow off his boots in the back kitchen, Miranda thought: Down in the cove, we'll be all on our own. There'll be no one near us. Not Caleb or Sylvia or Mrs. Brett. Winds and storms will be fiercer. Maybe there'll be polar bears.

Soon she was going to lose her brief home in the village. Only they had to move. Come summer, Magdalene Trewitt wanted her house back.

In March, Miranda's father went out duck hunting with the Borders brothers, all of them clad in snow-white jackets. Caleb Borders appeared at their door, snowshoes strapped to his boots, an extra pair in his mittened hands. He showed Miranda how to fit her boots into straps made out of pieces of old car inner tubes. Eagerly she trudged after him up the hill beyond the goat barn that led towards the metal rigging of the automated lighthouse. Pack ice is what the sea brings in, Caleb told her. Slob ice lies like a slushy skin over the water and moves with the waves. Ballycatters, those are the big pans of ice rafted at shore, their blue-green edges sharp as knives, and the slippery mounds of ice that salt spray sends to coat the shore rocks. He seemed to take pleasure in telling her these things. In a sudden rush of snow up on the hilltop, a dwy, said Caleb, they lay side by side and let the wind sift snow over them, the world growing more and more quiet.

Caleb's abrupt silences no longer felt rude. The curt intensity with which he liked to explain his world was becoming a shared pleasure. Miranda had seen his cousins tease him as they played shinny out on the ice of the harbour, all of them skating away from him except her, but Caleb didn't talk about this. She wished she could tell him more about her mother, who would have thrown herself into the snow beside them, laughing with delight, sweeping her arms like a snow angel as she stared up at the grey clouds. She'd told Caleb her mother's name was Jenny and she was a painter. She would never stop missing her. Never.

On March 15, a robin appeared in their yard. A robin already, her father said in surprise. He scribbled something in a notebook. Snow fell again in April, Sheila's Brush, the last storm of the winter season. Arctic ice began to drift south, earlier than in the old days, according to Sylvia.

In the sudden, intense heat of May, May month Caleb called it, Pat Green and Alan started work on the little house in the cove, along the road from Pat's house. They pulled off its rotted clapboard, wrapped the exterior, batted down insulation against the interior studs, rebuilt the walls with new electrical in them, connecting these to the batteries that would supply power to the house. Alan presented Miranda with leather work gloves and a hammer and screwdriver of her own, set her simple tasks. Learning to make things was as important as any other skill, he said. She nailed in baseboards. She painted primer on walls. In the evenings, he taught her to sew while mending a tear in his own jeans at her side.

Sometimes on weekends Caleb came out to join them, following her father and lanky Pat Green around like a puppy. He didn't seem to mind not being with his cousins. In the village, Miranda had heard his cousin Danny call Caleb names: Dirty and Smoked. When Caleb asked if she would ever go to school, she told him that the world was her school. She was learning about the wind and clouds and plants.

"Don't you know those things?" Puzzled, Caleb brushed waves of dark hair out of his eyes. Caleb didn't know the proper names of clouds like her father, but he knew that mackerel clouds brought wind and when woodsmoke doesn't rise, that's a sure sign of a storm coming. Miranda explained that what he called whisper clouds, her father called cirrus. The ones that brought rain, those were altostratus.

Kids were born to the goat does as caribou moss turned the hills lime green. Sylvia, who slept in the barn some nights, grew tense and short-tempered, caught up in the kidding. After Fleur gave birth one night at three, and Jewel the next morning, Sylvia allowed Miranda to climb into the stall to hold the tiny, newborn doelings, Fern, Willow, and Alder, the bucklings Bally and Catter. Caleb had named them.

One afternoon, as they scrambled along the shore path between Caleb's house and the cove, Caleb told Miranda how, the summer he was six, his mother had gone to work on a longliner. There wasn't much work to be had so why shouldn't a woman, if she was strong enough, go fishing. No man would take her on his boat at first, because of the bad luck of it, not even her brother Tom who fished, until Horatio Pine of Tom's Neck lost his brother to a slashed wrist and offered Sylvia a place on the crew of his boat *Starlight*. She lasted a season. True, there wasn't much fish to be had that year. But, Caleb said, it was being away from him for weeks at a time that proved too hard.

Out of the blue, as a black-backed gull flew past at head-height, Caleb asked Miranda how her mother had died. Something clanged inside her. What would her mother think to see her here, like this? If her mother had lived, would they have come here? Would her mother have wanted to live in such a place? In her room in Mrs. Magdalene's house, Miranda kept her mother's small painting perched on a dresser. Sometimes she vanished into it.

"In an accident," Miranda said.

Caleb seemed to be waiting for more. "Was it long ago?"

She shook her head, mouth full of all that couldn't be spoken, time travelling. On the anniversary of her mother's death, she and her father had found a sheltered place among the shore rocks between the village and the house in the cove. Just like that, the wind had died, and they'd been able to light the candle they brought with them. At home they lit more candles and said a prayer to honour her spirit. Now it was June month: roots like snakes underfoot, moist earth, berry plants blossoming. Her mother was Jewish, Miranda told Caleb. Then she asked him, "Is your father dead?"

She'd assumed he was. Caleb never spoke about his father. There was this equivalency between them: a missing parent.

"No," he said. "I don't know. My mother won't tell me a thing about him. Won't speak about him ever. Only he's not from around here, is he? You know what? I don't even know that. She won't say a word. He must have been something, right? He must've fetched up long enough in St. John's for something to happen. By the time I was born she'd moved to a house in the woods, that side — over there on the main island."

His light brown skin, his dark hair, his smallness. There was pain in him that he was covering with a jokey manner. Every so often Miranda caught a glimpse of Sylvia in his slim chin, the contours of his face. She, too, felt like an outsider but Caleb wore his difference more obviously.

When they got back to the village, to the puffy buns with jam that Sylvia had left on the kitchen table, Caleb asked Miranda to come upstairs to his room. This was a place she'd never been. When it rained they stayed in the kitchen or parlour or hung about in the barn with the goats or in the shed across the yard, which had its own wood stove, and where Caleb liked to do his homework, when he did it.

Caleb kept his bedroom very neat. From the bottom drawer of his dresser, he pulled out a cardboard box, removed the lid, and folded back a piece of red velvet to reveal a small curled animal foot, the fur rubbed nearly off the hard skin in places. A rabbit's foot, he told Miranda.

He said the only memory he had of his father was of a man's large hands slipping a pair of tiny rabbit-fur slippers, silky-soft, fur-side in, over his small feet. He must have been very young. In a cradle maybe? A glimpse of a man with brown skin, tight curls in his hair. It was his belief that his father had hunted the rabbit, made the slippers for him. He was certain the slippers had existed, though they'd vanished by the time he and his mother came to Blaze Island when he was two. If he asked his mother what had happened to them, she would say only that she had no idea. She didn't deny their existence. Besides, he still had the rabbit's foot. There were no pictures of his father to be found anywhere. He'd searched the house when his mother wasn't around. None of his relatives seemed to know anything about his father, though he knew they had their theories.

"You can hold it. Rub it for luck," Caleb said. Miranda took the little foot in her hand, touched the wizened skin and disappearing fur, understanding this for the act of trust it was.

"Who do you think your father was?"

A strange expression crossed Caleb's face. "I don't know," he said.

Miranda said, "My mother died in an accident. A car hit her. Last year."

"Oh," said Caleb as his face seized up.

July month: Miranda's new bedroom in the cove smelled of sawdust and cut wood. The walls were slats of wood laid sideways, painted a clean, calm white. A turquoise chair, fisherman's union green, stood in one corner. Above the dresser hung the small luminous painting by her mother, the landscape of another world. Out the window lay fields, then water, then bare hills on the far side of the cove. Miranda woke to the whoosh of waves and the bleating of Pat Green's lambs. Each morning she walked out into the field behind the house and scrambled over the rocks at field's end to where the sea burst in frothy waves. She named some of the largest rocks: after her mother, another Uma, another Craggy, and another one Mister Big. She gathered sea urchin shells. She flapped her wings and became a gull, learned that gannets were the white birds that dove like comets into the water. She ran into a wind that sculpted her limbs, enjoying a freedom unlike any she'd ever known, as long as she told her father where she was going and when she expected to return. When she did return, she stared in wonder at her muscular father as he hefted and nailed and sawed.

Now Pat and her father were talking of moving an old store shed that Pat wasn't using anymore across the land on skids. There was a gasoline generator set up outside the house, and a small portable solar panel for power until the bigger solar panels were delivered and installed. Sometimes Alan took a break to cut the grass around the house with the scythe he'd had delivered by mail order. When Miranda held its two wooden handles and tried to swing the metal blade, she could barely lift it, but her father made the scythe's movement fluid and fierce. He placed her hands into position, his sweaty body close, guiding her into a swing. When he stepped back, a smile flew across his ruddy face. You're not the girl who arrived here a year ago, he told her. This seemed to please him. And she wasn't.

Her father swung the scythe as if he couldn't bear to be still. He kept his beard trimmed short, his dark hair in waves, longer than it had ever been in the old life. Miranda's body, too, had grown lean and muscular. She stared at herself in her bedroom mirror, shocked at the sight. At times, her father turned broody and kept to himself. At other moments,

Miranda sensed a tremble of joy in him, satisfaction as he touched the fresh white clapboard of their house and eyed the fields all around them, no sign of other humans apart from a ruined house behind spruce trees on the far side of the cove. He took daily weather notes. He spoke about getting a pony. Or a dog. About bringing in hives for bees and covering one side of their roof with moss. He set up stakes in the place on the low slope behind their house where the land was rich and fertile, where he was going to dig a vegetable garden.

Here in the new, new life, Caleb dropped by almost every day. Sylvia, too, brought eggs and lettuces from her garden, jars of fresh goat milk. Sometimes Sylvia and Miranda's father went off on walks together, talking about bees or gardening, or they stayed in the new kitchen with its white walls, speaking of their children, while Caleb and Miranda flew about outside. Other times Sylvia took Miranda foraging along the shore for lovage, also called sea celery, which tasted like celery, wild parsley and sea rocket and beach pea and oyster leaf, all good to be mixed in a salad. Sylvia had a particular concentration when she foraged, an eye for every thing that grew.

For Miranda's eleventh birthday Sylvia baked a cake. The next day, Miranda watched Sylvia trench her potato beds, wielding a spade with a tough strength not unlike her father's. Handing Miranda the spade, Sylvia told her to give it a try. Here was another pleasure, to be able to dig in deep and turn the earth. Miranda set off by herself along the shore path, towards the cove, scrabbling like a goat over the rocks. This new confidence was becoming part of her, the swoon of being out on the land alone. At night, in bed, she fell asleep with her father creaking in the kitchen below, the smell of the sea on her hair and in her skin.

Bakeapples ripened early that year, and when they did, at the end of July, Sylvia invited the two of them berry picking, but Alan, who had spent the previous afternoon nailing new planks to the walls of Sylvia's goat barn, said he had to stay to do some work at the house. Only Miranda went with Sylvia and Caleb and Christine Brett to their family's bakeapple grounds, whose location, Caleb said, they shared with no one, so wasn't Miranda the lucky one. She felt lucky, charmed even, as they hiked inland, the ground sometimes marshy underfoot, until they were surrounded by a sea of small, star-shaped leaves with little orangeish berries protruding from them. Sylvia showed Miranda how to pluck only the cloudy-coloured berries, not the hard, still-yellow ones, and how to shuck them, separating the hull from the fruit with your fingernail as you picked, teaching her, in a different way than her father, how to live on the land. At the plunk of berries into the plastic tub, stiff west wind on her face, a rush of happiness seized Miranda, for the first time in a long time, guilt, then again a surge of undeniable happiness. She hoped her mother could forgive her for it.

She brought a bucket overflowing with berries back to her father, thrumming with delight. When, before leaving, she'd asked him why he had to stay behind, he said he was expecting a delivery. When Miranda asked of what, he said, equipment, but it was as if he were brushing her off. Now, out on the bridge of their new old house, he gathered her to him, running his calloused hands through her long hair, so much longer than it used to be. He told Miranda that he would cut it if she wanted and wouldn't if she didn't. "Do you like living here, my dear one?" There was a catch in his throat as he rocked her, hard and close.

"Yes," she told him. And again. "Yes."

"If only your mother could see us now."

"Yes," Miranda said.

"I'm doing all this for you," her father said, almost crushing her in his embrace, and Miranda held him tight in gratitude.

That night, they stepped outside together, holding hands. This, too, filled her with joy, as the two of them gazed up at the dark sky, the crazy vastness of the stars.

In the utility room the boxes that had been delivered to her father waited in a pile. He was going to set up a weather monitoring station, he told Miranda, so they could keep track of the weather. They'd keep talking to other people from around the island, gathering their weather stories, which would form their baseline data. He was going to create an island weather atlas, compile as much information as he could, as a resource for himself and others.

"Are you still a scientist?" Miranda asked. She was having trouble sharing her father's excitement. What he was doing now was different, he said, it was called citizen science.

For a week he didn't unpack the boxes. They had to squeeze around them to reach the refrigerator. He seemed to be pretending they weren't there and occupied himself reading the manual for the small wind turbine he was also installing.

Her father was at the table, buried in a thick sweater, manual open in front of him, when, one August afternoon, Miranda stepped into the kitchen.

"Dad. Mrs. Brett asked me to go with her across the bay tomorrow. She's taking the seven o'clock ferry and coming back again on the six o'clock. To get her hair done."

They'd been on the island for over a year. In all that time Miranda had not left the island once. Neither of them had. A day ago, for the first time since their arrival on Blaze Island, she'd heard her father laugh.

The ferry, she'd ride the ferry on a bright day, see a bit of the land on the far side, the bay itself, return. Most people went across regularly: to the malls in Gander, for medical appointments, to the dentist, the airport. Pat Green and his wife, Kimberley, went. Caleb and Sylvia almost never left the island, because of the goats and chickens, but even they had spent a week in St. John's, leaving Miranda and her father in charge of the animals. So why did her breath feel quaky and her fists ball up as she approached her father with this request?

Serious, even grave, he slapped shut the manual, pulled out a chair, sat her down beside him. "I'm sorry, sweetheart, but that won't be possible. Our life is here now. Other people will have different ways—but we only use gasoline for important things. Yes, we'll go stock up at the supermarket. And buy fish at the fish plant. We'll drive across the island now and again to talk to people about the weather. But on the whole, we'll try to live without going far. And we stay on the island. We've left the rest of the world behind, remember? We may look like outliers but soon others will begin to live this way again, sticking close to home. There are other people who don't leave the island—those sisters, you met them at Leo Borders's kitchen party, what's their name again? The man from Tom's Neck who used to lay shingles and fell off a roof and now makes a living playing the fiddle."

Miranda flushed with anger and frustration. All those people her father had mentioned, they were old people.

"You don't have to drive across, Mrs. Brett's driving."

"No, Miranda." Her father, with his sombre face, had never felt so implacable. There was wildness and freedom in the new life and there was a border, stern rules.

"Are we going to be here for a long time?" In that moment Miranda didn't know what she wanted. To leave? Never leave? Was the island a prison?

Something caught her father's eye. He tugged her by the hand, pulling her through the mud room and outside, into the wind-filled air. "Look," he exclaimed, "snow buntings!" A cascade of small white birds flew over them. "Yes, the plan is to stay here!"

Mid-morning after the storm: Caleb leaped off the quad, his boots, the legs of his coveralls spackled with mud. The back door to Cape House swung open on its hinges. Alarming. When he stepped inside, wind met him, wind where there shouldn't have been any. He followed the current into the parlour. The new windows that he and the old man had installed at the beginning of the previous summer, his pride, not to mention a big cut out of his bank account, had shattered, there and in the dining room across the hall. He sank to his knees, glass littering the newly sanded floors, glass and water and bucketfuls of heedless sunlight spilling all around him.

He found some plywood sheets to board up the frames, swept up the glass, mopped the floors. It was the best he could do. The windows could be replaced. But it would take money to buy new ones, money he didn't have, so the damage, while not ruinous, was ruinous for him.

These were the rooms that he'd been fixing up first, because they were the most beautiful, with their big bow windows on either side of the old front door that faced the sea. He'd spent nights camped in the parlour, where sheep had once settled and pissed, wrapped in a sleeping bag on the planks that he'd scrubbed until he was breathless, before sanding them silky. Waking at dawn, he'd stare out the window, into the violet light, the epic stretch of ocean pulling at him. Walking the rooms in wonder and contentment, he'd wanted only to share the pleasure with someone else. His mother. More than anyone else, the girl. He'd gone for broke with double-pane glass, sliders, wooden frames. There was a man in Shallow Bay who restored old windows but made them airtight. These windows shouldn't have been the ones to smash, with a storm out of the southeast. But there'd been those gusts from every direction. The sudden, violent pressure drop must have tugged the back door open, here as at his great-aunt's house, sucking air out of the rooms and pulling the pliant glass with them.

He was going to be late. Go right away, the old man had written in the note the girl had delivered earlier that morning. But the windows. Surely the old man would understand. Yet Caleb knew, from his encounter with those men the day before, that they were impatient to be off, especially Roy, the bossy one. Storms weren't convenient. There was supposed to be a meeting. Enclosed in the envelope addressed to him was a note Caleb was to deliver to Anna. If it was so necessary to reach the men in a hurry, though, why hadn't the old man rushed to them himself?

Still, here Caleb was now, tearing along the road to Tom's Neck. He'd come around Green Cove Pond on the trail before cutting back to the road at Cape House lane. Up in the Burnt Hills, beyond the washout, the road was fine. On its bare hilltop, to his left, the broken spine of the cellphone tower tipped, its support wires loose and dangling. Caleb stopped the quad long enough to tug off his helmet. He scarcely had to worry about traffic. The lack of cars suggested that people in Tom's Neck already knew about the breach in the road. Someone had tried to get through or the wind carried the news. A white-throated sparrow's song skipped to his ears. Beyond some goldenrod, the small bird darted from branch to branch, leaves turning ruddy as the seasons shifted.

In Tom's Neck, at Ruby's Convenience, partway around the open curve of the harbour, Caleb stopped again. The old man had asked him to buy fuel. That's what the bills in the envelope were for. Which was almost funny, given the old man's strictures about fuel use, yet here he was, as anxious not to run out of gasoline as the rest of them.

There were two gas pumps at Ruby's and a chugging gasoline generator off to one side. Ruby herself, in rubber boots, dyed blonde hair ripping about her cheeks, directed what traffic there was.

She couldn't hide her surprise at the sight of Caleb, come all the way from Pummelly.

"I was at Cape House, right, the old house I'm fixing up, this side of the sinkhole." Caleb freed the red jerry can from its bungee cord trap. "Sinkhole's big as a crater. Track around Green Cove Pond was some muddy. Lost two big windows at the house."

Ruby was saying something about wires being down on the road between Frenchman's Head and Shallow Bay. A town crew was working, but if they had to wait for a proper hydro crew from the other side who knew what day that would be, given the likely state of things over there.

"Loading ramp took a hit when the ferry came in to dock last night," said Aidan Burke, one of the ferry captains, waiting beside his tall truck. "The jammed ramp won't go up again. Managed to get over to the dock this morning, some debris on the road but passable. Boat's still in her berth and there's a bit of coverage over on bayside but can't get through to transport and unlikely anyone will be in a rush to think about us, let alone fly someone up to look at our boat or send another."

"So we're all castaways," said Ruby, without seeming fussed.

No phones. No power. No boat. No water from the taps. Gasoline vanishing. On the island, they were used to the ferry breaking down. It broke with some regularity and sometimes took days to fix or for a replacement boat to be found. In winter, ice sometimes froze the bay impassably or the wind got up so high that crossings were cancelled for a week or more. They were used to supplies dwindling in the general stores and in Pierce's supermarket, the only one on the island: no more meat or eggs or milk or store-bought bread or fresh fruit or vegetables come all the way from Ontario or California. Caleb and his mother were better off than most, with their own eggs and at least part of the year their own milk and cheese and vegetables. Even now, if the power outage were to last, his mother had ways to keep things cool in the old root cellar tucked into the hillside behind their house. They always kept a store of water on hand. If the contents of their freezer thawed, well, they still had the meat and fish they bottled each year.

Outside Bakeapple House, Teresa Blake, lithe and short-haired, in jeans and a T-shirt, was beating rugs hung over the laundry line with a broom. Forehead furrowed, she threw all her weight into each thwack.

"How's it going, Teresa?" Caleb called after parking the quad in the empty little gravel lot.

Teresa stopped her beating long enough to say, "How'd you get through?"

Presumably she'd heard about the broken road. If so, did this mean that Anna and the men had given up expecting him?

"Came through the barrens. How was the night here?"

"House swayed a little. These guests, my goodness, you'd think they'd never been in a bit of wind before."

Teresa was not quite his mother's age. Like his mother she'd once worked a government job in town. When Caleb had come to make the reservation for the old man, he'd caught her smoking in her vegetable patch with a sinewy woman named Kim from somewhere on the other side, the two of them vexed as teenagers at being caught. Caleb had seen them together before, walking along the road, slim Teresa, Kim with a motorcycle helmet slung over one arm, or sitting out on Teresa's bridge, arms brushing. In the last few weeks, sightings of Kim had ceased, and Teresa, in his last encounter with her, had been brittle and snappy.

"Are they in there now?" Caleb asked.

"Oh, no," Teresa said, "they're off."

"Off?" The word in his mouth nearly swallowed him. "Off where?"

"To check on their plane and see if they can find some coverage. I don't know what they're thinking. No one else has any. Even on the battery-operated radio—mostly static. Can't be good over there, can it? Margaret and I keep checking. But one of them, the one with the hair, says his phone is special. So they're after setting off with that woman, Anna, who seems to have some sense. I lent her my car. I've no idea when they'll be back."

The wave of relief was equally head-pounding. Not off as in off the island.

Like Cape House, Bakeapple House had been built by a long-ago ship's captain. Inside, a mahogany staircase rose in a fancy curve to the second floor. Teresa had told Caleb how her ship's captain, Noah Flett, rich off the salt fish, had modelled his stairs after some he'd spotted on a trading trip through the Bahamas. Her house was grander than Caleb's but his had better views. It seemed wildly unfair that her windows should be intact while his were broken.

Inside, voices drifted from behind the closed door that must lead to the kitchen. Margaret Hynes's voice for one. A generator chugged from the far side of the house. Smells wafting through the door made Caleb salivate. Fish broth. Biscuits. Really, on a day like today Margaret ought to be taking the men down to the beach, lighting a fire, and treating them to boiled tea and fried pork chops.

A commotion outside the front door snagged his attention. Roy Hansen was the first to enter, his appearance notably changed from the day before. He was still wearing the same corduroy jacket and sneakers, though there was no more silk cravat in his top pocket. His mane of hair looked windswept and uncombed rather than artfully dishevelled. He had the same air of authority but behind his sunglasses, his large face was taut and gloomy, cheeks unshaven. Len Hansen and Tony McIntosh stumbled through the door behind him, Anna at the rear. Caleb tried to catch her eye.

"How's it going?" he asked.

"Could be better." Without pausing, Roy passed Caleb and sank into a large, velvet-covered armchair in the middle of the sitting room.

"The road beyond here has a sinkhole in it," Caleb said. They might already know this, but he wanted to account for his tardiness. "On the other side of it, we're virtually cut off, road's gone, brook's a river. I had to make a great circle through the Burnt Hills, got stuck in the mud, was some struggle to free myself."

"Is that where your PI is?" Len Hansen asked Anna, his voice carrying from the hall. Caleb had no idea what a PI was.

"Out in the hills beyond," said Anna.

Len Hansen looked not quite as worse for wear as Roy, as if he'd combed his hair with his fingers. He kept patting the pockets of his crinkly jacket, likely searching for his phone. Tony McIntosh, who had the same scruffy air as the day before, went to join Len on the blue loveseat. "Did you find any coverage?" Caleb asked.

"A little," Roy said. When he looked up, his stare bored into Caleb. "We waited for you. Or some word."

"Yes." Caleb licked his lips. "Well, it took a bit of time to get here this morning. Apologies. No phone service, is there." He didn't know where to look. "So how are things out, you know, in the world?"

"Not good." Roy's gloominess was a miasma creeping through the room.

From the loveseat, Len said, "Roy's son appears to be missing."

"Well, now, I'm very sorry to hear that," said Caleb.

Roy said nothing, skin forming sinkholes beneath his eyes.

From the doorway, clad in jeans and a smoke-coloured sweater, Anna said, "He left a note for his housemates saying he was off to a wildlife refuge —"

"If he'd come with us, this would never have happened," said Roy.

"There was a huge storm surge along that part of the Massachusetts coast," Anna continued. "Apparently the land's still underwater, cabins and motels were swept away. His car's missing and he hasn't called or texted anyone. Roy received a message from his wife who'd had a message from his house-mates."

"Roy," said Len. "I still think you're leaping to conclusions. All you know is you haven't heard from him."

"Naoko asks him to let us know he's alive, what kind of child doesn't respond under such circumstances?"

"Maybe there isn't any reception where he is," Caleb said. "Service is out. Like here. Or else his phone died." Maybe the son didn't have a special kind of phone, like Roy's. There were perils to having a special kind of phone — news reached you that you didn't want — just as there were perils to not having one.

"He could borrow someone else's phone," Roy said. "A thirty-foot storm surge washes ashore right where he's supposed to be, water comes in for miles, utter inundation, scores of bodies dragged out to sea. Naoko tells me he went that way. What am I supposed to think?" He staggered out of the chair, leaving waves of disturbance in his wake. "Why would he do something like that?"

"Presumably he didn't know there was going to be a storm surge," said Len, while Tony flexed his fingers on the wooden armrest of the loveseat. "Roy, the young man has a point. Could be his phone is dead and there's no power to recharge it. Or there's no service."

Roy was staring furiously out the window as if he wished to alter either the weather or the view. "So —" he swerved back to the room, "what's with the meeting?"

"I need to speak to Anna for a moment," said Caleb.

It was a relief to be away from Roy Hansen's unrest, behind the French doors to the dining room, which Anna shut with a sharp click. She was somewhere between his age and his mother's. She lived in the UK but wasn't born there. That time Caleb had run into her on top of Bunker Hill during her first visit to the island, and asked her where she was from, she'd given a funny smile and, brushing the mauzy air from her eyelashes, said, The island of no trees. When Caleb asked if this was a real place, Anna, in her yellow rain jacket, had replied, Isn't it fascinating that all the shops on this island are named for the women who run them? Then she took off along the path, back towards the old man's house, a woman, but girlish and as nimble-footed as a fox.

"Sorry to be late," Caleb muttered, his stomach rumbling. "Where did you manage to find service?"

"Near the ferry dock."

"Are they going to be able to fly out today?"

"Roy wants to fly to Boston but I've a feeling nothing's going to be moving in that direction, is it. We stopped by the airstrip. The plane seems all right, except Roy noticed a dent in the fuselage that wasn't there before. Likely something flew through the air in the night and hit it. Obviously he's upset about that." They'd found Alf Harder at his house, Anna continued. He'd told them that without a phone signal there was no way for him to get hold of Gander flight control or for Roy to get a flight plan. Alf had his doubts as to whether the Gander airport would be open at all. Nor was there enough airline fuel on the island for a proper refuelling; with the ferry out of commission, there'd been no dangerous goods run that morning, which would have brought fuel over. "Alf doesn't think the St. John's airport will be open either, from what he gathered watching the news last night before the power went out."

"Text message for you," said Caleb, scrabbling in his pocket for the note addressed to Anna from the old man.

As she unfolded the crumpled paper, Anna's forehead kinked. "Tomorrow," she said. She didn't smile, she licked her lips. "Now Alan wants to postpone the meeting until tomorrow." This news seemed to unsettle her in a way the first postponement hadn't.

"Hard to imagine they'll be going anywhere, especially if they don't have fuel," said Caleb. "And if he wants to meet them in at the cabin—" Caleb was guessing this; in his note to Caleb the old man had said he was heading that way—"well, those paths will be some muddy, Anna. Treacherous even. Likely it's best to wait another day."

From the kitchen, Margaret Hynes exclaimed. Then came the softer echo of Della Burke, her niece, whom Caleb had gone to school with.

"Tell Alan I'll try. Did you speak to him this morning?"

Caleb shook his head and told Anna, without supplying further details, that he'd received a note as she had.

"I'll say the trails aren't passable. He's trapped out there. Or something. Roy won't be happy—" Anna's singsong voice held tightness in it. It was odd to feel a kinship with her, both of them compelled to follow the old man's orders, whatever they were. "He wants to get off the island as soon as he can." With a sigh Anna said, "You're going back to Pummelly now, are you?"

Caleb hadn't thought that far ahead. "I guess."

"Alan asks if I've seen Agnes. Agnes Watson. On the island. If you see him, tell him I haven't. Have you?"

"No." This was news. First, that Anna seemed to know Agnes Watson, who had also come to visit the old man. Second, that Agnes was somewhere on the island and the old man didn't know where she was.

Len Hansen and Tony McIntosh were on the moist lawn, Len pacing as if walking along a wire, Tony puffing on a cigarette. Flushed with relief at the thought that he was done — with luck, for the rest of the day — and leaving Anna to return to the parlour where Roy must be, Caleb scuffed through the front door, just as Len said something about someone named Conor, trapped in a motel in North Carolina.

"Well, you asked him to go down there, didn't you?" Tony replied. "To check on that spiffy new estate of yours. What did you expect?"

"He wasn't supposed to stay overnight and get in a car accident," said Len. "Anyway, he wanted to go. He built the place." There was petulance as well as anxiety in his voice.

"Sure hope it has pumps, Lennie, pretty exposed out there on Hatteras Island."

Both men turned at the creak of the door. Across the road, the harbour waters quivered, seaweed high on the rocks, a wooden stage, was it Edwin Harvey's, half-pitched into the water. Woodsmoke rising from the houses that weren't using gasoline generators pricked at Caleb's nostrils.

"So what's going on?" Len asked, thrusting his hands into two of the many pockets of his sports jacket.

"Anna's going to talk to you." Already Caleb felt surrounded as the men stepped close. It wasn't exactly menace but the power these men brought from elsewhere rose like a slippery wall.

"Tell us," said Tony, whose bluntness wielded its own kind of power.

"Well now, it looks like the meeting may be postponed until tomorrow."

"That's impossible," said Len.

Sometimes things that felt impossible became possible. Caleb knew this from experience. Things that you never wanted to happen did. His power, it seemed, was to be the one to announce that.

"Because of the storm. The flooding and the like."

"You got through, we got across the island. Granted we had to get around some downed wires, but we did," said Tony. After sucking his cigarette down to the filter, he dropped it under one foot and dug his heel into the grass, rubbing the fist of his other hand through his slicked-back hair.

"Well, yes," Caleb agreed, eyeing the crushed stub. "But now gas is rationed. It's running out. You haven't seen the bogs on the paths out in the hills."

"Bogs," said Len.

"Did you come from out there?" asked Tony.

"Thereabouts," said Caleb warily. "Only not as far."

"You came on that thing." Tony pointed at the mud-spattered quad. "Could we get to where he is on that?"

"That's right, yes. But you won't all fit on a quad."

"You can find us another one. Or the woman who runs this place can. We'll pay whatever we need to for gas. Or Len will. What I'm getting at is, if your director won't come to us today, why can't we go to him?"

A tumult rose in Caleb's brain. Whatever they were supposed to be doing together, the old man wanted it done tomorrow.

Len stared at the quad, his body retracting. "That's a lot of mud. And he mentioned bogs."

"Anna says you work for the company," Tony said to Caleb. "What exactly do you do?"

"I'm the site manager." Caleb touched one of the business cards the old man had given him, deep in the recesses of his pocket.

"What does that mean?" Tony demanded. Everything he said came out serrated, as if he wished to cut Caleb open like a steak. Or hit him with a stick.

"I look after some of the structures, do transport and the like," Caleb said desperately. Should he hand the bent business card to Tony? The old man had told him they were to be used in emergencies. Was this an emergency?

"Can we walk to where your director is?" asked Len. He at least was looking around, taking in water and road and the brilliant revelations of the sky.

"Well, now, that would be a very long and muddy walk."

"Here's the thing." Tony fixed his bluntness on Len. "It's a sad business, whatever's happening with Roy's son, I get it, but why should we wait till tomorrow? You need to seize the reins here, Lennie. Let Roy concentrate on the personal stuff and sorting the plane while we light out for the territory. We've got someone who can take us to this guy, their HQ—seems there's something in what they're developing. Even a patent if you make the right investment. They've got the goods, you got the jets to offer as a delivery system. You can make the move as well as Roy can. If you guys piss off, I swear someone else is going to muscle in here. You and me, Lennie, what do you say?"

So much passed across Len's face.

What was Tony's relationship to the Hansens, Caleb wondered. They seemed to know each other, yet they didn't exactly strike him as friends. In his cheap leather jacket, Tony seemed a creature of another species.

"So you can take us where we need to go?" Len loomed over Caleb.

"Yes," Caleb said, heart stuttering as a gull screamed. Why had he said that? Could he?

Uncertainty didn't leave Len Hansen. Certainty didn't seem to come naturally to him. Caleb, too, felt as if he were falling off the edge of a cliff.

"Okay, yeah, I guess that's a plan then," said Len.

"Lennie!" exclaimed Tony, before dropping his voice. "Show some enthusiasm. It's proactive brilliance."

"We'll go now?" asked Len.

"They'll be serving you your dinner soon," said Caleb.

"It's lunchtime," said Len.

"Margaret's creating a feast."

"We'll tell Roy we're setting off on a stroll." Len shook himself into resolution, drawing himself to his full height. "After lunch. To see some more of the island, that kind of thing."

"I'll look into procuring a vehicle," said Caleb, despite himself.

"Now we're talking." Tony's smile was thin and wide. "So we reconvene here in, like, an hour."

On the quad, Caleb sat, key in hand. He didn't start the engine. What had just happened? Here was his clearest thought: somehow he'd find a way to drive the two men along the road as far as it went. They'd get to talking, friendly and the like. The Hansens, Len Hansen, definitely had money. He, Caleb, needed money. He'd coax the men along the lane to Cape House up on its rocky height. The beauty of land and sea would draw them on. Tony had been talking about an investment. Wasn't an investment exactly what he, Caleb, needed?

. . .

Early one July morning, a month after she turned thirteen, Miranda hurried up to the vegetable bed to check on the seeds that she and her father had planted. There were the first feathers of carrots, and lettuce leaves that looked like lettuces. Everything had survived the sharp night. Achy with the world's promise, she raced back to the house. Inside, she tossed off hat and gloves. At the kitchen table, her father went on staring at whatever was on his laptop. The wood stove sparked. There was oatmeal on the electric stove, and it was burning. Miranda yanked the saucepan from the element. Coming up behind her father, she saw an image of water filling his screen, smooth and pallid under a pale sky. There was a pole in the water, a metal wand pointing up at a jaunty angle, from some kind of buoy, with a sign attached to it, which read, North Pole.

Only then did she notice the tears streaming down her father's cheeks. In the past she'd seen him sob with grief but not in a long time, and not these silent, steady tears, which threw her out of herself. When she reached to touch him, he scrubbed a hand across his cheeks and slammed the lid of the laptop so hard the computer leaped as the watery image disappeared.

"The oatmeal burned," Miranda said quakily. "I'll make some more." She wanted to comfort him. They were living the life he'd promised her, a life she loved. Wasn't part of the promise that they were to look out for each other and not be drawn away by things from elsewhere? That's what her father had insisted. He shouldn't break the rules he'd made for them both.

"What were you looking at?" she asked as her father stumbled to his feet.

"It's very warm in the north. It's been eighteen degrees in Iqaluit for days. It's above freezing at the pole. And only six degrees here." He gave an unconvincing laugh. "It shouldn't be nearly the same temperature here as at the pole. The warm air seems to be parked there."

"Is that really the North Pole?"

"It's a pond of melt water, from melting ice, not sea water, yes, at the pole, bigger than it's ever been. It's only July, the beginning of the melt season —"

He broke off and wouldn't meet her gaze. Occasionally her father said things that Miranda had the feeling he didn't mean to say to her, spoken because she was the only one nearby, words that he then wished to evade or deny. About thick, multi-year ice only being found in certain places now, near Greenland and Baffin Island, not all across the Arctic Sea. She'd caught him staring at a photo of a giant cruise ship floating on open water with jagged icebergs all around, the biggest cruise ship yet to make its way through the Northwest Passage, he said. One day he told her wistfully that he wished he could give her the air of the planet of his youth, air that had so much less carbon in it. When she pressed him, he said people were taking action to change things, just a little more slowly than he hoped.

For a year now, at her own insistence, Miranda had gone to school in the centre of the island, where, one day in the spring, their social studies teacher, Mr. Crosbie, had spoken to them about the gases accumulating in the atmosphere and warming the Earth. Tapping his paunch, Mr. Crosbie told them to turn off lights when they weren't in the room and avoid plastic bags when they shopped. When Mr. Crosbie asked if there were questions, Miranda kept her mouth shut. She tried not to think about melting ice. Already she was not like the others. She'd known it from the moment she entered the school, alongside Caleb. She didn't have a phone. She didn't watch YouTube. Everyone seemed to know she lived in a house with a wind turbine and helped her father gather weather measurements. The other girls didn't make fun of her but they left her to herself.

She had her father and Caleb and Sylvia for company, though it was impossible to imagine describing to anyone, even Caleb, what truly transfixed her father and troubled him sometimes. There were moments when simply by her presence she was able to comfort him. By bringing him tea, touching his shoulder, reminding him it was time to make supper. And sometimes not.

Standing in the middle of the room, her father looked so forlorn it frightened her.

"No one is doing anything—" he shouted.

He was out of the room before Miranda had a chance to catch her breath, the back door banging behind him.

By the time she made it out to the bridge, he was striding

away through the field that led to the shore. When she called out, he didn't stop or turn, he raked a hand through the air, as if waving her away. The gesture gutted her.

She was used to him going on walks by himself. He'd pack a water bottle and a piece of cheese or slice of jam bread and hike off on the track across the road that led inland, or along the path that led in a great circle around the headlands on the far side of the cove. Sometimes he took known trails and sometimes he broke them, came back covered in twigs and moss. He said he liked to walk until his very sense of time and self dissolved into rock and air. It was a good feeling, he said, a calming, even a necessary feeling, to lose the human self. When he returned after these particularly long walks, there was something cleansed and settled in him. Miranda, too, knew a version of that feeling, walking the shore path between cove and village, when she could gather herself into a still point that opened to every whisper of the land. Together they hiked out into the treeless barrens, to trout ponds and swimming holes where the water was dark and coppery. The lesson he wished to teach her above all was kindness, her father said as they lay drying themselves on the rocks beside a pond one day. To be kind to all things.

But he'd never left her like this. Far off now, he strode across the cove, his feet biting the hard-packed sand of the low-tide beach. Still he didn't turn. Then he was gone. Helplessly, Miranda waited a moment more: only the sound of waves breaking against rocks came to her.

Back in the burnt-smelling kitchen, she emptied the charred oatmeal into a bowl, told herself she would bring it to Caleb and Sylvia's yellow-eyed goats. The tea in the pot was cold and there was a skin forming over the tea in her father's abandoned mug. Miranda rinsed out the pot and set the kettle on to boil once more, every frail gesture existing only on the surface of things.

Her father's laptop lay on the table, a small flame. On her own laptop, an old and slower one that had once been her father's, she went mostly to sites about gardens. After an hour the Freedom timer stopped her from going anywhere at all. Sometimes her father showed her photographs—of Arctic landscapes, the ice he loved so much. Blue and sculptural. Blue ice came from older, deeper glaciers, he told her, the pressure of hundreds and thousands of years forcing the air out of the ice and leaving fewer reflective surfaces so that the red spectrum of sunlight was absorbed and the light released blue-green.

With her father gone, she could do what she wanted. Except there would be traces of any online path she took and she didn't know how to erase these traces. Gingerly Miranda opened the lid of the laptop. The image on screen blinked and refreshed itself. The pole. The calm, vast pool of water. Behind it—she pressed the cursor—her father's screensaver image of her laughing, dark-haired mother. Were things getting worse? With the weather? The world? Worse than her father let on?

He'd told her how, as a boy, he, Milan Wells, had always been the first out the door after a snowfall to shovel the walk and the driveway of their suburban Toronto bungalow, not just theirs but the sidewalks and drives of their neighbours and their neighbours' neighbours, too. He didn't care about getting paid, just loved being out in the snow. His two younger brothers, the uncles Johan and Simon whom Miranda had met long ago, thought him foolish and let him exhaust himself. One year, her grandparents, Magda of the gruff voice and wild-haired Richard, bought skis for the whole family and whenever it snowed took the boys skiing in the ravines near their home. They cut their own trails. All of them, even his parents, ignored the No Trespassing signs and scaled the fence of the local golf course, dropping their skis inside. They made great, gleeful circles around the golf course's sand traps and fourteen holes, now a tundra-like expanse. The golf course expeditions were some of his happiest childhood memories, her father had told her. They would have been possible only on a rare winter day now. As he grew older, Milan Wells realized that what he wanted more than anything was to learn about snow and ice, about polar ice and how it formed. This love was not like his love for her, Miranda knew, but it was profound.

One day, back in the old life, after he'd spoken out about the warming but before all their subsequent disasters, she'd come upon her father in his study. Setting aside his work, he'd talked to her about the problem of Arctic amplification: how the gases accumulating in the atmosphere created feedback loops that warmed polar regions more intensely than elsewhere. There was a record of this warming in the ice cores that he and his field team drilled: thick, blue layers of solid ice near the surface, a sign of longer and stronger summer snow melts that refroze as ice; all the coring revealed the same results, evidence consistent with the climate data.

Back up in the garden, alone among the lettuces, Miranda stared at all the small green things but her heart would not leap into them. Her lost mother's face appeared before her, more real than her own face, and Miranda called out, "What should l do?" Longing for her mother swept through her, an anguish so strong she doubled over.

At lunchtime, while she was cooking herself some scrambled eggs and wondering if she'd be able to eat them, the back door opened. When Sylvia came around the corner into the kitchen, in a man's jacket filmed with rain, disappointment lashed Miranda. There were more eggs in the wicker basket Sylvia carried, a jar of goat milk, and though Sylvia was drawing her into a strong hug, part of Miranda remained teetering on the other side of the room.

"You're on your own, are you, this fine morning," Sylvia said, rain shining on her cheekbones, speckles of rain in her flame-coloured hair. She glanced around the room, sharp-eyed, with a flicker of regret at Alan's absence. "Where's your father to?"

"Out for a walk," Miranda said as lightly as she could.

Only a few weeks before, the four of them had gone out on the water together, Sylvia and Caleb, Alan and Miranda, in Sylvia's brother Tom's speedboat, across the water to the Little Fish Islands — the last land before the vastness of open sea that stretched all the way to Greenland. No one lived on the Little Fish anymore, no human company for the puffins and turrs and eagles, though some families still kept fishing cabins and stayed overnight in the summer. They docked at a rickety stage, climbed up among the moss and harebells and eyebright, and while Caleb and Alan gathered driftwood from the little harbour, Sylvia and Miranda kept climbing, up to a stony lookout where the view was blustery and forever, sky and grey unfurling ocean, and Sylvia told Miranda something of what it had been like to go fishing, the hard work of it, out on the water for days. There's a place, she said, about thirty kilometres offshore where the smell of the land hits you, the smell of blackberries, we calls it, and oh how you welcome it after the cold air of the sea. There were some fish left, Sylvia said, but not like there'd been in the old days when her father and grandfather had fished for a living.

The four of them gathered around the leaping fire that Alan and Caleb had made, Sylvia nestling a blackened frying pan over the flames. She stirred salt pork in the pan until it crackled, before adding potatoes, onions, and fish that Alan and Miranda had caught on one of the food fishery days, out in a boat with Tom Borders. They'd both jigged, dropping the nylon line to the sea bottom, slipping it into one of the notches carved in the boat's side, pulling the taut line back and forth.

There used to be so many puffins, Sylvia said as she stirred, huge flocks of them everywhere. Nevertheless there were still puffins: a pair flew past, wings windmilling.

Almost like a family, the four of them gathered around the fire to eat Sylvia's delicious stew. Afterwards Alan stretched out, grinning like a contented cat, and complimented Sylvia on the food.

Leaving their parents behind, Caleb led Miranda up another slope, across the beautiful, desolate land, to a shed, unlocked, inside of which they found a Formica table, two chairs and a pair of foam mattresses in sleeping lofts tucked under the roof, an open package of PG Tips tea on a shelf beside an unopened packet of Purity biscuits. As they sat in the chairs of someone else's abandoned life, for a moment it was as if they became the parents, or adults anyhow, and this small shed on the edge of the ocean became their home. The possibility of a future hovered about Miranda, a life that was hers, theirs, whatever the weather, a life she could sense even if she couldn't yet see all of it. She and Caleb smiled at each other as these moments stretched all around them.

One evening, a few days after that, Alan came downstairs in a clean shirt, hair and beard washed and trimmed. He said that he and Sylvia were going out for dinner to the Chinese restaurant on the hilly road to the fish plant in the town of Blaze. "Call if you need me," he said quietly to Miranda. "I won't be late."

He stalled for a moment in the doorway before entering the sitting room where Miranda heard him whispering, as if to someone else. Perhaps he stood in front of the large painting by Miranda's mother that he'd hung there, the one of ghostly wolves running up Sixth Avenue.

After her father left, Miranda could have gone to see Caleb but her own confusion was something, along with her past, that she didn't wish to talk about. Abandoning a movie about dogs, she lay stretched out in bed. What did she want to happen? Sylvia had trained as a massage therapist. After dinner, would she offer Miranda's father a massage? He'd take off his shirt. Sylvia would rub his body with fragrant oil. Did Sylvia love her father? Did her father love Sylvia? And when her father did come back late, moving softly through the house, Miranda held her breath, sensing his furtive movements, the weight of his foot on the stairs, listening for some alteration in it.

At midsummer, a band came up from St. John's to play in the Parish Hall, and everyone in Pummelly danced, even Mary Green and old Wince Osmond. Alan and Sylvia danced together, Sylvia with rangy elegance, Alan with a stiffness he never used to have, and people made space around them, a promising space, until Miranda, who'd been dancing with Caleb, took her father's hand and he began to dance with her.

From the utility room, where she was stacking eggs in the egg tray, Sylvia called, "I'll be going to Pat's later to fetch some more wool if you wish to stop by." They'd already made one trip to Pat Green's to pick up big green garbage bags full of the wool that he'd sheared from his sheep. Sylvia was teaching Miranda how to card tufts of wool, washed but still greasy with lanolin, to prepare them for spinning. She'd given Miranda a pair of knitting needles.

"I can't today," said Miranda.

"Is everything all right?" Sylvia asked from the doorway.

"Yes," Miranda said. The cold wind jiggled the windows. A distant crow gave a guttural shriek. Her tongue stuck to the roof of her mouth, fixed there by Sylvia's penetrating stare. The melting waters at the pole spread all around them.

Sometimes Miranda wondered if Sylvia's kindness to her was all because of her father. Sylvia's longing was like another body in the room. But no, Sylvia's warmth was undoubtedly a true thing, the calm intimacy they shared when out foraging, the straightforward way that Sylvia had spoken to Miranda about menstruation, not, Sylvia said, because Miranda's father had asked her to do so, though when Miranda told him they'd spoken, he seemed glad.

Telling Sylvia that her father had run off after looking at a North Pole turned watery as far as the eye could see felt too risky. Sylvia might ask questions that Miranda was not prepared to answer.

Outside, perhaps an hour after Sylvia had left, when

Miranda turned to face the far field where the weather monitors stood, beyond the black rocks, out on the grey ocean floated an iceberg. Sliding southward, big as a castle, the water aquamarine and steely against the grey-white planes of the old ice. Glacier ice. White sky. Ice from Greenland that would keep travelling south until it melted.

There were more icebergs now than there used to be, Sylvia had said, at least some years. This summer, their third on the island, there had been a steady stream of them. The daily sight had turned Miranda's father brooding and quiet.

Surely he would be back in time to take the weather measurements. Four o'clock came and when he didn't appear, a deeper fear entered Miranda. Almost nine hours had passed. She grabbed the extra key to his office from the back of the kitchen utility drawer. Here in a place where no one locked their doors, where their own back door was always unlocked, he kept the office door locked at all times. Entering the small room gave her goosebumps: there was the line of black notebooks, their daily weather records. The notebook marking sea levels in the cove had its own shelf. Another, called The Book of Storms, was pressed beside a binder full of printouts of other people's weather stories, most of which Miranda had transcribed from her father's tapes. He'd created the online version of the Blaze Island Weather Atlas, uploading records and documents, tales of blizzards and gales and ferocious blows, which Miranda sometimes scrolled through, filled with private satisfaction, though, online, his name and hers were nowhere to be found. She wheeled past her father's two dulled computer screens, frantically turned over scraps of paper scattered on his desk, but nothing, nothing told her anything she wished to know. Notebook in hand, she hurried along the path to the monitors, past the wild phlox, the blue flag, the buttercups.

Later, out on the bridge, hugging her knees to her chest as the wind whipped up around her, she allowed herself the scariest thought: what if he didn't come back? Once her father had told her a story about a man in the Arctic whom a storm had driven so mad he'd tried to eat the wind. Here on Blaze Island, a man had walked into the woods in a snowstorm and was never seen again, according to old Harry Pratt. If she went out searching for her father, he might come back and find her missing, head out once more and lose himself. Yet out there, up among the tuckamore, the trout ponds, along the shore cliffs, *something* had happened to him.

At ten o'clock, clouds a thickness above the western horizon, a red band of light beneath, Miranda crawled into bed, shuddering as the house grew hollow around her.

Their first summer in the cove, back when she was ten and her father and Pat Green were renovating the small white house, Pat had loaned them a punt. After the men finished work for the day, Alan often liked to take the boat out and row the two of them, himself and Miranda, across to Seal Cove, a small half-moon of beach tucked along the cove's far shore. He would steer the boat towards the slip of sand where he and Miranda dragged the punt ashore. Spreading out a blanket, they drank homemade spruce-bud tea and ate biscuits. While her father read a magazine, Miranda gathered the tiniest shells and held them silky in her palm before bringing them to show her father.

One afternoon, Alan looked into the west and said, "Hey, Miranda, hop like a gazelle back into the boat, will you? That's fog, coming over the land, one of the new land fogs Harry Pratt was telling us about."

They were out on the water, halfway across the cove, when the fog reached them. They were in it, a cold room with no windows or doors. Not even a room, it was like being inside a body, swallowed. The moist fog touched Miranda's skin. It amplified the slop of water as her father lifted the oars and dove them back beneath the surface, the creak of the oars' wooden pegs turning on their tole pins. All other sounds retreated. Her father, who rowed with strong strokes, stared at the shore they'd left behind, while Miranda, in the stern, faced him and the land where they were headed. Which had vanished in the fog.

Her father held the raised oars, dripping, said he was listening for the sound of the far shore, asked Miranda if she saw anything. She didn't. Her father glanced over his shoulder. "It's a cove. We're halfway across. We have to hit the shore soon."

He kept rowing. Soon he was sweating, despite the cold, for the sun had gone and the temperature dropped. Miranda wrapped the blanket they'd brought around her shoulders. They were alone in this altered world, barely speaking. She kept her eyes on her father.

He stopped again, asked if she heard the sound of waves against the shore, yet no matter how hard she listened, all Miranda heard was the trill of water along the sides of the boat. The wind picked up, slapping water at the boat's wooden hull. The tide was going out, tugging at them, swells beneath them rising. Her feet grew cold. All this made her uneasy even as she told herself they'd be fine. Her father had promised to look after her.

"Can you tell me what time it is?" her father asked, his mouth sounding sticky and dry.

He'd left his cellphone behind because it needed recharging. Instead he'd removed the battery-operated clock from the kitchen wall and stuffed it in a plastic bag. The clock lay at Miranda's feet, ticking. When she pulled it out of the bag its ticking grew louder.

"Almost four."

They'd been out on the water not quite an hour. Would they miss the day's weather measurements? What would happen when it grew dark—if they were still out on the water? Why had they not reached the shore?

At last, Alan lifted the oars. Off to Miranda's right, not in front of them as they'd expected, water chugged and gurgled against rock. Ferociously Alan rowed towards the sound as Miranda craned into the fog's grey swirls. Black rocks loomed out of the blankness. She gave a shout. When her father looked, his body went rigid, before, with even more speed, he turned the boat around so the rocks were on Miranda's left, a craggy tumble veiled, revealed, as she held out her hand to keep the rocks in sight and stop them from coming too close, her father rowing against tide and wind, alongside the land.

Although it seemed like the rocks would go on forever, at last a stretch of stony pebbles appeared, and the white bobs of Martin Green's lobster pots on the water, the known world once more: this was the stretch of shore where they launched the punt, where they kept it hauled up in the grass beyond the landwash. Her father slid the bow in, pebbles scrabbling against hull. Stumbling into the knee-high water, he pulled Miranda and the boat to land. Her hair and skin were wet and Miranda held the blanket tightly around herself as she jumped from the bow. The relief of arrival was astounding. There, through the fog ahead of them, hovered a glimpse of white in the grey, their house, her home, and her heart leaped wholly towards it.

In her bed, in the empty house, curled under her quilt, Miranda cried. Two years before, they'd rowed themselves home, not out to sea. They'd come through that danger together yet where was her father now?

A little after eleven, the back door opened. She was downstairs in an instant, throwing herself at him in the indigo twilight. He smelled of the sea, salt air, spruce and juniper and lichen, there were twigs and stiff bits of dried moss in his damp sweater. He said nothing at first, simply held her tight.

It was as if he hadn't spoken in a long time. Running his hand through her hair, he said at last, "I'm here, Miranda. I love you so much. I will look after you, I promise."

She inhaled him through her shock, feeling the weight of his taut muscles within her embrace.

"Where did you go?"

What had he thought of doing? What had the weather made him think of doing? Whatever it was, he hadn't done it. *I will look after you whatever the weather.* He had made this vow before, yet it was as if he was saying the words for the first time. Something beneath his skin felt different.

—

For the rest of that summer and into the fall, Miranda watched her father carefully, the way you observe an animal in the wild. At first he was subdued, sapped back into a sadness he kept trying to yank himself out of. He went on long walks by himself, always telling Miranda in advance in which direction he was headed. Sometimes she'd catch him staring at desiccated fields in the Middle East on an online news site. Or raging wildfires in Australia or British Columbia or California. A new reticence took hold of him around Sylvia. He spent more time alone, holed up in his shed office. Did he dream of leaving the island, Miranda wondered. Sometimes she heard him shouting through the walls. He and Sylvia took fewer walks, the difference noticeable enough that one afternoon, as Miranda helped Sylvia make marshberry jam in her kitchen, Sylvia broke out with, "Your father seems preoccupied."

Painfully, all Miranda could do was agree.

All through the pack ice season of early spring, he busied himself drawing up plans for a cabin. In May, he and Miranda lit a candle to Jenny at the site, a remote spot close to the empty shore, along a path through the barrens and scrubby alder woods. With Pat Green's and sometimes Caleb's help, Alan began building. Other families had cabins dotted through the woods so to Miranda her father's plan seemed a hopeful thing. He ferried supplies in a wooden wagon hitched to the back of his quad: more solar panels, a composting toilet. The cabin, when Miranda visited, was smaller than their house, a main room, only one small bedroom. One afternoon, back at their house in the cove, Miranda came upon her father and Caleb loading the wooden wagon with more boxes. Computer equipment, Alan explained. As if trying to lessen her surprise, he said that he had an idea for a new weather monitoring experiment and would be using the cabin to work on it.

As if seeking to mollify Miranda's disappointment, he threw himself into building a chicken coop with a slanted roof in their yard. Soon they would have their own chickens, he promised. He transplanted saplings from the alder woods by the brook, snugging them into a row of holes he'd dug in the slope beyond the house. July came, and the fourth anniversary of their arrival.

A week later, as Miranda was laying kelp on the potato beds, wheels crunched to a stop on the gravel at the top of their lane. She started up at the unusual sound, just as a woman, slim and young, in a yellow rain jacket, climbed out of a parked white car. Though the stranger was still some distance off, Miranda sensed something purposeful in her manner. Checking a piece of paper, knapsack over her shoulder, she set off down the lane — their lane, in the direction of their house. No one from away had ever come to visit them — and the woman, wind tangling her sand-coloured hair, was surely not from the island. Miranda knocked over the bucket of kelp in her flight.

Her father had been scything in the yard. Strands of long grass lay all around yet there was no sign of him. She hammered on the door of his study just as he stepped out of the house in a clean T-shirt, his damp hair on end.

"Someone's coming," Miranda cried in alarm, but her father's eye was already caught, excitement erupting on his face, not dismay.

"Anna—"

On the far side of the yard, the woman dropped her bag, her face transforming in surprise as Alan strode towards her open-armed. "Milan, it's you. You're the one who asked me to come. You wrote me that letter."

They were inside the house, all three of them, the young woman touching the white walls, the wood stove, the fisherman's daybed under the cove-side window as if astonished to find herself where she was.

"Alan, I'll have to remember that, won't I?" Her accent was English mixed with somewhere else. When she smiled, her teeth shone. Girlish yet perhaps not as young as Miranda had first thought.

Alan flipped on the electric kettle. He set Anna's knapsack at the bottom of the stairs. This gesture sent a new pulse through Miranda. Was the stranger staying the night? It was late afternoon. Having just arrived, she was unlikely to be catching the last ferry off the island. Alan said he'd bring her rental car down the lane and park it beside theirs in the yard, out of sight.

"I met you once," Anna said to Miranda, loosening the wind from her hair with darting fingers. "You were quite young. It was at a garden party in Norwich, at your parents' house. You were rather amusingly running about holding an antique-looking house key. I was one of your father's post-docs at the East Anglia Climate Research Centre in those days. You're so grown up now."

The kettle had boiled but it was as if Miranda did not know how to make tea for someone who was a stranger to her, yet knew her father, who came trailing the past, who spoke the word *climate*, which she was not allowed to speak. Alan returned, a new lift in his step. Anna was the one taking mugs out of the cupboard while Miranda stalked into the utility room to fetch milk.

"I invited Anna to visit," her father called as Miranda returned, banging the milk jug onto the table. His gaze expanded beyond her to include Anna as well. "My invitation was a bit cryptic so I wasn't sure you'd show up."

"Grief will do strange things to you, really," Anna said. "I receive a letter from an unknown person, telling me it will be worth my while to find my way to some remote island on the far side of the Atlantic, and though I barely fly these days, I'm deranged enough to do as it says."

"Wise woman," said Miranda's father.

"Helpful that I have sort of a thing for remote islands, and I could stop off en route to a Polar Council conference, which, incidentally, is something I almost never do anymore, conference-going, I mean," said Anna, flashing her white smile once again. "Mostly we do these things via online video."

The three of them sat down to a dinner of capelin fried with butter, capelin that Miranda had gathered with Caleb and Sylvia only that morning. Right after breakfast Caleb had called Miranda, beyond excited. In the old days, the capelin, the little fish that whales feed on, used to wash ashore every year. Now it was a rare thing. Because the ocean water was warmer, Tom Borders had explained to Miranda, the capelin didn't need to come ashore to spawn. But when they did come, everyone in Pummelly grabbed plastic bags and buckets and raced out to UpABack Cove to gather them by the handful.

Miranda had filled a bag with tiny silvery fish, thanking them softly, and another bag with salt-scented kelp, sensing Sylvia's disappointment because her father hadn't come with them.

Now something fundamental about their life was altering, and without warning. There must be a reason her father had invited Anna to come all this way. The air was pregnant with unspoken things, with Anna and her father's desire to be alone together even as Anna told Miranda how she, too, had grown up on a tiny island, off the coast of Norway. If you kept staring out to sea, beyond Iceland, you'd come at last to some humps of land, including an island named after the weather. Her mother was an oceanographer, Anna said, her father a fisherman. The first time she saw a tree bigger than a shrub she was thirteen. Her parents had taken her to the mainland and the sight of these tall beings filled her with terror. She was convinced they were going to fall on her. The sound of wind through a forest was an incomprehensible roar.

Upstairs, the door to the spare room was pulled nearly shut, as it had been for days, though Miranda had not paid much attention until this moment. Something made her push the door open. Inside, the boxes were gone and there was a bed where there had never been a bed, an old wrought-iron frame, one she might have seen leaning against the outside of Leo Borders's house, only now the frame held a narrow mattress with a quilt tucked over it.

Her father might not have known for certain if Anna was coming, but he'd planned for her arrival. In the room, Miranda touched the quilt, the pillow, like a cat rubbing her scent on things. The smell of coffee wafted up through the floorboards into her own room directly above the kitchen, Anna's voice, and her father's, drifting up through the open seam around the metal chimney that climbed through her bedroom into the attic. They were washing dishes. Perhaps her father did not know how audible their voices were. When would he have stood, as Miranda was doing, listening to a conversation taking place beneath him?

"Did you burn the letter?" Alan kept his voice low, but it was impossible for Miranda not to hear his words.

"Of course," Anna said quietly. "Those were the instructions, weren't they, along with coming all the way here because the mysterious person who wrote the letter had something very important they wished to discuss."

"For various reasons I'm trying to hide my traces. I've always trusted you, Anna. You're a brilliant modeller and you go out in the field, that's a rare combination. I've always sensed the feeling in you too. When everything went down, Ian Petersen wrote to me — did you know this? — and told me I shouldn't have said what I did, that *we're in deep shit*. But we are. Come on. I know he was frightened, even suicidal after the attacks on our research. I know he spoke out in my defence, but these were his exact words, *You won't inspire anyone*. I'm sure things were tense in Norwich — I can't claim to know because I haven't been in touch with him or anyone else —. I left Princeton determined to ditch as much of that world as possible, find somewhere to be with my daughter that'll be safer when the truly bad weather hits. I'll abandon the science and concentrate on leading the kind of life we all ought to be living, that's what I told myself — then, last summer, when the temperature at the pole was so high, for days, and I thought, In a few more years most if not all of the summer sea ice will be gone—I broke down. I couldn't see my way forward—"

Miranda climbed quietly into bed. Should she squeak the mattress springs? Or cough? She pressed a pillow over her head until she couldn't breathe. When she pulled it off again, gasping, they must have returned to the table. Glasses chinked. Their soft voices only made her hearing grow more acute. Perhaps her father wasn't thinking about her at all.

"—in the spring, with Fletcher," Anna was saying. "We're trying to do as much as we can with wind and solar up on the ice sheet, but we have to fly in, don't we, and this spring, coming up the coast to Ilulissat, there was nothing but black water down below. On the ice so much of the surface is grey with soot from last summer's forest fires, and mushy, the sound of rushing water is everywhere. I heard it even in my sleep. Ten billion tons of ice lost every day—you know the figures. We need ground data desperately, remotely sensed data isn't enough. We never used to include ice sheet melt rates in the climate models because the melt happened so slowly but now we have to, don't we. The melt is happening so fast we can't keep up. Even if we can't say we believe a total retreat of the ice is inevitable—we deal in probabilities, and God forbid we should compromise our data—it's what I believe. What does one do with such a thought? With all the panic and the rage? When I come back to Norwich, everywhere I look I see ice melting while everyone else hops into their cars and orders their takeaway and flies off to Ibiza, all the silent deniers believing life can go on as usual. One night I woke up screaming out of a dream about a tidal bore of ocean water pouring over me."

The quilt pulled all the way over Miranda's head made the air stuffy even though the cloth around her was a comforting cocoon. Leaving her body behind, she floated out the window, into the night, skimming through the hills to Sylvia's house, to the room at the top of the stairs where Sylvia kept her folded-up massage table and where Miranda sometimes spent the night, where, from across the hall, Caleb occasionally moaned in his sleep and Sylvia slipped quietly from bed as the sun rose.

"What can we do?" her father asked Anna in the room below. "That's the question."

"And so—?" Anna said quietly.

"Anna," said her father. "Do you ever think about having a child?"

Anna gave a startled laugh. "I'd say it's highly unlikely."

"Are you with anyone these days, the Welshman—?"

"That was long ago."

"I never thought I would have a child," said Miranda's father in his own soft voice. "I never thought I wanted—Jenny wanted a child. Love changed me. There's hope even if a child increases the terror exponentially."

His words entered Miranda, lodged in her like a bubble of air.

"Having a child increases your carbon footprint, doesn't it. And you need to work a lot harder to hide your despair."

"Cynical Anna."

"Last month I went to meet my sister and nieces in London," Anna said. "Margot says she wants to show her daughters the world while she still can. They're eight and ten. I was describing to them how scientists have discovered ice sings at extremely low frequencies, these deep vibrations that make a sound, it's quite fantastic, isn't it, though when the ice warms it grows silent. I want them to know something about what's happening. But before I could say anything more, Margot stopped me. She told me not to speak of such things and asked Sofie, her oldest, to describe the paintings they'd just seen at the National Gallery."

"I've begun modelling," said Alan.

"Modelling for what?" asked Anna.

"Lowering the solar constant. The modelling's primitive, though I'm running as much RAM as I possibly can out here."

"How would you lower solar energy?"

"Right now I'm not modelling for that, only to see what happens if you do block the sun's rays, but I imagine by injecting something into the atmosphere. Some kind of reflective particulate. Say regionally, in the Arctic, even the eastern Arctic, you might use extremely long, thin pipes running skyward, suspended in the atmosphere attached to balloons, and pumps to propel particles up and out, create a haze that blocks sunlight, cools things down, helps preserve the ice."

"Alan, no."

"That's a blunt assessment."

"It's a pipe dream, literally. It's madness, bonkers, it does nothing to address the real issue of how to get the carbon out. It simply masks the problem. I know others are looking into this, but don't try to play God. Please."

"So you'd rather I sit by and watch my daughter's world burn? Not God, Anna. We're human, and we may need to throw everything we can at the problem. We don't even know yet what we might need, so why not at least pursue the thought experiment?"

"Because it's dangerous and illusory. There are other things we should be thinking about — and doing."

"You're implying I want to be doing this? What about the people dreaming of an ice-free Arctic, Anna. You know they're out there. The pipes and balloons, they're no substitute for changing human behaviour. I get it. I am saying they may be a useful tool in a desperate tool kit."

"I don't know," said Anna. "I don't know that I want to hear this."

"We don't know, Anna, that's the point. Listen, I can't go on living a quaint little off-grid life by the sea and that's it. All I'm thinking about for now is remote access to a mainframe. But I need a frontperson, a way to go in as someone else, because as far as the scientific world goes I've vanished. Right now I have no wish to reappear, in fact I've gotten very good at encryption and going in back doors since being out here. I've built a small place off in the woods specifically to do this work. It could be a new kind of collaboration. Don't say anything more, not now. Tomorrow I'll show you what I've been up to and you can tell me what you think."

. . .

The day after the storm, Miranda stood beside Leo Borders, near the brook as it rushed out of the spruce forest. A brown froth tossed itself over rocks and boulders and chunks of road tarmac, breaking open the known world. The wreck of Frank's car made goosebumps ripple down her neck. But the water was lower than it had been earlier in the morning and the tide was lower now, too. She lingered at the raw edge where, in the night, the force of the water had ripped through the road and left a gaping hole, while the sea, swollen by storm and tide and full moon, had rushed landward. Usually the brook ran through two drainage culverts. The collapsed road had crushed them both.

"Is the beach still under there somewhere?" Miranda asked Leo, gazing into the flood. How to connect this day to the one that had gone before? That had felt real. This did too.

"Or out in the cove." Leo shifted the brim of his ball cap. "Wind will bring the sand back if we're lucky."

Ella tugged at Miranda. She'd clipped the dog to her leash for the ride from the house in the cab of Leo Borders's truck, Leo and his quiet brother Tom in the front seat while she'd sat with Ella in the back. Her father and Frank came roaring up behind them on the quad, Frank behind her father, wearing Miranda's borrowed helmet.

Tom and Leo were clambering cheerfully into their orange rubber overalls. At the edge of the road, spikes of goldenrod shivered, the September sky a wash of cirrus cloud. Clusters of red berries trembled on a dogberry bush. Rubber work gloves tucked under her arm, Miranda pulled off a sprig of berries and wondered what colour of ink she might make from them.

That morning, on her way back from the village, she'd thought she heard the buzz of a drill from across the cove. Caleb would scarcely be working on the house today, would he? Unless there was damage. When her father arrived back from the cabin, he'd been anxious to know if either Miranda or Frank had seen Caleb, if Caleb had returned from whatever errand he was supposed to be running. But Frank said there'd been no sign of him while he'd been at the house on his own, and Caleb certainly hadn't shown himself since Miranda's return.

Whenever he could, Caleb spent hours working out at Cape House. Sometimes faint sounds blew across the cove or Miranda caught a glimpse of his small figure moving purposefully on the far side of the water, hauling pieces of wood or setting up a sawhorse. He never looked in her direction now. At least not when she was darting a glance at him. The work proceeded slowly because he was meticulous and only had so much time. And money. At this rate the renovations would take years. Since he'd left school, he'd been doing more work for her father, as well as everything he did for his mother, tending the garden and animals, setting wood in for winter, for his own house, theirs, her father's cabin.

Sometimes her mind carried her across the cove to where Caleb was. Sometimes, when she knew that Caleb was far away, when her father sent him off-island, say, she crossed the cove and set off along the lane to Cape House. This had to happen when her father, too, was far off, in at the cabin, working away on his weather-monitoring experiments.

Spruce trees hid the house from any far-off person who might have been passing on the road. Each time she snuck over to Cape House, Miranda knocked quietly, heart rocketing, and waited for the anticipated silence, before opening the door and slipping inside. She'd been coming to the house since childhood, long before Caleb had taken possession of the place, back in the days when the house had been inhabited by his uncle Charlie's sheep. As children, she and Caleb had wandered inside, hushed and excited, the rooms dark behind boarded-up windows, the sheep sometimes squeezing into the crawl space under the house, making a racket beneath the floorboards.

These days, she stayed only long enough to inspect whatever work Caleb had done since she'd last visited. In August, she'd stood at the parlour window, facing the lavender water, her eye caught by the distant breath of whales, a black fin breaching. To be able to see all this from your living room, that would be something. Was it longing or disquiet that shot through her then?

Caleb had begun stripping the wallpaper from the kitchen, layers and layers of it. In places the walls were already taken back to wood. It was impossible to be in the house and not be aware of his presence. Months before the break between them, Caleb had told her how, when the house first became his, he used to walk from room to uninsulated room, watching the wind move beneath the wallpaper. Being in the house filled Miranda with confusion. Her father had demanded that she stop talking to Caleb and she'd acquiesced. In the first weeks, her own anger and fear still high, the separation had felt justified. Later, she could have protested. Guilt touched her like sand. Sometimes missing Caleb gripped and shook her.

You can farm on this side of the cove, Caleb had said early the previous summer, his manner hesitant yet underscored with yearning. We'll farm together, Miranda. Yet when he tried to take her hand, she'd pulled back. Alone in the kitchen of Cape House, she poured a glass of spring water from the jug that Caleb kept on the kitchen counter, then used the dish towel hooked through a cupboard door handle to wipe all trace of herself from the glass. She returned the cup to the cupboard above the sink. Her hand hovered there. From outside, Ella gave a soft bark.

A noise at Miranda's back startled her. She was by the ferocious brook. Pat Green had just pulled up in his big grey truck. When she turned, Pat and his bristle-haired brother Brian were leaping out of the cab. The men gathered at the broken edge of the road, conferring, talking of dump trucks and earthmovers and how long it would take to get new drainage culverts, how much gravel infill would be needed. Tall and ungainly, Frank stood by himself staring into the gap, and though Miranda could have approached him, she didn't.

"Soon as the phones are working we'll be on it," said Leo. Miranda sometimes saw him in yellow hard hat and orange safety vest, directing a road crew, on her occasional trips to Pierce's supermarket in the middle of the island.

Frank's car was more exposed than it had been when Miranda and her father had peered at it that morning through binoculars. The wreck lay atop one of the crushed culverts, the windshield smashed, driver's side tilted in the air. Somehow in the wild dark of the storm, Frank's reflexes had been quick enough to open the window. He'd swum out through all the water heaving around him. Admiration travelled through Miranda as well as sympathetic fear, as if for an instant she'd been there with him.

From the cab of his truck, Leo Borders ordered Miranda to stand back, and reversed the truck close to the road's jagged edge. From the truck bed, Tom Borders and Miranda's father pulled a wooden frame made of two-by-fours and a pair of long metal ramps. Tom lowered himself implacably into the water, which rushed around his legs as he found his footing among the rocks. Alan followed, agile, then long-legged Pat and Brian, whose every movement had a sturdy roll. When Frank offered to help, the men shook him off. They set the metal ramps against the road's edge, Pat and Brian searching for purchase among the rocks, grinding the ramp ends until they were steady. When Leo's truck rolled forward, the others pushed at the car.

Haul, haul, haul, they cried, all of them loving a good emergency. And in this way the present continued to remake itself.

"Not sure you'll be able to resurrect this one," Leo Borders called once the wreck, streaming water, slid off the ramps and onto the road. "Looking at a car funeral, I'd say."

Beside Miranda, Frank pulled a key fob from his pocket. When he aimed it at the car, nothing happened.

"Strange the air bag didn't inflate. By the look of it you hit something in your tumble," said Alan.

"Good thing it didn't. Some hard to swim around an airbag, boy," said Pat Green, pulling off his gloves and rustling a hand through his greying hair. "Let's call it luck."

Streams drained from underneath the car. A submerged bag of some sort lay flung across the front passenger seat. When Frank tried the actual key in the lock, it wouldn't turn. Even when Miranda reached in through the window, the water cold through her rubber work gloves, and tried the door latch from the inside, the door didn't open. If it had, it would have released a flood. The men were talking about a file, wire, something to pry the door open, the problem with electronic systems. The car was not just a wreck but a ruin, sliding into the past. Pushing up his sweater sleeves, Frank leaned through the open window. Black characters wound up the paler skin of his left inner arm. A tattoo. What were they called? Not letters.

As he reached into the silty water, a bright strip of exposed skin and band of black underwear opened on his back. Miranda stepped back as if burned while Frank lifted out a soaked satchel with a long shoulder strap. He dropped the dripping bag with an air of self-consciousness as if, while being exposed, he was also trying to hide something.

Flipping the front seat forward, he tugged, through the driver's seat window, at something wedged behind it.

"Let me help," Miranda said. "I have gloves and they're probably too small for you." Once again her eye was caught by the tattoo, the black row of characters running over the soft skin towards Frank's wrist. What did they say? Her gloves were useless, given the depth of the water. She managed to find purchase, cold water oozing around her fingers. When the swollen bag released, the force sent her stumbling into Frank.

The men had found a wire and were approaching as, together, she and Frank struggled to squeeze the black canvas overnight bag through the driver's window. Sliding the wire through the top of the back door frame, the men jimmied the back door open. Water gushed onto the road. By now, the car seemed something ancient, accidental, like a dropstone.

"See you next time," said Leo Borders. Frank wiped his arms over his jeans before taking Leo's outstretched hand. He thanked all the men. Both sets of brothers climbed into their respective trucks and drove off, in the direction of Pummelly and civilization, leaving Miranda, her father, and Frank to themselves.

"I've another errand to run, if you don't mind," Alan said as soon as the others had vanished.

"Where?" Miranda asked, taken aback. She wanted her father to leave and she did not want him to go. His presence, alongside Frank's, made her feel acutely observed, yet the thought of being around Frank's curiosity, his persistent questions, and his body, without the security of her father, flustered her. She hadn't yet had a chance to talk to her father about Frank's questions.

"I'll try to get as far as Tom's Neck, see if I can locate Caleb."

"That's the next village?" Frank said amiably. "Can I come with you?"

For some reason, her father seemed caught out. "Best you stay here with Miranda. Stick close to the shore paths. Not sure what I'll find out there. I might not be able to get through, anyway."

"Is there another, um, quad we could use to do some exploring on our own?" Frank asked. "Accidentals could be anywhere."

"There's no other quad," Miranda said. Shouldn't Frank want to stay near the shore, if he was searching for blown-from-away birds? Then again, they had once come upon a scarlet tanager, a bird very far from home, in the woods after a storm. Another time, they had lifted an exhausted petrel from beneath a dogwood, taking the bird home and tending its small body in a bowl over warm water before releasing it back to sea.

"Miranda's likely got things she needs to do. Storm clean-up. Partridgeberries are ripening up in the hills. Isn't that right, Miranda?" said her father.

What about what she wanted? She was aware of all the hidden layers in her father's words. He didn't want Frank to accompany him. There were other people out there, the ones who'd flown in the day before, whomever he'd spoken to on the phone the previous evening—it was likely that he was trying to reach them. For his own reasons, he didn't wish Frank to know. There was no way for Miranda to say, and she hadn't had a moment alone with her father since his return from the cabin in which to ask, What do you want me to tell Frank if—? Or to inquire what her father was up to.

"I'll be back as soon as I can," Alan said. He kissed her cheek. "Take care of our guest. Good luck with the birds, Frank, and try not to walk into any more door frames."

Then her father was a disappearing sound, roaring into the woods, a little loss. Frank, with his dripping bags, cocked his head at her like a curious bird.

Miranda spoke to forestall him. "What was it like driving

here, trying to keep ahead of Hurricane Fernand?" When she released Ella from the bush where she'd secured the leash, Ella shook herself, as if casting off pent-up energy. Watching her made Miranda want to shake out all the strange new currents running through her as well.

Frank picked up his drenched bags. "There weren't really traffic jams, most people were *not* driving up the coast. I did have the thought, what if I got overtaken? By the hurricane, I mean. It was colossal on maps, I'd watched insane videos of its destruction of, you know, whole cities, and the sky was already gloomy and clouds were racing. Mostly I kept thinking how when I came back, nothing would look the way it did now. That felt eerie."

"Do you know if your roommates are okay — and your house? Can I carry something?"

Frank shook his head. "Haven't heard a thing — I can only hope. At least they're inland." He was staring into the distance and didn't seem all that interested in talking about his life.

"You know those micro-cells that sometimes blow through when weather fronts shift?" he said after a moment. "Those insane winds that don't last long but everything goes crazy. Maybe you don't get them out here but where I live they happen more now. Last summer one uprooted all these trees on my street, including the one in our yard, crushing cars, exposing root balls as big as, well, cars, which I guess is some kind of pointed message. Anyway, I expect whatever happened in the last couple of days, it'll be worse. Much worse. Won't it? Every now and again I wonder if I should have stayed."

Stayed? There was a drowned world out there, in Boston, and closer than Boston. That world pressed close. It was like someone laying a hand on Miranda. A hot touch. After a breath, she pointed to the alder saplings quickening on the low hills beyond the house, told Frank she and her father had planted all of them, and this seemed to make him more cheerful.

She wished she could tell Frank about her own journey north all those years ago, no doubt following some of the same roads he had, their own storms driving them onward. There were words in her mouth — only she couldn't speak them, given her pact with her father to keep the past hidden.

"Say, Miranda," said Frank, interrupting her thoughts. "Would you call this the end of the island?"

"The end? Islands don't really have ends. But — the road ends in Pummelly, you can't go any farther than the far side of the harbour, out on Careless Point. Why?"

"Someone told me to go to the end of the island." Frank spoke with a grin. He was changing the subject.

"I thought you wanted to go to Funk Island."

"Actually the end of this island feels a little more pressing."

The wind pushed hard at the back of Miranda's neck.

When Frank pulled off his sunglasses, she tensed. "Miranda, have you by any chance seen a couple of men around here, Americans, of course you wouldn't necessarily know that unless you spoke to them. Tall, they're both tall, one has longish hair, kind of a flamboyant demeanour, the other's more clean-cut. They might have blown in here in the last couple of days."

"After the storm or before? Are they birders?"

"Not birders," said Frank with a fugitive smile. "You could say they're my accidentals. I think they came here, I assume they arrived before the storm. They may even have left already. In which case I'm too late. I don't know why I thought I would just stumble across them. Is there, like, an airport here? They probably flew in on a small private jet."

A jet. The afternoon before, at that distant whirr of sound, Miranda had looked up from the garden to see a spark descending in a circle, an unusual sight, particularly before a storm. The airstrip was far off. In the middle of the island. In all her years on Blaze Island she had never been there. Then, as the storm blew in, she'd heard her father, on his phone, ask some unknown person, *How was your flight?* Now here was Frank, asking his own questions about strangers and arrivals. She'd seen no one who fit his description of the two men. So why was discomfort travelling up her spine? "I haven't seen them."

"What about your father? Do you think he has, or anyone in the village? Do you think there's a chance they're in the village, Pummelly, that's what it's called?"

Miranda said, "I really don't think those men were in Pummelly this morning. I'd have seen them or heard something." Someone would have mentioned word at Vera's general store or stopped by while she'd been having tea with Mary, yet her heart kept beating savagely.

There was an energy in her that wanted to make Frank look at her, to bring back that arrow of heat, to feel it shoot all the way through her, yet she also wanted to retreat as far from him as possible. He aroused too many feelings. There were things about him difficult to pull into focus. He was like a skipping stone. He'd arrived wearing a ratty, unravelling sweater yet the car he'd been driving was a shiny, new-model hybrid. He lived in a house with roommates and was looking for people who flew a private jet. A few other birders sometimes found their way to the island. Miranda had run into them in Green

Cove and out on the headlands. They clutched binoculars, carried cameras with telephoto lenses and seemed obsessed with birds at every moment.

"What's in that white house over there on the other side of the water?" Frank squinted at it. He had turned his attention back to the hills. The wind swept straight black hair across his forehead. Like a skipping stone, he sent out ripples. Even his gaze seemed to alter the world as Miranda knew it.

Sometimes she had imagined a stranger arriving, she had, yes, a stranger arriving just for her, a young man, beautiful and inviting, but the imagined stranger had never asked questions that provoked such internal tumult.

"It's Caleb Borders's house and he's renovating it but no one lives there now. Sorry, I really need to get to work." The abrupt words spilled out of her mouth, her feet already in motion.

"Miranda—" Frank called.

But she was racing down the lane away from him, Ella at her side, making for the red-black rocks and the sea on the far side of them.

. . .

Six months after Anna Turi's visit, Miranda begged her father to drive them across the wintry island to the shop in the town of Blaze where they had once purchased books about rocks and trees and flowers to be her schoolbooks, so that she could buy a notebook of her own. As she slipped the notebook under her mattress, wood stove ticking below, she made a private resolution. She, too, would keep a record of the weather. All kinds of weather.

Like the day two weeks later when, after a fierce sou'easter, all the men in Pummelly including her father walked up along shore to Pummelly Cove, out by the ocean. They walked, didn't ski or skidoo or snowshoe, because there was so little snow. Only rain had fallen as the wind howled, and not much rain at that, the wind blowing harder than it ever used to do in winter, Pat Green said. The sea, so high and ferocious, had toppled the big boulders that waves had been smoothing for centuries, toppled and cracked them. There were no ballycatters, no blue ice coating the tumbles of rocks, no turquoise pans rafting and reaching in frozen clashes for the sky, cutting off the hard and gnawing waves from the land. Miranda and Caleb and his cousins, who had followed the men, were there to observe their soberness and to be yelled at not to go close to the water. It was unsettling, even for Miranda—where was all the ice that had been there the year before?

Her father came home and wrote in The Book of Storms; he posted photographs of the broken rocks and storm details, including wind speed, to the online weather atlas. No doubt Harry Pratt wrote in his weather notebook, too. The next day Sylvia would walk out to observe the fallen rocks but rather than the rocks it was her father's moods that Miranda kept an eye on. He had been less morose since Anna's visit. Alongside the secrets of the past, new secrets were infiltrating their life, and these secrets included Anna, whose voice, by turns gruff and lilting, sometimes drifted from under the door of her father's study. He must be calling Anna over the internet, Miranda presumed. In the beginning, her father seemed to be trying to convince Anna of something. This was a tone. Most of their conversations took place at the cabin. Miranda had overheard him say as much. *I'll call you from the cabin.*

The new secrets pulled him away from the world right in front of him, so that it was up to her to tug him back. Come out and look at the sheet of ice over the cove. Let's go snowshoeing.

Then there was the day when dark-red blood flowed out of Miranda for the first time, another kind of weather. A Saturday afternoon, her father wasn't around. Miranda called Sylvia, as Sylvia had asked her to do, and Sylvia came over with supplies and raspberry leaf tea to ease the new throbbing from deep inside. With her capable hands, Sylvia wrapped Miranda in a quilt, gave her a pill to take if the pain didn't settle. With a brusque gentleness, she kissed the top of Miranda's head before departing. But the pain did settle and, after making a sketch in her notebook of the kitchen table and the mug holding the remains of the tea Sylvia had brought, Miranda went out. In her snowshoes she clumped along the shore path as far as the beach, a new landscape making space for itself inside her as the wind carved tufts and plains outside.

One March afternoon, hurrying through snow across the school parking lot to the open school bus doors, Caleb at her heels, Miranda noticed an older silver car pulled up on the far side of the lot, recognizable despite the film of snow covering it.

"What's your mother doing here?" Miranda called but Caleb didn't answer as they slid into their bus seat, Miranda at the window, Caleb by the aisle. Caleb, she said again. He had pulled out his phone.

At lunchtime Miranda often left the girls' conversations and went to find Caleb, knowing he'd most likely be by himself. At school her body felt stretched, as if it had distant vanishing points. Her new breasts set off a fizzing in her. Sometimes Caleb would be out on the borders of the soccer field on the other side of the road, scuffing around in his puffy jacket, and when she reached him, he'd look up and say, his manner friendly if not demonstrative, Oh hi, Miranda.

Caleb hadn't said anything about his mother being at the school or the library, housed in a small wooden building on the far side of the parking lot.

"She's working in the library now," said Caleb without looking up from his phone. A stubble of dark hairs traced the skin of his upper lip.

"Since when?"

"In the afternoons."

The library was only open in the afternoon, four days a week, and there had been a debate about whether it should stay open at all since fewer and fewer people were using it.

Windshield wipers flapping, the bus stopped on its way out of the lot. In the library window, lit by a row of fluorescent ceiling lights, visible through the shimmer of snow, stood Sylvia. Tall in a knitted cardigan and skirt, something Miranda had never seen her wear, she held a book in one hand, beside a metal cart full of books. She was staring hard, as if caught in a trap, as if she would far rather have been outside, striding along snowy slide paths.

Here was a difference between their two families, not spoken of but sensed: Miranda and her father lived frugally but had enough money for her father not to worry about paying work, whereas Sylvia, despite her proud self-sufficiency, had to fret.

Across the road from where the bus let Miranda off, fresh tire tracks entered the lane that led to her house. Two sets: her father had recently been somewhere and returned. The wind, gusting out of the north, pressed snow into hummocks against rocks and fencelines, scoured the field where the humming wind turbine stood, sang in the town power lines and pushed itself inside Miranda's coat. Soon the tire tracks would be obscured. Some days when the snow was particularly wild, her father came to meet her at the top of the lane, but there was no one in the house when she dropped her bag in the mud room, only the wind huffing in the chimney. She was about to head across the yard to her father's study when voices stopped her. Two, her father's and a woman's, outside, louder when Miranda stood between kitchen and sitting room, by the unused front door, at the foot of the stairs.

Not Sylvia. Obviously. Not any of their neighbours. Not an island voice at all.

The woman's voice approached through the wind's whine, solid yet with a flute-like timbre rising upward.

Three things happened, the voice said as Miranda strove to catch her words. Something about the national weather service asking for data. The eastern Arctic—. Wanted to hold a briefing. I was to be the spokesperson for our unit. Permission—. One higher up. Another—. No. No to holding the briefing at all. The government—. Political expediency. You can't speak about melting ice at a weather briefing. Ice may be melting but they've decided melting ice isn't weather.

A scientist, Miranda wondered as she stood rigid. Another visitor? She'd convinced herself that Anna's arrival was singular, and as such it had been possible to come to terms with it. Now what she had assumed to be exceptional seemed to be happening again, and again without warning.

"I got a call from my uncle Samuel," the woman continued, closer now, perhaps on the other side of the door, "the one who likes to play Moravian hymns on the trombone, did I ever tell you about him? In February he went partridge hunting, thinking he would have one good day before the weather turned, but he found nothing. The night he was out, it rained, a torrential rain, then a cold front blew through. In the morning he had to hack his way out of the ice on his tent. Ice on the ground's not weather, remember? Then he saw something strange. There were caribou. When he approached they didn't move. There are so few left up there now, and these ones were very thin. They were encased in ice. He said they looked like statues. The rain had frozen all over them. They were alive and calling to him. He had to use his rifle to hack them out. He watched them wander off, slipping and sliding, looking back at him with terrible sorrow. He says to me, *Agnes, you're a scientist, can't you do something?* He was always saying to my father, the ornithologist, whenever he came through Nain, *What good are scientists, with their analyses and their studying, they brought trouble when they first came, that's when the weather started changing.* But he's saying it differently now. All the melting permafrost, it's making his house tilt, like so many others. A pond he always used to guide himself has vanished, as if it never was. You can't look at the clouds and know the weather, it changes hour to hour. He says, desperately now, *Agnes, you have to do something, can't you do something?*

"I put down the phone. I can't decide whether to leave Ottawa, go home, back up north, or stay in Ottawa, gathering data no one will even let us talk about. When this mysterious letter arrives, unsigned but written by someone who seems to know me, I think it's one of the people from the weather service, wanting me to come and collaborate in secret. I decide I'll fly to Nain and from there to Gander with my brother, the pilot. I allow myself two flights north a year but even if I try to control my carbon budget, he's going to cancel it out many times over. What can you do, it's family. I sent the message saying I was coming—"

"—to an encrypted account, I can assure you."

"It was you standing there when I got off the ferry. You, my old professor, with that beard, but still."

"Old, Agnes?"

"Not so old?"

Miranda set out, through the back door, pushed her way around the near side of the house through the sifting snow. When she rounded the corner, they were almost on top of her, her father in his down jacket and snow-dusted wool cap, and, in a white down parka, a woman with a pale, moon-like face and vanishing smile, forehead fringed with pale brown hair, beneath a snow-tipped hat of silvery fur. The wind pushed them forward. Alan startled, the wind having kept Miranda's approach a secret. She'd unnerved him. Good.

Holding out his arm, he gathered Miranda beneath the warm wing of one shoulder. "Here's a dear friend of mine. And colleague. Agnes Watson, of Nain, Nunatsiavut, and Ottawa, Ontario. Didn't know until she showed up that she'd truly come all this way. Agnes, this is my wondrous daughter, Miranda."

Miranda's breath caught in her throat. With reserved curiosity, Agnes held out a mittened hand. Where Anna had a willowy toughness, Agnes's compact strength seemed to rise out of the ground. When she smiled, she didn't show any teeth at all. Her sealskin mitten gave off its own secret warmth.

"One day long ago," her father was saying, "back when we lived in Waterloo, Agnes knocked on the door of my office. She was a first-year undergrad, geography major, first year in the south. She wanted to know if she could take my upper-level class on the cryosphere, the science of ice and snow. I only had to talk to her for a few minutes before declaring yes, you must, you can teach me a thing or two. The next summer, there she was, up on the Devon Island ice sheet, the first undergrad we'd ever had join our research team, not to mention the first young female Inuk scientist. You've likely no idea how unusual that was. She's never looked back."

"I remember one day your father brought you with him to his office," Agnes said with a small smile. "He was carrying you on his back in a baby sling, like an amaut. And every time he said the word *ice*, you cried."

It couldn't be true, Miranda thought. Alan's phone rang. Tucking it under his hood, he stepped away from them into a gust of snow, leaving Miranda to contemplate this peculiar story and the stranger, who had known her father as a much younger man, up on the polar ice, the man in the red parka, known him from when she was only a little older than Miranda was — and in a way she never could.

"Why are you here?" she asked Agnes, unable to help herself.

Agnes said, "I study black carbon. All the particulate matter in the snow cover, all the dust that travels north through the air from forest fires and industry in the south and darkens the snow surface when it falls." Which wasn't exactly an answer.

"Off Charmer's Cove," Alan was saying. "Tomorrow morning, yes, if you have one to spare, I'll take one, with enormous gratitude."

To Agnes, he said, "That was our neighbour, Pat Green. He's going sealing tomorrow, weather willing, one of two in town still with a licence. If the catch is good, we'll have one."

At his words Agnes's strong face lit up with joy. "If I'd known there'd be seal hunting, I would have come quicker."

"Time for the weather measurements," Miranda said as loudly as she could.

The next morning, a Saturday, the whine of a motorboat woke Miranda. Out in the cove, Pat Green's speedboat plied a path through the open water between ice pans, two bundled figures in it. Across the hall, her father squeaked the floorboards, then knocked quietly on the spare room door, telling Agnes Watson he was on his way to meet Pat. Slipping back beneath the covers, Miranda listened to Agnes creak down the stairs after her father. Let them go. If the wind didn't pick up, she and Caleb would go skating. They'd snowshoe in on the trail across the road from their lane and set off in the direction of her father's cabin, but only go as far as Tucker's Pond. They'd bring a broom to brush away snow and a thermos of hot tea, jam tarts made by Caleb's mother, cheese sandwiches. At the insistence of both their parents, Caleb would first knot a long rope around himself. Leaving one end with Miranda on shore, he'd walk out and check the ice depth by carefully chipping a hole in its surface with a small axe. Four inches or more and they'd be fine, but they had to be careful, since just before New Year's Aloysius Morton, from the town of Blaze, had fallen through a pond he'd always skated on and died of hypothermia, the ice still thin after the year's slow freeze-up.

Out on the ice, Caleb would skate with sure strokes while Miranda's own skates cut fast tracks, her eyes keeping watch for cracks and bumps, her body growing loose and defiant. Out there, away from the awesome sea, the horizon being land and snow and twisted tuckamore, it was almost possible to forget she was on an island. She might even forget the changes that had entered her home, though other changes might touch her, the sudden cracks in Caleb's voice, the strange new warmth pushing out of her own body.

When Miranda slipped once more to the window, the two parkas, her father and Agnes, had reached the shore. Pat slid his boat up onto the landwash, Brian hauling a black body from it. She scribbled the date and time in her notebook, wondering all the while why her father had brought Agnes to the island, because it surely wasn't just to bring home a seal.

In bed, quilt pulled all the way over herself, she was interrupted moments later by a voice calling her name. From the foot of the stairs, her father shouted, "Miranda? Agnes wants to clean the seal down at the shore. Help me bring supplies."

"I'm going skating with Caleb," Miranda called back.

"Miranda, come with us this morning." Even when she pressed her hands to her ears, her father's voice penetrated, boyish and pleading, which made it hard, then impossible to refuse his desire for her to be with him.

In the kitchen, Alan thrust a mug of tea into her hands. "Drink up, sweetheart." He danced as he gathered tin foil, a carving knife, tossed things into the plastic wash basin. Passing Miranda his phone, he told her to send Caleb a message, and she sensed Caleb's disappointment like a kernel inside herself.

Out in the cold, bright air, snow winking at them, her father, bucket in one hand, grinned as he pulled their old wooden toboggan, not the bigger sled on runners that he took out into the woods to gather wood, his step light at her side. Miranda carried the basin, knife and foil and plastic bags jostling inside it, as they stepped into the footsteps that Agnes and her father had made in the snow.

Usually seal meat came to them bottled or frozen. It wasn't that Miranda hadn't seen the butchered carcasses of creatures before: deer, rabbit, duck. Fish she'd caught herself, though she had never entirely got used to the feeling of eating the soft, sweet flesh of something she had killed. Why, she wondered, did her father insistently want her with him when he had Agnes for company?

The seal lay on his back in the snow, just above the line of pebbles, a sprawl of red slowly leaking beneath him. A harp seal, a year old probably, what Pat Green called a bedlamer. With a close-lipped smile that appeared then vanished, Agnes teased that if she'd known there'd be seal hunting, she'd have brought her ulu. She said she'd already warmed some snow with her breath and given the seal a few drops of fresh water to drink. Miranda's father nodded, as if this was something he'd expected her to do.

You drop fresh snow in a dead seal's mouth so its soul will not go thirsty, Agnes told Miranda. She and her mother used to process seals by the shore in Nain, she said, seals that her uncles would hunt and bring in for them.

"When I was a child, my brothers and I used to play on a pebbly beach like this one," Agnes said, "building landscapes out of stones, while our mother was at work."

"Sweetheart," said Alan, beckoning to Miranda as Agnes threw her jacket into the snow. No longer wearing her sealskin mitts but their dishwashing gloves, Agnes crouched over the seal and carved a thick line through the centre of his body, opening the skin and flesh and fat beneath. Moving with strength and tender care, she exposed the pale cage of the seal's ribs and ribbons of intestine. She cut off the flippers. Deftly she cut away the pelt, gently sliding it free of the blubber beneath. The body was a seal and by now not a seal. Blood drifted across the white snow.

In spring and summer, seals sometimes visited the cove, their bashful heads bobbing. During their second summer in the little white house, one particular seal had come every day.

They believed it to be the same seal, and because the creature came alone, Miranda's father decided it was a he. Miranda, just turned twelve, named him Lucky. After three weeks of daily visits, the seal vanished, and no matter how often Miranda walked the path her father had scythed through the grass to the shore and searched the water, she saw no further sign of him. She stared at the sea-lapped rock not far from shore that looked like a seal head but it did not turn into one. Most likely the fish he'd fed on had gone elsewhere, her father said, but the loss of Lucky's gleaming head and inquisitive gaze left Miranda keening.

One night, waking to a moon so full and bright it turned the white walls of her bedroom azure, Miranda slipped from bed. Outside, the water in the cove was smooth as glass and the shadow of the white house fell across the grass nearly as darkly as during the day. Out on the blue-black rocks where she and her father had come to watch the seal, she sang, hoping her voice might lure him.

A sound made her turn. A wild man burst towards her, shirtless, in jeans and boots. Her father's face contorted, contorting again at the sight of her.

"Miranda—get back here right now." His voice made her grip the rocks all the harder, his face full of expressions she could barely fathom.

"It's so beautiful," she said, wanting him to see what she saw. No seal, yet the moonlight made a world more spectacular than any she'd encountered.

"Off the rocks. The tide's high." His voice was hoarse and broke in pieces. When he held out a hand, Miranda took it, his hold like a vice. She told him how she never wanted to leave this place, never, never, certain this was what he wanted to hear, even as she was terrified he might crush her.

Back in her room, he pulled her close. "I woke up and had no idea where you were," he said in his strange, hoarse voice. "Never go out by yourself at night. Never down to the water in the dark. I might have lost you, too."

Above the icy cove, gulls scored the air, alive, the sea so quiet apart from the sloshing as Agnes rinsed the seal skin at the water's edge, the water curdled with puffs of red. Miranda's hands, her breath. Alive.

Then it was her father's turn to tug out the long ropes of intestines, handfuls of them, his arms bloody now, too, asking Agnes what to do, as if their roles had reversed and he were her assistant.

"Nowadays, when there's no longer ice near shore, and the seals stay out at sea, hunting's harder for everyone," Agnes said. "Boats have to go farther, that takes more gas, and when the ice breaks up early, it disperses the seals."

"They lose their breeding platforms," Alan said, lowering the intestines into a bucket. "Do you remember that time we went sealing together up on Baffin Island?"

Agnes nodded. "You and your 20/22 distance vision. Everyone wanted to hunt with you because you spotted creatures across the water before anyone else could." With a wistful grin, she reached deep inside the cavity of the seal's body and pulled out a shining bulb.

When Miranda brought the basin, Agnes held the dripping bulb over it. "It's the seal's heart," her father said as Agnes cut a slice of the shininess and held it out to Miranda on the edge of the knife blade.

"We're giving thanks to the seal for the gift of his life," Agnes said.

Miranda was to take the slice of heart from Agnes's blood-stained fingers. This much she understood. The past was all around them, her father's past, Agnes's past, the seal's past, though her father's longing was wrapped up in this present moment, too. He wanted her to share in whatever this was. So how could she not take the slice of seal heart from Agnes? Miranda placed the slice on her tongue. Blood and muscle. Grief. Now Agnes was cutting another slice, which she held out to Alan, one more for herself. There were tears in her father's eyes and on Agnes's cheeks. They were eating a body so close to swimming through the sea. A lost body, gift and loss. Heat and wind filled Miranda's mouth, her throat.

The whole house smelled of seal, pungent and dense, despite the vinegar and baking soda her father was using to soak the seal meat. There was seal meat on every kitchen surface, zip-lock bags out for freezing, a pot boiling on the stove, her father stirring whatever was in the pot, Agnes turning from the kitchen counter to offer Miranda small cubes of seal blubber held out at the end of a knife.

Mittens on, Miranda was ready to set off for Caleb's when Alan called out, "Would you mind going back down to the shore? Seems we left the carving knife there and with luck the tide hasn't stolen it."

Soon Agnes and her father would be alone, talking about

whatever their own business was. Outside, the air was cool and free of seal smell. Calming. More pack ice had entered the cove, the pans winking turquoise, undulating with the swells beneath, the sea ice that had broken up in the Arctic and been tugged south by the Labrador Current, travelling along with the seals. Here, too, the pack ice no longer came to shore some years. When it did, the ice was wondrous, mesmerizing, appearing so suddenly, and, when the wind shifted, vanishing as quickly, pulled back to the horizon. Even out at sea, the strong, white field of ice was a riveting presence. The sea ice spoke in many voices, it groaned and crackled and softly sifted, and when it filled the cove, the whole world went silent.

The knife was on top of a rock, right by the water's edge. The tide was creeping in, water lapping almost invisibly beneath the thinnest skin of ice. There was still blood among the lonely pebbles and, pulling off her glove, Miranda crouched to touch that slickness. In the quiet, she pressed the sharp tip of the knife blade to her skin and the whisper of this pain was satisfying.

Approaching the house, she was stopped by the sound of voices: Agnes and her father were out on the bridge, a rope of seal intestine swinging from their laundry line.

"What do you tell her?" Agnes asked.

"I tell her some of what's going on," Alan said. "Not all, obviously, something of the science, a little of what may lie ahead. I'm teaching her practical knowledge, survival skills, about the natural world. Berry picking. Planting. This morning, too, it's all part of her education. I want to bring her back to the land, hoping perhaps that's the best preparation for whatever's coming."

"You'll stay here," Agnes said.

"Just breathe this air. How could I, how could we, leave that?"

"You asked me here. Why? Apart from, you know, procuring me some country food."

"I've been monitoring the weather out here, as I told you, keeping track of what's happening in this place. More and more I've been wondering what might be done to save the ice, stop catastrophic ice-sheet melt and sea-level rise, all these things that, as you know, are already happening right across the Arctic."

"Set all the oil barons loose on melting ice floes and make everyone else return to a subsistence life."

"If that doesn't happen, Agnes? Even if it does, what if things are so far gone we still need to intervene more aggressively, cool things down by, say, injecting something into the atmosphere—possibly sulfate aerosols, which would circulate rapidly in the stratosphere and reflect back incoming sunlight. I've been modelling. Others are, too, but out here I've been working largely on my own. A risky proposition, injecting atmospheric particulates, admittedly, but could we not conceive it as a necessary form of care, an act of reparation for all the damage done?"

"Change the atmosphere by adding more dirt to it, and change it knowingly? Is that a form of care?"

"If the situation's grave enough."

"I've heard people talk about making clouds."

"Spraying water particles lower down in the troposphere, but this would be higher up, to reflect incoming sunlight. Possibly reducing global temperatures, that's the goal. Because nothing's happening, is it? What about all those fires in Siberia last summer? How many died in that heat wave across India? And the droughts in Kenya that have gone on for how many years? Still the engines of business crank on and atmospheric carbon goes up and up."

"More forest fires and more industry means more clouds of black carbon," Agnes said. "The dirtiest clouds on Earth someone called them. When the soot falls onto the snow—I'll pick up a handful—you can see how all the feathery crystals have turned into small, dark grains that don't reflect light, just absorb more heat."

"So do we not have a responsibility to see what might be done? To save the world? Protect the snow and ice? Out of a kind of love? Others are talking about spreading giant swathes of white cloth over ice sheets or setting up huge reflective mirrors on their surface, but a stratospheric global haze of particulate matter might be more effective. Could such a plan work on a smaller scale? Regionally? We don't know yet. Here's where I could use your help. All that data on the snow and ice pack you say no one wants—Agnes, I want it. We can make use of it together, create a baseline data set of the most up-to-date ground-truth data for this region, here, in Labrador, and Nunatsiavut."

Their words drifted towards Miranda, settled over her like dust.

"Who would do this particulate injecting, Alan? People like you? And where?"

"Issues of governance are crucial, obviously. Tricky. Governance and consent. Particulates don't pay attention to borders any more than the weather does. But perhaps those who will be most affected should have some say?"

The back door closed. Their voices vanished.

—

"Who's your visitor, Miranda?" Sylvia asked. The kettle was boiling on the far side of Sylvia's kitchen. Miranda and Caleb had dropped their skates inside the back door before heading up to the barn to feed the goats. There Miranda, still flushed with exertion, had climbed into the pen to press her nose to the noses of Fleur and Jewel, whose pregnant bellies swelled, while Caleb forked hay from the loft. As they left, Caleb said, brushing her arm, that he had to fetch something from the shed, the shed being his den, where his woodworking tools hung on the wall in a neat row.

Sylvia's words filled Miranda with unease. Red hair pinned loosely atop her head, Sylvia pinched tufts of dried spruce needles and nettle and raspberry leaves, strong hands moving deftly—grimly—from bowls to fill a row of mason jars on the table.

If people ask, Alan had said, as in Miranda's mind they were bound to, simply say Agnes is an old friend of mine. Caleb had asked about the woman with the sealskin hat as they'd snowshoed in to the pond, and Miranda had told him what her father had said. Inuk. Lives in Ontario. Back in the summer, Sylvia had asked about Anna, with a surprise that mirrored Miranda's own. Again as if she couldn't help herself, Sylvia had wondered aloud why Miranda's father now spent so much time holed up in his cabin, what did Miranda think?

The changing weather brushed at the edges of everything like fur.

"Pat Green brought in a good catch this morning, didn't he," Sylvia said with a keen stare from across the table. "I gather your father took one."

"Yes," Miranda said.

The long velvet curtain closing off the kitchen from the breezeway billowed as boots clumped through the back door. The next moment, a man plunged into the kitchen.

"Hello, Alan," said Sylvia, straightening up, caught out as Miranda herself was.

"How's it going, Sylvia?" He'd taken off his boots but not his down jacket, his feet bulging in wool socks, car keys still in his hand, his beard trimmed the day of Agnes's arrival. Preoccupied, he made no attempt at charm in Sylvia's presence. "All right, Miranda, let's go."

She'd called her father on Caleb's phone and left a message, telling him she'd be at Caleb and Sylvia's for supper. "I'm staying here," Miranda said.

In Sylvia's house they would eat venison stew with dumplings, deer meat brought back by Caleb's uncle Leo from a hunting trip over to the other side, the stew's spicy aroma already filling Miranda's nose. Afterwards they'd lounge in the parlour, enclosed by the folds of the red velvet curtains, maybe watch a movie on one of the old silver DVDs Sylvia had kicking about, and everything would feel like the old days, when the three of them used to do this frequently. Miranda longed for the old days. Maybe, if she were tired and lazy enough, she would curl up and fall asleep on the daybed in the room at the top of the stairs, where Sylvia might kiss her good night, a perfect combination of being like a mother yet not a mother, and it would be as if she were floating in a safe ship at sea all through the night.

"What you mean is, Yes, Dad, I'm coming," Alan said, because he did not want her to be here where Sylvia might ply her with questions about Agnes.

"You're welcome to stay for supper as well, Alan, there's plenty of food," said Sylvia. Her voice, while light, held what sounded like a challenge rather than the teasing warmth of earlier years.

"Can't, I'm afraid. Come on, Miranda." There was an abruptness in him different than the tentative abruptness of his first encounters with Sylvia. It seemed to border on anger, to be resisting something that Sylvia was trying to bottle but which kept escaping into the room.

"Here's something I marvel at," Sylvia said. "Why is it, Alan, that when you have a friend visiting, such a rare occurrence, mind you, you never invite us to meet them? You're welcome to bring your new friend by. Even tonight, we might all sit down together. If they've come from far off, why not bring them here and let us show them some hospitality? We're friendly." Colour rose in Sylvia's cheeks.

"I've left something on the stove, Sylvia. Our visitor and I, we'd bore you, honestly—all we do is talk about the weather."

"The weather?" Sylvia slung her arms across her chest. "We're all interested in the weather, aren't we? You and I have spoken about how queer it can be."

"Anyway," Alan said curtly, "I've no desire to bother you." Yet his face was saying something else. There was a struggle in him. Perturbation. Conflict. Guilt.

"No desire?" Sylvia threw back her head with a raucous laugh. "No desire to bother me? Well, thank you, Alan, I must say, for clearing up that point of confusion."

"Miranda, let's go."

"Why exactly are these women here? Friends, you say, yet, whenever I ask, why do you always act as though I shouldn't be asking?" Sylvia had raised her voice. "Why lead me on, Alan?"

Miranda didn't want to move. There *was* secrecy in her father. Her toes curled tight. She didn't want to be left in the room with Sylvia's anger either.

"Lead you on?" Miranda had never seen her father shout at Sylvia. Something in Sylvia froze, as if aware she'd gone too far. "I've never done that. You know what, Sylvia, I'm fed up with all the innuendo and haranguing. Good night."

In the breezeway, stumbling after her father, Miranda fumbled for her skates in the dark. She was in the yard, which was darkening, Sylvia calling her father's name at Miranda's back. The rooster crowed. The tears in her eyes might be Sylvia's tears or even her father's. A fist pummelled her stomach from the inside. Could they not go back in time? Five minutes, a month, a year or two?

Their old car, running off its electric battery, was quiet as it reversed across the yard, so quiet that perhaps Caleb didn't hear it until he stepped out of the shed, the doorway lit behind him, something small in his hand, likely something he'd carved. He'd begun to whittle creatures out of pieces of driftwood: a crouched fox, loping wolf, diving seal, swimming polar bear. Cutting boards shaped like whales and dried salt cod. He'd sell them too, setting up a summer stand at roadside, though he'd told Miranda tourists sometimes found it odd to buy souvenirs from a local who looked like him. A silhouette in the doorway, it was impossible to see his face and impossible not to feel how his initial pleasure and expectation as he stepped through the door immediately turned to distress as the car tugged Miranda away from him.

Her father didn't stop. Perhaps he hadn't even seen Caleb. Past Christine Brett's B&B they went. Mrs. Magdalene's boarded-up house was a smear on the far side of the road.

The snowy yards. Her father remained silent and closed in on himself. Something was being broken. Miranda's hands closed into fists. She wished to be far away, out on the ice with the seals, away from this moment, which she would mark in her notebook, date, time, the storm of it.

. . .

Seated on his quad in front of Teresa Blake's guest house, Tony and Len having disappeared back inside, Caleb wondered where he was going to get a car, not a quad or a truck. What he needed was a vehicle big enough to carry the two men, yet small enough that no one in Tom's Neck, seeing him sail by at the wheel, was going to swivel their head and say, What's Caleb Borders doing driving Earl Patton's Dodge Ram out of town? And who's in there with him?

Anna had expected him to go back to Pummelly but he wasn't going to do that. With a glance over his shoulder, Caleb set off on foot across the lawn. Inside the back door of Bakeapple House, he placed his big boots beside a pert black pair with chains looped around the heels that had to belong to Margaret Hynes's niece, Della Burke, working in the kitchen alongside Margaret. When Caleb looked up, Margaret herself loomed on the far side of the kitchen doorway, a thick orange extension cord snaking past her feet, knife brandished in her hand, while, outside, the generator roared.

"Caleb Borders, if you come any closer, a gulch is going to open up and swallow you whole."

"How's it going there, Margaret?" Caleb had to raise his voice to make himself heard above an ocean of sound:

generator meeting kitchen hubbub. Margaret wasn't tall but she emanated strength, her bottle-brown hair snared within a hairnet.

At the far counter, red kerchief tied over her hair—saving her from the fate of having to wear a dreaded hairnet like her aunt—Della turned. Mouth open in surprise, she was on the cusp of dropping a spoonful of whiteness onto two crab cakes cooked to a golden crispiness. Beside them lay a pale nest that to Caleb's eye looked suspiciously like caribou moss. Was it? You had to boil that moss before you ate it. Otherwise it was poisonous. Presumably Margaret knew to do that.

"Well, then, are you gone yet, boy?" Margaret barked, knife held high.

In the background, Caleb's ear brought into focus another sound. A radio. Yes, a small battery-operated radio was propped on the windowsill beside the stove—Teresa had spoken of one that morning. At this distance, it was impossible to hear anything more than a buzz and crackle adding to the general uproar: whirring fan, spit of grease.

"Any news from out there?" Caleb asked Margaret.

"Not good," she said. "Now go."

"Anything from the Avalon, Gander?"

"Surely you have a fondness for that head of yours and those fine hands. Della, grab those cakes before they burn!"

"I need to speak to Della," Caleb cried, distracted nevertheless by the word of no good news, because, from the coverage of previous hurricanes and other natural disasters, he knew how reports began with one confirmed death or two before climbing into the hundreds, even thousands. This one had begun in the hundreds so now what? And here they were still trying to hold onto the ordinary.

He'd hooked Della's attention at any rate. "It has to do with the guests," he called across the gulch separating them. "The very important guests."

Margaret lowered the knife. "One minute, then," she said, grabbing back her spatula in disgust as Della hurried to join Caleb, stepping over the extension cord that powered the fuse box, pulling her T-shirt down over the black leggings that clasped her wide thighs.

He wasted no time. "I need to borrow your car."

When he saw how instantly crestfallen she looked, he realized Della must have thought he had a specific plan for her, something that might lift her out of the drudgery of her aunt's kitchen. Beyond Della, Margaret was nudging more crab cakes onto a plate with the tender devotion others reserved for babies.

"I need to take them somewhere, and it's too far to walk. One of them's already going off with the blonde woman, Anna, in Teresa's car. It's for the other two."

"There's a sinkhole down along the Pummelly Road, in Green Cove."

"You think I don't know that? My car's on the far side of it. I have a can of gas, Della. I'll replace any I use and more."

In school Della Burke, shy as she was, would have ignored him, like all the others. It was something agreed upon by everyone. Was it because of his missing father, the colour of his skin? He was the castaway. Sensing this had made Caleb cranky or mute, which only made things worse. His solitude grew profound. With all their classmates gone, though, things were different. There was a vulnerability, an ache in Della, owner of a little Chevy four-door.

"Be a sweetheart, Dell."

"If anything happens to my car, Caleb Borders, your arse will be whipped." But she was still plump Della Burke, scrabbling obediently in her shiny black handbag, which hung from a chain that matched the ones on her little black boots. From the bag she pulled a car key.

"You're a wonder, Della," Caleb said, as she handed the key over.

"We're hardly finding a station on that radio," she told him with sudden, conspiratorial gravity. "Nothing at all."

He didn't drive the quad to Della's house, figuring it would attract less attention if he left the quad where it was. As Caleb hurried along the main road, he grew aware of footsteps, swift-paced, approaching from his rear. Someone with a spectacularly quiet tread was sticking close, not trying to make a wide berth around him.

Hunched in an oilskin jacket, brimmed cap pulled down over his forehead, sunglasses a mask across his eyes, the old man pulled in stride with him. The old man's furtiveness did nothing to cancel out his air of authority. "Now where are you off to?" he asked softly, so close in Caleb's ear that Caleb's heart sprang from his chest.

They were coming up to the turnoff that led down a slope to the government wharf, its long arm stretching into the harbour. Two boats were moored alongside the wharf, the cabin cruiser that Owen Freake used for tours whenever eager visitors came to the island and Pete Decker's small fishing boat, *White Foam*. The aluminum speedboats often berthed at the wharf had been pulled to land before the storm. Across the harbour, at the fish plant, Tom Borders's longliner and others waited in a row for the sea, which still had the force of the storm in it, to settle. Those boats — the money they cost. Caleb had heard his uncle muttering about the expense of fishing these days.

The old man's touch, neither rough nor gentle as he steered Caleb by the elbow onto the turnoff, made Caleb recoil. On the wharf they would be less observed. There would be no one to overhear them.

A little over a year ago, though it seemed much longer now, one very early July morning when the sky was still dark and the moon full and shining, they'd come down to this wharf together, Caleb, the old man, and the old man's third visitor, Arun Mudalnayake. That time, too, there'd been secrecy.

Before dawn, they'd arrived in the old man's car, the old man and Arun in the front, Caleb in the back, balancing on his lap a mysterious object with gauges and computer readouts, a small solar panel, and a row of tiny nozzles. It was about the heft of a medium-sized dog and the old man had been constructing it all winter in his store, as he'd constructed a smaller version the year before. Don't let it jiggle or bounce, he'd warned, only half-joking as he entrusted what he called the module to Caleb for the journey. In the face of the old man's obvious anxiety, Caleb was as careful with the peculiar object as if it were made of glass.

Arun had arrived the previous day. Caleb had been the one to drive across and pick him up, a slim figure waiting by the Gander airport curb in down jacket and gloves, despite the relative mildness of fifteen degrees, his skin a good shade darker than Caleb's, which aroused Caleb's interest.

Arun hadn't said much on the rainy drive back to the coast, preferring to stare out the window or doze. He must have been older than he looked, which was about fourteen. A faint scent of cologne hovered about the collar of the crisp white shirt glimpsed beneath his jacket. He'd flown up from Boston. He did say that he worked in a lab at a university and that, in another year, he was supposed to move back to Colombo, Sri Lanka, to help run his father's computer-chip factory. Last summer, the grass in Colombo had been so hot it burned his feet, he said, the blades as sharp as glass. The huge floods from Cyclone Mala—had Caleb heard about them, how they'd crashed like the long-ago tsunami over the southern coast. On the ferry Arun didn't want to leave the car until Caleb told him they all had to go upstairs.

With the old man, as they made the drive through the dark from Pummelly to Tom's Neck, Arun was more talkative. Perhaps because of the dark and because he had nothing to add to the conversation, they spoke as though they had forgotten Caleb was there. About sulfate particles versus calcium carbonate or diamond dust or water droplets when it came to optimal reflectivity and dispersal rates, the question of dispersion in the troposphere versus the stratosphere, whether to create more clouds at lower elevations that cooled with their albedo or a thin, high reflective haze that would enclose the Earth. There'd be losses, inevitably, as well as gains. If a haze, then no more pure sunny days, for one. Sulfate particles might eat away more of the ozone layer, calcium carbonate particles wouldn't.

"There it is, there it is, the double-edged sword of the sulfate particle," exclaimed Arun, the dark hair at the back of his neck bristling as he spoke. "Exactly what it is that got me thinking, can we engineer a particle that will take the good stuff from the sulfates, the reflectivity, na, the uniformity of dispersal, the ability to stay aloft for some time? And not the bad."

"It's a clever name you've given your nanoparticle, Skyspex," —or was it *Skyspecks*, Caleb had no idea—"I presume you've taken out a patent on the name as well as the idea itself," the old man said.

Outside the car window, blue ponds and moonlit trees flew past.

"I truly hope, based on the modelling and the lab results, it will rival the sulfates for dispersal and staying aloft, but in the lab of course we're not able to simulate all the interactions—"

"—of the air. Ah, indeed, there's the rub," said the old man.

"Yes, yes, the mysteries of cloud and aerosol interactions—"

"Anyway, I'm glad you were willing to come all this way to have our conversation. The sprayer's rudimentary but functional, proof, fingers crossed, it's still possible to build something useful in a shed. I'm fully aware of the restrictions about actual geoengineering experiments in the field, don't think I'm not. Of course, one can't go out and start chucking particulates into the atmosphere—on the other hand, people have been making clouds for a long time. Those guys pumping smoke from a boat to mimic shipping exhaust, who made enough cloud cover to create a cooling effect fifty times greater than the warming from their emissions? Basically a geoengineering experiment. Even artists have made clouds. All we're trying to demonstrate is that the sprayer functions. And gather, as I mentioned, some necessary documentation."

They made the turn and were gliding down towards the

government wharf where Pete Decker stood waiting for them. The floodlights picked out his stocky figure pacing beside his truck. In the car's back seat, his skin blue in the dark, Caleb touched the metal of the module gently, musing on what he'd heard. He assumed the old man must have paid Pete Decker handsomely for whatever they were up to and likely for his silence.

As Caleb and Arun unloaded more equipment from the trunk, two pressurized gas cylinders, boxes, and, from the trailer hitched to the car, a wooden spool wrapped with coils of extremely thin lime-green tubing, the old man stood on the wharf directing them, all the while cradling the module.

"This is for the weather monitoring then, is it?" Pete Decker said amiably. Caleb had to presume this was what the old man had told Pete, even though part of his mind went, *Weather monitoring?*

Weather monitoring was what the old man had told him to offer his mother as the reason for this early morning trip. Tell her I need your help. But the old man had not wanted Caleb to tell his mother that he'd picked up Arun Mudalnayake while on the Gander run to buy supplies. Let's keep that to ourselves. It was awkward navigating between his mother and the old man now that the two of them no longer spoke. There'd been other arguments before the one that broke them. His mother had called the old man shifty to his face. Able to think only for himself. After they stopped speaking, Caleb sensed he was overhearing an internal conversation his mother was having as she shoved a pan into the oven or boiled goat milk for yogurt at the stove. He knew she felt aggrieved. Betrayed. Something had happened that she couldn't or didn't want to get over.

The old man had secrets, true enough. The fact that he seemed to be entrusting Caleb with some of them made Caleb feel close to the old man, honoured and emboldened and gratified, likewise closer to the girl. Even if the girl didn't know everything he and the old man did together, a magical web spun itself around the three of them.

From the deck of the *White Foam*, Pete held out a hand and helped Caleb scramble aboard. With the greatest of care, Arun and the old man passed the module into Caleb's waiting arms.

They were lucky. The weather had turned the day before. It was clear and likely to stay so for a few days. With a thermos of coffee at his side, Pete settled himself in the wheelhouse. They set off as the light grew. The Little Fish Islands, materializing as a dark line of rock on the horizon, looked a thousand kilometres away. In the cabin, Arun and the old man set to work inflating a small weather balloon with gas from the smaller of the cylinders. They attached the module to the balloon and the lime-green tubing to the module; a line of tubing descended from the module to the spool, now locked to a winch on deck. It would be Caleb's job to turn the winch.

Water droplets, the old man said, pointing to the larger cylinder, as if he wished to make sure Caleb understood this. Once the length of tubing had been unspooled into the air, the droplets would be pumped up through the tubing to the module where a blower would push them into the sky, the nozzles being no wider than two human hairs, droplets so tiny they would rise even higher and hang suspended.

We're studying clouds, the old man said to Caleb, again as if he wanted to make sure this was clear and perhaps so that Caleb didn't imagine other things.

The sky had turned pink in the east. Farther out at sea, icebergs floated past, one shaped like a horse, another a fish, mauve and turquoise in the dove-coloured light. The old man was gruff with his instructions, no doubt because he was caught up in what they were doing. As Caleb turned the winch, lifting balloon and module higher, he excused the gruffness. Slow down, Caleb! For God's sake!

Arun, who had pulled his hood over his head and tightened it under his chin, nervously eyed the module and the swell of the waves through his tinted glasses. They were settled out on the water, the motor quieted. Once the tubing was extended as far as the old man wished, and attached to the second pressurized cylinder, it was Arun's job to monitor the pump while the old man checked readouts on a small computer pad, calling out, *Size of vapour plume! Rough number of particulates!* Every few minutes he stopped to take photographs.

Caleb's hands grew cold. There seemed to be a problem with the readouts. The old man's head and Arun's knotted close. The ocean rose and fell beneath the deck. Speckled cod flicked through the deep water and part of Caleb descended with them, down to the dark ocean floor, the pressure of water a weight all over his limbless body, gills puffing like tender accordions. Farther out, humpback whales exhaled umbrellas of vapour. Would the Coast Guard wonder what they were up to? All at once Caleb was instructed to reel the module back in. *Gently!* Gulls flew close, curious to see if they had caught anything edible, which made the old man mutter nervously and shout at them. It turned out, after some discussion, that one of the nozzles was blocked.

As more icebergs floated past, Arun came to stand beside Caleb on the rear deck while the old man went to consult with Pete up in the wheelhouse. Arun said he'd never seen an iceberg before the previous evening when he'd walked into Green Cove with Dr. Wells to inspect a small one beached on the sand.

"Dr. Wells?" Caleb said.

Arun flinched, offering no answer other than, "And now icebergs are everywhere."

"I'd say," Caleb said. "It's a good year for them." A wave of cold air blew at them from one distant blue mountain. He let the *doctor* thing go. Obviously the old man wasn't an actual doctor.

Arun frowned. "Are they not from Greenland?"

"Most of them are, that's right."

"So it's not good there's so many of them, is it? Don't you think precarious regions like islands ought to have the means to protect themselves from—from what might be coming? The floods, the storms, the rising seas?" Arun spoke in a fervent undertone, as if confiding a thought close to his heart. "At the very least we must find a way to call attention to our possibly terrible fates."

Caleb wondered what Arun meant by *possibly terrible fates.* How terrible? He breathed in the scent of Arun's skin. What the old man had said in the car about people making clouds that cooled fifty times more than the heat created by a ship at sea, that might be useful. What else had he said—there might be no more purely sunny days like this one?

"Thing is, I'd rather be on an island, this island, than anywhere else," Caleb said. Sometimes he dreamed of travelling south, to places, islands where people might look more like him; each time, though, something tugged him back to this land.

"Pete Decker told me there are hundreds of icebergs stranded over on the other side of the island," said Arun.

In Vera's general store in Pummelly, Caleb had heard thousands, stretching as far as the eye could see, more than anyone could ever remember being calmed there. Dan McGrath himself had driven across to the town of Blaze to take a look at them. An idea sprang into Caleb's mind. He'd been searching for weeks for a way to enact an extraordinary plan, a way to bring the girl closer than ever. Now the best course yet stretched clear before him.

He was on the government wharf in Tom's Neck. The day after the unexpected storm. In searing mid-September sunlight. With the old man who, in his oilskin jacket and sunglasses, had swerved him away from the road, brought him down here, asked him something. The past was all around them. Caleb tried to push it away. The day he'd taken the girl out in speedboat to see the icebergs, she'd seemed less upset by the time they finally docked in Pummelly, and Caleb, who had turned the boat towards the far shore, true, and not listened when the girl begged him not to do this, had allowed himself to believe he'd been forgiven. Until a few hours later, when the old man texted him and ordered Caleb to meet him down at the beach in Green Cove. There, out of sight and earshot of all others, the old man reared up, and though he never touched Caleb, his anger was so strong as to make Caleb feel he were being whipped and shaken. There in the soft sand as the tide crept towards them. *You crossed a line, Caleb. You know she's not to leave the island. Taking someone somewhere against their will, that's called kidnapping. Hitting them, it's called assault.*

Hitting them? On the beach, as the old man's words sundered life as he knew it, Caleb's shocked mouth opened in grief and despair and self-defence but only air poured out.

Nevertheless the old man hadn't fired him. Nor, despite his pain, had Caleb quit his job because quitting would have been a worse fate. It would have cut him off even further from the girl.

He was on the wharf, and in an hour he was to meet the two men, Len and Tony. They were a thread leading him forward, into the future. Thankfully, Della's car key was stuffed deep in the pocket of his coveralls, not clutched in his hand.

What was it the old man had asked him — *where are you off to?*

"To fetch something for Margaret Hynes," Caleb replied, an answer, he hoped, that didn't strain credulity too much.

"Did you entertain any thought of returning to Green Cove to let me know if you were able to deliver my message to Anna — ? How about filling me in on the state of things with our visitors, especially since I've recently promoted you and given you a raise?"

It would have been flippant to say, What was the point, since the old man was clearly not at the house in Green Cove, now was he?

"The windows — the new bow windows at Cape House, the ones we installed, they smashed last night in the storm." All the desolation of this rose in Caleb again.

"I'm truly sorry, Caleb. That was a shocking barometric pressure drop, it took Mary Green's roof, as I'm sure you know. I'll come out and take a look if you like, but today I need you to focus on the tasks at hand. It's critical."

Hearing new warmth in the old man's voice, the old man

who never seemed to care about the colour of Caleb's skin, Caleb kicked at the thick wood of the wharf. He explained about the men's trip to the ferry dock with Anna, where they'd found a wisp of phone coverage and the man named Roy had picked up some messages, including one that said his son was missing.

At this the old man perked up, all his coiled physical energy a giant, magnetizing force. He even pulled off his sunglasses.

"What happened to him?"

"Roy thinks he got swept out to sea in a storm surge that came in over a wildlife refuge where he was."

"Roy knows this how?"

"His wife sent him a text." Roy's wife had a foreign name. Japanese? Presumably the old man knew this already.

"I see," said the old man with something of the energy a hive of buzzing bees might make. "Thanks for that information, Caleb."

They were hard upon the *White Foam*'s moorings, the boat tugging at the creaking ropes. The old man was contemplating something with furious intensity, the creases at the corners of his eyes appearing and disappearing. The lines on his face were deeper than they used to be, his cheeks hollowed above his speckled beard. Whenever he was with the old man for any length of time, especially when the girl herself was nowhere nearby, a question took form in Caleb and began to press hard then harder against his tongue. Dare he ask the old man if he could speak to his daughter once again? Assert that his penance had gone on long enough?

"Any word back from Anna?" the old man asked.

She'd agreed to the further delay, Caleb told him, and decided not to mention Anna's reluctance though he added that the men did not seem happy about being held up on the island for another day, not happy at all. In any case, they didn't have enough fuel to leave, nor was Roy able to get a flight plan.

"It's not likely they would be happy," the old man said. "Roy especially, even more given his missing son. It's perversely helpful that the hurricane is engineering delays for me, saving me from certain kinds of ingenuity. It's a good thing for a man like Roy Hansen to discover he can't always make the world do what he wants when he wants it."

Long ago, in the days when he had first gone hunting with the old man, the two of them crouching together behind a gaze built of stones at shore, the old man had taken it upon himself to teach Caleb bits of science, things Caleb didn't learn in school. Once, as they waited for a flock of eiders to appear, the old man had said that the world would be a very different place if the carbon particles accumulating in the atmosphere were something people could see, like a red mist spreading in the sky, growing redder year by year, if bright red trails poured out of jet engines. Now and again, Caleb tried to imagine a world like that. Red skies. Red mist. Growing redder.

The old man could be caring one moment, ferocious the next. And he harboured mysteries, as in what exactly he was up to with his visitors and all the computer equipment he kept stashed at his cabin, not to mention balloons in the sky and tubing. Caleb's mother surely wasn't wrong to be wondering, even if she didn't know about the balloons.

"Alan—" It was the possibility of kindness that made Caleb speak the old man's name, the most urgent question filling his mouth, "Did you come to Tom's Neck to meet the men?"

"No." A new concern gripped the old man's face. "Don't say

a word to them about seeing me. I'm checking up on things. Checking up on you as it happens."

"Why are the men here?" Caleb's heart galloped as he asked this.

"To learn something about islands." The old man spoke so quickly Caleb wondered if he was telling the truth.

Why was it so hard to utter the question he wanted to ask most of all? "Do you have any news from the other side?"

"I'm as cut off as you are."

Now, the voice inside him kept urging—there was no one around them on the wharf as they stood close under the bright, redeeming sky.

Once, it had seemed like the old man was courting Caleb's mother. Or his mother was courting the old man. Then things, which looked like they were going one way between the two of them had gone another, and despite a house full of his mother's sorrow and rage, Caleb had breathed a huge sigh of relief. Because if the old man had really been on his way to becoming a father, this would have made the girl a sister. If so, what was Caleb to do with his dreams, the way he woke with a boner between his legs and the girl's name on his lips, whispered aloud as he imagined licking every speck of her body?

So, while it had been a terrible thing when his mother and the girl's father stopped speaking and began to act as if each were dead to the other, it had launched him into a wide new world of hope.

Once, as they stood together atop the grassy cliffs of the headlands, out beyond the trail that led to Cape House, the girl, with her soft breasts and sometimes feral manner, had blurted to Caleb that she thought he was more like her father than his own mother. A north wind punched their faces as they faced the churning sea and Caleb had to ask, puzzling, What do you mean? They were both wiry and muscular and had dark hair, the girl said. But there seemed to be more. Your moods, the girl blurted. Then Caleb did not know what to think.

"I have to go." As he faced the old man on the wharf, a salt taste filled Caleb's mouth. They'd gone to school dances together, himself and the girl. They'd danced, before retreating bashfully to the sidelines. He'd held her hand and he would do so again.

Yet there was also this: his hour was shrinking and he had to get to Cape House to prepare it for the men. Once he'd secured his investment, then, only then would he ask his question of the old man and go further: describe the beautiful future he'd prepared for his daughter. Storms or no storms. Surely then the old man would relent.

Caleb touched Della's car key in the depth of his pocket, the balls of his feet pressed hard into the dock. "Is there anything else?"

"Stop by the house end of the afternoon, once you've done whatever you're doing for Margaret. One last thing—have you by any chance seen Agnes Watson amid your wanderings?"

"No," Caleb said truthfully, as everything in him wobbled with unease.

"Keep an eye out please. If you do, tell her to come to the house."

Agnes Watson was the only other person Caleb had met whose footfall was as quiet as the old man's. She'd surprised him, once, up in the snowy hills. He had finished checking his rabbit snares and was staring out at the white sea. The gulls were returning. He searched for seals. Someone stood beside him. He'd heard nothing. The woman staying at the Wells's place, Inuk, the girl had said, who along with the old man had taken one of Pat Green's seals the morning before, was wearing what must be the old man's snowshoes. Their turquoise meshing glowed. She disconcerted him in a totally different way than the other woman, Anna. Agnes had a solid strength entirely different from Anna's silvery gestures. It was like turning to discover yourself beside a caribou. When Caleb asked Agnes what she was doing on the island, she said something he didn't understand. Sila.

"It means breath and air and mind and weather. The living world. A silanigtalersarput is someone who sees clearly in the darkness and knows the weather and ice."

Agnes said, "There are people out there who don't believe ice and snow are weather. We are entering times of dangerous weather and that weather is inside us as well as outside."

. . .

Miranda came to a halt at the edge of the far field. Pieces of storm wreckage lay strewn about where the flooding waves had tossed them the night before: strips of aluminum siding, driftwood, a plastic fishing buoy, a toilet seat. Breath burst from her lungs. Having dashed away from Frank, she was not going to look back and see what he was doing. Sleeves still wet from pulling things out of his car, she tugged on her blue rubber gloves and set to work, dragging one end of the piece of siding to the place where she would make two piles, the burnable and unburnable. They would have to find a way to get rid of the unburnable later.

How far had the siding travelled, from Pummelly, the island, or afar? What about the toilet seat? She didn't want to think about the fact that there had never been storm wreckage in this field before. It felt good to throw herself into movement, be only a swing of muscle, steer herself away from her cascade of feelings, the flux of everything in and around her. The altered world. She grabbed a piece of driftwood as Ella sniffed at it. Her mind would not stop racing over what Frank had told her — two Americans, why would Americans be on the island now?

It was impossible, dragging the driftwood, not to catch a flicker of lime green out of the corner of her eye. Miranda turned her back again. Haul, haul, haul. Clouds flew overhead. The reek of kelp was thick in her nose, rust-red kelp covered the rocks all along the shore, the air tugging at the salt smell. The kelp needed to be gathered before the tide rose again and pulled it all back out to sea. When she looked up, Frank was beyond the row of conifers, on the footpath that led into the fields. With a hitch in his stride, he stopped at the first weather monitor, Marty, the insect-like one, peered at it without touching. A ripple of emotion travelled through Miranda, misgiving and something else. The next time she looked, Frank was standing in front of the second monitor, inspecting the little white house on its pole, which was technically called a Stevenson screen but they called Iceland. Even farther out, the wind sock continued its jittery dance. Suddenly it seemed pointless to run away from him. She did not want to run away from him, even though she was glad he was a good distance off.

Closer still, Frank called out, "Miranda, do you need any help?"

"Not really," she called back. She pulled off her gloves and wiped an arm across her forehead. "Except for the kelp."

When Ella trotted up to him, tail wagging, Frank ruffled her black fur. Kicking at the toilet seat she'd dropped on top of the siding, he asked Miranda where she thought it came from.

"Hard to say. The sea brings strange gifts." And then, "The water was really high last night, higher than it's ever been."

"Ever?"

Frank's face kept shifting, it was full of so many things,

maybe new vulnerabilities alongside old ones. He looked about to say one thing, then, with a quick frown, changed his mind. Something else opened in him, demanding her attention.

"Miranda," he said. "Can I tell you something?" He didn't wait for her reply. "I think my father's on the island."

"Your father?" Once more the whole world gave a great tilt.

"And my uncle. The Americans I was talking about, that's them."

His father. "Why would your father be on Blaze Island?"

"It's kind of a long story. It'd be best if we can go somewhere we won't be disturbed. I know we're out in a field and all but if your father came back it would be awkward because I'd really like to explain all this just to you."

"You told us you were looking for birds."

"Let me explain some more, then you can judge me." A gull flew overhead, its shadow travelling over them both.

A story came to Miranda, one her father had told her those first summers in the cove, lying in bed beside her, holding her hand. He said he'd heard the story long ago from Inuit hunters with whom he'd gone sealing while he, in return, had offered them stories about selkies who shed their seal skins and took human form. Agnes Watson had recounted a different version of the tale on the day they'd processed the seal, after Miranda had returned from the shore with the forgotten knife.

A young woman refuses to marry any of the young men in her village. One day a good-looking stranger appears, and she agrees to marry him. As soon as they are married, her husband turns into a large seabird and carries the young woman away to an island across the sea. One day, missing his daughter, her father sets off across the sea in his skin boat. Upon reaching the island, he begs his daughter, who has grown bored of her life, fed nothing but fish and often left alone by her seabird husband, to come away with him. She agrees, but when he discovers the girl missing, her husband, a powerful magician, grows angry and flies after them, swooping so close to the father's little boat that his wings cause a great storm. The father throws his daughter overboard, offering her back to her bird husband, but the daughter clings to the side of the boat, pleading with her father to rescue her. Her desperate father chops off the first knuckles of her fingers, which fall into the water and become seals. Still she clings to the boat, pleading. He chops off the next joints, which become walruses. Finally he chops off the last joints of her fingers, which transform into whales, and the girl sinks to the depths of the ocean to become Sedna, mother of the sea, stirrer of storms, and protectress of all sea creatures. When at last he reaches home, her father collapses on shore, filled with remorse, and lets the tide sweep him out to join his daughter.

Once, as he kissed her good night, Miranda's father had added something else: The waters all around us, these are Sedna's seas.

Still dizzy with Frank's revelation, Miranda wedged her gloves under a rock, one that the sea must have moved, because it hadn't been in the field the day before. It was as if she had come to a decision without knowing how. She whistled to

Ella and called, "This way." Filled with anxiety flecked with excitement, she led Frank past a copper-coloured pond frilled with tiny waves to the big mound of boulders where cove met sea. Here were the rocks she'd named as a child, Sharp One and Craggy, the one with flecks of quartz that she'd called Jenny after her mother.

The shore path led into a gulch and up the winding slope of Bunker Hill, where Americans had built a bunker to watch for German submarines in the Atlantic, long ago during the Second World War. That's what Pat Green had told her. Ella darted ahead, while Miranda scrambled over the skittering pebbles, Frank at her heels.

At the summit, there was nothing left of the bunker but a cement slab crumbling under the dazzling sky. Miranda waited for Frank to catch his breath, to take in where he really was. Her world spread out below them, the silvery cove, her little white house with its moss-covered roof on one side and solar panels on the other, the familiar view she loved to paint and sketch. Over there on the far shore a small, thin polar bear had swum to land the previous spring as Miranda watched apprehensively through binoculars. Awesome, she heard Frank whisper. She stared at him. The disruptive stranger, he seemed entranced, and Miranda felt herself pulled out of her own body, allowed to see the world below through Frank's eyes. The next moment, he'd pulled up the binoculars still dangling around his neck. Again she caught a slip of the black marks, closer now. His tattoo. Possibly it was best to let Frank discover for himself that there was no scientific research station across the cove. Instead she mentioned the polar bear. Which made Frank go taut.

"There are polar bears on this island?"

"Rarely. Only in the spring. They swim ashore from ice floes."

Then she had to promise him that there really, really were no polar bears on the island now.

"You have to cross your heart."

She crossed her heart. "Is your father a scientist?" she asked as Frank trained his binoculars on the broken cell tower.

The face he turned on her then was so extraordinary in its mixture of disbelief and rearrangement and private hilarity that Miranda barely knew what to make of it.

"No," was all Frank said.

Earlier, he'd mentioned his father arriving by plane. As far as Miranda knew, there'd been only the one small plane circling to land the day before. Her father seemed to have spoken to someone arriving on that flight. Did that mean her father knew Frank's father? This thought was so perplexing, Miranda had to swerve in the other direction, to face Pummelly's ring of houses spread around its double harbour, *like ventricles of a heart*, Caleb had said to her once. Beyond the village, UpABack Cove glittered. Beyond that, the island's rocky shoreline curved out of sight. Frank had dropped the binoculars, following her gaze, and Miranda felt him breathe in and out, as if momentarily letting go of whatever gripped him, allowing the sky above and the water all around to imprint themselves on him.

She led him down the hill's far side, faster now, where the path wound through mounds of partridgeberries, shiny greenery and red berries scattered among the rocks. While Ella sniffed at a fox's whitened skull, Miranda stopped to pick some of the roundest, ripest berries, offering the little red globes to Frank. Who was Frank's father and why was he on Blaze Island? Was she sure she wanted to know? Frank's mouth exclaimed at the tartness, but the next moment he was crouching to pick more himself, they were both stuffing berries into their mouths, until Frank's prior urgency to tell her his story overtook him and he stood up.

Farther along the path, the rocks flattened out before tumbling at the shore into more boulders, the land part of an ancient volcano now tipped on its side. Off to the left, over a small pool tucked in a rock dip, rose a handful of bigger boulders. Miranda led Frank this way. Here was a place she sometimes came when she wanted to be truly by herself, hidden by slabs of granite and gabbro yet within easy reach of her house, invisible from the path that led between cove and village, out of reach of anyone who might come in search of her. She leaped over the pool. Their boots made wallowing sounds as they landed. Here they were close to the waves and their smashing spray, the granite wet with it. Finding a seat on the damp, flat surface, boulder at her back, Miranda patted the rock beside her and Frank sat, crossing his ankles, the rips in his jeans revealing crescent slices of bare knee. With a glance at her, he began to speak.

"Let's get this first part over with. My father. You know Tempus Airlines and Roy Hansen, the man who founded it. The name Hansen, remind you of anything?" There was a bite in his tone that took Miranda aback.

"I don't know anything about Tempus Airlines. Or Roy Hansen," she said.

Once more Frank's face contorted. Miranda had an

impression of a thousand faces crossing his quick and mobile face, volatility and disbelief, and then Frank said, "Are you sure?" She couldn't tell if he was angry or about to laugh.

Embarrassed, Miranda squeezed her hands. She'd brought him to her secret place and now his febrile energy was twisting it. "I don't fly. I haven't since I was two, so I don't really pay attention to airlines. We don't leave the island. Everything we need is here."

"Really?"

Actually, she told him, she went fishing, she'd been as far as the Little Fish, pointing to the misted, rocky humps that lay at the horizon, and once out into the bay, so it wasn't strictly true that she'd never left. Also, he might as well know this now, she didn't own a cellphone, didn't want one either, she didn't live the way other people lived. But the name, Hansen, Hansen, it was rocketing through her, making its own connections —

Frank leaped to his feet. "Okay, I get that, a totally admirable commitment to the local, and the cellphone thing, truly noble — but, like, Roy Hansen, of that band the Echo Men, they were famous — before our time, I guess. Then he goes on to fall in love with flying and, you know, figures out a way to buy one airline, then another. Next thing, he's this mega celebrity-entrepreneur, an American darling."

She was putting together the trembling pieces that were there to be put together, even if she'd never heard of this man in her life. "That's your father? Your father owns an airline company?" If so, didn't this make Frank's father the enemy of everything her own father believed in?

Frank's body seemed to imply that he was waiting for something. A wave shot through him. He swung his arms and bent over with a huff of breath, which made Ella come running from wherever she was. Frank rose up, shaking his head. Laughing? "It's the most awesome thing that you have no idea who my father is."

Scrambling to her feet, Miranda barely knew what to say or ask. Again a warning sliver of danger entered her. Danger. Spray leaped in front of them, drops brushing her face. "Why would your father be on Blaze Island?"

"Can we back up a bit?" Frank said. "Can I tell you a little more first? Yes, my father's this total venture capitalist who makes—steals—obscene amounts of money and people say he only has to touch things for them to turn to gold, though I should add he's had more than a few business busts in his time. And I really do live with housemates in, like, a co-op in an old house in Somerville, or I did, if it hasn't floated away."

His words broke over Miranda as she stared at the flecks of quartz and feldspar winking in the granite. His mother was a famous Japanese American jewellery designer, Naoko Tanaka, Frank said. Naturally Miranda had never heard of her, either. His father had grown up white and half-Irish and poor in Columbus, Ohio. At least one of them, his sister Keiko, had inherited the capitalist gene—Frank got the recessive, activist one. *I came into the world this way.*

His mother was there in Frank's face, his cheekbones, his eyes, his black hair. That's what Miranda was seeing. And the tattoo. Japanese characters on the inner skin of his forearm, even closer now, close enough to touch. Perhaps Frank's lanky height came from his father. So he had a mother and a father, a sister, and the life he was describing hurtled him a million miles away from her.

"When I was twelve," Frank said, "they sent me away to boarding school for the first time. I kept getting into trouble because I went around telling all the other kids that capitalism was a form of cancer, unstoppable growth, right, or a brain-wasting disease like BSE, and would kill them, them and their parents, too.

"When I got kicked out of that school, my parents decided to try again. I went along with it because I thought school would be better than living at home, which by then meant their palace of a Manhattan apartment, not that either of them was there much, they're always taking off in some private jet for one of their many houses — or a beach or someone's yacht. Just being in that apartment made me feel complicit in, like, everything. Me, half the time alone in this humongous space. They didn't want to leave me there either because they were frightened I'd start giving things away. So, this time, back at school, I started organizing rallies for basic income and tax-the-rich policies. It was in the middle of the Great Recession.

"That's when I met Colson Barnett, this brilliant philosophy teacher and poet who grew up black and poor in Detroit, and through some twist of fate ended up teaching kids like me, nurturing the closet and not-so-closet anarcho-Marxist nihilists. Colson decided to take me under his wing, so to speak. Birding is a thing Colson loves. He said it's hard to be angry when you're out in the woods even though the birds are vanishing and birders who look like him are a rarer breed than that. Because I admired Colson so much for being nothing like my father, I went along with him, forest bathing and birdwatching in the woods of New Hampshire. That's how I know what I know about birds."

When Frank's jacket brushed Miranda's arm, a dart sped through her.

"Anyway, to speed everything up, a few months ago, I received a letter, an actual letter in the mail, addressed to me, handwritten, which made it possibly creepy but so unusual I had to open it. I get kooky stuff sent to me sometimes, people trying to reach my dad, like fan letters, even hate mail."

Frank kept glancing across intently, as if while spilling all these things he was simultaneously trying hard to take her in, too. "Miranda, do you know what solar geoengineering is? Solar radiation management, does that mean anything to you?"

On the edge of the flat rocks, by the little pool, Ella gave a bark. Of warning? They weren't hidden standing where they were, as they would have been if seated, tucked against the boulders. Anyone coming up over Lighthouse Hill from town would be able to spot their two figures among the red rocks. One distant figure, then another rose above the crest of the hill, two women, one tall with a flood of hair.

"I'll be right back," Miranda said, breath loud in her ears. Ella had gone running towards the women. The tall one, Sylvia, turned and retreated out of sight, leaving Christine Brett, in slacks and windbreaker, to continue down the near side of the hill with sturdy purpose, making her way along the winding path until she was close enough to call, "Miranda, do you know where Caleb's at? We've not seen him since this morning. He was supposed to bring a can of gasoline back for us."

"He's running an errand for my father," Miranda shouted, reddening. The wind boxed her ears. She felt Christine take in Frank's presence, wherever he was behind her. Frank's attention was a new skin all over her. The next moment, as if reading her mind, Christine was asking if that was the American who'd driven into the flood, and Miranda called back yes. She almost stumbled on the rocks under her feet, the sense of worlds colliding was so intense.

A look of concern crossed Frank's face when she returned. "Are you all right?"

"Let's move off a ways."

He followed her back up the slope to a flat place below the summit of Bunker Hill. Down in the cove there was, as yet, no sign of her father's quad. Across the cove rose the emphatic presence of Cape House. Miranda touched the rock beneath her to make sure it was still there.

"One other thing you need to know is my father has set up this foundation to fund research into tech innovations like alternative airline fuels and carbon sequestration plants." Frank hugged his chest as they halted. "Things that make it look like he cares deeply about the problem of the climate, about greenhouse gas build-up, which is completely hypocritical, given all the emissions spewing from his planes — and his desire to launch a mission to Mars, I kid you not. He's got a wing of his foundation devoted to that, too. Basically he's this carbon pirate and he won't stop, he wants to keep expanding."

Somehow they were back on top of Bunker Hill. There was fervour and vulnerability in Frank's stance along with an acerbic twitching at the corners of his mouth. "Miranda? Do you want me to stop talking? You have a peculiar expression on your face. It's truly not my intention to disturb your beautiful life."

Everything came at her acutely, shifts of moisture and air pressure as the air touched Frank's face, the way he spoke her father's forbidden word *climate*, all these new and uncontrollable feelings.

It was as if she'd been living in a bubble. It was a beautiful bubble, yes, a bubble that she and her father had created. Frank was outside it, punching at its membrane with his words. Moments before, he'd told her how, at college, he left his freshmen dorm one day to join the occupy movement in New York, protesting and living in a tent for weeks, before running off to do the same in London. He could fly for free and he'd taken advantage of this — *for only the best reasons, Miranda* — adding his body and voice to protests in Rio and Lima, protests against the capitalist barons who ruled the world, who believed in infinite growth and would gouge every corner of the Earth to attain it, who kept all the money for themselves leaving wreckage for everyone else, which meant of course his father. As he spoke, Miranda pictured this: the barons, crowds of protesting people, Frank with a knapsack over his back, wearing his ratty sweater, racing from place to place to be with so many others. Had the other protesters known who his father was, she asked. Some did, Frank said, some didn't.

She'd heard vaguely of the things that Frank described but she'd allowed the outer world to fall away because it had torn a life from her and it felt good to let it go. The exhilaration, the hope in those crowds, it was like a drug, Frank said. He'd been arrested in London and tear-gassed in Hong Kong. His father, disgusted, had cut off contact with him for months. In the past year, he'd stopped flying, mostly — *Miranda, I swear* — and was working for a local co-op in Boston, whose workers were fighting to reclaim their factory, which had made plastic takeout dishes; they wanted to retool it to make compostable or even edible ones. It was as if, while offering this account of himself, Frank was trying to hold his long limbs together, to stop them from flying off. There was a pain in him that Miranda couldn't place or reach.

She ought to tell him that the world she knew was nothing like this and had more than people in it: wind and trees and plants, she was someone who spoke to plants and considered trees her kin. In retreat you could make your own life. Escape some of the world's horrors. Frank was a disturber. This was what he did. He was full of indignation. And yet: Miranda felt like a curious fawn at the edge of the widest clearing.

On top of Bunker Hill, Frank stood without speaking.

"Just tell me what you want to tell me," Miranda said.

She had to step close to hear him say, "Are you sure?" Close enough for him to see her nod.

The touch he gave her then was no doubt meant as reassurance, yet it sent a ricochet of dizziness through her.

"What was in the letter?" Miranda asked, her voice so breathless she had to repeat the words.

This time Frank was the one who first stepped onto the path. "It was sent to me by someone named Anouk Sand. I didn't know if that was a man's name or a woman's. What the letter said was that my father, through his innovation fund, has plans to back this private company involved in solar radiation management research."

"What does that mean?" Miranda heard herself ask as the echo of other overheard words streamed through her.

"You spray tons of particulate matter up into the stratosphere, most likely from jets, so all the little particles create a haze, which wraps the Earth. The sun's rays bounce off the particles and are reflected back into space. Supposedly this prevents temperatures from rising so fast. Kind of like what happens with a volcano, when it spews volcanic dust and the dust forms a cloud that stays in the atmosphere for years, and makes temperatures drop. Except the atmosphere is extremely unpredictable, so there's a big risk, say, if you spray sulfur particles, of increasing the hole in the ozone layer and generally disturbing weather patterns even more, causing more floods and droughts, especially, like, in equatorial regions, or messing with major ocean currents. But it's alluring because the technology's basically there, and the weather, well it's pretty hard to disagree with the fact that it's growing wilder all the time.

"Any experiments in the field, even small ones, are highly contested, since there's only one atmosphere, and what happens if things mess up? Because, all things considered, the technology's fairly easy to implement, there's actually not much to stop rogue nations, or some private dude with a ton of money, from deciding, Hey, I'm going to do something about all this crazy weather. I'm sure you can see where I'm going, like it's totally the kind of thing my father would be jonesing for. Specialized jets to carry the stuff into space, thousands of flights a year for years? Which is what people are talking about. Oh my God, he'd want to believe it's our salvation. And he'd want to be the one bringing it about."

They'd reached the gulch, where the water sucked in and out with ferocity and residual storm force, hollowing out the old rock into a great, round bowl as it had done for eons before humans had been around to see it, and likely would for eons more. It was possible to stand for a moment staring into its depths and wonder anxiously, without saying anything at all, what the future might bring. Frank fell silent. There was heat inside Miranda, pressure building up behind her ribs.

Why would her father have anything to do with a man like Frank's father? With a plan like what Frank had just described? Had she ever heard him discuss anything of this nature? Jets? Frank's father doing the spraying? One night only months before, leaning over her in bed, her father had kissed her forehead and whispered strange words. *I do nothing but in care of thee.* How far would he go in his experiments? What did it mean for the life to come if even here she wasn't safe?

Once her father had explained to Miranda how all the carbon humans had put into the atmosphere was like water in a bathtub. Even if you turned off the tap, the water level wouldn't go down or would at least take a very long time to drain, as if the drain were only open the tiniest bit. The past, human actions in the recent past, would linger in the sky above them. For a long time, he'd said. One day, left on her own, she'd gone leafing through one of his books and discovered the truth: some of the carbon gases would stay in the atmosphere for hundreds of thousands of years.

"Was there more in the letter?" Miranda asked Frank as a flicker of disturbance passed through her.

"It said this private company, Assisted Radiation Interception Engineering Limited, ARIEL for short, is doing some research up on this remote island off the coast of Canada, private research, and my father had plans to go up there to meet with the company about investing in it. The letter even named dates. I had no idea why this person was writing to me, why they thought I'd want to know, if any of it was even true. But once I knew, I couldn't unknow it. Knowing, I couldn't ignore it, could I? There was no easy way to track this person down—no address of any sort. I couldn't find anything on-line about the company either, which I guess isn't surprising because if you're doing this kind of research privately, you'd want to keep your operations far out of sight.

"My father was supposed to be flying through Boston. Sometimes he texts me when he's coming to town. Mostly I tell him I'm busy, but this time I suggested meeting up. Meanwhile, I was trying frantically to bone up on SRM tech-nology—that's solar radiation management in the lingo. I wasn't sure exactly what I was going to do, but in this hotel bar I managed to ask him what he thought about it. Enticing, is what he said. He got this look on his face I've seen before. The next thing I know he's asking if I'm interested in going on a little expedition with him and my uncle Leonard, who's his younger brother and kind of his yes man. Maybe he thought I'd undergone a conversion, back to the techno-corporate side. He was cagey with details, but the dates matched those in the letter. Hurricane Fernand was already forming in the Caribbean. He said he was going regardless. I said yes, then, after this sleepless night, thought, I can't do it.

"The letter was still gnawing at me, though. It was like this person wanted me to go, complete with the instruction, Go to the end of the island. So I thought, maybe I should take off after all. I left, driving like a maniac, as you know, and here I am, despite almost dying in that flood. Maybe my father never made it. Or this project isn't happening here? That makes no sense. Why am I here? Help me, Miranda."

She had no idea how to answer. How confused and helpless Frank looked, shoulders pulled tight as he faced her.

Somehow they had ended up back in the field by the kelp-covered rocks. Her father had left her alone with this person, who, despite the awfulness of some of what he'd told her, did not sound despairing.

"Why do you want to find your father?"

"What he's planning is so nightmarish it shouldn't be allowed to happen."

"What if—if things get so bad we need something like this to protect us? At least for a while." All around her swirled the turbulent haze of other people's plans. Her own feelings were a pack of surging clouds. A mist of particles in the air: she tried to imagine it. A week ago, her father had come running up to the garden, where Miranda had been pulling up onions, and, face aghast, told her the museum her mother had loved more than any other, in the foothills of Los Angeles, where unstoppable brush fires had been razing neighbourhoods for days, had gone up in smoke. Panic lurched through her at the news. In far-off Australia, he said as if he couldn't help himself, the city of Sydney was threatened by wildfires, too, its skies turned sizzling orange. "If it's an emergency?"

"Not like this, Miranda."

In front of them were the piles of storm wreckage she'd gathered, the storm-flattened grass, the rocks the violent sea had moved in the night. Frank walked to the shore. From the nearest rocks he scooped an armful of kelp and asked where he should put it. Carry it into the field, Miranda told him distractedly, gathering an armful herself and burying her nose in a reek so strong it made her forget everything else.

"Do you think I should talk to your father about all this?" Frank asked.

"Don't do that." She spoke faster and more firmly than she'd intended. Her first instinct was to protect her father, to deny his secrets, and in doing so protect herself. The trail that led around back of Green Cove Pond, the one her father had taken, would be muddy, and the flat bank of stratus cloud rising out of the south made it look like a shower was coming. Surely he'd be back soon. She could send Frank away. He'd be on foot and have no idea where he was going. All she had to do was point him in that direction.

If he left, her world would contract again. Did she want that? Yes, and yet, in the deepest part of her, she did not. "Yesterday afternoon I saw a small plane coming in to land."

"You did?" Frank was all over her in an instant. "Where? What time? How small a plane? What did it look like? Are you sure you haven't seen it take off?"

A car, a rust-coloured compact, came speeding down the road from Telephone Hill, remarkable for being the only car Miranda had seen approaching the cove that day. Either someone didn't know about the washout or was planning to inspect it. The car looked vaguely familiar, one she must sometimes have seen parked outside Pierce's supermarket, a car from Tom's Neck. Sensing the shift in her attention, Frank turned as the car vanished into the alder trees and mountain ash on the lower stretch of the slope near Cape House lane. It didn't reappear. Without her needing to ask, Frank handed over the binoculars.

Miranda searched for rust-coloured metal among the green. Something, no, someone was moving along the lane, dark head bobbing. Flattened by the binoculars' focus, Caleb looked particularly purposeful and intense.

"It's Caleb Borders," she explained, her head filled with a new throb, that Caleb was likely going to work on Cape House, that he must have finished whatever he was doing for her father.

"What kind of work does Caleb do for your father, Miranda?"

"Runs errands. Cuts wood, delivers things." Describing Caleb with such dispassion made each word feel like a betrayal. Her heart flew out to him. Still, it was a shock to hear herself say, "We can ask Caleb if he knows anything."

Why? Why had she done that? Because Caleb might indeed know something about the plane or Frank's father. Have heard something.

And yet. Wasn't it perverse to suggest speaking to Caleb when she wasn't supposed to talk to him at all? Only she, too, needed to know about the plane and who was on it. Despite all that had happened between them, Caleb might understand this urgency and be entreated to help.

Tucked up against the grassy mound of the root cellar in the near field lay their white punt, held down by stones lodged under the gunwales and magically untouched by the storm. With luck the two sets of oars her father had temporarily stowed in the dark, earthy cave of the root cellar would still be there.

"Can you row?" Miranda asked Frank. Everything in her clarified around the conviction that she needed to find the courage to speak to Caleb herself.

. . .

From his perch on a ladder propped against the wall of Cape
House, Caleb heard the most astonishing sound. A voice,
tussled away from him by the wind and pushed out to sea,
a voice that hadn't addressed him in more than a year, was
calling his name. A miracle. Pleasure and relief almost made
him fall.

He stumbled down the rungs. He'd been extracting the
screws he'd inserted only that morning to hold boards over
the now-exposed windows whose glass had broken in the
storm. With a screwdriver, the cordless drill having run out
of power. Because it made no sense to bring Len Hansen
and Tony McIntosh to Cape House only to show them rooms
shuttered in darkness while being forced to describe the thrill
of the view.

Walking towards him, Miranda was asking what had happened to his windows, had the storm broken them?

"Yes," Caleb said feverishly.

His voice broke, happy in his throat, blood warming every
part of him. Now, once more, he could say her name. Her dark
hair flowed from beneath her blue wool cap. Her cheeks were
pink, as if she'd been exerting herself, and no doubt because
she was nervous, which aroused a tenderness in Caleb so huge

it threatened to dissolve him altogether. In the months since he'd last had the chance to really look at her, she'd grown older, her face finding a new slenderness over the bones. Those lips. He reached out a hand. He would have knelt in front of her. Seeing her was like being pelted with stones. It struck him that she had appeared from the direction of the headlands, not from the side of the house that faced the road, which was unusual. Up on the ladder, back to the water, he wouldn't have seen her if she'd come in boat.

"Is it okay to talk?" The warmth of her questions was a resumption of all that was. Things that had been broken were unbreaking themselves.

"Yes," Caleb said again. He wanted to shout it.

It didn't matter what she had told her father about their journey out on the water that day. He would forgive her for it. Time curved around them like a bowl. Off to Caleb's left, a chipping sparrow landed on an alder branch and a fox, curled with her bushy tail around her, flicked her ears at the rustle of small animals digging in the earth. He had to incorporate all this into the moment, these awarenesses that came to him unbidden, although when he had told Miranda about such experiences she'd said it wasn't so strange. Caleb's heart sang with the conviction, always held in his deepest places, that somehow they would find their way to this moment. The future thrummed in his body, their future knitted together out of the past. He loved her. He always had.

Someone else was stepping out of the spruce trees and alder woods, from the footpath onto the grass. A young man, thin and long-limbed, with wind-strewn black hair and pale brown skin. His eager lope shattered the moment like glass.

The hair rose at the back of Caleb's neck. Was this the

other American, the young fellow who'd crashed his car in the cove? What right did he have to be slamming into a moment as precious and longed-for as this?

Miranda was saying something. It was hard to hear her over the pounding of blood in his ears. Frank. The stranger's name, the stranger who was holding out his hand in the misguided assumption that he, Caleb, was going to shake it. A new unpredictability whipped around him. The stranger's smile was full of the oppressive assurance of someone convinced that everyone he meets will smile right back.

"Caleb, can you help us?" Miranda said.

There was intimacy in her appeal, she was so close, even as the word *us* went ripping through Caleb. What did she mean by it? She was saying something about the airstrip, wondering who had come in on that plane. Her eyes were agitated, and for the life of him he couldn't decipher what was in them.

"Do you know anything?" she asked. "Frank's looking for people. He thinks they might have flown in yesterday. I told him I thought you might know something about them, you might be able to help."

"Two Americans," the young man was saying in his American voice, "very tall, one has this, like, shock of white hair."

It could not be that she had broken the silence between them, defied her father, simply in order to help someone else, even as Caleb quaked at the horror of this convergence — what did this stranger want with the other men, what did she want with them?

"Why ask me? Why not ask your father?"

What cracked, bruised part of him, buried deep inside, erupted in a shout?

—

The shock of that shout was still in him when a rain cloud opened over Caleb as he pelted along Cape House lane, away from the house, away from the girl and the stranger, and all he felt, as the rain soaked him, was, *I deserve this.* He raised his face to the sky and yelled the words aloud.

Shouting was the worst thing he could have done, yet he'd done it. Why? He ran until he found himself back at Della's car, parked at the mouth of the lane. He tried to push away those terrible moments. On foot, he went on, in the direction of Pummelly, clambering over the washout's jagged edge. Current swift against his boots, he grabbed chunks of concrete to keep his balance as he fought the water and rock-strewn ground, lunging his way across. He brought failure on himself. He wanted to step on rocks and crack his feet open. Sometime in the night, the stranger had escaped from all of this, why should he be the lucky one, his wreck of a car hauled out and glittering on the washout's far side.

Beyond a copse of alders, the cove opened, a mess of storm debris rising in the landwash, sticks, wood, more wood, nylon rope, plastic, and beyond it, slate-coloured water swelling over the place where the old man had once shouted at him. Out on the water, the girl — again it was too painful to say her name — and the stranger in the little white boat, pulled hard against wind and tide. She was out there, unreachable, unless Caleb ran down her lane and met the two of them at shore. Which was impossible. What was he going to say to her now? Shout at her again? Besides, her father's quad was pulled up near the house, and the sight made Caleb gag.

At his own house, no sooner had he tugged off his boots than his mother was looming in the kitchen doorway, like an island when the air pressure sank, the world still so full of parents. She must have been outdoors not long before because a trace of wind clung to her hair.

"My, look who it is," she said, Caleb's breath still heaving.

"How's it going, Mom? Did you make it round to Mary Green's?"

"Now where would you be coming from in such a hurry?"

"Fetching a few things."

She threw out an arm, barring his way. "Fetching what things, Caleb? For whom?"

"Doing a bit of tidying up at Cape House."

She stood before him, tall and insistent, a keen one, his mother, with her sharp eyes and intellect and pride and temper, the flames of her hair streaked now with ashes. Hard to get anything past her, even as she relentlessly kept things from him.

"Tidying, Caleb? What are you about?"

He'd never been able to talk to her about his dream of a future with the girl at his side, at first because his own dream so hugely interfered with hers. And then because of her unvoiced disapproval. She might not like the father anymore but she liked the girl, she always had. So why, why would his mother not want him to love the girl and the girl to love him back and live with him in the house he was making ready for them both? He didn't know why, only he sensed his mother's resistance. With a dive, Caleb scooted under her outstretched arm, past the waving velvet curtain.

"Fixing things up for my visitors." He shouldn't have said that.

"Visitors? What visitors might those be? Caleb, please tell me this isn't something Alan Wells has roped you into."

Thankfully the fridge was on the other side of the room. Dark when Caleb opened the door because there was no power. As fast as he could, he stuffed a packet of cheese in the pocket of his coveralls. Opened the freezer door. He was trying to come up with a plan, a Plan B, on the spot. A small bag of ice stung when he shoved it under his arm. He unhooked a small cast-iron saucepan from those hanging beside the stove.

"Mom, listen, I'll tell you everything when it's over, all right?"

She hated her library job because almost no one ever came to the library except for the girl and Charlize Petton, who claimed to have read every book on the shelves, and Joe Cluett, who didn't own a computer or a cellphone, and himself sometimes to visit his lonely mother. The emptiness of the library made her despair.

If this hadn't been a day of storm cleanup, she might have been out in the hills or taking her brother Tom's speedboat out to one of the uninhabited Little Blaze Islands in the bay to go berry picking. Though his mother had shown less interest in picking berries than she used to, last year and this. Oh, she still picked, but there was a listlessness in her, a hardness to her lanky, careless beauty, as if she were doing things now only because she had to, not because of her commitment to the old ways.

The queer weather disturbed her, growing queerer with every year. She spent more time in her armchair, staring out to sea, or taking the car and driving off who knew where. The rain was no longer the same rain, she said. The wind, harsh as it was, used to be something you could depend on. Now, she said, it was as undependable as most human beings were.

In the parlour liquor cabinet was a bottle of Scotch that Caleb knew she never drank. The old man had brought it long ago, in the days when he and Caleb's mother would sometimes sit and drink together, the old man with his Scotch whisky, his mother her beloved Irish.

"Caleb, put that bottle back." A deeper sharpness had entered her voice.

"You'll never drink it. It's wasted here."

"Put it back, I said." She'd left the kitchen doorway and was striding towards him, and Caleb had the sudden fear that she was about to hit him.

"I'll put it back if you tell me who my father was."

This made her blanch as he knew it would and stopped her in her tracks. The skin grew tight across her cheekbones. "Caleb, you know I can't do that. I made a promise."

"Bad promises aren't ones you have to keep."

"He's no part of our lives, that's the way it is."

"Do you look at me and see him?" What did she see? How often he had wondered this even as the ferocity of her love wrapped him round.

"Long ago, I had to make a choice, Caleb, between you and a man who told me he had no wish to be a father. Either it would break him, he said, or he'd inflict harm as he'd had harm inflicted on him. I've told you this. He agreed I had a choice, but if I chose you, he would disappear, and I'd have to do my part to make him disappear. So I've kept my promise to say nothing about him. I chose you."

Given the chance, Caleb still searched the house for clues. Whatever she was hiding, he trusted she wouldn't have picked a monster. A Labrador trapper, oil-rig worker, man from a Caribbean island, some kind of footloose charmer, who'd dreamed since boyhood of finding a new life in the North. Most often this was what he allowed himself to imagine. But why did her stubbornness never waver, as if she were determined, above all, to be true to some younger, hopeful, even more stubborn version of herself? The girl at least had a mother, even if her mother was dead.

"He made me slippers," Caleb said. Sometimes his own mother hugged him so tight he feared his bones would snap.

"Slippers?"

"Rabbit-fur slippers and a rabbit-foot charm. He gave them to me, I remember, he slipped them over my feet."

"Oh, Caleb, no. We'd moved out of town by then, into the house in the woods. Other people came to help me, those were made for you by someone else." Her colour had risen, he didn't know what that meant, only the soft dream he'd harboured, of the man leaning gently over him, whispering oh so tenderly as he slid Caleb's tiny feet into the warmth of fur, went out like a failed match.

"Was he Trinidadian? Dominican?"

"Put down the bottle, Caleb."

In the future, he'd make tea for the girl and bring it to her in bed, as his mother had once done for him. There was such pleasure in the long twinning of their lives. That they should go on entwining, it was everything. Outside Cape House, after breakfast, the girl would slip two fingers between her teeth and whistle the strong note that made her dog come running from wherever she was. Beside her hovered the mist of a child. A child. Surely it was possible. He'd be a father, the kind he'd never had. He'd still dream of his missing father but all this would be enough. If she wanted, there'd be room for his mother in the big house, too. A rocking chair in the parlour, where she might sit by the wood stove and stare out to sea for as long as she liked. Drink her whiskey. Caleb would look after her, build walls that were tight and firm and clasped her close, make a home, keep the harsh and changing weather outside.

"I'm doing this for you," Caleb shouted as he fled.

"You're late," Tony McIntosh called from the lawn of Teresa Blake's guesthouse. And Caleb, who had just pulled into the gravel parking spot and stepped out of Della's rust-coloured car, was very late.

So many things had happened since he'd last set eyes on the men that Caleb felt ghostly. Everything repeated itself. Len Hansen was pacing across the grass. Rufus, Teresa's old Lab, who appeared to have moved a body's length to the west, twitched in his sleep.

There was no sign of Roy or Anna, which was some relief.

Tony dragged on his cigarette, down to the filter, the nub glowing like a fiery star. Len paused in his pacing, charged with impatience, as if he wasn't sure whether to confront Caleb or bolt. He was wearing the shoes he'd had on when Caleb picked the men up from the airport the afternoon before, in the mists of time before the storm had come. Black loafers with tassels. He'll want boots, Caleb thought, but said nothing.

This time, when Tony ground his cigarette into the earth, Caleb bent to pick the butt from the grass.

"So I encountered some unexpected delays, see," Caleb said, aware that his damp overalls gave off a fetid smell. "It's that kind of day. But, look, I've found us a vehicle."

"You're lucky we waited," Tony said with an irritable hauteur that made Caleb wonder why he was acting not only like his boss but the boss of all things. Once more Len checked his non-functioning phone, before mentioning that Roy and Anna had driven back to the ferry dock since Roy was determined to find a way off the island as soon as possible. With a glance at the car, Len asked anxiously if there would be walking and Caleb said not much.

The two men safely ensconced in the back seat, Caleb circled around the harbour, the way he'd just come, past Ruby's Convenience, where a handwritten sign on a piece of cardboard now read, No Water or Gas. When he asked the men how their dinner had been, hopeful for some good news, both men shrugged — as if the meal, no doubt splendid, had already vaporized.

A young fellow, Caleb told them, sentenced to hang for stealing a horse, had managed to escape prison, flee England, fetch up on Blaze Island, and live long enough to give the village of Tom's Neck its name — seeing as how his neck and all his other body parts were spared. As an innkeeper, Caleb would want to tell his guests such stories.

When his grandmother and sisters were young and power first came to the island, Caleb said, each family had been given a light bulb.

"One light bulb?" Len seemed stricken by disbelief. "What good is that?"

Tony, after doing some internal computation, said, "Like, you mean, sixty years ago? There was no electricity here before then? That's insane."

Yet with the power out, and limited gasoline to fuel generators, they might soon be reduced to candles once again.

When Caleb tried to ply the men for more information about the after-effects of Hurricane Fernand, they could tell him little more than what he knew, the states of emergency declared, how it would take decades to recover, although, Len insisted, that was bound to be an exaggeration.

"What's your occupation?" Caleb asked Tony, glancing back to catch a glimpse of the man's protuberant face as he took the turn that led out of town. He wanted them to think him friendly. He wanted them to confide in him.

"Professor," said Tony.

Caleb had to muffle his surprise.

"Of economics," Len chimed in. "Tony's famous for his articulation of the virtues of neo-liberalism, deregulation, an expert in the petroleum economy. Also once famous because of a blog."

"About economics?"

"The climate," said Len almost lazily. "Tony's always been prepared to say necessary things about the, let's call them, known unknowns and unknown unknowns, introducing doubts when doubts seem useful. Though these days he's a little more *sotto voce* about all that."

"*Realpolitik, realpolitik*, that's how it goes," said Tony.

It sounded as if, one way or another, Tony did have some interest in the weather.

"Len's the CFO of the company and Roy's the CEO, in case you haven't figured that out, and I'm one of their beloved advisers," Tony added from behind Caleb's head, "but in a behind-the-scenes kind of way, so keep that between you, us, and the fence post."

The company. No one had yet told Caleb what the company was.

Outside the car, along the winding road to Pummelly, ponds glittered. Steady Pond. Dutchman's Pond. Nell's Pond. Tuckamore stumped across the Burnt Hills, where there had once been forests until the trees were cut down for firewood or burned to cinders where they stood.

"Your PI's out there in a bunker?" Len asked.

A bunker? Whoever had said bunker? The only one Caleb knew of had once stood atop Bunker Hill, long before his time.

"Yes," he said over his shoulder as Tony muttered about Roy's bunker, underground in Kansas.

They were approaching the bare crest of Telephone Hill where the broken cellphone tower listed, cables swinging in the breeze. Though it was hard to miss, Caleb wasn't about to call the men's attention to it. His plan was to bring them to Cape House. Then what? Behind him, Len was describing a house with huge plate-glass windows facing the sea. "The landscape's nothing like this, it's on a sandbar."

"Or was," said Tony. "Sorry, Len, hoping for the best."

Len kept on, "The thing about dating an architect is Conor's so attentive to environmental specifics, like making sure the walls are resistant to wind thrust, up to 180 miles per hour. I know Fernand was clocked going through the Outer Banks at 200, but the walls are supposed to bend, and the house is up on stilts, to help in floods."

"Stilts," said Tony. "Pardon my ignorance, Len, but, when there's no flood, how do you get out the front door?"

Caleb had got as far in his planning as the part where Len Hansen, obviously keen on architecture — great! — won over by the quality of his renovations and the swoon of a blood-red sunset from the windows of Cape House, offered him all the money he needed to complete his renovation work.

"What's that?" Len cried in alarm.

Past the solitary hulk of the erratic Ghost Rock, they were coming up to Cape House lane. Ahead of them, at the bottom of the road's slope, the raw edges of pavement gaped around the hole in the road where chunks of upturned tarmac tipped like incisors and water still bustled out to sea.

"Road's washed out," Caleb said.

"I can see that," said Len. "But what are we going to do about it?"

"Oh, we don't need to go that far," Caleb said, pulling the car to a halt on the road's shoulder. He scarcely had to worry about the car being seen and if anyone did spot it, abandoned here at roadside, no one would identify it as his. When he climbed out, the men followed, eager, like released zoo animals.

Trunk raised, Caleb was stuffing the bottle of Scotch, along with the other supplies, into the reusable shopping bag that Della had helpfully left him, the kind they all used now that Pierce's supermarket no longer offered plastic ones, when Tony's acrid breath poured over his cheek.

"Lookee here. Len, he's got a Laphroaig. Sweet, how old, let me see."

"Later." Caleb wedged the bag under his arm.

"What else is in there?" asked Len.

"Delicacies," Caleb told him.

The road would likely remain empty. Nevertheless he wanted them out of sight as soon as possible, anxious that no one stumble across them or even spot them from afar. He had the uncanny sensation of the old man spying on them from somewhere in the hills. Checking up on things, as the old man had said he was doing earlier in Tom's Neck. What kind of things did the old man want or not want to happen to the men? They were here to learn about islands, he'd said, and whether that was true or not, Caleb was intent on showing them something of the island.

"This way," he said.

"I thought you said it was that way." Len peered behind them into the Burnt Hills as Caleb set off along rutted Cape House lane. The afternoon was drawing on, the sun settling into the west, whisper clouds rolling and dissolving across the aqua sky. Though he felt Len and Tony exchange a look behind his back, they had no choice but to follow him.

Almost immediately there were puddles, soon one large enough to engulf the lane's width.

In his black loafers, Len halted as if on the shore of an inland sea. Thickets swelled along the lane's verges. The only way across, if you didn't wish to walk through the middle of the puddle, as Caleb in his rubber boots had done, was to squelch through the mud at the edge, as Tony, in his low leather boots, was doing.

"Is the whole path going to be like this?" Len's forehead knitted in a frown.

"A touch of rain last night, wasn't there," said Caleb. "Lane's not safe to drive in a car."

"Should've kept those rubber boots on, Len," said Tony. "Don't know why you changed."

"I thought we were going in a vehicle. I'm not wearing rubber boots to a business meeting," snapped Len, who, Caleb noted, had also added a dress shirt and purple tie beneath his sweater.

"Could've carried the shoes. Just sayin'," said Tony.

"Is it far?" Len asked, raising his voice across the puddle.

"Not so far," said Caleb.

"Take off your shoes and go barefoot," said Tony with a nearly malicious grin, watching the spectacle of Len's hesitation from the safety of the puddle's far side. "Or maybe that one will carry you."

"Me?" said Caleb, stunned by the suggestion. Tony, barely taller than he was, had more weight on him though perhaps less muscle. And — *that one?*

Then again, if he did Len Hansen this favour, it was another reason for Len to look kindly on him, even be in his debt. Which was how Caleb came to wade back across the puddle, heft Len onto his back, a stiff weight, Len's arms nearly choking him as Caleb clutched the man's sinewy thighs and forded him across.

On their left appeared a row of weathered longers, the upright spruce poles that enclosed what had once been his uncle Charlie's potato patch. On the right, more longers surrounded his uncle Leo's former vegetable garden. Uncle Charlie was out west, Leo said he was too busy with the roadwork during growing season, though it could be he'd also fallen out of the inclination to dig and trench and plant.

A rabbit, hearing their approach, fled in terror into the bushes. Waves soughed against rocks, invisible beyond Uncle Leo's overgrown field. When they startled a murder of crows congregated on fence posts, the birds flew up with guttural caws over the field that Caleb himself was resurrecting. At the sound, Len shrieked.

"Labrador tea." Caleb held out a sprig and squeezed it between thumb and forefinger to release its piney scent. Here was a small marvel: Len took the sprig and actually sniffed it.

"What sort of man is your boss?" asked Tony, breathing smoke in the rear.

"Powerful," said Caleb after a moment.

"Like, is he straightforward, clever, does he play games?"

"All of the above." Caleb slid a hand into his pocket to touch the crumpled business card.

"Do we know for certain he'll be there?" Len stared fitfully up at the sky just as the rare needle of a plane caught sunlight, threading itself through the blue, and, as Caleb watched, everything in Len went rigid as if he'd seen a ghost or wished to turn into an arrow and shoot skyward.

"He'll be there later," said Caleb.

"Later? How much later?" Tony asked sharply.

"A couple of hours maybe." Caleb needed to stall them. His ideal would be for them to arrive at Cape House, which was not far off, as the light and the wind quieted and fading sunlight spread across ocean and sky. He anticipated certain queries, given that Cape House was no bunker and didn't resemble an office, but he'd say he'd made an arrangement for his boss to meet them there. It was closer. He'd show them around, explain his renovation project. To a man like Len, the money Caleb needed would be less than nothing. After Len was seduced and that deal sown up, they'd wait for the old man to show. Only he wouldn't. Then it would be up to Caleb to say with a shrug, Unfortunately something must have come up. It was a plan full of holes but the best he'd been able to come up with.

"How did you get through to him without a phone?" Len asked, at Caleb's side.

"Pigeons," said Caleb.

"Pigeons?" Tony stopped in his tracks. "Are you kidding me?"

"Works even when power's out," said Caleb, a new recklessness streaking through him. Now, as they came up to the end of the lane and the abandoned firepit, where teenagers used to come and light bonfires, far from the eyes of others, less so now that he was often close by working at Cape House and because there were fewer teenagers all the time, Caleb said, "Here's where we have a little pause to refresh."

The house was a short distance ahead of them, as yet invisible on the other side of a grove of spruce. With every step, he drew closer to the scene of his disastrous encounter with the girl hours before. He wanted to reach Cape House and never get there at all. Near the firepit, a few pieces of driftwood lay about, branches Caleb himself had dragged up from shore, thinking to carve with them or burn them, and these, along with wood from a ragged pile of old fencing gathered at the end of the lane, could be used to start a fire. "It's an island thing," Caleb said to the men. "Thought I'd offer you a boil-up."

"If it involves the Laphroaig, I might be coerced, even if we are en route to a business meeting," said Tony. "It's not so warm around here."

"I don't know," said Len. "Maybe we should keep going. Can you absolutely confirm this meeting's going to happen?"

"Laphroaig, Lennie," said Tony. "A sip, then we're on our way. Strike while the iron is hot, remember?"

"I'd simply like to know the location of the iron and how hot it actually is," said Len.

Caleb pulled out the bottle. He got a fire going with spruce tips, pieces of bark and sticks and spruce needles scavenged from the ground, Tony McIntosh's lighter, a splash of Scotch for good luck. Don't waste the stuff, Tony cried, grabbing the bottle from Caleb. A nice blaze blew up, crackling. Good thing the teenagers, his classmates and others before them, had set out stumps to sit on.

He handed the men empty jars he'd pinched to use for drinking, and presented a jar of his mother's bakeapple jam to Len as a gift. Amazing that he'd managed to grab this much, what with his furious mother at his heels as he raced out of the house. As if put out by the lack of gift for him, Tony glared from his stump, and when Caleb asked for the bottle back, Tony said, I'll serve. While he poured generous dollops into his own jar and Len's, he slopped only a modest portion into Caleb's.

Then again, Caleb never drank. He hadn't been intending to. This was something else he and the girl shared, that had separated them from the sixteen others in their class at school. Having watched his mother drink herself into darkness sometimes, Caleb had decided that was enough. The girl said she didn't like the taste of alcohol. Yet, after swirling the liquid that Tony had given him, Caleb slugged it back. A flame caught at the back of his throat, seared a cavity deep inside him. Who cared that Tony was shaking his head; the drink pushed away the past, which was good enough.

"How about some of that ice?" Tony asked.

Caleb slammed a sharp rock against the small slab to see if the force would break off slivers.

"It's iceberg ice, see." Which meant it was very hard. Showing them its blueish cast, Caleb told them about the icebergs that floated past in summer and sometimes foundered on the shore, breaking into growlers like this one, right by his house. Turned out neither of them had ever seen an iceberg.

"We're looking to lease gates at one of the new Greenland airports, talking to the locals, possibly investing in infrastructure, now the ice sheet's melting and traffic's ramping up," Len said, accepting a sliver of ice in his drink. "We're in, ready for the opening resource and tourism market." He held up his glass and considered it. "Not a bad way to melt ice."

"Are you buying up some of that newly green land, Lennie?" said Tony. "Heard there's diamonds under it. Got to get in there ahead of the Chinese now things are really warming."

Len gave Tony a peculiar look.

"Warming schwarming," Tony said loudly. "Okay, clearly there's some warming going on, at least near the poles, we just don't know what's causing it, most likely natural cycles, so we take advantage of it rather than acting like some new apocalyptic religion has taken hold, as is happening with some people." He poured himself more Scotch and slurped from it.

Caleb asked the men if they wanted tea. The flames seemed unusually hot and wild. Smoke might be visible from across the cove, but he wasn't going to think about that. The wind had come round, blowing at them out of the north, a colder wind, pushing smoke at Caleb, making the men cough and forcing them to move. The men didn't want tea. Bread? The men didn't want bread either. Len touched his phone, its shape visible through his pocket. The jam was stuffed in another pocket. A lock of hair blew into Len's eyes. He looked like a boy as he pulled out his phone and took a picture of the fire, which suggested that he was having a fine time despite the knotted muscles of his throat. Len turned to Tony, though he seemed to be speaking as much to the flames.

"In his last text, Conor said the motel still had power, despite the flooding, and as long as there was power, he was going to hang out in bed and watch porn, so at least he still sounded like himself."

"Say there," Tony said to Caleb. "Have you ever noticed something like a haze over the sky around here? Something that persists, even for a few days?"

"A haze," said Caleb cautiously. "Well, now, we get all sorts of clouds out here, many in one day."

This time Tony poured Caleb a larger ration of Scotch. The liquid filled Caleb's mouth with an odour like gasoline, liquefying his limbs and pushing the girl even farther off.

"What about the weather, say in the last year, been any cooler than usual?"

"Well, now, last winter was brutal," Caleb said. And it had been. The storm they'd all thought was Sheila's Brush, the last big storm of the season, had dumped a metre of snow on them at the end of April then been followed by another sudden snowstorm the second week of May, wind so high Uncle Leo had been pushed off the road in his truck, not knowing where the road was. His cellphone dead, he'd only been rescued when someone saw his antenna sticking out of a snowbank. A week later the weather had turned toxically hot, before temperatures plummeted again.

Tony gave Len a look both querying and confirming. "Could be they're doing some private, small-scale regional particulate releasing up here. Under-the-radar field experiments. They mentioned small-scale field experiments in that prospectus, didn't they?"

Len swallowed a mouthful of Scotch and nodded. Clouds stretched in yellow bands and every place else Caleb looked the sky was a different blue: milky, slate, azure. The sun had settled into the hills.

"I have a house—" Caleb began.

Only Len was saying to Tony, "You know how Roy used to protect me, back in Columbus, when we were boys? He'd beat up other boys, the ones who always shoved me around, but he made me steal for him, like from corner stores, and buy him tickets to ball games, that was the trade-off."

"I'm working on a house," Caleb tried again. Then he said, "I think we should go now."

This brought both men swiftly to their feet. Sunlight fell like a fever over the hills on the other side of the cove, where the little white house stood, but on this side shadows were growing. Caleb banked the fire. It felt like men were dancing on top of his brain, while at the edges of his vision trees grew blurry. They were going to lose the beautiful reddening light. Tony, who still held the Laphroaig bottle, seemed to have no intention of handing it back. It's my gift, he said with something like real malice and a gleam of sharp teeth. Then Tony decided he had to piss and told the others to go ahead while he made sure the fire was truly out with a gush of liquid so loud it unnerved Caleb as the embers hissed.

And here, across the grass that Caleb had cut days before, borrowing the old man's scythe, was the house, his refuge, his skin. One day, he'd buy a scythe of his own. Unlike this morning, the back door was not swinging open. From this angle, you couldn't see the damage to the front. Caleb did not want to look across the cove to where in the still-bright light, solar panels would be shining from the roof of the girl's house. From there, anyone looking in this direction might see him and the men. What was the worst that could happen? If the old man, catching sight of the three of them, came racing over on his quad, in the men's eyes that would be a grand thing. As long as Caleb got in his pitch to Len first.

The new clapboard shone. The old back door, sanded and slicked with a new coat of green paint, welcomed them from the top of the new bridge that Caleb had built.

"This is your headquarters? This?" said Len.

"This is my house," Caleb said. "The one I'm renovating and turning into a guesthouse, see, so it will be my livelihood, so I can stay on the island. A boutique inn kind of thing, only a few guests needed, keep my carbon footprint low, but treat them right, give them a unique experience, chance to live close to land and sea in a remote place, eat food grown right here on the premises or gathered in these hills — local meat and fish. Sheep that graze right here, cod hand-caught in these waters. Grow kelp in the ocean as a carbon off-set."

At least the Scotch was making the words flow out of him. As they approached, Caleb told Len how Cape House had been built by a wealthy ship's captain but had fallen into disrepair until Caleb had seen it as his very own mission to bring the place back to life. He wasn't born here, no, his mother was, her people were from the island, not his father's. Yet this place was his home, his everything. The light, the pinking clouds above them were perfect.

"This is where we're meeting your director?" Len asked as Caleb beckoned the men inside.

The north wind hit them as soon as they stepped into the kitchen, pouring from the parlour and the dining room where the glassless window frames opened to the relentless sea.

The kitchen was a work zone of sawhorses and planks and boards and Caleb's equipment bag. He'd tidied the planks. He told Len how he'd installed a new pump, big expense, but now, when he fired up the generator, beautiful spring water poured from the taps. He kept a jug filled at all times. Do you want to try some, practically an elixir, it is. A burst of happiness surged through him, happiness and hope.

"But I'm in need of more money to help with the renovations," Caleb went on. "And recently I experienced a setback, see?" He directed Len and Tony into the wide and beautiful parlour. Uncle Charlie's old wood stove squatted in a corner. In time he'd buy one of the new ones that burned a single log for hours. Only that morning, he'd been sweeping broken glass from the floor and mopping up the sea's soaking spray.

Outside, clouds were massing—the headlands stretched off into the distance, bands of sunlight yellowing their grassy, mossy humps, the rocky shore of the cove ribboning out to the implacable ocean.

"The storm last night took out my windows, when the air pressure did that crazy drop? I'm doing all this on my own. So I could use an investment from someone who cares about such places, you know, who understands the beauty of living close to the sea. Like yourself."

"Me?" Len Hansen drew tight inside his jacket, perplexity gripping his mouth.

"Yes," Caleb said. "With an investment, you could come back and be my first guest. Bring a companion. You have to imagine the room with proper windows, all snug and cozy, with a fire going, right, and the view, nothing like it, is there."

"You'd have to pay me to come back here," muttered Tony. He took another slug of whiskey straight from the bottle, lips kissing the rim. "Do you have spreadsheets, cost-benefit analysis, five-year plan? Can't make a pitch to a capitalist without these things. He's not a charity."

"I can put something together," said Caleb. "Any amount will help. I'm also planning to start a GoFundMe."

"Anyway," said Tony, "Len's already here about an investment."

"Tony," said Len with a sharpness that jolted Caleb.

"He works for the company," Tony said. "He's got to know something. We're supposed to be plying him for information, remember? Have they or have they not done any actual field experiments with this engineered particulate? Will it do what they say it will? They had some pretty pictures and graphs in that online prospectus they sent you but we're here, in situ, what more can we find out?"

"Len's in the airline business, isn't he," Tony said to Caleb, before Len could utter a word, "and airlines don't like colossal storms like Fernand, which has kind of wrecked civilization up and down the east coast, at least temporarily. It's not good for business, not good that Manhattan's underwater, or Miami. Len and Roy have pumps running day and night at their headquarters down in Naples, Florida."

"We're moving to Chicago," said Len.

"Right, so that's why they're interested in what the ARIEL project is up to, spraying the little specks up in the atmosphere to cool things down, *ergo* you have a way to control the thermostat. Len here works out a deal to provide a fleet of modified jets to do the spraying, and, voila, we're set, finger on the knob. You're ready to go, aren't you, Lennie? Nudge, nudge, maybe there'll be a cut in it for me."

"You would do the spraying?" Caleb said to Len, who suddenly seemed gaunt and full of angles.

"Keep the technology in the hands of those who know how to employ it best, are nimble, and not beholden to the masses," said Tony.

"It would be our contribution to sustaining life as we know it," said Len.

"And keeping yourself in business," said Tony.

One sunny day two summers ago, July month, a year before his trip out in boat with the girl to see the icebergs and only a few months after Caleb had acquired Cape House from his uncle, he was working out at the house when who should appear but the old man, stepping towards him through the grove of spruce.

The old man had been out to visit a few times, and even had ideas about how the work should be done. There was a new kind of interior insulation, he'd told Caleb, made of wool, high R-values, fire retardant, moisture absorbing; it wouldn't be the cheapest, but, if Caleb were interested, he'd help defray the cost.

Because there was no rain in the forecast, Caleb wanted to get the old clapboard off the exterior walls as soon as possible so that he could nail up a layer of Tyvek wrap. As he worked, he dreamed—these the earliest, most exuberant days of his dreaming. Only the day before he'd seen a caribou doe three times in the vicinity of Cape House, certain it was the same doe, her limbs sliding into his, her presence undoubtedly a form of luck. Before vanishing along the path to the headlands, the old man asked Caleb if he wanted an extra hand the next morning, and Caleb said yes, joyously.

Bright and early, they rode out together on the quads, their wooden trailers banging behind them, carrying out more of Caleb's building supplies. The air was calm. Stouts flew at them but not many. When Caleb opened the back door to Cape House, he was startled to find a cardboard box in the entry. The old man told him not to worry, it was his, he'd brought it over earlier by car. It's fragile so don't bump into it, please. It's en route to somewhere else. This was puzzling, yet moments later they were both outside, gathering splintered clapboard into a pile.

Late morning, the old man glanced at his phone and said, "Do you remember Anna Turi, who visited three years ago? She's on the noon ferry and will be meeting us here."

"Here?"

Anna, whom Caleb had sometimes heard in internet conversations with the old man, their voices floating through the cabin window as he dropped off a load of wood. Anna, who spoke of equations and grid sizes, to whom he'd once heard the old man say *I owe you so much* with such rawness it stopped Caleb in his tracks. Well, now, Anna was coming back.

They drove both quads with their empty trailers down the trail and parked them near the firepit. The old man set off on foot in the direction of the road, leaving Caleb to ponder the mystery of Anna's reappearance while listening to the shrill whistles of sanderlings on the beach, down a slope and out of sight from where he was. Moments later, a small white van nosed along the lane towards him.

A figure leaped out of the driver's side, in a knitted cap and outdoor clothes, waving as if, although they'd met only twice — in the kitchen of the old man's house and on top of Bunker Hill — Anna remembered exactly who Caleb was.

From the rear of the van, they unloaded equipment into the trailers: long metal cylinders, like the ones the old man used to inflate the small weather balloon he sent aloft every evening, the gas cylinders that Caleb now picked up and returned for him in Gander. Only these cylinders were bigger. A coil of hose with a nozzle on the end, a large metal spool thickly wound with lime-green tubing thin as a wire, a cardboard box smaller than the one the old man had dropped off at Cape House, a large metal winch, big enough to house the spool, with a handled wheel attached to it. Anna was strong, despite her slightness. Caleb watched her hands move, quick as leaves.

From Cape House, Anna was going to walk, carrying the box the old man had brought over that morning, while Caleb on his quad followed the old man on his, past Seal Cove with its curve of sand, out through the fields where Caleb's uncle's sheep had once grazed. The afternoon sun hung high above them. Whisper clouds tufted and dissolved. So as not to jounce the trailers or leave Anna far behind, they drove slowly. Nevertheless the old man kept glancing over his shoulder.

Occasional tourists walked the footpath but so rarely they were unlikely to run into anyone. Lobster season had ended so Martin Green would no longer be coming into the cove to check his traps. The person most likely to spot them was the girl, yet when Caleb glanced across the cove there was no sign of her.

Before they reached the headlands and their cliff-like rise towards the sea, they cut northeast through fields and came at last to Sheep's Cove, where there had once been a settlement and before that where Beothuk had stopped to forage and light campfires. The weathered ribs of a rotted boat were the only sign of former human habitation. Waves roughed the sea ahead but the air in the grass was calm, protected by the headlands to the northwest and the bare hills to the south. Bakeapples were beginning to ripen. Caleb stooped to pick a few. Ghosts sighed in the grass. Anna set down her burden gently, before searching for something. For what, Caleb asked. Sharp objects, she replied.

Next thing, the old man was handing each of them a pair of thin white cotton gloves. Like the others, Caleb slipped his on. All this seemed peculiar but, whatever, it was his job.

With a knife, the old man slit open the smaller cardboard box taken from the back of the van. From it he pulled out something encased in filmy plastic, which, when the old man broke the plastic open, revealed layers of very thin folded fabric. Caleb and Anna were to hold the fabric in their gloved hands, so that it didn't snag or tear, the material expanding between them as they walked away from each other. All this was as baffling as any task Caleb had yet performed for the old man, including hauling all that computer equipment in to his cabin. Their careful steps felt like a ritual, even though Anna, across from Caleb, kept staring distractedly out to sea. There were no icebergs. It had been a slow summer for them, wind keeping them far offshore. The flat form was a balloon, Caleb realized once it had gained a shape, bigger than the old man's regular weather balloons.

With Caleb and Anna still holding the fabric's edges, the old man fastened the nozzle at the end of the hose to the balloon's narrow end. The hose was connected to the first of the long canisters, which lay on its side in the grass. When the old man turned a valve, gas hissed and entered the fabric.

Slowly the balloon swelled, the helium inside its skin tugging at Caleb's hands as the balloon gained the urge to rise. The larger the balloon grew, the smaller he felt, until, released from their hands, the balloon floated as large as a house above their heads.

Before the balloon was fully expanded, the old man opened the box that Anna had carried with such care and lifted out an object that Caleb recognized immediately. The old man had been tinkering with it in his work shed for months. It resembled nothing so much as a tiny snowblower with a row of very small nozzles on one side. Inside its shell were propeller wings that would spin like those of a fan. A rectangular casing attached to the snowblower housed a circuit board and, the old man said, pointing to another rectangular section, Here's the pump. Attached to the contraption was the small solar panel that would power it. As Caleb wandered about, the old man and Anna secured the contraption to the base of the balloon so that it dangled, the lime-green tubing attached to the contraption, the spool fitted onto the winch, which would unwind the tubing, and the balloon, into the air.

Anna fussed with a small notebook computer while the old man took pictures. To Caleb, the whole scene seemed fantastical.

"Here's where we show how low-tech and low-cost an intervention might be—and local. Though you'd still want some kind of scientific consortium deploying it, even for regional use, plus some kind of intergovernmental approval. Ideally," the old man said.

"I didn't think any of this was about living in an ideal world," said Anna, frowning.

"Some of the technical issues might be resolved by engineering a purpose-specific particle — there's a team in the US working on something like that right now, one of the lead researchers, he's young, from Sri Lanka, a cloud physicist as well as a nanoengineer, which seems like an enticing combination. I'm planning to contact him. I certainly never thought I'd be spending this much time and energy thinking about clouds and particulates when I began a career in paleoclimatology."

The old man covered his phone with his hand, peering at the photographs he'd taken. "Even something small-scale would need to be implemented over a decadal span, or centuries," he continued. "Years and years. We need a technology that stable. Which *is* hard to imagine, isn't it? Sudden termination could be disastrous. So one needs to have an exit strategy — and simultaneous technologies for carbon sequestration and plans for massively reducing carbon use. There's a lot of cognitive dissonance running around, I'll be the first to admit. And magical thinking, okay, yes. So I've been doing a lot of pondering, Anna. Here's the thing, what if we reconfigure the nature of the experiment?"

"Reconfigure it?" Anna looked up in bewilderment. "What do you mean?"

"Make this more of a conceptual project."

"Conceptual how, Alan?" Anna seemed genuinely taken aback.

"We still need this field experiment, or this prototype of a prototype of a field experiment, or conceptual field experiment. But we reframe things. Reframe them to focus on altering the human instead of the atmospheric. There might be less of an issue of oversight, which I know is a big concern of yours. Intention changes everything. Let's see what happens if our intention changes. What we require is evidence of an experiment, to capture someone's attention. Documentation that we're up to something, that's the main thing."

The old man sent Caleb to check on the winch while he and Anna spoke quietly and fiercely. *Him? Really?* Was what Caleb overheard Anna say when he drew close again. Then the two of them broke off as if the argument engrossing them had been settled.

It seemed they were about to leave. How was that possible? Surely they were going to do something with the balloon—let it rise into the sky, pump something up through the length of tubing into the snowblower suspended high in the air so that it spritzed out of the nozzles, pushed by the small, spinning propeller wings? The old man spoke about the wind dropping off as the sun set, which, given that a soft northwesterly was blowing, it would, Caleb knew. The evening would be clear and calm with a full moon.

At Cape House, the old man told Anna she could pull the van around to his side of the cove, park in his yard, or else he'd simply meet her back at the site in a couple of hours. He made no mention of bringing Caleb along. Pointedly, he told Caleb he was free for the rest of the day, and though it was perplexing to feel disappointed, Caleb did, despite the fact that his mother needed him at home.

Later, much later, he would take a break from massaging bawling Lola as his mother tugged two blood- and mucus-covered doelings into the world, and make a dash up the path beyond the goat barn to the top of Lighthouse Hill. There, squinting into the duckish light, the western sky fading to juniper blue, he'd glimpse the far-off, unmistakable silhouette of the balloon rising, though there was no one nearby other than his mother, stripped to her undershirt in the goat barn, blood all over her arms, who might have confirmed the sight. Was that the mist of a small cloud or did he imagine it? By the time Caleb made it back out to Sheep's Cove, after Fern had given birth to a buckling and a doeling, a day had passed, and there was no sign, other than trampled grass, that anything unusual had happened out there at all.

Outside Cape House, after the old man had roared off, Anna asked Caleb playfully if he would give her a tour. It's still a wreck, Caleb protested, pleased nevertheless. Two weeks before, he and the girl had been shovelling out sheep shit. There was no running water. Anna said she didn't care, she was used to living rough for months at a time, out on the ice — she broke off, as if she shouldn't have mentioned this.

They rappelled up the broken staircase to the second floor, where Anna peered into the biggest room, and announced that if she were a guest, this was where she'd want to stay. With a smile she lay down on the filthy floor, as if there were indeed a bed beneath her, and a glimpse of the longed-for future unfurled itself in front of Caleb.

He had opened his mouth to ask her about the balloon when Anna broke in on his thoughts. "Will you live out here by yourself?"

Shaking his head, he blushed because, her gaze burrowing into him, it was as if Anna had guessed his innermost secret.

At moments, a fog rolled over her, as if someone close to her were dying. They were downstairs, in the parlour, about to leave, when Anna hesitated. "Can I give you a hug?"

A hug? Imaginary nippers crawled all over his skin. Mutely Caleb nodded, and Anna gathered him close, so close the pores of her pale skin were visible, the sharp line of her chin. The next moment, she kissed him on the forehead, a kiss that Caleb would never have the courage to mention to the girl.

"May it all work out as you wish," she whispered. "Whatever happens, you'll need to be brave."

Outside Cape House, at dusk, Caleb vomited into the grass, the two men crashing about inside like the intruders they really were. The sea's strong rote was in him, waves heaving and booming. From the bushes a fox scented him, raised her lips and bared her teeth, before slinking off in disgust. What had Tony McIntosh just said? They would be in charge of spraying a haze into the sky. These men. Roy, more obsessed with his son than the rest of the world, manic to get back into the air, Len, who seemed as swayable as grass in the wind, which left Tony, licking his lips, hands on the puppet strings. The old man had said, *Conceptual experiment.* He'd said, *Weather monitoring.* He'd said all kinds of things, but he'd never suggested the weather would end up in the hands of men like these. Jets, an endless fleet of them, altering the sky. Those field experiments, which Tony seemed so keen to find out more about, surely they were the ones Caleb himself had been involved in, out in Sheep's Cove with Anna and the old man, on the boat with Arun. The old man had made him part of this.

Once more Caleb's stomach heaved. He had to get up. Go back inside the place he'd believed would never betray him, yet the new weather was battering it, traces of his encounter with the girl lay all over the house, and now these men were stomping through it, threatening to leave destruction in their wake. The clouds, the constantly shifting clouds looked the same as they always had. Who knew what they really were? Maybe there was already an invisible haze up there somewhere. He was a cloud, dissolving, looking down on all that was. Across the cove, a huge yellow moon rose, a gull screamed, insects rustled, the fox scented rabbit, and though these men might not know it, everything, everything was alive.

From upstairs, where Caleb had told the men not to go, came a shriek from Tony and the sound of splintering. He must have fallen through one of the broken floorboards. Taller than ever, mud on his trouser legs, spruce needles in his hair, Len reared over Caleb in the kitchen.

"Have you been leading us on the whole time?" Len's face was white and any trace of sympathy had drained from it.

Tony appeared in front of Caleb, pushing him up against the wall, hands at his throat, crying, "Where are the particulates? Forget your boss. Take us to the lab. There's gotta be a lab. They manufacture them here, right? So we can get our hands on them ourselves."

The whump of the back door made them all jump.

It wasn't the old man who emerged from the shadows but Anna in black boots and jeans and white trench coat, an actual flashlight, not her phone, held in one hand. Her teeth glittered and she did not look happy as she shone the flashlight beam right into Caleb's eyes. "So this is where you are." She might have walked all the way from Tom's Neck, spotted the parked car, followed their footsteps. She, too, had betrayed him, playing along at the old man's game.

Be brave, she'd said to Caleb, standing right in this room, and given him a kiss, but what kind of bravery was possible when, whichever way he turned, darkness and more darkness gathered all around him?

. . .

From the punt, halfway across the cove, Miranda pushed into each stroke, Frank rowing with her, both of them facing where they'd come from, backs to what lay ahead. On their way over, as they'd heaved the oars in their tole pins, she had watched her father's quad roar down the lane. His sharp-eyed stare had followed them but Miranda wasn't able to lift a hand to wave, and anyway waving wasn't what she felt like doing. Where would he think they were going?

From inside the house, through the salt-smeared windows, he'd have been able to see them pull at last around the lip of land that led into Seal Cove where he and she used to go ashore. If he kept watching, he'd have glimpsed them on the shore path, approaching Cape House and Caleb — as he'd expressly forbidden Miranda from doing.

Yet why did her father have the right to determine who she spoke to and when? The idea now seemed outlandish. All Miranda had told Frank as they rowed, uncertain where her loyalties lay, was that there were difficulties between the two families, which made her nervous about talking to Caleb. It seemed hard to imagine telling Frank that her father had forbidden her from speaking to him, because Frank might reasonably ask why she had given in to her father's orders for so long without resistance. Then, when she broke her father's rule and approached Caleb outside Cape House, Caleb had yelled at her, and run away, which made her desire to move beyond the break feel like the wrong one.

Once they were on the far side of the cove, Frank had wanted to keep going. Could they reach the road beyond the washout and walk to the next village, what was it called, it had a funny name. Miranda yearned to return home. The pull felt like it was exerted by her father and she didn't know how to resist it. At last, with Frank's agreement, they set off back across the water, fighting tide and wind, and staggered ashore, their legs like jelly.

At the house, her father greeted them, a host welcoming long-lost guests, and didn't ask Miranda what she'd been up to, which surprised her, but at least his silence didn't force her to lie.

As she entered the kitchen, arms and hands aching from the row, everything felt altered — who her father was, who Frank was, who she was. Was it really the same room? The same life? A plume of steam rose from the kettle. It was as if she needed to re-encounter her father in the light of Frank's words, reassess him, assure herself that he was still her father. To be in the same room with him was instantly like being touched. He was dropping tea bags into the pot. Was he truly planning something in collusion with Frank's father? Had he really brought Frank's father to the island?

"Hard lop out there," Alan said as Ella lapped from her water bowl. "Still a following sea —" which meant the sea still had the force of the storm in it. "You must have got some exercise. Seen any accidentals, Frank?"

Did he think this was why they'd crossed the cove? Possibly. Yes. Of course. Miranda had forgotten about the birds.

"Not yet, but I'm not giving up." Frank examined his palms, which had blisters on them, and the sight sent Miranda speeding upstairs to scrabble for blister bandages in the bathroom cabinet.

From below she heard her father say, "You'll have a few scars by the time you leave this place," to which Frank replied something about being wounded for a good cause.

They were both at the table, nursing mugs of tea, when she returned, and her father was asking Frank, "So what has Miranda taught you?"

"Some things about the wind," Frank said, his black hair tufted and his cheeks wind-chapped, looking up at her with a sly grin.

She couldn't keep her eyes off Frank or her father. Nothing was what it seemed. Frank, a billionaire's son, sat in her kitchen, in a wool sweater knit by Mary Green, pressing a blister bandage to his palm, hiding the true reason for his arrival. Her father, rumpled and bearded, who kept an eye on the weather always, had likely conducted a few weather-related experiments, but was he actually looking for a way to cover the entire planet in a haze of tiny particles in order to cool the air? Everything felt incredible, indescribable. Even when her father handed her a steaming mug of tea, Miranda was too restless to sit. Yet with every step she took, she bumped into another secret.

Somehow she had to find a way to speak to her father about all this, ask him questions. But not in front of Frank. It was like knowing things without knowing what she knew, knowing without thinking. She'd overheard snippets over the years. Her father must intuit this. What did he think she understood? Did he believe he'd truly wrapped her in a haze that kept out so much, so much about the weather that surrounded them and pressed on every element of their lives? How deeply was the world in trouble? Did her father, pulling back the tea towel to check on the rising bread dough he'd somehow whipped up in their absence, have any idea who Frank really was? Someone had sent Frank a letter. Her father had sent other people mysterious letters. Did this mean he'd sent Frank a letter — Miranda couldn't decide, though the thought was dizzying.

Her father asked Frank, "So what do you think of our set-up out here?"

"Awesome. Your self-sufficiency's amazing. And your food security. Miranda was showing me her vegetable garden. I hope I have a chance to taste some of its bounty." Nevertheless Frank cast a glance over his shoulder at the rifle in its rack above the kitchen door.

"Can you imagine living such a life in a place like this?"

"Can I?" Frank faltered. "I don't know. I've —"

Her father interrupted Frank by rising to his feet. "Frank, I've a yen to show you something. Stay where you are and close your eyes. Wait, I have a better idea. Stay there. Keep your eyes closed. Miranda?"

He whispered in her ear. Her father was often asking people to do things. Giving orders. Asking her to do things. This struck Miranda with sudden force. Only that morning she'd run his errand into Pummelly without question, delivered his message to Caleb. Why did her father need a scarf? She could refuse him, but she went into the mud room, pulled from a hook a mauve scarf she'd knitted and brought it obediently back to the kitchen, ashamed of herself.

When Alan attempted to wrap the scarf around Frank's eyes, Frank jumped to his feet, head hurtling towards the rafters. "What are you doing?"

"Indulge my whimsy here, Frank. I want to give you a particular sensory experience, compel you to focus on something other than sight, and since I barely know you, I'm not convinced, when I ask you to close your eyes, that I can trust you not to peek. How trustworthy are you really, Frank?"

"No blindfold," said Frank. "No bondage in the middle of the afternoon, thanks very much. I'll keep my eyes closed, I promise."

Frank's eyelids flickered as, from the utility room, came the suction of the freezer door opening and shutting, the metallic clang of hammer against chisel, the knock of chisel against ice. With her father out of the room, Frank could have opened his eyes and offered Miranda a querying look, but he didn't. The next moment her father returned, bearing a saucer full of ice chips, like a magician, calling attention one place while something more crucial was no doubt happening somewhere else.

When he asked Frank to open his mouth, again Frank started to his feet, eyes wide open.

"Come on, Frank. Why so paranoid? You'd think I was trying to poison you."

Maybe it was in Frank's nature to question any figure of authority, Miranda thought.

"It's ice," her father said. "I'll take a chip, Miranda here will take one. We'll each put an ice chip on our tongue."

Her father was someone who liked exercising authority.

Had he always been this way or had it become more pronounced since they'd come to the island or was it simply that
Miranda was noticing this aspect of him with new acuteness,
a sudden pressure against her sternum?

"It really is just ice, I promise," she said, placing an ice chip
on her own tongue where it fizzed and softly popped. Open
eyes fixed on her now, as if to say, I'm trusting you, which felt
like both gift and burden, Frank did as she did.

"All I want you to do, Frank, is tell me where the ice comes
from." Alan set the saucer on the table.

"Where it comes from."

"That's right."

"I'm assuming water is not the answer."

"Let's just say it's not the answer I'm looking for."

"Okay, you want somewhere spatial, like geographic, like
a place?"

"Partly geographic and partly material, I'd say."

"That's oblique, and the answer is probably not out of
your freezer or your tap, so, like, your yard in the middle of
winter?"

"In the general direction yet not correct, I'm afraid. Feel
it in your mouth. Let yourself pay attention to it."

"It tastes a bit salty," Frank said after a minute, the ice
giving him a lisp. Every so often his gaze checked in with
Miranda, as if seeking guidance or reassurance, which hollowed out a new space inside her. "Does it come from the sea?"

"Warmer," Alan said with a catch in his voice that Miranda
heard clearly. She understood in part what her father was up
to, even if his methods seemed bizarre.

The first iceberg she'd seen, her first summer in the cove,
had been a huge blue slab, like a broken-off piece of a giant's

wall that gained turquoise glints and a bright glaze as it melted in the sunlight, floating slowly past and vanishing southerly into the misty air. She'd been awestruck at the sight. Then, as the years passed, she'd grown used to seeing them. No, it was impossible ever to grow truly used to the icebergs even when it became commonplace to step out the door on an early summer day, look towards the ocean, and there one was, tugged along by the current, slowly twisting, dense white, then porous aquamarine as the light shifted. Some years there were so many, a steady stream for weeks and weeks, far out or closer, craggy, sepulchral, growing shiny in the sun as they melted. Never more icebergs than the summer before last, when she and Caleb had taken the speedboat out to look at all those marooned in the bay. This year there'd been almost none, the icebergs melting farther north or far offshore. Suddenly, unable to bear any longer her father's game, if that was what it was, or Frank's befuddlement, Miranda burst out, "It's iceberg ice, from off the Greenland ice sheet, that floats south and washes into the cove."

"That's right," said her father, who, if surprised by her outburst, didn't show it.

Frank's face transformed again, this time into an expression of childlike wonder. He pulled the nearly melted chip out of his mouth.

"We gather the bits that come ashore in summer," Miranda said.

"No point in wasting the wreckage," said her father. "Better to honour it somehow before it goes. Here, look." He poured a glass of water, dropped in a piece of ice and held the glass to the light. "See how the ice fizzes and bubbles? That's little bursts of ten-thousand-year-old air being released, air that has far less carbon dioxide in it than ours today. In a sense, from where we are, in this room, staring at those bubbles, we're looking across the stretch of time in which humans have enjoyed a stable climate here on Earth."

The bubbles rose to the surface and burst, air of the past dissolving into air of the present, as the ice melted in Miranda's mouth and in the glass. Something that had existed for ten thousand years suddenly no longer was: it was jolting to imagine. And, the word her father had forbidden her from uttering since coming to the island, *climate*—her father had just spoken it.

"Only I'm afraid the stability of this climate will not be something you'll inherit," he went on quietly. "As more and more of the ice melts. We need the ice to maintain our elemental home, Frank, and we may need to do whatever we can to preserve it. Those of your generation, both of you, may be required to show ever greater ingenuity and resolution when it comes to caring for it, it and the rest of this good world—

"Anyway, thanks for allowing me to indulge in this odd little ritual. Let's all close our eyes—you, too, Miranda—and contemplate the ice as it dissolves in us, ancient microbes and all. Let your boundaries blur, Frank, let yourself become transformed by the ice, and when you go back into the world, remember the ice, consider how whatever you do will affect it. Up here in these parts, facing the North Atlantic, it's harder to forget."

"Ancient microbes," said Frank after a moment, eyes still closed. "Do I need to be concerned about them swimming inside me?"

"When I used to work up on the ice, leading research teams in the Canadian Arctic, or in Greenland, drilling ice cores to study their climatic record," Alan said, "we boiled our water from glacial snow, drank glacial runoff when we could. Think of the cleanliness of that water, Frank, how little plastic is in it."

These words, too, were astonishing, her father pulling back the cloak in which he wrapped himself to let a bright piece of his past shine through. He'd never done this with anyone other than Anna and Agnes and Arun since he and Miranda had come to Blaze Island. Other borders seemed to be breaking down. Cores brought to the surface. And he'd done this in front of Frank, of all people.

"So you are a scientist," Frank said meditatively, as if the ice were working on him like a drug.

"I was," said Alan. "I am."

"I spend a lot of time thinking about social injustice and the redistribution of capital," Frank murmured, eyelids twitching, "and what it will take to achieve it. Sometimes I think it will take an epic disaster, I even find myself wishing for that. But then the disaster's already happening, it's been happening for a long time, so I guess the question is, how bad is it going to get?"

"Hard to know," said Alan.

It was as if they were talking only to each other now, her father fixed on Frank's intent face, Frank focused on the ice. Miranda slipped from the room. Even when her father called her back, she kept going.

The trip had started out beautifully enough. July month, an afternoon so calm it was astonishing. Caleb had called Miranda on the land line, caught her just as she stepped into the house. "Let's go see all the icebergs stranded in the bay, Miranda. We may never again see the like."

She'd heard about the hundreds of icebergs, and so, abandoning her gardening gloves and shovel, she said yes immediately. With an old, brimmed ball cap planted on her head, she set off at a run to meet Caleb down at Pummelly's government wharf. She'd turned eighteen the month before. Sometimes, on a calm day, Caleb was able to borrow a speedboat from his uncle, and her father made no objections as long as Caleb had his phone and they actually wore their life jackets and didn't go too far. Caleb had made a point of learning the water by heart, pestering his uncles until they taught him the old names of shoals and trap berths, the places you needed to know before GPS. Sometimes he recited these to Miranda: there's Turrs' Rocks, there's Muddy Ledge, out there's Round Head Ground, Shoal Spot, Green's Ground, The Razor, The Stone, Eastern Shoal. They'd motor into coves reachable only by water, spots Caleb knew about, pull up the boat and picnic.

The previous summer, sitting with arms wrapped around folded knees, wind freshening over them, they had talked about their plans for when school ended, neither of them with any intention of leaving the island. Miranda, her body simultaneously restless and calmed, spoke of her desire to farm, and Caleb about his new plans for Cape House. They were on a small, rocky islet in the middle of Shallow Bay the day he suggested they might farm together. There were all the untended fields on his side of Green Cove where the Borders family had worked their plots for generations. There was loneliness in him and desire. She, too, had wondered who his father was. As he spoke, Caleb stared at the rock on which they sat as if he were contemplating a move he couldn't bring himself to make. Squall clouds blustered out of the south. His voice stumbled, his hand reaching out. "And we can do more together, if you wish, Miranda."

It was a long way around the island to where the icebergs were, past Sheep's Cove and Auk Point and Tom's Neck, past the wide mouth of Shallow Bay, past Herring Cove, the green mound of Bear Head, then the hilly harbour of the town of Blaze. It was hard to talk while in the boat, Caleb at the tiller in the stern, Miranda on the bench in front of him, riding the swells like the wild creatures they were, their speed creating its own wind, the constant thwack of wave against boat a percussive register of their passage. Not speaking hardly mattered—she was happy to drink in the air and be splendidly free from all that usually surrounded her.

Far at their backs, icebergs floated slowly past out on the Labrador Current, shimmering in a heat haze at the horizon. When they came at last around the volcanic mound of Blaze Head, rising like a giant's skull out of the water, there were the masses of icebergs that Caleb had promised and that Miranda's father had mentioned at supper the evening before: icebergs filling the entire breadth of the bay, stretching northward as far as the eye could see, so many, it was impossible to count. Large ones tall as houses, small ones like pale creatures. The blue of the sky had turned dull white under a haze of cirrus cloud and still the icebergs glistened, every colour in the spectrum of blue and green: cobalt, turquoise, aquamarine, emerald. From one angle they looked like one thing, from another something else. As the icebergs turned, they revealed arches, hollows, ponds, fissures. It was hard to know how to describe them other than to compare them to other things: this one's a castle, no, no, a dragon. There were no words. Some swayed, unbalanced by their melting. Drafts of cold air billowed from them. For long moments, the two of them sat in the boat, motor idling, and, awed into silence, they did no more than stare.

The icebergs were as old as the ice her father had once studied. Could some of them actually be the same ice? Layers of thousands of years, their own lives nothing but a film on top, yet the icebergs had come here to dissolve. How little time it took for eternities to vanish. Gone. The thought sank into Miranda. Could you say an iceberg was dying? They'd come here to die? Her father might say so. Or Anna Turi. Or Agnes Watson. Here they were, witnessing that death. The death of the world. Their world. *Them*? This was what her father feared. The death of the world as they knew it. The icebergs floated mutely in the heat. Their presence seemed to speak and pose a question.

Miranda asked Caleb to go closer, could they. Mindful of the depths that lay beneath the icebergs' surfaces, the risk that one might tip and founder, he motored slowly in among the nearer ones. Her body quailed and yearned—for what? Something turned over deep inside her. The air was colder now. The icebergs creaked. Some distance off, a crack sounded, harsh as a bullet, and a chunk broke from a great crag and with a crash tumbled into froth, its fall pushing the whole mass sideways, a wave surging in their direction.

Swiftly, Caleb turned the boat and drove them away from the icebergs, southward, into the open water of the bay. Miranda swung a glance over her shoulder. Shouldn't they be going the other way, back, which meant northward around the island and so home? When she shouted at Caleb, asking him where he was headed, he seemed not to hear. Nor did he stop but kept motoring into the bay, the bow now fixed on the distant green shore. Tensing, Miranda shouted again and this time Caleb cut back the motor. With a bright smile, he said, "I thought we'd take a little trip. An adventure, Miranda. It's truly the day for it. Just the two of us. A trip across the bay."

"Across the bay?"

"My cousin Ger's on the three o'clock. He'll pick us up on bayside and take us into town. Or we'll call a cab. We'll go out for a meal, whatever you wish, Miranda."

"What if my father finds out, if someone sees us and tells him?"

"We'll ask them not to. Everyone already thinks it strange. That you never leave. You can't, for any reason. Why shouldn't you, Miranda, one afternoon, you're eighteen, where's the harm in it? It'll be some fun, I promise."

In her first years at the island school, girls, Brianna Morton, Caitlyn Harvey, others, sometimes asked her to come along when their mothers agreed to drive them in to the Gander malls, but when Miranda always said no, they stopped asking. She became known as the girl who didn't leave. Couldn't, wouldn't. The only one. When people asked why, she said she and her father didn't. Always Caleb had accepted this aspect of her life without ridicule or protest. Would she be like this forever? Maybe. The bond she shared with her father was strong, though, yes, she had sometimes asked Caleb to describe Gander to her, the airport, or St. John's with its brightly painted houses and steep streets. Phoneless, she had sometimes looked at the world through his phone and texted her father on it or together she and Caleb had watched a movie on its tiny screen.

She had never flouted her father's rules, understanding the reasons he gave for them. They had all they needed on the island. More people needed to live as close to home as they did.

Danger had driven them to Blaze Island. As far as Miranda could tell, from overhearing her father's conversations, from her own brief forays online, the outer world hadn't altered. The deniers were still there, even growing stronger, heat intensifying, storms worsening, most people going on as before while the blanket of gases accumulated above them all. To leave the island was to take a step back towards all that.

"I can't go over there," Miranda said. The sun had broken through its haze and warmth poured down on them. Off in the distance beyond Caleb, the silent chorus of icebergs floated over the water. Above their heads, terns squeaked and tore through the air.

"If your father finds out, tell him you wanted to go."

"I can't, Caleb. Please don't make me."

Every particle in Miranda's body stiffened at the thought, and if it made her seem foolish, she didn't care. Yes, her father would be angry. Yes, he had a temper. But it was more than that. She wanted to be back on the island, feet on that ground, feel every particular of that place around her, its tremulous shelter a small thing to set against the deepest fears.

There was something else, another seam in her. She didn't want to go across the bay with Caleb. Something stopped her. They had stared at the melting icebergs—and now he wanted to go to a restaurant? If they found themselves sitting across from each other, Caleb might reach for her fingers or slide a hand under the table to touch her thigh, and she didn't know what to do with the confusion of feelings these imaginings aroused. Yet, unless she leaped into the freezing water and swam, so cold it might kill her, she was dependent on Caleb to get back, familiar Caleb in his coveralls perched in the stern, squinting beneath his ball cap and smiling an unnerving smile, hand on the tiller, still revving the engine.

"What's wrong with you, Miranda?" He was trying to be teasing, but she sensed his frustration.

He took off, speeding them once more away from the island and into the bay, southward, to where the still-invisible Adieu ferry dock must be. When Miranda lurched towards him, he pushed her back.

"Get off me."

"Take me back, Caleb."

She was shouting, but some new hardness in him wished only to have its way. Again he revved the engine, the boat smacking the water, and as the distant shore grew closer, Miranda's panic rose. This time when she lunged, almost stumbling into Caleb, she grabbed the tiller, the boat rocking precipitously. When Caleb pushed her back, harder this time, she tumbled over the metal bench, landing on the boat bottom where the life jackets lay, biting the inside of her cheek with the shock.

"Jesus, Miranda!" Caleb, too, was shouting. "What are you trying to do, tip the boat and drown us?"

Her chest stung from the force of his push. He'd grabbed the tiller back and righted their course, slowed the engine, thankfully. Bilge water soaked her jeans and her tailbone burned. She clambered over the two benches towards the bow seat, as far as she could be from Caleb, who had at least turned their course. How could you know someone and not know them at all?

Only now was he asking her, his face full of concern and remorse, "Are you all right, Miranda?"

All the way back to Pummelly harbour, he kept calling, across the length of the boat, forehead crumpled with anxiety, more like the Caleb Miranda thought she knew, telling her how sorry he was, begging her not to tell her father, the frightened outsider, insisting he hadn't meant to hurt her. "Are you all right?"

Huddled in the bow, she touched her tongue to the place in her mouth where the skin was broken, felt the sting of Caleb's hand on her chest, tried to breathe through her shock.

When she got home, her father was still at the cabin with his third visitor, Arun Mudalnayake, but as soon as he returned and they headed out to take the weather measurements, he seemed to sense something was wrong. But Arun with the nervous stare was with them, and Miranda had no intention of saying anything in front of him. It was while she was feeding the hens in their run that her father cornered her and asked what the matter was. Concern emanated from him.

"Caleb tried to take me across the bay. When I refused to go, he hit me." Miranda heaved out a breath. She didn't know how to talk about the icebergs. The lingering pain in her chest felt like a bruise coming in.

"Caleb hit you?"

She had the full weight of her father's attention now.

Anger and self-righteousness and the desire to cause

pain were a confusing fire. "We were out in Tom Borders's speedboat."

"He tried to take you across the bay?"

What had she expected would happen then? When she confirmed these things with a nod. She was still her father's daughter. She, too, had the power to break apart a life.

Two weeks after the boat trip out into the bay with Caleb, on an afternoon when she knew Caleb to be busy elsewhere, Miranda knocked on Sylvia's door. It was a relief when Sylvia opened it.

Sylvia didn't offer a hug, she asked if Miranda wished for tea. Her kitchen table was littered with the last of the rhubarb stalks, a bucket for the discarded leaves beneath. Sylvia took up her seat and knife again, chopping with strong, deliberate strokes, cutting up stalks for jam while Miranda took out mugs and tea bags and a jar of goat's milk from the fridge, as she'd done so often before, finding it impossible to speak until Sylvia spoke for her. "Are you going to tell me your version of what happened out in boat, Miranda?"

Miranda's hands shook as she held her mug. "Caleb tried to take me to the other side, against my will."

"Your will? I thought it was your father's."

Couldn't the two be the same thing, Miranda wondered. "I tried to grab the tiller, because I didn't want to go across the bay, and Caleb shoved me back onto the bench, hard enough to bruise my chest."

"I'm not excusing my son's actions, Miranda, only wondering why your father thinks Caleb hit you."

It was hard to own up to the words. "That's what I told him."

"I see," Sylvia said quietly. "Now why would you put it like that?"

"Because he hurt me," Miranda said.

"I see," was all Sylvia said.

There were things it felt impossible to talk about with either Sylvia or her father. Caleb's longing. When they'd kissed, during the winter months in his shed and then, when summer came, by the rock called the Devil's Chair, up along back shore, Miranda hadn't said no, wanting to know what it would feel like and what would change when she opened her mouth to Caleb's tongue. Caleb's lips were soft, on her face and neck, hers on his, her tongue in his mouth. Yet, despite her curiosity, she'd felt like they were playing a game and part of her remained outside it.

One evening at the beginning of the summer, Caleb brought a blanket out to the parlour at Cape House and with great ceremony laid it on the planks. The sight made her skin grow cool. Sliding his hands under her shirt, he'd fondled her nipples and, hands under his shirt, she'd grazed his bare ribs, their bodies pressed tight enough for Miranda to feel the bulge in his crotch, her skin pale against his. Something in her had pulled back in dismay, because Caleb still felt like a brother and no matter how she tried to imagine otherwise, she couldn't shake this feeling. She'd run all the way home, without him, through the twilight.

Yet, sitting at the table in Sylvia's kitchen, she felt the wide breadth of Caleb's absence in her life and the growing fear that she had wronged him.

—

Miranda clambered up the slope to the garden, leaving Frank and her father in the house.

Always when she'd allowed herself to think about the future it had been shaped by the contours of the past: how else did you envision what was to come other than by reconfiguring what you knew? There were days when, swayed by Caleb's suggestions, she had imagined living with him on the far side of the cove even as another part of her retracted from the dream. She had assumed that somehow Caleb and Sylvia would be in her life forever. What she loved would always continue, how could it not? More often she'd seen herself living in the little white house in Green Cove with her father and Ella, taking care of her father, because he needed her to do this. She'd ruffle Ella's fur, meet her brown-eyed stare. There'd be more animals, because she wanted more, she would tend the land, build a bigger greenhouse, listen and note each time the wind shifted, there would be order and safety in such a life, in its deep choreographies and self-sufficiencies, in being responsive to sea and sky and the wild and ragged weather growing wilder all around them. There had been ruptures and alterations, but nothing had shaken her fundamental belief in the continuity of this life, given to her after the biggest rupture of all, the catastrophes that had sent the two of them fleeing to the island: everything here was proof that, despite grief, a new life could be made. Even the rupture of losing Caleb, painful as it was, had somehow been bearable. She'd gone on. They all had. Now, though, the world looked so different she wasn't sure she could step back into the body she'd inhabited only a day ago.

She was searching for salvageable leaves among the storm-pummelled lettuces and arugula when a shift in the air made Miranda scramble to her feet. Someone was on the other side of the garden fence, town-side. Sylvia was standing there, tall, her red and grey-streaked hair blazing, a groove notched between her eyebrows where the light hit, Sylvia who hadn't come near their house for over four years, since her break with Miranda's father.

Her father was the one who'd cut off contact first; then Sylvia, in retaliation, had done the same. Despite this, Sylvia had not cropped Miranda from her life, and this had felt like grace, that Sylvia still welcomed Miranda into her home, took her foraging, offered solace. Then, when her father declared that she was no longer to speak to Caleb nor Caleb to her, Miranda was convinced Sylvia would turn her back as well. Even after their awkward conversation in Sylvia's kitchen, she and Sylvia had gone berry picking together, cared for the year's new kids in the goat barn, carded the wool from Pat Green's sheep. Not as often to be sure, there was a new distance and wariness, since the invisible presences of both Miranda's father and Caleb now lay between them, but Sylvia's warmth didn't altogether vanish. This had calmed Miranda. She hadn't entirely destroyed what had been, although she sensed a turn in Sylvia's feelings for her, a new note that felt like pity.

Over the fence, Sylvia wished Miranda a good evening and Miranda, wiping her hands on her jeans, wished Sylvia the same. Everything was civil, yet there had to be something pressing to compel Sylvia to come out this way. Sylvia was staring at the ripped plastic flapping from the greenhouse.

Was it storm damage? Miranda said it was. Yet this could not be why Sylvia had come.

"Miranda, I wouldn't be asking you this if I didn't have concern, but do you have any idea what my son might be doing for your father today?"

The question filled Miranda with confusion; Sylvia had never before asked her about Caleb's work. All she could utter was that earlier Caleb had been at Cape House. Sylvia's next question was even more alarming.

"Do you know who flew into the airstrip yesterday? Are they friends of your father's, by some chance?"

Miranda's tongue clung to the roof of her mouth. Why should Sylvia want to know this so badly that she'd walked all this way? Would she have come to the house if she hadn't found Miranda in the garden? "I don't know." Which was a sort-of truth.

"I've a request to make of you." It was as if Sylvia had only now reached the real reason for her arrival. There was something severe about her manner, even regal. "I've come to ask you to have nothing more to do with my son."

Did Sylvia know about their botched encounter that afternoon at Cape House? If so, why would Sylvia be asking questions about Caleb's work or the visitors that she might have asked of Caleb, unless he'd refused to answer. Something had raised Sylvia's suspicions higher than ever. "But I don't—"

"Nevertheless, I'm asking you," Sylvia said with the same stern air.

There was something confounding about Sylvia's insistence. Here was someone else demanding Miranda acquiesce, like a child. Yet Sylvia's demand had affliction in it, as well as protectiveness, and in making it, Sylvia was asking Miranda to look clearly into herself, at all that she'd done, what she was doing.

"Why should I promise?"

"Because you'll hurt him whatever you do. Miranda, can you not see that?"

No matter how much she yearned to throw herself into Sylvia's arms, press her cheek against Sylvia's sweater, wait for the old kindness to arise, it was not possible. Sylvia had a great, invisible knife. With it she was cleaving the air between them, cutting it as sharply as cloth, slicing the past from the present and the present from the past, severing an imagined future. When Sylvia turned, it was as if she were pulling herself away for good.

Frank and Alan were in the yard, staring up at the flapping wind flag, the green rectangle of cloth tugged by the south-westerly, Alan teaching Frank an old wind rhyme.

"Wind in the north, no sailor should go forth."

Frank repeated the words.

"Wind in the east, not fit for man or beast."

They waved at Miranda as she approached, garden basket over her arm, the disturbance of Sylvia's words swimming in her, loss streaming past on all sides.

"Wind in the south brings bait into the fish's mouth," said Alan. "Miranda, tell us the last one."

"Wind in the west, that one is the best." But she didn't stop in her passage towards the bridge and through the back door.

"Wind decides everything," she heard her father say to Frank. There was no sign that in her absence Frank had asked her father probing questions about scientific research stations or an artificial haze in the sky or his own father. This was one more thing that threw Miranda off-kilter. Having set the basket full of greens on the counter, she found she couldn't stay in the house after all: she needed to know what her father and Frank were up to.

They had moved to the shed, where, door open, the muscular older man was explaining to the lanky young one how their power set-up worked: the solar panels attached to the western roof, the one bolted to the rocks by his study, the wind turbine, how they all connected to this storehouse of batteries.

Across the yard, Miranda scrabbled in the laying box for eggs for their supper, and Ella pressed close, as if she at least sensed Miranda's turmoil. Frank and her father were chatting about harnessing tidal power and small-scale wind farms and community energy grids and how that could work out here, and Frank was gesticulating excitedly. Why was her father showing Frank the mechanics of their survival and why was Frank, who organized protests and lived in a co-op in Boston and was surely going to vanish as soon as he could, acting so interested?

When her father shouted to her that it was time to take the weather measurements, Miranda went with them. She listened as her father explained to Frank what a Stevenson screen and an anemometer were, the wind sock dancing complicated patterns that the border between sea and land made of the air, and Miranda felt like a wind sock rippling.

Supper was the omelette her father cooked, the kale Miranda stir-fried, a sliced tomato she'd grown, and when her father pulled out a bottle of Norwegian vodka brought by

Anna Turi on her last visit and asked Miranda if she wanted some, she said yes. Frank ate hungrily, eyes on Alan as he told the story of crawling through the yard at night through Hurricane Jose. With a certain self-consciousness, Frank described huddling in a bunker on an unnamed Caribbean island while the house, well, mansion, really, above his head was torn to pieces, and Miranda spoke of the thunderstorm that had come to the island the previous July, the first in years, its huge clouds and violent stabs of lightning slowly moving across the land, how strange it had been to hear the rumble of thunder after so long. "When did you last hear thunder — before you came to the island?" Frank downed a mouthful of vodka with a sliver of iceberg in it.

Springing to his feet, Alan said, "Let's go outside and watch the sun set, shall we?" Pink light was already staining the white walls, moving across the planks and fading instant by instant.

They walked out into the grass and there, facing the cove and the western hills, her father threw an arm around each of them.

"Look, smoke." Miranda pointed to the faint plume on the far side of the cove. Was Caleb burning things in the firepit? It seemed an odd time to be doing so. But she was distracted, by the squeeze of her father's hand, by Frank's reckless exclamations about the beauty of the sky, by all that could be lost or was being lost, by Frank, tucked against her father's shoulder, saying, "You know what, I think I really could live out here," though likely he was drunk on vodka, the whirlwinds of the day, her father's conviviality. The words meant nothing. Nevertheless, her father smiled as if with secret satisfaction.

—

Miranda woke in darkness. She was riding a fierce wind. The changes were not going to stop. Someone was moving about below her, and the small sounds would have been reassuring, except that it was only a little after five a.m. Whoever was below had lit a fire. Heat ticked in the metal chimney on the far side of the room, the ticks speeding up. Miranda whispered to Ella not to stir.

Through the half-open door of her father's bedroom, she took in the tussle of his empty bedclothes, reading glasses tossed atop his dresser. Always there had been secrets in this house, and she had surrendered to her father's desire for them, the things they'd kept hidden about their past, other things he'd attempted to hide from her and she'd allowed herself to ignore, but a new impatience surged as if she were struggling to climb over the fence that encircled her.

Downstairs, in his coveralls, eating a slice of toast at the counter, her father turned sharply at the sound of her footsteps. "Miranda, what are you doing up?"

"Couldn't sleep." She kept her voice as low as his. He'd made only the one mug, not a pot, and everything in his posture made her presence an intrusion. He wasn't welcoming her, she was merely slowing his escape.

"Why don't you go back to bed? There's no need for you to be up so early."

But she was wide awake. "Where are you off to?"

His face relaxed into a smile. "To see if by some miracle I can access the internet at the cabin."

"Can I come with you?"

It was an impulsive thought, and he said no before adding, "There's no need for that."

"Why not if I want to? Are you meeting someone?"

He shook his head. "Best to have one of us stay with our guest." Our guest, she thought, and then, more possessively, *my* guest. Something else gnawed: Would her father lie to her? Had he before, would he again? Did her own safety make the lies justifiable?

"Dad—the plane that landed at the airstrip the day before yesterday, who was on it and what are they doing here?"

Her father gulped down the dregs of his tea and set his mug in the sink.

"Miranda, I need you to sit tight for a bit. Can you do that for me?"

He was ruffling her hair, asking her to do something for him once again. She shook herself free, some essential part of her refusing to be deterred, a new resolve forming in her throat.

"Why won't you answer me? I'm supposed to do what you want but you're always hiding things from me—saying we should never leave then inviting people here and going off with them. What are you actually doing? Whatever you're up to, it isn't just weather monitoring, is it?"

"Miranda." He stepped into the middle of the room. "If I've kept secrets, it's only been for your own good. Things are in such a precarious state. I'm trying, from this out-of-the-way corner of the world, to do everything I can—"

"What if I don't want to be protected like that?"

He didn't have an answer, other than to show her that she'd jarred him. When he hugged her, the strength of his embrace stopped her mouth even as she struggled to say more. The next moment, with a rustle of jacket and shudder of boot, her father was gone, leaving her alone once more, if not entirely alone, given Frank asleep upstairs.

—

Outside, Miranda called sharply to Ella as the wind bit her cheeks and raced through her long underwear, tangling at the place where her calves met her boots. Her father hadn't taken the quad. Even so, he'd vanished.

When she threw open the henhouse door and, with a whiff of ammonia, the girls burst into the run, flexing their speckled feathers, the sight of their ordinary hunger made tears spring into her eyes. Rosie, Mottle, June. A band of lemon light gathered along the eastern hills. What was going to happen? What should she do? The island was her home, the only home she had. Yet it no longer felt like the home she knew. Someone laid a hand on her forearm, and all the breath swept out of her.

"Miranda, it's all right now, it's all right," Caleb said.

She'd missed his approach, the wind rushing at her ears. Off about her own business, Ella only now galloped close, tail wagging, because Caleb, to her, was no intruder. Nostrils working, could Ella smell the wildness in him? He looked as dishevelled as Miranda had ever seen him, hair askew, mud on his coveralls, sweat in his clothes, possibly sleepless, a white moon, just past full, hanging in the sky behind him. Had he by chance spent the night at Cape House and had some new calamity befallen him there? He'd shouted at her the previous afternoon and now his touch on her arm set off a flapping through her, despite the gentleness of his voice. She was in nothing but sweater and boots and long underwear and needed to pee.

"Not meaning to frighten you, Miranda." There was the unpredictable in Caleb. Strong passions blew out of him. He was scanning about as if expecting her father to charge out of the house, still playing by those rules. It was only then that Miranda remembered Sylvia's words and the promise that Sylvia had attempted to extract from her the evening before, of which Caleb seemed oblivious.

"My father's not here," she said, and this seemed to relieve him.

"Where's he to?"

"He went out. I don't know when he'll be back."

"For a walk at this hour?"

"To the cabin, he said, but I'm not sure." Maybe she shouldn't be telling Caleb these things. Then again, he worked for her father. She had the strongest longing for their old unrecoverable companionship. She still trusted Caleb, loved him. Her almost-brother. Could she try again to ask him what he knew, ask for his confidence, tell him her concerns?

"Miranda, I've come to warn you, your father's up to dangerous things."

Once more the earth beneath her feet heaved, and her skin retracted at his words. "What do you mean?"

"Those men he's brought here—"

"Brought them?"

"Yes, Miranda, they're here to make a deal about some way to alter the weather all over the world and make it just the way they want it, I swear. They're meeting with your father this morning. They're ruthless and they want to make money off it. Has your father ever, *ever* talked to you about this?"

Once more the top of her head was turning. Here was Caleb repeating Frank's crazy words, only Caleb was going further. "How do you know my father's—"

"I took two of them out yesterday evening, Miranda,

and they got to talking. They were telling me things. They threatened me. I realized, I've helped him—"

"Helped how?"

"Experiments. I didn't know. Miranda, you have to come away with me."

He was close beside her, as close as they'd been in over a year, close enough that she smelled the sourness on him, took in the little pockmarks on his skin. But the undoable moments on the boat were also inside them. And the afternoon before, the sight of her with Frank had made him so angry.

"You can do whatever you want, Miranda, not what your father wants. We can make a good life across the cove, a life of our own, you know that. She's a good house. There's space to grow things. And beauty. We'll have all we need. For years. Free yourself, Miranda. You know how much you want this."

Her body trembled. As the light grew, robins flew overhead, not just one or two but a great flock. "Caleb, I'm sorry for what I did, and what I said, and then for all the silence." Once they'd sat together at a Formica table in a tiny shack out on one of the Little Fish Islands, and she'd dreamed of a life just like the one he described, when it was still possible to imagine a future that resembled the past, when they were two outsiders claiming a world for themselves. "But I can't come with you."

"What do you mean?" He stood bereft, while she tried to determine what new courage was required of her.

"I can't be who you want."

"You have to get used to the new way, Miranda. Things will change."

He slid his fingers into hers, skin cold and damp, and squeezed, and she squeezed back, before extracting her fingers from his. When he placed a hand on her arm, her pulse hammered. Holding tight, he tugged, as if he would drag her somewhere.

She backed away from him, which felt like running. She held onto the doorknob from inside the house because there was no lock, but there was no sound of Caleb following her up onto the bridge. No stirring from Frank either. Only Ella, loudly lapping from her water bowl, Ella whose barks had made Caleb turn, distracting him long enough for Miranda to wrench herself free. Upstairs, she didn't bother to knock before bursting into the spare room.

Frank lay sprawled on his back, naked, the sheets and quilt in a tangle on the floor, Miranda's entry waking him so suddenly he bolted to his feet. Staggering to avoid the ceiling, he attempted to wrench the sheet from its mound and cover himself while Ella sniffed and Miranda stared.

All that skin. She tumbled from one tumult into another. There were bruises all over his body, which was nothing like her father's body, what of it she'd ever seen. Or Caleb's body. The room smelled of Frank's sleep. The sun was rising, pulling yellow over the hills from the east. Surely Frank could sense her agitation, although he seemed to be surfacing slowly out of whatever dreams or dreamless state had gripped him. He seated himself carefully on the edge of the bed as if he still wasn't sure where he was—what explanation was she to offer for bursting in?

"Did you really mean it last night when you said you could live here—here in this house? With my father?"

In response, Frank offered her a dreamy grin. "Would you like that?"

"No," Miranda said firmly.

And Frank laughed, which made Miranda laugh as well, even though she barely knew why, yet somehow the laugh was a release.

She wanted to touch him, touch all of him. There wasn't time. She shouldn't even be imagining these things. Stepping close, she ran her fingers over the line of black characters tattooed along the inside of Frank's left forearm, how soft and smooth his skin was, pale brown, nearly hairless. He would get cold soon, in the raw morning air, and cover himself. He was ephemeral, not of her world, and soon he would disappear.

"What does this mean?"

"Oh," Frank said as they both looked at his tattoo. "It doesn't say noodles or dog or terrible mistake in case you're wondering. It's inspired by something my mother used to say to me. Like when I would get furious at my father and harangue him about why he didn't pay more taxes. I'd call him a swindler and a thief, and she'd take me aside and say, Frank, please be more productively disobedient. I believe she meant, Don't be so reactive. So when I asked her how that might be translated into kanji she said it was impossible but she wrote this out for me instead. *Gihan.* The character *gi* means justice or morality, and *han* means rebel or outlaw, so like righteous rebel. I can live with that."

When Miranda ran her thumb over the characters, 叛義, the touch went all the way through her, into the deepest places. Frank twisted his fingers so they were laced against hers, a delicate pressure. He yawned and smiled again. This was the feel of her fingers on his lips. Nothing, nothing had ever been like it.

Miranda couldn't stop the words from bursting out. "I think my father's doing something with your father."

Frank struggled to his feet. So much was competing in her: his skin, the ferocious surface of her own skin. Her father had left the house about an hour ago, she said. He'd told her to stay with their guest. Didn't that mean she was free to go anywhere Frank went? Her body followed every movement of his body.

Wait, there was more. Her father was a climate scientist. How liberating, after so long, to say the words. He'd been attacked by climate-change deniers. Her mother had been hit by a car and died. In Princeton, New Jersey. Nine years ago. They'd fled and hidden themselves away on Blaze Island.

Shortly after they arrived, Miranda said, she and her father had borrowed a book of poems from the library. There was one poem in particular they'd loved and memorized and sometimes recited to each other, sitting by the shore. It was sombre but beautiful, a poem spoken by a father to a daughter, by a man facing death who also looks out on the new lands of a new life from his wrecked ship, and somehow the poem had felt like an echo of their own journey. It was by a man named T.S. Eliot, she said, from a book called *The Ariel Poems*, and she'd seen it lying on top of her father's dresser only that morning. As far as she knew, it was still there.

"Caleb Borders came by and said my father's meeting the men from the plane."

"We should go." Frank dropped the sheet and seemed unabashed, now, at Miranda seeing him naked, even with an erection, as he tugged on his black boxers. "I think I remember when that ruckus happened, with your father. Crazy. And now he wants to engineer the air."

He was still so close, close enough to touch, the room small enough they had to squeeze around each other, and he was touching her, kissing her, were they not kissing each other, the bed taking up so much space, and Ella sprawled on it, panting.

Had her father written the letter that had drawn Frank to the island? Was her father the enigmatic Anouk Sand, who, for his own reasons, had brought Frank here and thrown him in her way? He had directed all this, offering Frank to her as a gift or distraction, to keep her occupied while he did what he wanted.

The repulsive idea rose in her and Miranda backed out of the room, aghast, leaving Frank in his ripped jeans, staring at her as he yanked his arms into his own bedraggled sweater. His face pulled into a question mark. "What?"

She had a choice. Run out of the house, down the lane, clamber alone over the broken road. Who was going to stop her? Where would she go? Anywhere she could reach. Her chest was a cloud chamber, churning. Why did the new bring so much loss? But she was ready to throw herself into whatever lay ahead. Into who knew what weather. Possibly her father had imagined this: there were things she could learn from Frank, and he from her. And she had. She was learning with every moment. She needed to know all she could. Here was another thing she knew: she didn't want to make a new world alone. There had to be others and she would seek them. They had to build a world together. One, two, a crowd, as many as possible. Who else was out there?

"We have to find our fathers—" Frank shouted, dashing ahead of her.

"There are other things we have to do, too," Miranda shouted back.

. . .

Caleb stumbled down the lane. This time, meeting the girl
in her yard with the dawn light growing, there'd been no
shouting. This time she'd been the one to tear herself away.
Eyes burning, when he came to the road, he turned in the
direction of the washout and Green Cove, back the way he'd
come, past the wreckage of the stranger's blue car. Once
again, he scrambled over chunks of pavement, boulders, the
broken world, through water that was lower now, its ferocity
becoming a remembered shock. On the far side, still some
distance off, Della Burke's dew-speckled compact waited where
Caleb had parked it the previous evening, when he'd brought
the two men to his home-in-progress, still caught up in the
fervent, ludicrous belief that Len Hansen would be his saviour.
How far he was from that hope now.

Caleb had no idea how Anna had returned the two men to
Tom's Neck after she'd burst in on them. He'd been in no state
to drive anywhere and Anna hadn't asked. They must have
stumbled along the road in the dark, past looming rocks and
glimmering ponds, Anna herding the men unforgivingly with
her flashlight. There was a twinge of vicarious relish in the
thought of the men's drunken discomfort, their being slapped
about by the cold night air. Caleb touched the sore place at

his throat—had Tony McIntosh really tried to strangle him? Once they'd departed, Caleb had collapsed on the fisherman's daybed in the corner of the Cape House kitchen, wind roving over him. At dawn he'd blundered outside, gripped by the conviction that he had to go to the girl—tell her all that he knew.

At the sight of Della's car, Caleb patted his pockets. Mercifully, he hadn't lost the key. Inside, he rested his aching forehead on the steering wheel. The car's cool interior smelled of air freshener, old smoke, and the sea. The sun came up and its warmth caressed him. The rote of the waves filled his ears. At a bird's piercing cry, he raised his eyes.

A flock flew past, circling, searching for the sand that hadn't yet returned. Curlews, their long, curved bills unmistakable, flying down from the north, on their way south for the winter. Early. They shouldn't yet be here.

What would the particulates the old man and those others planned to spray into the atmosphere mean to the curlews? Could the haze harm them? But the new, man-made weather was already tossing the curlews about.

Caleb let his mind move into the curlews, into the swift, steady pounding of their hearts. There was calm in it. Still grief-stricken, he turned the key in the ignition and Della's car shuddered to mechanical life, gasoline flowing through its veins. He had no clear thought as to where he would go until, reaching the rutted, gravel access road that led through the barrens to the crest of Telephone Hill, he took the turn.

Leaving the car where the bumpy lane ended, he walked the last stretch to reach the perimeter fencing that enclosed the metal cellphone tower. Above him, its broken support cables clanked mournfully in the wind around its spindly, canting height. One of its receptor panels hung loose in the air. He didn't care about the tower. Instead Caleb poured all his awareness into the lichen that crawled in the slowest circles across the granite, the soft mounds of moss, the masses of crowberry bushes, the little flies, the coppery water of the ponds that dotted the barrens. Seeking consolation. And advice. The old man was out there somewhere. If he and the other men were going to meet, presumably this morning, they would have to travel across the land, and, from up here, their tiny figures would be impossible to miss.

He'd wait them out: he had all the patience he needed to sit tight until he saw something.

Once more the new knowledge gleaned the night before tore through him: the man-made haze; these men, who wanted the weather to do whatever they wished, who might use violence to get their way. Who wanted to make money off whatever this new technology was, an engineered particle. Was that not something the old man and Arun had spoken of in his presence? Hadn't the old man spoken of patents as well? So was the old man, despite all his concern about changing weather and melting ice, looking to get rich alongside the Hansens? How deep did his deceptions go? Whatever experiments he'd been conducting, whatever trial particulates he'd sprayed into the air from his homemade pumps through that lime-green tubing attached to floating balloons, he'd done it here, on Blaze Island, meaning Caleb himself and all that he loved—this small place vast enough it had once taken days to cross, where there might yet be rocks no human had set eyes on, where fish had once been so plentiful you could practically scoop a hand into the water to catch one—they were at the heart of the experiment. When the old man had said to him, Tread lightly on the land, and, Find your home and stay close to it, he'd listened. Oh, such a good student he'd been. And look where it had got him.

He'd eaten so little in the past day, drunk more than he'd eaten. His head throbbed. But there were Labrador tea bushes just out of reach and his mother's words, some of the old wisdom, returned. Chew the leaves to settle your stomach. Stumbling to his feet, Caleb pushed a sprig, bitter and aromatic, into his mouth.

There were bright red partridgeberries at his feet, dotting the rocks. Spitting out the leaves, Caleb gathered them, the fattest and juiciest ones, leaving the pale pink ones to ripen. Here was something. Their tartness made his stomach quiver but they stayed down. The dizziness that had rocked him began to settle. The land was a hand at his back. A warmth that held him.

Only two days ago, before the storm — how could it be only two days? — he'd come upon old Wince Osmond, out on the rocks by Wells Lane, flat on his stomach, picking the first berries. Caleb had halted at the sight, a man lying on his stomach amid the rocks. Raising his head, old Wince had told him how he'd just had an operation and couldn't yet bend his right knee, but that wasn't about to stop him picking for the wife.

He would never be able to tell the girl this story.

The sun had risen above the hills. Far off, if he stared towards the water, the solar panels on the shore side of the little white house glowed as the moon sank. The wind turbine spun in its field, wind flag rippling into the northeast. The weather monitors on the far side of the house were out of sight but trees climbed the slope to where the girl's garden was. Trees that might one day make a new, small forest. How benign it all looked. How much of his life had been touched by a place now utterly inaccessible.

Locked in the trunk of Della's car was a thing Caleb had set there and nearly forgotten. The previous morning, he'd filled a can of gas at Vera's store in Pummelly. He'd left that can with Pat Green to give to his uncle Leo to pass on to his mother and great-aunt. Caleb hoped Leo had done so. Midday he'd filled the old man's jerry can in Tom's Neck, then transferred that container, still full of gas, from the back of his quad to the trunk of Della's car. Where it still lay.

Once more Caleb patted the pockets of his coveralls for the key. Back at the car, he blessed Della Burke who smoked and kept a lighter on the little shelf in front of the emergency brake, even if she might be beyond furious with him, wondering if he'd run off with her car for good. Caleb pressed the key to release the trunk. There were some rags in its depths and he grabbed a couple of these before lifting out the red plastic container full of gas.

When someone spoke his name, he dropped the can as if it were on fire.

He recognized Agnes Watson immediately, for all that he hadn't seen her in years. Her curious, compressed energy, which had once made him feel as if he were standing near a caribou, travelled towards him. At the top of the track, in a jacket the colour of sand, she was smaller than he remembered, her brown hair, or what he could see of it beneath her wool hat, longer, a dark fringe spackling her forehead.

"When did you get to the island?" Caleb demanded.

In response, Agnes crunched up the lane with her deliberate stride. He'd not seen or heard any sign of a vehicle from the direction of the road, but Caleb knew of Agnes's propensity for walking great distances across the land.

One snowy afternoon four years before, he and his cousin Ger were running an errand in Gerald's truck to the hardware store in middle island, when Caleb had spotted a figure walking along the highway between Harbour Islands and Shallow Bay. This was the day after Agnes Watson had surprised him out on the slide paths, when he'd snowshoed in to check on his rabbit snares rather than borrowing one of his uncles' Ski-doos. Once again, as she walked along the road's narrow shoulder, made even narrower by the drifting snow, Agnes was wearing a snow-white jacket, which seemed pure foolishness, except that a red knapsack slung over her back made a bright and moving flare, and her sealskin hat and mitts stood out as well. Gerald didn't want to stop but Caleb said they ought to. He told Ger the woman was staying with Alan Wells. When they pulled up in front of her, Agnes thanked them for the offer of a ride, but said if it was no bother, she preferred to walk, her narrowed eyes turning back to the still, white expanse of the iced-in sea.

She made his skin stiffen, as she faced him on Telephone Hill. She'd arrived the night of the storm, she told him, on the last ferry, made it as far as Shallow Bay before pulling off the road. She'd used the jack in the spare tire set of her rental car to break into the disused Anglican church.

"Out of gas?" Agnes asked, nodding at the jerry can. Caleb didn't know what to say. He heaved shut the trunk of Della's car and picked up the plastic container.

"Everyone's running out of gas," he managed, shifting from foot to foot. "What are you doing this way?"

"Out for a walk. Hoping to meet you." Agnes offered a thin smile.

"Where did you spend the night?"

"At the shore."

"The shore? What shore?"

"On what sand is left in Green Cove." This was utterly perplexing, yet when Caleb looked closer, he spotted traces of sand clinging to her jeans and speckling Agnes's wool hat. So while he'd been up at Cape House, she'd been not far off. Water must practically have been lapping at her toes.

"Now why would you do that?"

"I had it in mind to speak to Alan but saw he had a guest" —she must mean the young American—"and this morning he left so early I had no chance. Then you showed up in the yard. And I wanted to greet and sing to the sea."

It was unnerving, to discover such a private, rending moment had been observed, if at a distance, by someone engaged in their own private moment. Agnes had an air of mournful exhaustion. There were dark stains under her eyes, as if, not surprisingly, she'd barely slept. "I heard the car start and head up the hill, so I followed the sound, saw it parked up here from the road. Thought you might be able to tell me what's going on."

"Me?" Caleb said in astonishment. "Is that right? You're one of his team, on that fancy project, aren't you? You ought to be the one telling me."

The long, contemplative look that Agnes gave him was not unlike the look she'd offered the wintry day they'd met on the slide path. Then, Caleb had felt her taking in the colour of his skin, darker than her own, and the curiosity he'd felt from Agnes had not been like the estranging curiosity of others around him. When she'd asked him who his people were, he'd told her his mother's were from the island. As for his father's, well, could be Papua New Guinea or Paraguay for all he knew, smoked Irish was what most people around here called people like him, and when Agnes nodded, Caleb felt no judgment from her.

"What do you know, Caleb?" Agnes asked now.

"What do I know? I reckon it's not weather monitoring going on here, is it, the particle haze, the deal with these men. Why all the secrecy, why doesn't he want to be seen, why is he so frantic they not know his name?"

"Can I tell you a story?" Agnes asked.

"No time for that now." Because, truly, if he was to do as he planned, he needed to be on his way.

"Last winter the ice in the bay where I come from didn't freeze up until February," Agnes said. "That's months later than in the old days, months, not weeks. The temperature of the sea up there is rising faster than almost anywhere in the world. Twelve people fell through the ice last winter and had to be rescued, including my youngest uncle. Hunters can't get to their cabins because the ice isn't safe to travel on and they can't get out on the land. My cousin Eli's involved in a project placing sensors into the ice and on the runners of sleds as a warning system that will alert people when and where the ice gets thin. Better adapt than die, he says, and better we all work together. In the past, scientists came up, including my own father, who's a Scottish ornithologist. Like the rest of them, he looked around, did his thing, and took off. That's what I liked about Alan from the first time I met him, he kept coming back, he listened to what the elders had to say about the weather, and he was better than most about sharing his data."

Caleb shifted from foot to foot.

"Kappiasuvunga. That means, I am afraid, in my mother's language," Agnes said. "Once there was a man who studied the ice. He and his team of researchers and students, including me, drilled deep into glaciers. We brought up ice cores, a record of ice over thousands of years, but what we observed of the recent past was troubling. When this man told the world what he feared, other people became so afraid they threatened to bomb the place where he worked and kill him. So he vanished, leaving everything behind. Meanwhile, people's behaviour didn't change and weather patterns grew more violent and unpredictable. Even in the place he'd fled to, this man's fear grew. Other people's fear grew elsewhere as the ice kept melting. So he began to wonder, Is there something we can do to save the ice? He reached out to others who love the snow and ice as much as he does and know how much we need it—"

Caleb was aware of her lips, the sand grains on Agnes's cheek. "You're talking about him. Alan Wells." He'd felt her love that day, as they stood together beside a grove of wind-battered spruce trees, staring out over the white, still sea, how love of the ice was like blood to her.

"If you want to find out if what I've said is true, you'll need to search for him under a different name. It's Milan Wells."

Well, now. It was like encountering the same person only they were wearing a different skin. Bomb threats. People had tried to kill him. Which was a shocking discovery, though if Agnes thought the news would elicit his sympathy, she was wrong.

"I've thought and thought about what Alan proposed—" Agnes said.

"Not just him but you!" Caleb shouted, gas can sloshing at his side.

"Maybe there would be an application, a spraying program workable on a local scale, that might specifically target the ice and not need to be global or so intrusive. I hoped for something, I wanted to believe, but I've come to think the desire for such a thing, his desire, even his fear, it's corrupting. In reaching out to these men, in whatever way, there's still a risk—. One of my aunts said to me, Don't act out of despair. Caleb, where are you going with that gas can?"

A path led away across the flat rocks. He couldn't stop himself from turning back once more.

"How bad is it out there?"

"Out where?"

"Across the bay, everywhere else." He needed to know and no one seemed able to tell him.

"I came from Nain, not from down south. I took the ferry past Rigolet and Hopedale, hitched a ride from St. Anthony to Gander, picked up the rental car there. It's not going to be so good on the other side now, is it, where Fernand went through, though up north we still have smoke in our eyes from all the forest fires that won't stop burning in Quebec, and the sun when it shines is bronze like bog myrtle in the fall."

Not long before the power went out at his great-aunt's, the weather channel had announced another hurricane forming in the Caribbean. Where was that one now? Maybe what he wanted to know was, Is it so bad out there as to be unimaginable?

Caleb took off at a run. There was a path around the perimeter fencing and from there another track led off through the mounds of rust-stained rock scraped by ancient ice and wind and bared by fire. Out of the northwest, from the direction of Tom's Neck, something tiny and moving—human?—caught his eye.

The gas can, an awkward weight, tugged at his side. The ground underfoot was still wet and puddled with mud, and protruding rocks were there to be tripped over. His own steps shuddered loud. The wind had shifted into the south so that he was running into it, not a wild wind, yet strong enough to pummel his ears. Rolling banks of cumulus cloud filled the sky, a window of blue among them. A squall cloud hung veil-like in the distance, taunting him. Already his stomach was cramping.

Anger remained a pulse, alongside exhaustion. His mother's voice rose, all the times she'd tried to warn him about what Alan Wells was up to. Her fear, her suspicions. He's not to be trusted. He should have listened to her. Yes. Caleb spat and spat again.

When the weight of the gas can felt like it would pull his shoulder out of its socket, Caleb slung the can into his other hand. A tawny fox, ahead on the path, bottle-brush tail straight out, bolted at the thud of his steps and the tattered breaths he couldn't quiet. There was no sound of Agnes behind him, which didn't mean she wasn't back there, and he was leaving a trail of footsteps it would be impossible to miss.

Coming over a rise, Caleb plunged to a stop. The musk caught him, then the sight. A caribou stag stood in the path, one branch-like rack of antler rising from his head. Caleb knew this stag. In winter, he'd seen the same creature from the road, near Shallow Bay, feeding among the rocks, shaggy and white-coated, ribs showing, notable because of the single antler, only a scar where the other had been. Now the stag was in his brownish summer coat, not yet moulting. There were others close by, caribou brought to the island in the years before his mother was born. Now there were fewer all the time, coyotes hunting them, the lichen they ate growing ever more slowly. Caleb sensed their presence, but it was the stag who held him in the mutual, nearly unbearable pressure of seeing and being seen.

He shook himself out and, grabbing the can again, charged forward, a pair of coyotes out there too, trotting along another path.

At each fork, Caleb bore to the southeast. Off on his right appeared a clearing where the Green brothers had been cutting wood, trimming the hewn trunks before teepeeing them to dry. There were more trees around him now, juniper and black spruce and tamarack. The next fork led to Frenchman's Pond where the old man had taught himself and the girl to swim, the water's taste as sweet and dense as tea.

That way led to Martin Green's cabin, Martin who like his uncle Charlie now worked out west in the oil. Crane operator, he was. His cousin Danny was training to pilot an oil tanker, one of those that travelled up and down the coast between the eastern oil platforms. That's where the work and the money were. For now. Burning oil spewed carbon into the air. On and on the ever-more-tumultuous weather ran through all of them.

Past a tangle of raspberry cane, through another stand of alders, there at last was the spare wooden frame of the old man's cabin, which Caleb had helped Pat Green and the old man build, with its view across another plain of rock and out to sea. No lights shone inside. The curtains remained drawn. No smoke rose from the chimney. What was being asked of him? To see through space and time, to feel all the pain he could in a world stripped of illusion? Was pain the price of clarity? What lay on the other side of pain?

Muscles spasming, Caleb swore at himself, fingers so numb it became a feat to unlatch the circle of interlocking teeth on the gas can's black plastic cap.

The cabin was the place where the old man kept his most prized equipment, the multiple screens, the tall metal storage units, secure behind the locked door, and data too, backed up no doubt, but the equipment housed all his secret plans, and the cabin itself was made of wood.

On the bridge, Caleb sloshed gasoline against the boards of the walls. The doorknob, which he didn't try, was rusty from exposure to salt winds and no doubt the wood was damp after all the rain the hurricane had dumped on them. He would circle the cabin first. The smell of the gas swilling around him made him gag, but the old man would see the flames and for a brief, victorious moment he—Caleb Borders—he, too, would be seen.

He was around back of the house, sloshing a stream of gasoline over that wall, slopping gasoline all over himself as well, when someone knocked him to his knees from behind and sent him sprawling. An arm, not his, righted the toppled container that glugged gasoline into the spongy ground. Caleb struggled to break free of the grip that pressed his chest to the earth, catching a glimpse of blue coverall as a knee dug into his back. Hard hands clasped his wrists and pulled his shoulders tight. He yelled.

He heard the old man's voice. "It's become aggravating how much you keep interfering with my plans, Caleb."

"I'm messing with *your* plans?" At that, the old man, who had reserves of muscular strength Caleb seemed not to have, gave him a blow hard enough to stun him, and held him down while binding his wrists with something that felt like cloth.

He couldn't believe this, the old man was actually gagging him with more of the ripped sheet, tightening the cloth in a knot behind his head, so close that each flex of the man's body, each taut heave of purpose and huff of breath felt like an echo of his own.

"It won't be for too long," the old man said, patting Caleb on the shoulder as he hauled him upright and pushed him towards a spruce tree, then, with two neat kicks that made Caleb's knees buckle once more, lowered him to the ground. With another strip of sheet, the old man tied him to the trunk.

. . .

Over rocks and mud they ran, Ella loping ahead, tongue at a rakish loll, Frank behind Miranda until she lost the sound of him and turned to find him doubled over, voice barely audible between gasps. *I need a break.* He seemed close to stumbling, and Miranda, too, was breathless enough that it was hard to speak. Pulling a jar of water out of her knapsack, she passed it over and Frank drank in grateful gulps.

In the mud ahead of them a single set of boot treads imprinted themselves over quad tracks laid the day before, footprints that, Miranda was certain as she knelt over them, belonged to her father. So he had gone to the cabin as he'd told her. Yet there were no other tracks, so where were the men from the plane whom Caleb had insisted her father was meeting — Frank's father and uncle, according to Frank, who were supposed to be signing a deal to back her own father's research into cooling the Earth with a haze of tiny droplets. A stop-gap measure, she thought her father had said, yet Caleb had told her the men were in it to make money, and he'd called them ruthless. She had no idea how to square the circle if there was a circle to be squared. Was her father deceiving her, or lost in a sea of self-contradictions? He'd spoken on the phone to someone who'd flown in and knew who Agnes Watson and Arun Mudalnayake were. Arun was supposed to have come to the island but was stuck in Boston, Agnes might be somewhere nearby, which left Anna; where was she?

Whatever they were up to, the ARIEL project that Frank had described, based on something someone had outlined to him in a letter, she and Frank and Caleb, too, would have to live with the consequences: even worse weather, more droughts or floods, altered winds. In the aftermath, however far-fetched all this was, they'd be here, picking up the pieces.

Yet what she really wanted to explain to Frank, who'd thrown himself into a patch of crowberries, was how the world kept expanding. Perilously, necessarily, and he was part of this magnificent yet terrifying alteration, the surging, the unravelling, whatever it was.

"Miranda?" Frank stared up at the shifting clouds. "Did I tell you my father's offered me a seat on his Mars expedition? If things get bad around here. All of this is like a huge gamble to him, if the Earth thing works, great, if it doesn't, the chosen few will be whisked away to a place where there's no breathable air and there was, like, water a million years ago, where we won't be able to go outside and there's no way back. Doesn't that sound fabulous? Want me to ask him if you can come, too?" When Ella licked his sweaty face, Frank pushed her away with bursts of breath. "You want me to ask him about dogs? Take my word for it, Ella, you don't want to go there."

He was on his feet again, loose-limbed in his jeans and bedraggled sweater, one of Miranda's knitted hats clamped on his head. Now he was telling her how, for his eleventh birthday his father had organized a paintball party, sent out all the invitations before Frank knew a thing, and, on the day of the party, when Frank refused to go, his father had grown so angry Frank was convinced he was going to throw him down the stairs.

They were jogging. Even now, Frank said, his father was looking to buy out another airline and start another discount subsidiary— *as a democratizing venture*. He gave a hard laugh. "As if already having a footprint big enough to leave a mark on the geological record isn't enough, it has to be the biggest footprint possible because insatiability is all he can imagine. Even if it brings on a firestorm, he's convinced he'll survive it. Or else he's just desperate to be loved."

He stumbled once more to a halt. "But I'm giving you the wrong impression. I'm leaving out his phenomenal animal magnetism. You'll see. Everyone flocks to him. He used to play stadiums with thousands and thousands of people cheering. I've seen the videos, the total adulation. His generosity. He wants to give me everything he didn't have as a kid but the deal is I have to be masochistically grateful, and when I'm not it slays him because he's such a narcissist. He taught me how to sail, we'd go out on one of his boats together or wander along the shore of this island he owns, searching for the green flash that happens sometimes, you must know, when the sun sets over the ocean—"

"Have you seen it?"

Frank held out a hand. "You're my green flash, Miranda. You're my accidental. Maybe we don't need to go anywhere. We stop right now and hang out here, just the two of us."

When she slipped her gloved hand into his, the new and thrilling electricity jolted through her. It caught at her too, the desperate desire to let everything else fall away. She squeezed again. "Later. First we have to find out what they're up to."

And here was a path forking off to the right, through tamarack and spruce, leading into the hills, and there in the soft dirt—following the lead of Ella's nose, Miranda knelt over a confusion of footprints, coming from the fork and continuing along the path ahead. "What if they've already done whatever they're doing and we're too late?" she cried with a rush of helplessness.

"We'll still find a way to stop them," said Frank. He seemed both young and old as, with a touch of his hand to her back, he was the one reassuring her.

The cabin stood on a plain of rock, trees and solar panels at the rear. The building was unassumingly small and grey, a cottage Miranda might have called it once, the place for which her father had half-abandoned her. Out on the bridge a woman in a yellow rain jacket paced. Anna Turi, yes, it was surely Anna's willowy frame and ardent stare. Anna stiffened at the sight of them. Her alarm seemed at first to be concern, as if they were running towards her bearing news of disaster from somewhere else, only as they drew closer, they transformed into the danger, and when they came stumbling up to the cabin's front steps, she threw out her arms to stop them.

"You can't go in there, Miranda," Anna said fiercely.

"Anna, I have to speak to my father."

Sweaty and red-cheeked, Frank plunged under one of Anna's outstretched arms, Ella scrambling after him onto the bridge.

"Please let me through," Miranda cried. What could she possibly say to convince wide-eyed Anna, her father's collaborator, who no doubt had the strength if she wanted to pin

Miranda in place, to let her pass? Yet a pained tenderness seized Anna's face and, with a waver, she dropped her arms.

On the bridge, the smell of gasoline billowed up from the planks as Frank fought the rusty door handle. Of course the door would be locked. Would they have to break through a window to reach their own fathers? What would they find? But when Frank gave the door one more shove, the handle released, practically throwing them inside.

In the dim room, where the flowered curtains had barely been opened, four men sat around a wooden table. At the rear, her father shifted silently at their tumbled entrance. But it was the man to his right, with the shock of white-blonde hair, broad-shouldered, signing something with a stylus on an electronic pad, who seized Miranda's attention, who seemed to occupy so much space that he obliterated the other men with him.

Roy Hansen's large features were surrounded by dark troughs of skin. Unshaven, his bristled cheeks in no way detracted from his handsomeness. Where was he in Frank, or Frank in him? Miranda strained to find something. The lips. The air of bold ardour. Airline magnate, carbon pirate, Roy seemed both invincible and intensely childlike, more childlike than Frank, and the combination was mesmerizing and uncanny.

"Don't sign anything," Frank shouted. At his lunge through the dimness towards the table, such an ordinary table, his father thrust himself to his feet, taller than Frank and blistering with outrage.

"What the hell?"

By the door, Miranda knew herself to be invisible to all but her own father's slitted gaze. All eyes were on Frank reaching for the computer pad, only the man in a red nylon jacket, his back to Miranda, grabbed the pad before Frank could and clutched it like a birthday present to his chest. On the far side of the table, a man with receding, slicked-back hair and a thick stare hidden behind glasses looked ready to pounce. Towering above them all, Frank's father ordered Frank to remove his hat. Before Frank could do a thing, his father surged forward and ripped the wool hat from Frank's head. The next moment he was smothering Frank in his arms.

Fury still seemed to pour from Roy Hansen, only it couldn't simply be fury. "What are you doing here? You're supposed to be dead." He was shaking Frank as if Frank were a doll in his grip, and Frank, whose black hair lay plastered damp against his forehead, whose chest still shuddered from their run, seemed at first to go limp in his father's hands.

"I'm not dead," said Frank in a squeaky voice that he struggled to break free of. "It was a long drive, I almost drowned at the end, but I'm here."

"Why the hell didn't you fly in with us?"

"I didn't want to come with you, I want to stop you." Frank's voice gained strength as Miranda sent all her breath towards him.

"Stop us from what?" Kindness had entered Roy, or guile, his smile giving off brilliant flashes that seemed determined to seduce them all. "You don't even know why I'm here."

He had tucked Frank close to his shoulder — was the gentleness real? When Miranda tried to catch Frank's eye, he seemed far off, caught in a struggle. Was it love that turned his father into a fierce and gaping mouth, a mouth that wanted to swallow Frank whole, because Frank was his and there to be possessed?

"So why don't you tell me?" Frank said, just as new footsteps thundered onto the bridge and shouts burst outside the door at Miranda's back.

Anna's voice—and Caleb's? Miranda had no sooner hauled barking Ella into the corner where the propane camping stove and kitchen cupboards were than the door swung open again.

"That's the end of all experiments, all right?" Caleb cried. "No more spraying anything on this island."

The odour of gasoline, already strong in the room, grew stronger, the smell pouring from Caleb's dirty coveralls, which must, for some reason, be saturated with it. There were spruce needles in his hair and crease marks on his cheeks, and at his arrival, as if this time taken by surprise, Alan leaped to his feet.

"I want you off my island." Caleb's gaze veered into Miranda's and kept moving. There was something shocking about the ease with which he passed her by in order to concentrate on the men, as if, amid all this cacophony and chaos, he had become unreal to her, and she to him, and this made her shiver.

The knock was as startling as any other intrusion. Equally startling was Caleb turning to open the door. Agnes Watson, watchful and determined and not seen by Miranda since that early spring visit when she'd carved up a seal at shore, stood on the threshold with Anna Turi.

"Agnes, you're here." Alan's face lit up with joy. "I was really beginning to worry what had happened to you."

"Yes, I'm here," Agnes said, wiping her forehead with one arm, though her own response was more muted than his.

"Did one of you release him?"

"I did," Agnes said. "You think I was going to leave him tied up like that?"

"It was temporary, to allow us to get some work done here."

"Not a good idea, Alan," said Agnes. There were strips of what looked like ripped sheet dangling from her jacket pockets. "Why shouldn't he hear what you have to say?"

Caleb's face quickened.

"Absolutely," said Alan, whose own expression remained inscrutable to Miranda as he took in the rebuke of Agnes's words, "as long as you promise, Caleb, not to disrupt things."

"I'll give you a few moments," Caleb said gruffly, and when he ducked his head, Miranda recalled the gesture from the long-ago night when they'd first met. Caleb had been a boy then. Now he moved with the energy of one sensing his possible authority.

"Why don't you all find a seat?" Alan said. "It's a bit cramped in here but we ought to be able to make this work."

There was enough light coming in around the curtains for them to see each other. Miranda tugged open the curtain above the sink but didn't turn on the overhead light, while at her side, Ella's nose kept working, taking in the barrage of scents along with the painful stink of gasoline. The room was thick with odours of human sweat, an undernote of damp, the wood stove unlit. Anna and Agnes settled together on the daybed on the far side of the room, Anna touching Agnes's shoulder, their clothes releasing trace notes of spruce and blackberry and outdoor air. Frank's father returned to his seat as Frank, with a glance at Miranda, dragged her father's desk chair from the corner of the room where her father's desk bulked in the shadows, along with its four darkened monitors and the metal blocks of all his data-filled hard drives.

"Caleb?" said Alan.

"I'll stand," said Caleb from the doorway.

"We're in the middle of a private meeting." The man in the red nylon jacket spoke plaintively from the near end of the table. His sulky gaze and twitchy lips radiated hostility. He must, Miranda realized, be Frank's uncle. "Can you not ask all these interlopers to leave?"

"Actually I can't," said Alan. "Things haven't gone as planned, but here's where we find ourselves, apart from my collaborator who remains trapped in Boston, but isn't this how it goes, these days, that we're relentlessly called upon to respond to the new unpredictabilities."

Had her father expected that she and Frank would find their way here, Miranda wondered, and find their way here together? Surely he hadn't planned for Caleb's sudden, dramatic entry.

As the man wearing glasses muttered something, Alan introduced Anna and Agnes as his colleagues: Anna Turi, climate modeller from Vaeroy Island by way of Norwich, England, Agnes Watson, geographer and climatologist, formerly of Ottawa, now back in Nain, Nunatsiavut, and could they spare a moment to hope that Arun Mudalnayake, Sri Lankan cloud physicist and nanoengineer, trapped in his Cambridge lab by Hurricane Fernand, was safe.

Agnes's face remained uneasy. Frank's uncle noted that others were also trapped. Alan nodded, fixing on him intently, and said indeed they were.

Her father had his own stealthy power, Miranda thought as she crouched on the floor by the stove. Somehow they'd all arrived here and he was surveying them not only across a small room but a vastness of many, moving landscapes. He was out on a sea of shifting and colliding ice pans, trying to keep his balance while leaping across the pans as if his life and so much more depended on it. She felt the shifting deep inside. He did not seem in control of anything, and this lack of control was reassuring, despite all that hung in the balance, accompanied as it was by his keen vigilance. Alan touched his lips. He stood and paced, running a hand through his greying beard.

"I could show you maps, graphs, some modelling data, data from our proto-experiments, but instead I'd like you all to imagine something," he said, at which Roy made a peculiar sound.

"Air. Water vapour condensing around billions of tiny particles to form clouds, which never stop moving and reforming. We model using sets of equations to represent sections of hundreds of kilometres of the Earth's atmosphere and super-computers evolve the grids forward in time. But real clouds are usually no more than a kilometre or two, and volatile, wisps of vapour and particles, some existing for no more than moments. It's extremely difficult to capture with any degree of accuracy in a computational model what clouds really are.

"Over the years, Anna and I have run models attempting to determine possible kinds and sizes of particle we might introduce into the atmosphere and the possible reflective haze that might result, how the particulates might behave up there, up among the high cirrus clouds. We have to consider clouds in all our climate models, high clouds and low. They're extremely hard to model because simultaneously large and small, and climate change itself is shifting the atmospheric patterns. The complexity of clouds—it's one of our biggest unknowns. It's not actually all that difficult to shoot particulates into the stratosphere, but to create a uniform global reflective coverage and sustain it? Even regionally—there's a huge amount of research still to be done. Is it possible to create coverage that has some beneficial effect on the snow pack, not to mention the world's whole weather system? Is it possible to do so without causing irreparable harm? In the air and on the ground? Who would ensure the safety of such a program and how? I can't tell you with any certainty at all. We're very, very far away from knowing this."

"Wait a minute," said Roy. "You brought us all the way here to tell us you can't do something?"

"I invited you here as part of an experiment."

"To invest in a promising research and development project," said Roy.

"Roy, let me ask you a question. Why did you come?"

With an exhalation of impatience, Roy said, "Out of a desire to support evolving technologies, which will help us create a more robust and sustainable future. And tackle the carbon problem. I'm doing you a favour—"

"Me a favour, Roy?"

"I'm willing to offer you considerable financial backing—"

"We are willing—" Frank's uncle attempted to say in a smaller voice, which Miranda's father interrupted.

"You would be doing this for me? I hardly think so. And what I, what we, proposed to you won't tackle the carbon problem, only bandage it. The gases will go on accumulating, which all the studies we provided to you make clear. If we do something like this, it's got to be alongside robust decarbonization and carbon sequestration. Or else—what if the spraying ended suddenly, for who knows what reason, and there's nothing to protect us from all the still-soaring emissions waiting for us in the atmosphere? Our past, the past still hanging there up above us. In any case, do you really think the best way to proceed with something so risky and of such global import is via a small cabal of us, holed up in a cabin on a remote and windswept island?"

"We've put up with a hell of a lot of capriciousness to end up in this shack, which is not, I can assure you, what we thought we were coming to. If you wanna talk about being misled—"

"I invited you to see if you'd come. As I said, that was part of the experiment—it became the core of the experiment. And you came, Roy, you and Leonard and Tony. Not even a hurricane on the scale of Fernand was going to stop you, even as it went on hammering the seaboard, smashing cities, infrastructure, airports one by one. Possibly it made you more eager to come, am I right? Possibly it amplified your perception of the need to do something about our precarious predicament, which is only getting worse. Roy and Leonard, you even signed what Tony McIntosh called *my worthless preamble*, because there's something you want here, isn't there? Anna, can you—"

How did it happen that Anna came to be holding the electronic pad, which Frank's uncle Leonard had been clutching? He must have set it down and quick-fingered Anna, having picked it up, passed the pad to Alan, who, squinting, held it out far enough to read without his reading glasses. "*We confirm the evidence for human activities raising the temperature at the Earth's surface has reached a 'five-sigma' level of certainty, that is to say a probability of 'virtually certain,' or 99.999 per cent.* That's scientific language for there's no room for equivocation. None. Perhaps the wording sounds a bit fussy, since we've known this for years, yet it remains surprisingly difficult to get people to confirm it or act like it's true. Why do you think that is, Roy?"

Leaving his perch, Frank approached Alan and said, "Can I see that?"

When Alan handed him the pad, Frank stared at it. As if he didn't know what to do next, he stuffed the pad under his sweater, tucked into the waist of his jeans. With an amused smile Alan let him. Frank's father sat playing with a gold fountain pen, as if not looking at Frank were a way to dismiss him and turn him into a prankster. "Uncle Len," said Frank, "how about passing over that piece of paper I saw you fold up and put in your jacket pocket?"

"Oh, give it to him, Len," said Roy. "It's just a piece of paper. The digital file can be demolished and the signed hard copy can be ripped to pieces when we get it back."

"If you get it back," said Frank. "But, Dad, why would you want to destroy it? Really it would be more of a start if you acknowledged the extent of your own contribution to the destruction of the world as we know it. What do you think about that?"

"Roy, listen," said Alan. "What if I now reveal our aerosol intervention may work after all, there's real promise of a cooling method without significant harm in this engineered particulate and balloon technology we've been studying—but as a prerequisite for coming on board, and our accepting your backing, you must agree to decarbonize your company as swiftly as possible. Not only yours but the whole airline industry. Airline manufacturers, civil, military—the works. Perhaps that will mean shutting things down, at least in the short term, until a zero-carbon fuel source can be found. If it can be. Shrinking your footprint. No more growth. No more backing any oil and gas projects either. Surely you have enough money to live on by now, Roy. You could stop what you're doing tomorrow, give most of it away, and still have enough. Make a model of yourself. Globally. Roy Hansen of Tempus Airlines. You're a powerful man and a persuasive one, galvanizing even. Forget Mars. You could begin to change this world. Maybe you can even convince your pal Tony here, who's done so much damage. That's why I brought you—"

"He might agree, he might even go out and say these things, but would he actually do them—" said Frank.

Chair legs shrieked as Roy rose once more to his feet. "What right do you have—" only the steely voice of the third man cut over his.

"I know who you are." Across the table this man, the man named Tony, stood as well, loudly sucking in air. "You introduced yourself as Alan Wells, but that's not the name you used to go by, is it, when, if I remember correctly, you headed up some Arctic climate centre down in the States. Took me longer than it should have to put the pieces together, Wells, because you look a little more ravaged now." The man scrubbed his cheeks as if miming a beard.

A small, hard belly protruded beneath his shiny leather jacket and there was something eerily persistent about his smile. Miranda had seen him before. He, too, had looked younger, his hair darker and there'd been more of it. He'd worn different glasses then, but his blunt, pugilist's face had imprinted itself on her.

Nine years before, in their Princeton living room, her mother had grabbed the remote and switched the television off, her body shielding Miranda from the images that still glowed there of the climate-change denier and her father while the voices of that man and the studio audience bounced off the walls. *No proof, no proof.* Then they were in the yard. Breathe, said Miranda's beautiful mother, Jenny. There was dew beneath their feet and a tremble of cherry blossoms all around them, and her mother was holding Miranda's hand. This moment, too, would live on inside Miranda, it was there in the cabin with her, even though a month after speaking these words her mother would be dead.

"You're Milan Wells, the climate scientist from Princeton." The man's face began to rearrange itself. "I thought you were some kind of fraud artist. Perhaps you are."

"Should I know you?" asked Roy, looming over Miranda's father.

"We had a little contretemps once upon a time," said Tony from across the table, lifting his chin, at which Miranda's father gave a bitter laugh.

"A contretemps, is that what you call it, Tony? By which I presume you mean attacking scientific consensus and making me your whipping boy? Even if you weren't personally responsible for the death threats against me and my daughter, for the death of my wife, you created the atmosphere for them."

Death threats—against her? The rage of Miranda's father crackled like lightning in the air. Old fears, newly sharpened, pressed beneath Miranda's ribs. How had she not known this? Her father met Miranda's gaze and held it: he was trying to release his anger, let it dissolve into particles and drift. He was offering her an apology, for what, how much, she wasn't yet sure.

"Len consults Tony more than I do, not always wisely. It was Len's idea to bring him along," said Roy.

"I thought it was your idea," Len said gauntly. Every tendon in his body seemed to be engaged in trying to protect himself.

"Sometimes Len goes a bit rogue, Roy," said Tony. "He had this idea to cut you out of whatever R&D investment you were planning to make here. I've been trying to talk him out of it."

"It was my idea to bring Tony," Miranda's father said as Len blanched. Only the smallest flicker at the corner of Roy's eyes seemed to acknowledge what he'd heard. "I brought you here, Roy, because of your connection to Tony, because while you say one thing publicly, you've supported him and others, the ones who've sown so much discord and doubt. I brought you to an island so you can feel what it's like to live on one, to see what the place might do to you, if you might lose yourselves and in the process find yourselves. I brought Frank here —"

"What the fuck does that mean?" Roy shouted.

Miranda scrambled to her feet beside the stove. "I forgive you," she said to Tony, "even though you helped destroy my life." She didn't know where the words came from. Were Tony's actions truly forgivable? Had her father wanted her to meet him, and him to meet her? Anger rose in her as well. She knew that she was speaking not only to Tony, though perhaps her words entered him, because he gave a shudder. He was staring at her as if she were an alien being.

Everyone in the room had turned in her direction. Her toes curled in her boots. Ella panted at her feet. Sweat streamed down the inside of her oilskin jacket.

Roy was the one demanding, "Who are you?"

"I'm Miranda Wells." She wanted to get the words out before her father spoke for her. "I'm Milan's daughter. You stole something from me," she said to Tony, "but we found a way to remake ourselves, my father and I. You stole something too," she said to Frank's father. "The air, and you want to go on stealing it."

In response, Roy offered her one of his charismatic smiles. "How do you know my son? You arrived with him, didn't you? I assumed you were some new inamorata he'd seduced with his clever, idealistic talk and dragged along for the ride."

Frank's shame was a silent, high-pitched scream rising out of the top of his head. He, too, seemed to be trying to overcome rage and calm himself, drawing on the new, steady cord that stretched tight between them, which made Miranda feel supple and strong.

And there was Caleb, silent for so long, his torn attention reaching Miranda alongside Roy's belligerent flailing for control. Part of her reached out an invisible hand to Caleb through the mayhem, offering her own apology for all that was lost, for the fact that there would still be pain.

"Frank crashed his car in the cove near where I live —" Miranda said.

"Miranda, rescued me — She's been showing me her life. Transforming me."

Roy turned to Frank, his mouth working, as if aiming for deprecating amusement and failing to hide utter perplexity.

Caleb said, "I reckon you have a lot to say to each other, but I'm still waiting for a promise, isn't that right? You need to make my deal. No more experiments. Because look what I've got."

When he held up the box of matches and shook them, a

needle of disquiet sped down Miranda's back. So that's what Caleb had darted to grab, moments before, reaching across the counter in front of her. One of the boxes her father kept there to light the wood stove.

"Can't miss that smell of gasoline, can you," said Caleb, and there was hardness in his face. "So I spread some all around this cabin. Then I encountered a small delay, but thankfully I was liberated. A lighter was removed from my person, but look what I found. Good thing is, fuel's had a chance to soak into the wood. There's a camping stove over there, behind Miranda, see, and if I turn the knob, we'll have gas inside and outside. Almost everything's flammable, I'd say. What I want, it's very simple. No experiments, no spraying of any cloud haze, and then all of you, off my island."

All of them. Why was it a shock to hear Caleb include her with the others? She'd made a choice to turn away from all he'd offered. Her actions, too, had consequences. Yet, to Miranda, his rejection was a form of pain.

"Caleb, give me the matches," said Alan as if speaking to a child.

"Now why would I do that?" Caleb gave an unchildlike laugh.

Caught between counter and doorway, Miranda was the one closest to Caleb, cutting him off from the camping stove, but before she could make up her mind what to do, Caleb, with a glance at her and an eddy of wind, slipped out the door.

All the unease in the room ratcheted upward, yet no one moved, as if everyone were listening to the sound of Caleb's footsteps on the bridge, then the ensuing silence, the air thick with the possibility of what Caleb might do next, as if they were simply waiting for the smell of smoke to manifest and enact their doom. It was Frank who moved first, only once he was at the door, he did the most astonishing thing: he turned the lock.

"Frank, what kind of game are you playing?" Frank's father, now, seemed unable to laugh.

"I'm not playing a game." Some of his father's mocking bravado had entered Frank. "I'm trying to enhance our focus, all the better to meditate on our predicament."

"Are you frightened, Roy?" Where did this voice come from and where had she found this audacity? Her voice, Miranda's voice, daring to speak to Frank's formidable father this way, even as she poured trust into Frank, whose motives she had to believe in, and into Caleb, who would not hurt them, he would not.

As if breaking from a trance, Roy slung a white canvas knapsack over one shoulder and said, "Are you ready then, Len? Let's get the hell out of here, because clearly there's nothing for us in this mess. Someone wants us to leave? Can't get out of here fast enough." He seemed intent on ignoring Miranda's question.

"You're on an island, Roy," said Alan. "When you leave this cabin, you'll still be on an island. Frank, would you mind unlocking the door?"

Though Frank did so without dispute, he did not move from the doorway, so that anyone attempting an escape would run right into him.

"Anna, are you ready?" Roy ignored Miranda's father as well.

"You are frightened," said Miranda, and the look that Roy turned on her then was like nothing she'd ever experienced. There was no bluster or pretence in it: looking into him was like falling down a well, into the depths of someone's self-annihilating terror and having to use all the strength she possessed to claw her way up again.

The room itself was brightening. Pushing open the curtains on the far side of the door, Anna seemed to be searching outside for Caleb. Agnes zipped up her jacket and settled her wool hat back over her wide forehead with the air of someone mustering purpose.

"Alan — Milan, I hardly know what to call you now," said Agnes. "I came all the way here to Blaze Island intending to tell you something. Each time I tried to find you, there was an interruption, but before we go any further, I need to make clear, I want out of this project. That's what I came here to say. Your project isn't mine. I moved home. And now I'm going back home, to where the ice is truly melting, to concentrate on what needs to be done up there."

"You're free to go, Agnes."

"Nakummek," Agnes said quietly, her eyes on Miranda's father. Then she said, "Mr. Hansen, I invite you to come on a journey with me."

"Alas, that may not be possible," said Roy, shifting from foot to foot.

"Yet here's my invitation," said Agnes. "To come with me out onto the sea ice this winter. You, too, Milan, if you wish. It will be a long trip to reach me if you don't fly. The ice itself will be very thin and the trip will be very dangerous, but we'll have sensors under the treads of our sled to show us where the strongest ice is."

"Anna," Roy said once again. "I'm really done with this madness."

"Just so you know, I've filmed all this." Alan gestured

towards one of the dark screens in the dark corner. "There'll be a record of what occurred here and everything you've said, Roy. I intend to show the world."

To this Roy said nothing. It was as if Miranda's father had said nothing. Roy's body contained violence, though, and her father had neither his height nor obvious force.

Agnes pressed Anna's arm. Something passed between them, emboldening, confirming, that made Anna's dark eyebrows stand out even more sharply, emphatic marks in her pale face. "There's a path, isn't there, Roy. You're more than capable of finding the way yourselves."

"Come on, Anna, you brought us here."

All three men were shrinking, Frank's uncle Leonard growing more abject by the moment. Tony, who had finished wiping his glasses on his shirt tail, was scribbling what looked like frantic calculations on a sheet of paper. Could Miranda bring herself to pity them amid the chaos of this new world? Her chest tightened. Was that the smell of smoke?

"But I'm not taking you back," said Anna. "When you get to the guesthouse, what will you do then, Roy? How are you going to get the fuel you need to fly out? Communications systems are still down, aren't they. The East Coast is underwater. Nothing's moving. How do you intend to get a flight path?"

"I'll figure it out. One of my many, many talents. That's fine, Anna, if you're abandoning us. There's a seat for you on board, Frank, isn't this your lucky day?"

His father laid a large hand on Frank's shoulder and Miranda couldn't bear to watch: Frank would leave. Before they'd had a chance to—he'd give in to his father because he couldn't help himself. Until she heard his voice as he broke from his father's clutches.

"Sorry, Dad, I'm going wherever Miranda goes."

"Miranda?" said Roy, as if he were staring through a telescope at a far-off star. "And what might Miranda's plans be?"

"I don't know yet." Her father's astonishment landed on her, too. It split him open. What had he imagined? That she would stay with him forever in the refuge he'd created for her, their now-fractured haven. That he would leave while pressing her to stay—with Frank to keep her company? How many months ago had it been that, stepping through the damp spring twilight, Miranda had heard Anna's voice eddying out of her father's study along with tendrils of woodsmoke. You could go back, you know, Anna had said. You don't need to be a ghost. Open another research institute. You've been completely vindicated.

Standing stock-still in the yard while the roar of waves grew ever louder, Miranda had waited for her father's response. Here was the thing she'd never allowed herself to imagine. Could this life, too, vanish into mist? No, Anna, her father had said at last with a long sigh. And even if I were to leave, I could never go back to that.

When had she stopped feeling like his shadow or he like hers? Was there a moment upon which she could lay a finger and say, here? She, the child her father had not known he wanted until she arrived, whose being filled him with terror as well as love. Now it was up to her to step free of the conjoined life that had bound them together for so long.

In the doorway, Frank held up a lighter. Where had it come from? Could it be the one Caleb had lost? Frank flicked it, and, when a small flame burst to life, he waved the lighter in the air. "See this, Dad? If you don't do what you've been asked to do — do everything you can to cut carbon and get everyone else to do it too, as fast as possible — I'll set myself on fire. You don't believe me? There's only one way to find out. You'd risk my life — but then you're already doing that every day." He held the flame to the tattered cuff of his sweater, the wool igniting, smoldering, the bright flame of the lighter ever closer to his wrist.

Miranda's breath snagged as Roy dove for Frank. Before his father reached him, Frank mashed his arm against the counter. In the stunned silence, the smell of burned animal hair filled the room. Frank's father said nothing. Steadily Frank met Miranda's gaze.

Something pushed her past the cluster of frightened men, past Frank, through the door and into the open air. The wind met her on the bridge, surging out of the southeast, bearing the scent of rain and as yet no whiff of smoke. Waves were a warp and woof of sound. Ella took off at a gallop. Every inhale brought more wind into Miranda's body. Breathe in, breathe out, and with each breath love swelled amid the turmoil. Fear. Need. Joy. Shock. The island was her world and the world was an island, full of people like these, and others. The lost ones and the dead. Trees. Birds. Broken things. The seams of her body expanded, alive to all possible feelings. Panic. Hope. What would happen next? *No proof.* In a moment, there would be men stumbling through the Burnt Hills, the tremulous pulse of Frank nearby, her father peering towards the north as if tugged in that direction, Anna Turi setting out with Agnes Watson across the granite flats that led into the scrubby woods. Would her father leave the island? Would she?

Soon Caleb would reach his house beside the sea, his breath a ragged scrape across his chest. Stripping off his filthy coveralls like an old skin, he would make his way into the parlour where the wind poured through the glassless windows. Picking berries out in the hills, Sylvia would look up, sensing a shift in the weather. A fox would trot through the long grass. Out in the cove waves turned like schools of fish. Clouds swirled. Rocks crumbled. A trace of sand returned.

EPILOGUE

Some nights the storm door would pull free of its latch and bang. Some days the wind was so strong we couldn't leave the house. Even in summer, the wood floors were cold first thing in the morning. Wind from the southeast brought rain, from the southwest fine air, from the south were our warm winds; northwest meant cool but fair, northeast bitter weather. The ocean water shifted with the air. The waves swung round like flocks of birds. A storm moves in a circle. If you know the wind you know the land. Wind decides everything.

There were glassy days, too, yet on the island wind was the room we lived in. The grasses in the fields followed the wind, bent with its breath, pushed one way or another.

The sea was full of mirages. Rocky islets no more than protuberances above the waves lengthened into cliffs. Icebergs doubled in size. Stretches of sea folded themselves upward and turned into sky. Things altered as we watched. Sometimes the islets in the distance loomed. Then it was as if they not only grew but floated close across the sea. You'd think you could walk to them. This was a sign of a low-pressure system approaching, which would bring a bit of weather.

In winter, the wind blew horizontal. Tearing hard across the barrens, it caught up the snow, dug out hollows, covered them over. We stared hard, trying to figure out where we truly were.

In March, the sea ice arrived. The wind called through the broken pack ice that undulated on the surface of the water in cove and harbour. The wind ground pieces of ice together, made them groan, rafted slabs into turquoise ridges at the shore. Some years there was so much ice, some years less. In May the icebergs returned, travelling south, a silent crush of them, then fewer and fewer.

We remember all this.

Change is clear after it happens.

ACKNOWLEDGEMENTS

My profoundest thanks to the Tilting Culture and Recreation Society for the gift of return visits to the Jennifer Keefe Studio and the Reardon House in Sandy Cove. Without your generosity and support, this novel would not exist. In the earliest days of my dreaming about the book, when I was still in search of an island, some good spirit pointed me in the direction of Tilting, at the far end of Fogo Island. The Canada Council supported my first research trip to Fogo Island through a travel grant. Particular thanks to Jim McGrath, who made sure my residencies ran smoothly, and to the Keefe family for making the beautiful gift of the Jenny Keefe Studio available to artists.

Thank you to everyone in Tilting for making me feel so welcome over the past eight years — and to all those on Fogo Island who shared stories and answered my many questions about wind, weather, climate change, words, birds, and how many men it takes to pull a car out of a brook, including Al Dwyer, Roy Dwyer, Christine Dwyer, Mary Keefe, Frank Keefe, Cathy Keefe, Martin McGrath, Maureen and Phil Foley, Paddy Barry, Winston Osmond, and Bob Blake. There is a village of voices in this novel. Special thanks to Mona Brown for her foraging wisdom and Holly Hogan and Bonnie McCay Merritt for bird lore. To M'Liz Keefe for friendship and her artist's descriptions of the Fogo Island landscape. To Jack Stanley and Vida Simon for their weather stories. To Cheryl Blake for her ongoing generosity and hospitality. To Dave Anthony for my first tour of the island and a place to stay in his family trailer in Burnt Point, Seldom, during my very first days on the island. Thanks to the land itself and the voices that arise from it.

Heartfelt thanks to Dan Murphy, who not only extended invitations on behalf of TRACS but went above and beyond at every stage to help me bring the novel to fruition — answering questions right until the end, reading the manuscript, and offering both scientific and practical know-how, even helping me land on the name of my fictional island. May sweet sou'westerlies blow on you, Dan!

Thanks to those who offered their expertise in scientific matters, with particular thanks to Jason Blackstock and Holly Buck, not only for their climate-engineering knowledge but their astute thoughts about how climate engineering might find its way into a novel. To Sean Low for helping to bring me to CEC14, the 2014 Climate Engineering Conference in Berlin. To Dr. Chris Derksen for sharing his Arctic field experiences.

This book owes a great debt to my sister, Elizabeth Bush, climate scientist and brilliant science communicator, whose conversations helped inspire the novel, who read the manuscript more than once, offered invaluable scientific consults and was a necessary sounding board in so many ways. All mistakes are my own.

To Kelly and Emma O'Brien, for your own thoughtful responses to the climate crisis. Emma, one of Miranda's school assignments may resemble one of yours.

To Angus Andersen, for his glimpses of life in Nain and the Inuktitut language. To Caitlyn Baikie, inspirational young female Inuk scientist.

To Ted Goossen, for linguistic advice on Frank's tattoo.

I am indebted more than I can say to those who read the manuscript in progress, each offering their particular wisdoms: André Alexis, Amanda Lewis, Brian Brett (who made time during an intense residency committed to his own work; bless you, Brian), Shani Mootoo, Brad Kessler, Darren Hynes. Thanks to Reneltta Arluk, for bringing an Inuk eye to the novel. Mike Hoolboom read the manuscript multiple times and his unflagging faith (alongside his crucial editorial advice) saw me through from start to finish.

To Susan M. Gaines, director of the Fiction Meets Science program at the University of Bremen and the FMS residency for writers at the Hanse-Wissenschaftskolleg in Delmenhorst, Germany—my fellowship could not have come at a more propitious time. The novel found its end here.

This is a work of fiction inspired by a play full of magic, set in a world where science and magical thinking vie with each other and are sometimes on a terrifying collision course. The novel draws on the work of actual scientists and scientific research, including the climate-engineering research of Canadian scientist David Keith, now at Harvard. His slim book *A Case for Climate Engineering* (MIT Press, 2013) was a useful reference as was Jeff Tollefson's article about Keith's work, "The Sun Dimmers" (*Nature* 563 (November 29, 2018): 613-15). The climate-engineering listserv was an invaluable, constantly updating resource. When imagining Alan's "conceptual experiment," I drew loosely on the example of a group of retired Silicon Valley scientists attempting to build their own machine that sprays aerosolized particles, also the cloud-making art of Karolina Sobecka. I want to acknowledge the work of ice climatologist Dr. Jason Box and his Dark Snow Project on the Greenland ice sheet (darksnow.org), as well as his blunt speaking out about the dangers of the climate crisis. Among the many sources consulted as research for this novel I'd like to cite Clive Hamilton's *Earthmasters: The Dawn of the Age of Climate Engineering* (Yale, 2013) and William Marsden's *Fools Rule: Inside the Failed Politics of Climate Change* (Vintage Canada, 2011, 2012).

Thanks to my editor, Bethany Gibson, for, as ever, her empathetic and astonishingly acute editorial eye. Thanks to Paula Sarson, copy editor extraordinaire, and everyone at Goose Lane Editions. To my agent, Samantha Haywood, whose enthusiasm and belief buoy me always. You make it all possible.

CATHERINE BUSH is the author of four previous novels, including the Canada Reads long-listed *Accusation*, the Trillium Award short-listed *Claire's Head*, and the national bestselling *The Rules of Engagement*, which was also a *New York Times* Notable Book and a *Globe and Mail* Best Book of the Year. She has been a Fiction Meets Science Fellow at the HWK in Germany and has spoken internationally about addressing the climate crisis through fiction. An associate professor at the University of Guelph and Coordinator of the Guelph Creative Writing MFA, she lives in Toronto and eastern Ontario. *Blaze Island* is her fifth novel.